An Ellora's Cave

www.ellorascave.com

Fury

ISBN 9781419965432
ALL RIGHTS RESERVED.
Fury Copyright © 2011 Laurann Dohner
Edited by Shannon Combs and Pamela Campbell.
Cover art by Syneca.

Electronic book publication July 2011
Trade paperback publication 2011

LAURANN DOHNER

FURY

ELLORA'S CAVE
ROMANTICA®
WWW.ELLORASCAVE.COM

FURY

Dedication

❧

To Mr. Laurann, who always supported my writing even when I used to do it on an ancient word processor. He never complained about my late nights typing away or thought it was silly to write stories just because it made me happy. I wrote my first book in 1993, continued to write dozens more of them over the years in my free time, and this series is one that became an obsession of mine when I started it in 2001. I didn't even consider getting published until 2009.

This is also to the readers who sent me many emails asking what I used to write, because it made me go back, re-read those books I'd written in the past and salvage this series. I'd also like to thank my wonderful editors, Pamela Campbell and Shannon Combs. They have taught me so much, continue to believe in me, and are an endless source of support. Last but not least, my thanks to everyone at Ellora's Cave for giving an unknown author a chance. Dreams really do come true!

Prologue

sð

"Shit," Ellie muttered under her breath, watching the man restrained against the wall inside the next room. Every time she sneaked into the viewing room it depressed her but she couldn't stay way.

She knew he couldn't see her through the two-way glass and yet he seemed to be looking right at her. Her gaze skimmed over his bare chest and the straining muscles of his well-defined physique. His large biceps bunched while he pulled on the chains, rage evident on his features as he fought them.

Sympathy and compassion made her ache for him. His determination showed regardless of how he'd been stripped of his freedom and dignity. He had to know the futility of his actions yet he still struggled. Her hand lifted to touch the wood frame under the glass. She wished she could soothe him by showing him that someone cared. Most of all, she wanted to get him out of the hellish prison that contained him. He deserved to be free.

Movement in the corner of the room drew her attention away from the man who haunted her thoughts day and night. Fear made her heart race as a technician entered the room. Jacob Alter had to be one of the most callous, unfeeling monsters who worked for Mercile Industries. The asshole actually enjoyed inflicting pain on the test subjects. He especially targeted this one with his brand of cruelty. A month before, the big man chained against the wall had broken Jacob's nose when Jacob had gotten too close to the elbow of the restrained test subject. Ellie knew it had been well deserved. The bruising still shadowed Jacob's face as he flashed an evil grin toward his intended victim. He planned to inflict more painful testing upon him.

"Hello, 416." Jacob chuckled, an unpleasant sound. "I hear you pissed off Doctor Trent. You know what that means, right?" Jacob placed a tan case about the size of a bowling bag on top of the exam table in the corner. It made a loud thump. "It means I get to do something I've wanted for a really long time. You're going to suffer today." He glanced up at the security camera in the corner and waved his hand over his throat in a cutting motion.

"Shit, shit, shit," Ellie chanted softly as panic seized her. She'd heard of inmates being tortured when they really angered one of the doctors. Jacob obviously didn't want to record whatever horrible thing he had planned for 416. It had to be really bad.

Jacob cocked his head, continued to stare up into the corner, and then grinned before he turned to face 416.

"The camera is off now. No record is being made of this. What Doctor Trent doesn't know is that you are going to have a horrible accident, you freak. You shouldn't have fucked with me. I warned you that I'd take you out." He grabbed the bag he'd carried into the room. "Nobody breaks my nose and lives. I knew it would only be a matter of time before you would be punished. I just bided my time." He pulled out a syringe. "You're going to die, you bastard!"

This can't be happening, Ellie thought. She hadn't struggled through the daily nightmare life had become for the past two months only to lose 416 now. She'd lived in constant fear of being discovered as a spy but witnessing 416's continual defiance had given her the strength to face each day. For him she'd taken dangerous risks to collect enough evidence to set him and the other prisoners free.

In fact, she half expected the security guards to come after her at any second. She'd become so frantic to collect real proof of what happened at the research facility that she'd committed an insane stunt half an hour before. She'd stolen one of the doctor's badges to sneak into the woman's office to download files off the computer. If security reviewed the surveillance tapes she'd be caught for sure. They would arrest her immediately and make her fate as grim as 416's. They both would be dead by the end of the day.

She wavered between doing something incredibly stupid to attempt to save him and following orders from her real boss to never interfere. She'd finally obtained enough damning evidence to possibly free the forced test subjects. She had an opportunity of smuggling something out at the end of her shift if she just kept her head down, her mouth shut, and didn't draw the attention of anyone. It would mean doing nothing while Jacob murdered the man restrained to the wall.

Her gaze locked on 416. Out of all the prisoners, she wanted to free him the most. He had kept her up nights since she'd been transferred to the illegal drug research facility Mercile Industries ran. 416 had become the last image she saw before she drifted to sleep every night. Sometimes, she admitted, he even featured a starring role in her dreams. Her decision quickly slammed into place. It would be unacceptable to just watch this happen. It would break her heart. She couldn't live with it if she did not even attempt to save him.

"You're not going to be able to fight me this time. You're going to be defenseless. I want you to know you're going to die." Jacob's voice grew harsh. "But not before I hurt you, animal."

Ellie spun around, no plan in mind, but desperate now to save 416. She fled the room, forced her movements to slow when she stepped out into the hallway, more than aware of the security cameras located there, and stopped at the supply room to grab a testing kit. It would raise suspicion if she just entered the cell without a valid reason. She yanked the tackle box-sized plastic container out of the cabinet where they were stored and tried not to appear as frantic as she felt when she entered the hallway again, but knew she needed to hurry to

416's holding cell before Jacob had time to do something horrible.

"Ellie!"

She froze, her eyes widening, and then slowly turned. Doctor Brennor, a tall redheaded man, stepped out of one of the rooms holding a chart. "Yes?"

"Did you get that mouth swab from 321?"

"I did." She held still even though she wanted to spin and run away.

"Good. Did you drop it off at the lab?"

"Of course."

He reached up with his free hand to rub the back of his neck. "Long day, isn't it? Are you wishing it were the weekend already? I am."

Shut up, she ordered him silently, *so I can go.* She shrugged. "I like work. Speaking of, I need to take a blood sample. It's a stat order."

"Yeah. Sure." His gaze drifted down her body. "Do you want to go out to dinner with me tomorrow night?"

It stunned her for a split second that he'd ask her on a date. "I have a boyfriend," she lied easily. The idea of going out with anyone who worked for Mercile made her nauseous. "But thanks for asking."

His mouth tensed and the friendly light cooled in his green eyes. "I see. Fine. Go. I have to update reports." He turned to head in the opposite direction and strode away. "I do too much damn paperwork," he grumbled before disappearing around a corner.

Cameras are watching me, Ellie remembered, resisting the urge to sprint down the hallway. She strolled casually to 416's cell as if she didn't have a care in the world. At least she hoped that was the appearance she gave.

Dear God, she prayed silently, *let me reach him in time!* Her fingers trembled as she punched in the code on the digital lock. The door beeped when it accepted her numbers and the steel bars made a distinctive sound as they slid away, allowing her to open the door. She entered the room quickly.

She forced a smile she didn't feel. "I'm here to take a blood sample."

The door automatically closed behind her, the locking pins slammed into place to seal her inside the cell, and a quick, sharp buzz sounded to underscore that fact. She took in the scene and gasped at the pure horror she witnessed.

416 wasn't chained to the wall anymore. He was stretched out on the hard, cold concrete floor, facedown. The chains secured to his wrists had been locked to one of the pins cemented into the floor, forcing his arms high above his head while his legs were shackled to the wall. Jacob had removed the restrained man's pants—they were a balled-up white pile on the floor—and he was on his knees between 416's spread thighs, which were forced apart by the way he'd been bound.

It took her only seconds to realize what horrific thing she'd interrupted. Jacob sat back on his heels, frozen, stunned as well by her sudden appearance, but he recovered faster than she could. He dropped the instrument of torture, what appeared to be one of the guard's batons to the concrete floor, and tried to rise. He grabbed for his unfastened pants, trying to close them, cursing. Ellie reacted.

"You sick bastard!"

She sprang into action before she thought, the hard plastic case gripped so tightly in her fist that it dug painfully into her palm, and swung it with all the strength she could muster. It smashed into Jacob's face. He reeled back, cried out, but Ellie didn't stop when he hit the floor. She ended up dropping onto his body, straddled his belly, her body pinning his down, and grabbed the kit with both hands. Pure rage drove her to batter him with it. He tried to defend his face but after a few hits, his hands slumped to the floor.

"You monster," she panted, hit him again, and then realized how bloodied his face had become. She stopped, her entire body shaking, and stared in horror at the technician.

Her gaze lifted away from his smashed nose and mouth, to the kit. Blood smeared all over the side she'd used to bash him repeatedly. She dropped it on the floor, in shock, and eased her weight off the downed man. His chest wasn't moving.

"Oh God," she gasped. She reached for his throat, a moan tearing from her parted lips, and felt for a pulse. She couldn't find one. "Oh God, Oh God, Oh God," she chanted, certain she'd killed him.

She turned and stared at 416, just remembering him. He faced her, his eyes were open, his cheek against the concrete, and he blinked. He'd watched what she'd done. Her hands shook and she glanced down at them.

I just killed Jacob. Her gaze drifted back to the horrific sight of the monster she'd attacked in a fit of pure rage. *He deserved it.* She tried to sooth her panicked mind. *Think. They are going to come in here and find him. They'll know I killed him. They'll drag me away, torture me to find out why I interfered, and they'll kill me. The evidence will never reach my handler. Think, goddamn it, Ellie!*

She peered up at the camera. Usually a red light blinked but this one didn't. It wasn't on. The guard had followed Jacob's instructions. No one but 416 had witnessed what had really taken place. She had no idea how long those cameras would remain off but she assumed they would until Jacob ordered them to start monitoring the prisoner again. She swallowed hard and rose to her knees. All her focus shifted to the man who watched her so intently, helpless on the floor.

"It's going to be okay," she crooned to him.

The test subjects were dangerous. She'd been warned a hundred times that sometimes the chains that restrained them broke. Mercile Industries had illegally altered human beings with animal genetics somehow, made them stronger than normal humans, and even their appearances had been changed. Testing facility assistants and some doctors had been killed by the people they'd helped create. She'd silently cheered at hearing that news but then, she hated everyone who worked inside the secret facility, performing illegal experiments. Mercile Industries was a drug research and development company that would do anything to make a buck.

She watched 416 cautiously as she allowed her gaze to roam over his naked body. His back rose and fell with his breathing but besides blinking, he didn't otherwise move. She noticed a red mark on his side. With his arms stretched upward she could see it clearly. Ellie hesitated. He could kill her if he broke a chain.

He is worth saving. She repeated that silent chant a few times while she worked up the nerve to inch closer to his downed body. She'd already decided to put her life on the line when she'd agreed to work undercover, understanding the real possibility that she might not survive. Lives were all too often taken in the name of science. This company only cared about money and they needed to be stopped.

"I'm not going to hurt you," she promised him. Her hand brushed next to the mark and anger stirred. Jacob had jabbed him hard enough with a needle to leave a dime sized injury. Her gaze shifted to his face. "He drugged you?"

The male didn't answer but she didn't really expect him to. She knew they could talk, had heard some of them curse and threaten staff as she'd drawn blood, but this one had never spoken to her. The times she'd entered his cell, he hadn't even growled at her. He'd silently watched her approach, occasionally sniffed at her, but his dark brown gaze always fixed on her every movement. She swallowed again, taking note of his hot skin, and wondered if he were sick. He felt feverish to her.

"It's going to be okay. He's dead. He can't hurt you anymore."

Her hand left him and she crawled a little down his body. She winced at the sight of what Jacob had done to him. His ass was red from blows from the baton. Jacob had beaten him with it on his buttocks, inner thighs and the backs of his legs. She clenched her teeth. She hadn't arrived in time to prevent another horror either. The sight of blood near his rectum assured her that Jacob had been doing exactly what she'd assumed. He'd used the baton to sexually assault 416.

Rage gripped her again as she shot a murderous glare at the dead man. His pants were still open and his flaccid cock showed, covered in a condom. She didn't see blood on him. That small relief, that she'd arrived before he'd raped his victim, helped slightly. A growl emanated from 416.

"Easy," she crooned. "You're bleeding. Let me take a look. I'm a nurse."

She didn't bother rushing for the corner cabinet to get gloves. She wasn't sure how much time she had. With only a slight hesitation, she lifted her leg over the man's thick, muscular thigh to get a better view, and peered down at a rounded, beefy ass. Her hands touched him softly, spread the cheeks enough to check the damage, but it looked minimal, considering.

"I'm so sorry for what he did. It doesn't appear he got—" Her voice died. To say Jacob hadn't raped him much or seemed not to have penetrated him deeply sounded horrific to even note. This shouldn't have happened at all. "You're going to be fine." *At least physically*, she amended. Her hands released his ass.

She moved from between his spread thighs to crawl up next to his body and leaned down to study his features. He watched her and she couldn't miss the look of rage. His lips parted to reveal sharp fangs. He snarled at her, a little louder than the mild growl he'd given her before. His body didn't move though.

Dear God, he has canines. She could see the sharper teeth at close range. *Like a dog's or maybe a vampire's.* She guessed it had probably been some kind of canine breed. It could account for the terrifying growl that erupted from the back of his throat that eerily resembled a vicious dog. She hesitated, afraid he'd snap at her with those sharp teeth if she got too close.

"Easy," she urged again. "I'm not going to hurt you."

Peering into his eyes told her a few things. His pupils were unusually large and he seemed a little confused. Jacob had obviously drugged him pretty strongly but she had no idea what he'd used. The powerful guy sprawled on the floor probably *couldn't* move. He'd have fought otherwise when Jacob had assaulted him. He lay meekly next to her but his eyes were lively and another growl tore from his slightly parted lips. She tried not to shiver from the sight of his sharp fangs.

"Did he do anything else to you? Did he mention what drug he gave you?"

416 stopped growling but he didn't say anything. It made her wonder if he could speak. The drug might be preventing him from doing more than making throat noises. Ellie knew she'd have to check him over, do it quickly, and think a way out of the mess she'd created by rushing to 416's cell. The security cameras would have recorded her going into the room.

She opened the metal pin cemented into the floor to release the arm chains that held him flat to the floor and grunted as she pushed the large male onto his back. He was very tall and had to weigh at least two hundred sixty pounds or so. She tried hard not to gawk at his wide chest or the fact that he didn't have on any clothes.

Ellie took note of how tan he appeared and determined it had to be his natural skin tone since they kept him below ground. His coloring never changed. With his dark-brown hair and deep-chocolate eye color she thought he had to be a good portion Native American. Of course she couldn't miss the fact that he was a great deal bigger than any Native Americans she'd ever seen. She guessed he had German or some other husky, tall ancestry too.

He wasn't handsome in any conventional sense, his cheekbones so pronounced they made him appear too harsh. Some might not consider him good-looking but he was quite exotically beautiful. She guessed the bone structure might be caused by whatever genetic altering had been done to him. He looked human but not quite fully so. With his hate-filled glare and the tense jaw, it gave him a snarling appearance, which he actually did the moment Ellie inched closer. The deep growl made her pause, heart pounding, and fear shot through her. He looked intensely masculine and rough, projecting how dangerous he could be. It disturbed her that she found him extremely attractive. She couldn't deny how his muscular body and pure masculine magnetism drew her to him.

If he regained movement she'd die. She knew that and he probably wished he could get his hands on her. She glanced across the room to stare at the cracked and peeling white paint that ran the length of the room on the floor by the door. The staff called it the kill line. All test subjects were shackled by each limb. Though they were strong enough to break chains occasionally, none had ever broken all four at once. They only needed one free limb to kill. She sat inside the kill zone with an enraged, huge male whose two arms were chained but they weren't connected to anything anymore. That realization made her want to crawl away from him but she resisted the urge.

He's worth saving. She nodded. *He needs help. Check him over, do what you can for him, and pray no one walks in here. Yeah.* She could just hope the drugs didn't wear off immediately. He'd probably snap her neck before she could beg for her life. He had to hate everyone who worked for Mercile and he had a damn good reason. Her gaze landed on Jacob's dead body, her teeth clenched, and she forced her gaze to return to 416. *See how hurt he is.*

Red marks marred his stomach. Her fingers traced the proof that Jacob had punched him there. She felt his ribcage where more marks showed. She didn't feel any broken bones. His belly had firm, hard muscles even while he lay lax, but she didn't feel anything that would suggest internal bleeding. She tried to stay professional but her fingertips lingered a little too long as she traced an integrate pattern of muscle groups. She couldn't deny touching him affected her as a woman. He was forbidden, dangerous, and sexy.

Her gaze lowered to his pelvic area, unable not to look at the male she found so appealing, and she gasped. She moved before she thought, gripped his slightly engorged cock, and worked the painful looking bands down the shaft. She tried to be gentle but Jacob had tightly wrapped a thick piece of rubber around the man's penis a few times. She managed to work it loose and threw the offensive thing away as soon as she got it off. Her fingers gently massaged the reddened skin before she realized how inappropriate the action was. Her gaze lingered there, realized that, even mostly soft, he was impressive. Blood flow had been painfully constricted and prevented from reaching the shaft.

"That son of a bitch," she muttered, cursing Jacob for doing such a horrible, vicious thing. Her cheeks warmed when she realized what she'd done. More embarrassment slammed her when she realized how her body responded to touching him, even just to remove the offensive implement of torture. She'd been handling his cock.

416 growled. Her gaze flicked up to his face. He watched her with dark, furious eyes. She realized she cradled him still inside her palm and released his cock quickly. "Sorry! I had to remove it." She glanced down at his appendage and saw the line where the rubber band had injured him was still red and angry looking. "I'm sure it will be okay."

She hoped so anyway. Jacob had obviously done it to hurt 416. If left that way too long, lack of blood supply to his cock would have done severe damage, but of course that bastard had planned to kill him. *It would be a horrible crime to disfigure such a sexy guy.* That thought made her want to groan and made her more aware that her body responded to the naked male sprawled in front of her. She mentally shook that line of thought away, couldn't afford to go there, and needed to stop looking at his bare body.

She bit her lip, thinking hard about how to get them out of the mess they were in. She needed to be free to leave work after her shift and get the data she'd stolen to her handler. Her gaze flicked to the dead guy once more. He lay there, bloody, on the concrete where she'd left him, the cause of his death obviously the blunt-force trauma from pounding his nose with the kit. She'd experienced pure rage to do so much damage. It could be mistaken for damage from a fist. Her gut twisted.

"Shit. I can only see one way out of this." She met 416's angry gaze. "I'm sorry about this. I have no choice." She hesitated, wanted to tell him who she really was, why she had to do something horrific to him, but didn't dare. *What if he tells them? He could. He has no reason to trust anyone who works here. I'm safer if I just have him assume the worst.*

416 had been certain Ellie would never harm him. Panic jolted through him from head to toe when she apologized to him for her intent. He tried to move but his body refused to budge. He could move his eyes, blink, and swallow. A few growls had come forth but he couldn't talk. *Does she plan to kill me now? Then why did she take out the technician who attacked me?*

Anyone but her, 416 thought frantically, worried he may die helpless, on the floor of his cell. He inhaled the clean scent of the woman who never failed to stir his body. Ellie always came to him sweetly, her touch gentle, and her gaze kind when she'd taken samples from him. She'd been the only human he'd ever met who gave him warm, honest smiles, and he'd even looked forward to the times she entered his domain. He'd trusted her not to hurt him. She was the only person who could walk inside his cell without him tensing up in anticipation of dread, pain, or humiliation.

He saw fear lurking in her beautiful blue gaze as she stared at him and it wrenched his heart just a little. He'd purposely never threatened her or snarled as he did the other technicians who approached him. Until today. The idea of terrifying her had made him feel regret. It would have ended the smiles that he'd grown to appreciate when she'd begun working there. It hadn't been long. He had no concept of time but she hadn't been a part of his life until recently.

His body started to respond to her presence when his cock twitched. It made him suffer pain, throb from whatever the male had done to him, but the movement he felt made him hope that the rest of his body would recover soon as well. Ellie did things to him, made him long to touch her blonde hair and press his nose against her throat to inhale her wonderful scent. He sometimes dreamed about her under him, naked, with him free from his chains. He longed to touch and taste every inch of her body, to hear her voice and learn everything about the woman who fascinated him on every level.

The sound of her voice had always been music to his ears. He wanted to see her smile, learn her laugh and a hundred questions filled his head that he wanted to ask her to know more about the woman who had captured his soul. Her skin appeared unbelievably soft and smelled so good, too good. But now she had stated that she planned to harm him.

It was the worst kind of cruelty and painful betrayal roared through him. He also felt shame at what she'd witnessed. She'd saved him from being raped by the dead male but knew of the suffering he'd taken, the indignity of the human's cruelty. It pained him to know she'd never look at him again without that image lurking inside her memories. It hurt him on many levels and enraged him. They'd even managed to take away his fantasy of her ever regarding him as a sexual male.

He snarled again in an attempt to scare her, to prevent her from doing whatever she planned. His body refused to work, his limbs unresponsive, but he knew he wouldn't kill her even if he did manage to break free. He'd just throw her away to a safe distance past the line to prevent the temptation of following what his instincts demanded. He wanted her in ways he knew weren't possible for a prisoner and his captor.

He watched her rise to her feet and move out of his line of view. When she'd turned him onto his back, it blocked his view of the dead man. He tried to turn his head but couldn't. He heard her though, smelled her, and heard strange noises. *What is she doing?*

He had no clue but he dreaded it. All the humans were cruel. They showed no mercy. It still stunned him that she'd killed his attacker—for two reasons. First, she had done it to stop his assault and second, she wasn't a big woman. She'd taken down a male. He may have misjudged the female. He'd believed her soft, delicate, but she'd attacked a fully grown male in a wild and brutal assault. His heart raced. He tried desperately to move his limbs but they remained unresponsive.

"You're a worthless bastard. I hate you. I want you to know that," Ellie hissed.

His mind accepted her words, pain gripped him, but he wasn't stunned by it. He'd known everyone who worked inside the testing facility considered them nothing more than breathing flesh to abuse. Why he'd thought she'd be any different had been a mistake on his part.

Stupid and unforgivable. Fury gripped him and his finger twitched. He moved his mouth, a silent snarl trapped inside his throat, and promised he'd get even with the woman for fooling him into believing she was different.

"You're a worthless bastard. I hate you. I want you to know that." She just hoped that wherever Jacob had gone after death, he could still hear her. She wanted him to know what she thought of him. She wasn't sorry she'd killed Jacob. It messed with her mind but she figured she'd get over it soon enough. He didn't deserve her guilty feelings.

20

Ellie cleaned the kit, studied it, and didn't spot any traces of Jacob's blood. The case had dented but she doubted anyone would notice that fact right away. She hid the bloody tissues she'd cleaned it with inside the kit. She had to touch his body and grimaced as she tugged his pants down more to fully expose the condom he'd put on to leave no doubt of his intentions.

Ellie tried to calm the rising panic growing inside her. Her gaze drifted to 416 on the floor. He hadn't moved an inch, thankfully, and she still breathed because of it. She could only pray that her plan worked and that what she'd been told was true. He was too valuable to kill. The doctors and staff would abuse them but Jacob had planned to kill 416 against Doctor Trent's orders.

He will be fine. I have to believe that.

She removed another tissue from the kit and wiped some of the still-fresh blood from the floor. She turned to face 416. *Will he hate me for doing this? Probably.* She just didn't have a choice. They'd never allow her to leave the underground facility if they suspected her of Jacob's death. She didn't even dare tell 416 what she planned to do. If he told anyone, they'd secure her, demand answers, and she'd never reach the surface. She needed to be able to avoid all suspicion to save him and all the other test subjects.

She found the needle that Jacob had used. Luckily he'd recapped the thing after he'd injected 416. She hated to risk 416 getting an infection, but she had no choice but to reuse the needle. She hoped Jacob had not let it touch anything before recapping it. Ellie hesitated. Once done, there would be no going back.

She moved quickly before she could change her mind. She crouched by 416 and wiped the bloodied napkin over his knuckles and hands, smearing Jacob's blood there. She refused to glance at his face while she framed him for murder. She just couldn't.

They wouldn't kill him. Those guys killed techs sometimes. She'd heard that plenty, yet they were still alive. *They don't kill test subjects. They are too valuable. He'll be fine.* She chanted that inside her head.

She rose, dumped the last bit of blood evidence into the kit and removed the syringe from where she'd placed it inside the case, and turned. She hated to hurt him. Tears filled her eyes. He lay there helpless. She wanted to hug him even if he wished her dead. Someone should show him compassion but it couldn't be her at that moment. Someone needed to take the blame for Jacob's death to make sure she could leave unmolested to get that data to her handler. Once they received enough proof, a judge would issue search warrants. The testing facility would be searched, the test subjects discovered, and Mercile Industries would be exposed for all the dirty secrets they hid from the world.

She crouched over 416. His beautiful but angry dark gaze focused on her. Rage burned in his intense glare. She swallowed the bile that rose at what she had to do to him next. "I'm sorry. Really. I have to do this to you."

"I'll kill you," he rasped. One hand flopped on the floor next to her. "I swear this!" His throat worked. "I will kill you with my bare hands."

Fear gripped her that he would do just that, he had obviously started to regain control of his body. She looked down to find the injection site that Jacob had used. She jabbed the needle in, the suppressor already locked down from the original injection, and then lurched to her feet without giving 416 another glance even as he snarled from the pain she'd just inflicted.

She yanked up her kit, ran at the wall next to the door, and turned her face at the last second before she slammed into it. Pain exploded down her cheek. Her knees threatened to buckle and the taste of blood filled her mouth. She didn't have a mirror but it reminded her of the observation room. What if someone had stepped in there and witnessed what had taken place? She figured, if that were the case, security would have already flooded the room to arrest her.

She hoped her face looked as bad as it felt. Her fingers shook as she punched in the code to the door. It beeped, the steel rods inside the door slid, and the door popped open as she desperately jerked on it. She stumbled out of the room, the door slammed automatically behind her, and the sharp buzz confirmed that it was locked. She collapsed to her knees in the hallway, turned her head to locate the security camera, and screamed.

"Help! Oh God! Help!"

Seconds passed and seemed to grow to a least a minute before the sound of running, booted feet reached her ears. Four security guards turned into the corridor, coming at a dead run. The men panted when they slowed and stared at her in confusion.

"I walked into the room to take a blood sample," she sobbed. "Jacob was sexually assaulting the test subject. He attacked me." Her hand rose to her face where it throbbed. "I think I passed out and when I came around I saw 416 break his arm chains free. Jacob stabbed him with a needle but whatever he gave him didn't take effect fast enough. I think he's dead! I think that thing killed him before it collapsed to the floor."

God forgive me, she silently prayed as her mouth closed. The security guards grabbed for their Taser guns, one of them fumbling to press in a code to get the doors open, and then they rushed inside 416's cell. The door sealed behind them. Another security team arrived, along with some of the medical staff. It was Doctor Brennor who treated her in one of the employee rooms. He looked grim as he cleaned her mouth.

"You'll be fine."

She nodded. "What will they do to 416? I can't believe Jacob was doing that to him. It's wrong."

Anger tightened the redheaded doctor's mouth when he frowned. "I know. We made these *things* to find cures for diseases that animals are naturally immune or resistant to. And to prevent diseases from crossing from animals to humans ever again. Do you know how much damn money they cost us create? The staff should use hookers if they want to get off, not expensive test subjects."

Ellie had to lock her jaw and lower her gaze not to show him how disgusted, horrified, and enraged his cold assessment of living, breathing people made her.

"Now we're making a bundle off them testing drugs we've cooked up to enhance the military and fitness freaks." He turned away to tear off his gloves. "Have you seen how damn big we've made them? How strong? We trained them to fight just to show what is possible to do to humans and how much damage they can take with the new batch of rapid-healing medicines. Do you know how many billions of dollars in contracts we're looking at? How much money we've already made so far? They are our prototypes. Showing what we can make them do, how fast, strong, and lethal they are is going to be the research for Mercile that blows our competitors out of the water. Every guy will want to buy what we've stirred up. That damn Jacob could have cost us a prime one. He's too valuable to take risks with."

Her eyes closed to hide her relieved tears. They wouldn't kill 416. She'd made the right choice. He may hate her for framing him for murder but he'd live. Now she just needed to leave after her shift, hand over the evidence she'd stolen, and save him the only way she could. She would help bring Mercile Industries to justice.

"Hey," Doctor Brennor sighed. "Sorry. I'm talking about money and you just survived a traumatic experience. Why don't you go home? You should take the rest of the day off. Hell, call in sick tomorrow."

She opened her eyes and met his gaze, hiding how desperately she hated him. "Thank you." Her voice trembled. "I was scared."

He gripped her arm, rubbed it, and smiled. "I could visit your home to check on you later." His gaze lowered to her breasts. "You shouldn't be alone."

"I have a boyfriend," she lied again.

He released her. "Fine. Go. I'll tell security I'm sending you home early."

He spun away, walked to the phone, and Ellie watched him. She hoped he got life in prison. It would serve him right.

Chapter One
Southern California
Eleven Months later

ഔ

Ellie sighed and adjusted her headphones to a more comfortable position. Heavy metal music poured out of the MP3 player she dropped into the front pocket of her cotton capri pants. The warm temperatures made her sweat even at eleven o'clock at night, despite the very slight breeze that fanned her skin. She glanced toward the open windows. The air-conditioning system of the dorm had gone out again. The maintenance teams were still fixing glitches on the newly constructed building.

She approached the balcony doors she tended to leave open and stepped outside to enjoy a nice breeze to help cool her overheated body. She sipped the cold water from the small plastic bottle she'd grabbed from the mini-fridge when she'd entered her apartment. She leaned against the railing to stare down at Homeland from her perch on the third floor. She'd just finished her nightly workout. The breeze felt heavenly on her skin. Her attention strayed to the security walls approximately fifty yards ahead.

They towered thirty feet high and guards patrolled the perimeter on the catwalks overhead. Below her stretched grass and a few trees that made a park-like setting between the dorm building and the outer wall. The new five-thousand-acre Homeland had just been completed and Ellie had spent her second day living there. No one strolled along the sidewalk that twisted through the grass and trees below.

The very quiet building disturbed her a bit but she'd been warned to expect it. Most of the women hadn't been moved into the dorm yet but once they were, Ellie hoped everything would go smoothly. She really wanted to make sure Homeland worked according to plan. It would house the survivors from Mercile Industries, an oasis from the rest of the world where they could live, and adjust to freedom within a safe community. They needed a safe haven.

She'd only known about Mercile Industries running one illegal testing facility but once it had been raided, three more existing ones had been discovered. She closed her eyes, still sickened over the number of victims involved that had been reported on the news coverage over the past months. Those testing facilities had been raided by government and law enforcement agencies, the victims now released, but not all of them had survived long enough to be rescued. The numbers of dead subjects were in the hundreds and those losses had broken her heart.

Ellie forced her eyes open. Two years prior she'd worked at Mercile's administrative building when she'd been approached by Officer Victor Helio. He had explained there were rumors about a secret research facility that forced human beings into being test subjects for illegal drugs. The police had tried to get undercover agents imbedded inside Mercile but they'd refused to hire anyone from the outside. As an existing employee she didn't raise suspicion when she'd asked for a transfer to one of their research and development testing facilities. She'd been so horrified by the concept of humans suffering that she'd agreed to spy for them. It had taken six months to be granted the request and months more to gain access to the lower floors of the research building, but then she'd met 416 and others living their hellish existences. She'd been proud of her part in bringing down the original testing facility. She'd risked her life to smuggle out those files but it had been enough evidence to have a judge grant search warrants that resulted in a full assault on the facility.

She sighed. Classified information and victim-protection policies were the terms she heard every time she'd asked about *him*. She knew some of the subjects hadn't survived the actual rescue from her testing facility. They'd been murdered before law enforcement breached the most secure lower areas where a lot of the victims had been kept. For all she knew, 416 had died floors below the surface, locked inside his cell, never knowing help had tried to reach him. It broke her heart to consider that possibility.

Ellie jerked the headphones from her ears, turned off her MP3 player and dropped them on the desk, fighting back the anguish she suffered every time she thought of 416. She'd wanted to be there when the warrants were served, to stand guard outside his door to protect him. She owed him that and so much more. She'd begged Officer Helio to allow it, but he'd refused. She wasn't law enforcement and she'd been firmly told they wouldn't risk an informant they needed testimony from to make their case against Mercile.

"Shit," she cursed.

She couldn't forget those dark eyes, the look on 416's face when she'd abandoned him that day inside his cell, or the way he'd growled at her. She'd only wanted to save his life but he had no way of knowing why she'd allowed him to take the blame for that technician's death. He must have thought her monstrous and cruel. Hot tears blinded her but she blinked rapidly to hold them at bay. She'd cried buckets of them since that awful day she'd left him on the floor.

The Homeland-issued phone rang, startling her. Her cell phone was her only contact to the outside world but no one called her on it. She'd distanced herself from her friends and family. Everything about her life had changed while working those months for that testing facility. She could no longer tolerate her divorced parents using her as a weapon against each other or tearing into her over her own divorce. There were genuine problems with the world and her time could be spent making a real difference. Now her focus centered on helping the New Species and it gave her a sense of worth by doing something to right a wrong. It gave meaning to her life and that's what she needed most. She answered the phone on the second ring.

"Ellie Brower."

"Ms. Brower, it's Cody Parks with security. I'm calling to inform you that we have a late transit arriving with four women. They were compromised at the hotel and we just received notification they are here."

"I'm on my way to the door now." She hung up.

Damn. The media must have somehow found out four of the rescued women are in the area. Protocol stated that, if a flight came in after dark, the victims should be placed with guards at a hotel to be transferred to Homeland during daylight hours. Security had deemed it easier to protect them while in transit during that time but obviously hiding the survivors inside a hotel hadn't been as smart as they'd thought. She could only hope the women hadn't been overly traumatized by whatever had happened. The real world could be frightening enough for those poor survivors without media vultures circling them with their shouted questions and flashing cameras.

It took mere seconds to slip on her shoes and grab her security card. Ellie left her room and purposely avoided the elevator. The thing moved too slowly for her patience. She jogged down the flights of stairs to the entryway. The windows were clear but were made of a type of glass that was strong enough to withstand abuse of the worst sort. Outside she spotted four women approaching the entry with two guards trailing behind, carrying four suitcases. She increased her pace.

Cody Parks, the "go to" man in security, greeted her with a smile. "Evening, Ms. Brower. Sorry for the late arrival of our newest residents."

Ellie smiled. She directed her focus to the Amazon-like women. The shortest of the four stood at least six feet tall. There were already ten women living inside the dorm, all of whom were tall, muscular types as well. Ellie felt short and tiny compared to them. Her smile widened as she glanced at each one but none of them returned the gesture. They looked tired, angry and out of sorts. Sympathy welled inside Ellie.

"Welcome to your new home." Ellie spoke softly. "I know you have been through a lot but you're safe here. I'm Ellie, your house mother."

Two of the women frowned. One woman, the tallest and most kick-ass-looking one of the small group, glared. The fourth one, a blonde, spoke.

"Our what?"

"Your house mother. It's just a title," Ellie explained quickly. "I'm not really trying to be your mother. I'm the one you will come to with problems, if you have questions, or if you need something. I'm here to help you in any way possible. You can talk to me about anything and I'll always listen."

"A head doctor," the shortest, dark-haired woman snapped. She barred her sharp teeth at Ellie.

"No," Ellie corrected. "I have basic nursing skills but I'm not a doctor. I know all of you had to see therapists. I've had to see a few of them myself and I hate them too." She gave them a sympathetic expression. "I'll show you to your rooms, give you a short tour around the dorm, and we'll get you settled. I—"

"Ms. Brower," Cody Parks interrupted.

Ellie turned her attention on him as the women walked through the doors. They glanced around the large entryway toward the living-room area. She knew they needed a few minutes to get their bearings.

"Yes?"

"There's been a meeting called in twenty minutes. They requested you be in attendance since you're in charge of the female housing. The head of their new council demanded to be briefed fully on Homeland. He wants to make certain his people aren't being mistreated in any way. He just got appointed to the position and needs the reassurance."

Dismay filled Ellie. "But it's so late. I'd like to get them settled and it will take longer than that."

"I understand but he showed up with them and stated it was important." The man's gaze held Ellie's. "It's imperative they know we are with them on this all the way to make everything smoother for them to transfer into a normal setting. He's worried."

She hesitated. New Species had been separated, sent to different secured locations after they'd been freed, until Homeland finally had been made ready to accept them as a large group. It would be their permanent home for the foreseeable future. The guy had valid reasons to worry about the safety and well-being of his people.

"Of course. Let me get them taken care of and I'll be right there. Is the meeting being held inside the conference room at the main office?"

He nodded. Ellie closed the door between them. The alarm beeped instantly to assure her the automatic locks were in place. While security was tight, it could never be strict enough, not after the way the media had converged on the survivors of those testing facilities. They were constantly trying to breach the perimeter to obtain pictures of the victims now that they had a fixed location where some of them would be.

The government had started the process of implementing a law to ban the media from revealing their photographs to protect the New Species. They were victims who had the right to be shielded from the press. There were also hate groups who didn't believe New Species should be considered human with equal rights, opposed them being given Homeland, and gathered outside the gates to protest.

She strode forward, going on autopilot, as she gave a short tour of the lower floor of the dorm. It housed a conference room for meetings, two large living-room areas, a roomy kitchen for cooking, a dining area that could host fifty, one large bathroom with four stalls, and a full library. The second and third floors housed mini apartments. They each contained a small bedroom, a living room, a private bath, and a kitchenette.

Ellie led the women to their rooms, side by side and across from each other on the second floor. She'd learned to do that in the two days she'd been handling the incoming women. They had to be frightened, not that they would admit it, but they did want to stay close to each other. Ellie knew the women had gone through unspeakable horrors and now they had a completely different one thrust upon them, something totally foreign. Freedom could be a terrifying experience after a lifetime of being test specimens.

"If you get hungry, there are cold drinks and food inside the silver metal boxes by the sink." She didn't call them refrigerators. She'd learned early on that they didn't know what those were. "There are ten other women here on the second floor so if you hear noises, please don't be alarmed. They are from different places." *Testing facilities*, she thought. "But they are your people. The building is secured so no one can get inside who isn't supposed to be here. You're completely safe."

The women who stood in the hallway were examining her as if she were a bug. Ellie sighed, used to it, unfortunately. They didn't trust outsiders—that being anyone who hadn't been reared as a test experiment.

"I will be on the third floor when I return from the meeting I need to attend. My room number is posted on the wall by the elevator. Just come to me for anything you need or if you have any questions. I am here to help you and I want to do that. Do you have anything you want to ask me before I go?"

The four women didn't speak. The tallest one spun on her heel to stalk into one of the rooms Ellie had just shown them. The other three followed and the door shut firmly with Ellie on the other side of it. None of the women seemed to want anything to do with her but she hoped that would change with time.

Ellie stared down at her outfit—running shoes, the black, cotton capris and a light-blue tank top. Her hair was secured in a ponytail. She knew she probably should change to something more professional but a glance at her watch assured her there wasn't enough time. She had to run to make the meeting. Ellie darted for the stairs.

The main offices were located near the front of Homeland. Each dorm and building had been assigned golf carts. Ellie drove hers to the front parking spaces and turned off the engine. She glanced at her watch again with a soft curse, certain she'd be late. Cody hadn't given her an exact time but twenty minutes had passed. She ran for the front double doors. She slowed to a walk when she spotted the armed security guard posted at the building. She didn't know him yet.

"Hello. I'm Ellie Brower. I'm the female dorm house mother. Cody Parks said there's a meeting I'm supposed to attend."

The man tensed and his hand gripped his weapon at his hip, while he glared. Ellie slowly reached into the front pocket of her pants to pull out her security card. It not only opened doors but it had her picture on it to identify her as an employee. She stepped closer to hold it out for his inspection.

The guard accepted her card, examined it carefully, and then handed it back. "Go inside to the left conference room. Are you familiar with where that is, Ms. Brower?"

"Yes, I am. Thank you."

Ellie inched around the man and entered the main office. She jogged down the long hallway and headed for the double doors where no guards were posted. She grabbed the handle, gave it a firm jerk to open the heavy door, and stepped inside.

The darkness of the room surprised her. The overhead lights were off and only scones dimly lit the walls. She couldn't see well but the soft rumble of many voices assured her the room had filled with people.

Two security guards turned instantly and grabbed for their guns. She met their alarmed expressions with a calm smile. Her hands lifted out away from her body to show them she held nothing threatening but her security card. The room became utterly silent. She didn't dare turn her attention away from the two men with their hands curved around their weapons.

"I'm Ellie Brower, house mother of the female dorm, and I come in peace."

Neither guard smiled at her attempted joke. One of the guards kept his hand on the gun at his waist while the other man came forward to yank her card from her hand. She didn't move while he examined it and then nodded.

"Take a seat. You're late." He offered the card back.

Ellie took her badge and returned it to her pocket. She had to move around the guard since he decided to remain, blocking her way. She took a few steps beyond him and peered at the people standing inside the room.

Darren Artino, the head of Homeland security, and Director Boris were also present. The director frowned as he closed the distance between them. She flinched when he glared at her outfit, silently communicating his disapproval of how was she dressed.

"I didn't have time to change," she explained. "I had four women to settle in and less than twenty minutes to do that before getting here. I wasn't given any notice they were arriving until they were at the door."

The tense lines around Director Boris' mouth eased. "Fine, Ellie. Next time, dress properly. You look as though you just walked out of the gym."

"Close," she admitted. "Would you like me to turn the lights up? It's dim inside here."

"No." Director Boris sighed. "Some of the council members prefer it this way."

Ellie instantly understood. She'd been informed that some of the survivors had spent years locked inside darkened cells, resulting in oversensitivity to bright light. She'd outfitted some of the apartments with those female survivors in mind, had even gone out to buy them sunglasses to put inside their rooms so they could wear them in the common areas of the dorm, and had dimmer switches added to some rooms for adjustable lighting. She spent a lot of time considering New Species feelings and needs to be good at her job, something that had become a near obsession for her.

She recognized a few more faces near her as she glanced around. She smiled at Mike Torres, from the male dorm, when he winked at her. He seemed to be a nice guy in his early thirties who had flirted with her during the first meeting, the day Ellie had arrived. The employee who'd given Ellie the rundown of her duties as dorm mother stood next to him. Dominic Zort nodded curtly. His job, in general, seemed to be keeping the departments cooperating and he did most of the hiring.

Movement from of the corner of her eye caught her attention. She turned. Someone moved in her direction from across the room but being the shortest person surrounded by a group of taller men didn't help her identify who approached.

"Ellie?" Director Boris drew her focus back to him. "We'll sit down over there."

"Sure." She took a step to follow Director Boris.

"*You*," a male voice snarled roughly from behind her.

Ellie attempted to spin around to see who the scary voice belonged to but someone grabbed her. She made a sound, a mixture between a grunt and a gasp, but then her body lifted from the floor. Strong arms twisted her in the air. Pain shot through her back and the air was knocked from her lungs. Her eyes widened as she stared up into the face of one enraged...416.

Chapter Two

ഇ

416 growled at Ellie, revealing his sharp canine teeth, and she realized her arms hurt where he gripped them above her elbows. He had slammed her flat on her back on top of one of the conference tables. He bent over her, his enraged face inches above hers, and the anger poured from his dark gaze. Pure terror flooded Ellie.

Her mouth opened but nothing came out. She sucked in air. He snarled louder, held her down tighter.

"What the hell? Let her go!" Director Boris gasped.

Ellie saw movement all around her from her side vision but she didn't dare turn her focus away from the dark, furious glare of 416. He looked as if he was ready to tear her throat out with his sharp teeth, which hovered inches from it. Her heart pounded so hard she wondered if it would explode from her ribs. He'd survived and would kill her just the way he'd promised he would if ever given the chance.

"Let her go," a male voice demanded firmly in a steely tone.

"What the hell is going on?" That came from another man who sounded shocked and whiny.

"Fury, let her go," another man ordered in an unusually deep voice.

Fury's rage-filled glare shifted away from Ellie's terrified gaze when he jerked his head to the side. He growled at someone behind him.

"No. This is between me and her. Back away."

Ellie swiped her tongue across her dry lips, relieved she could breathe again. The hands on her arms were bruising and it hurt enough that tears flooded her eyes. Fury glowered at someone behind him who kept his focus off her. Despite being in a room full of men, she knew she'd die in front of them when his attention returned to her.

"Let her go, Fury." The male voice grew deeper, to a menacing growl. "Please."

"She's one of them," Fury snarled. "She worked as a tech inside the testing facility. Back off now. It's my right for vengeance."

A distinctive noise cut through the room and Ellie's eyes widened. She recognized the sound of a shotgun being pumped. She swallowed the lump that formed in her throat, afraid they might shoot him to save her. *Damn it.* She wouldn't allow that to happen. All the terror dissipated at her concern for his life. She'd saved him once and she would do it again.

"It's okay." She spoke as loudly as she could. Her voice broke but she got the words out. "Don't hurt him. Nobody shoot. Please."

"Ellie?" Director Boris inched closer. "What is he talking about?"

Ellie gasped when her tormentor turned his head to glare down at her again. A chill ran down her spine from his cold, intense gaze and the knowledge that he would definitely carry out his threat. She had no doubt that he'd kill her on top of the table in front of everyone present.

"Fury," another male voice growled. "Release the woman. We'll settle this reasonably."

"Mine," Fury snarled, obviously so angry he couldn't talk in a normal tone. His fingers tightened even more.

Tears slid from her eyes to roll down the sides of her face but she didn't make a sound. She feared it would upset everyone around them, especially whoever had pumped the shotgun she'd heard.

"Ellie?" Dominic Zort sounded close. "You were an informant, weren't you?"

She swallowed a moan of pain. Fury softly growled and his hands were brutal on her arms.

"Yes," she gasped. "I know him."

The growl deepened inside Fury's throat to a vicious snarl.

"Fury!" A man rasped the word. "Release that woman now!"

Fury's grip eased but he didn't relinquish his hold. He moved back a few inches though. He didn't hover all the way over her body and his lips pressed together to hide his canine teeth. He took deep breaths through his nose but he didn't look away from Ellie.

Fury. Yeah, the new name fits the look in his eyes.

"She was already on Mercile's medical staff. She was sent undercover when rumors about the original testing facility surfaced. We tried to get undercover agents embedded inside Mercile but they were never hired. I think she was the on-site nurse at their corporate office. It took a lot of hard work for her to get transferred into that hellish place to discover if the rumors were true. She smuggled out enough proof to get us the warrants that were served on the first testing facility." Dominic Zort spoke quickly. "I didn't know she'd met any of your people, Justice. I wasn't her handler but Victor Helio didn't write anything in the file to indicate she had harmed any New Species or had interacted with them. I never would have hired her to work with your people if I thought any of them knew her personally." Dominic Zort's voice remained calm and cool. "Her name is Ellie Brower and she's the one who runs the women's dorm. She risked her life every day to spy on Mercile for us, Justice. She knew they would kill her if they realized she only took that job to gain proof of what they were doing."

"Let her go." Justice's tone lightened but it held the authority of an order. "Ease up, Fury. I understand. Did you hear what the man said? She worked there to help them gather proof of our existence. She helped save our people."

Fury didn't release Ellie and he continued to glower down at her. She stared back at him, certain he didn't care why she'd been there. She knew he hated her for framing him for Jacob's death and she didn't blame him for it. She had done it to save his life but that didn't alleviate the guilt of the crime committed against him.

"Ellie?" Director Boris spoke. "What was your exact job at the research facility and what did you do to this man?"

Shit. Ellie swallowed. She watched Fury's eyes darken even more, turning from a chocolate brown to near black. "I just assisted when needed," she explained softly. "I kept a lot of the charts on the test results from the blood and saliva samples they had me draw."

"Why does he hate you so much? Did you personally hurt him somehow?" Director Boris voice rose in outrage. "Did you harm them?"

Ellie stared into Fury's tense, lined face. If she'd been sexually assaulted, she wouldn't want it flaunted about. He had been a proud male and it probably wasn't something he wanted to share with the entire room. She'd have to tell everyone why she'd killed the technician if she admitted what she'd done to make Fury so angry. She hesitated. His eyes narrowed to slits as the growl rumbling from his chest became louder.

"Don't," Fury ordered.

"Fury?" Justice spoke. The man had an unusually deep voice. "What did she do to make you want to hurt her so much? Did she force you to take their drugs?"

"Ellie, tell us now," Director Boris demanded.

"I had to do tests," she lied. "I had to inflict pain on him." That part was truthful. She knew what she'd done had to have caused him emotional distress on top of what Jacob had done to him while he'd lain helpless on that floor of his cell. "He also didn't like me taking samples from him."

He snarled at her in response.

She didn't look away from him once, her gaze locked with his. "I'm so sorry but I didn't have a choice. I knew help was coming if I could just smuggle out the evidence. I did what I had to do to rescue you. You were so close to getting a chance at freedom." More tears spilled down the sides of her face. "I am so very sorry. I just wanted to save you."

Fury had the woman who had betrayed him in his grasp. He couldn't believe he had found Ellie again, she worked at Homeland, and his hands were actually on her. He had his freedom now, was no longer helpless, and he battled with himself over what he should do to her. A small part of him wanted to snap her neck while the rest of him wanted to pull her against his body and hold her. Either way, he didn't want to release her. Self-disgust welled at his conflicting emotions after what she'd done to him inside his cell. He'd never forget that day or the one that followed.

Justice demanded again that he release Ellie but his hands refused to let go. That she'd dare be where New Species were supposed to be safe from their tormentors enraged him. She'd been the worst, with her pretty blue eyes that had lured him into a sense of trust that she'd never do him harm. His fingers flexed on her soft skin as he inhaled her scent that had haunted him many nights.

Her pale-blue gaze seemed more beautiful than he remembered and he inwardly flinched while he watched tears pool inside her eyes and slip down the sides of her face, knowing he hurt her. He battled with the knowledge that he had the right to get revenge but at the same time hated to cause her pain. When she spoke up to tell everyone not to hurt him, it confused him more. Ellie had to be his enemy so why did she attempt to protect him?

"Fury," Justice whispered. "She's a woman."

No one needed to tell him Ellie's sex. Her sweet scent of strawberries and vanilla made him want to groan, to bury his nose against her skin and investigate exactly where it originated from. He wondered if her hair products or her body wash gave off the tempting smells. It angered him more that he wanted to find out.

It stunned him to learn she had been working against his enemy. It did matter to him why she'd been at the testing facility but he couldn't let go of his sense of betrayal over her leaving him inside that cell to face the consequences of her actions.

Didn't she realize what she'd done or how he'd been harmed? But he didn't want her to tell the truth about what she'd done to anger him so much. Too many questions would be asked. He had enough shame. He didn't want anyone to know how deeply his humiliation ran when it came to feeling helpless all those years he was locked up and the abuse he'd suffered in his lifetime.

He was New Species, in control of his mind and body, though he'd been a prisoner. He couldn't have prevented the technician from attacking him but as he'd lain there helpless, still traumatized from what had been done to him, and his body had responded to Ellie being so close to him. She'd turned him on despite the horrible situation. He had not wanted to react to her that way. It only made her betrayal even more unforgivable. He'd lowered his guard and then she'd harmed him. He acknowledged that he'd lost control again when he'd mindlessly grabbed her and now refused to release her.

The pain revealed by her features finally made him understand how strongly he gripped her arms and it horrified him, realizing he'd bruised her tender skin. He should want to kill her but instead he wished to massage out the pain, even apologize, and it disgusted him. He had earned the honored job of being second in command of his people, an example to

Species of how they could live in peace with humans, yet he stood over a terrified small woman who had haunted him since he'd been freed.

He'd always wondered what had become of her. He'd even used his new authority to read through the list of Mercile employees arrested. He'd fantasized about walking into her cell and...watching her, just to see her again. A snarl tore from his throat and he knew he needed to get away from her before he lost what little control he'd regained.

He needed to think, to get a grip on whatever had gone wrong inside his mind when it came to Ellie. He usually kept his reason, remained calm regardless of his circumstances, and others considered him good natured. His people depended upon him to remain that way. He'd chosen his name for what he kept in his heart but outwardly he hid it well. Usually.

He stared down at Ellie and ordered his hands to open, regardless of how his instincts screamed to keep hold of her. Fury's grip loosened and he released Ellie as if her touch burned him then he spun around and shoved people out of his way.

Ellie lay immobile on top of the table until someone touched her leg. She was shocked that Fury had allowed her to live. Darren Artino moved next to her, his touch gentle as he pulled her into a sitting position. Ellie glanced at the stunned faces of the men who surrounded her. She quickly wiped away her tears, amazed to be alive. She searched for Fury but he'd vanished.

"Ms. Brower?"

The man who spoke stood about as tall as Fury. He had wide shoulders and his long hair had been swept back into a ponytail. His eyes were an appealing dark bluish-black and oddly shaped, similar to a cat's. He dressed in a tailored suit but nothing could hide the dangerous vibes he projected while he remained a few feet from her.

"I apologize for Fury's…" He paused. "Attack on you. I'm Justice North and I will make sure Fury is punished for what he's done here. Did he harm you?" His exotic, unnerving gaze slowly skimmed down her body.

"I'm fine," Ellie lied softly.

Her heart broke into pieces that the man she had grown obsessed with had just walked away. She resisted the urge to run after Fury, beg him to listen to her, and apologize again for what she'd once done to him. She wanted to make it right with him so badly she ached. She realized that doing that would be impossible as she stared up at the large male who blocked her path. He currently posed a threat to Fury and she needed to handle the situation before it escalated.

Ellie attempted not to openly gawk at the good-looking man with the fascinating eyes. "Please don't punish him." She would beg if that's what it took. It was the least she could do to make sure Fury didn't get in any kind of trouble. "His anger is warranted. Trust me. I wouldn't have blamed him if he'd killed me."

Shock paled the man's features while he blinked at her a few times. His shoulders, broad as they were, seemed to relax. "Perhaps you should be excused from this meeting. You've had a trauma and I'm sure someone here could fill you in on what will be discussed at your convenience tomorrow, after you've had time to recover."

Director Boris moved forward. "We shall remove her from Homeland immediately, Mr. North. Please accept our apologies."

Dread spread through Ellie. She'd moved to a new state to be a part of the project to assimilate New Species into a normal way of living but now she'd lose that job. She didn't blame Director Boris for firing her, considering the circumstances. Homeland had been given to the New Species to be a safe haven from the abuse they'd suffered. Having a walking reminder on the premises would violate that concept.

Justice frowned as he stared down at Director Boris. "Firing her won't be necessary. She saved our people from the testing facilities and we won't thank her for that selflessness by taking her away from something she helped make possible. It's not our way to do that. This is our Homeland, is it not?"

Director Boris' mouth popped open from shock. "But Fury hates her and he's your second in command."

"Fury will deal with his anger." Justice glanced at Ellie then. The harsh expression eased from his features and softened. "Go rest, Ms. Brower. Your job is secure. You can continue to run the women's sleeping dorm. You have been quite refreshing with your candor and I appreciate your understanding of Fury's behavior."

Ellie knew to escape when given the opportunity. She eased off the table. Her knees trembled but held her weight once she stood. She kept her head down, her gaze on the floor, and strode quickly toward the empty hallway. She paused outside the conference room, leaned against the wall and then covered her face. Her entire body shook. It took a minute to pull her frayed emotions together.

Ellie finally moved, dropped her hands to her sides, and exited the outer door. 416 had survived but now he had taken the name Fury. Worse, he had to be Justice North's second in command. She shivered when she stepped outside. The armed guard frowned at her but didn't say anything as she moved toward her golf cart.

Justice headed the New Species Organization. His people had voted him to lead them, the face and voice of New Species as a whole, but they'd also appointed council members to represent groups of the survivors, thus helping him do his new job. One survivor from each of the four testing facilities had become a member. The NSO as they titled themselves, had proclaimed their own government order when they'd been assured the United States would back them on having free rein to structure their independence.

The fact that the government had unknowingly funded those testing facilities with large research grants had gone a long way to make Uncle Sam bend over backward to be accommodating with anything they asked for. They'd used taxpayer's money to help create New Species and continue the horrific research that had been done on them for decades in the name of perfecting prescription drugs and vaccines. A lot of money had exchanged hands at the expense of the suffering of New Species. The newly built military base had been gifted to them as their Homeland, rumored to be the government's grand gesture to save face and garner favor with public opinion overall.

Ellie parked the golf cart in front of the dorm and climbed out. She rubbed her aching arms and hurried toward the front doors. She had nearly reached them when the hair on the back of her neck prickled. She stilled after she pulled out her ID card and slowly peered over her shoulder.

A man lurked under the shadow of a tree across the street, just a dim outline of a figure, but Ellie sensed him watching her. She knew it had to be Fury. She stood there staring at him. She held her ground and he held his while neither of them moved.

Ellie bit her lip, wondering if she should approach him. She could apologize again for what she'd done to him and maybe explain in more detail until he understand her actions fully that day inside his cell. Indecision kept her in place while she struggled with the need to talk to him and the fear that he hadn't calmed down.

He didn't move and she couldn't make her legs respond to go to him. The memory of his rage, of his hands squeezing her flesh, changed her mind about talking to him at that moment. Fear motivated her to face the door, swipe her key card, and hurry inside the dorm. She made sure the locks slid into place before dashing for the elevator.

An eerie silence settled into the dorm late at night. She entered the elevator with the sensation of being watched. With walls of glass, she knew he could see her from where he stood outside. The doors shut firmly to put her out of view of the street and Ellie sagged against the wall. Would he let it go? She didn't know but now he knew where she lived. He also worked at Homeland and probably lived in one of the housing units built just blocks away for the council and high-ranking members of the New Species.

Damn.

The elevator dinged when it opened on the third floor where she currently was the only resident. Once more women were transferred to the dorm, the rooms would fill up until the building would be full of life on every level. She suddenly minded being alone up there a lot.

The building was secure, she reminded herself. The only people who had access to the building were the women living there and the security guards assigned to guard it. Not even a member of the council had access. Fury wouldn't be able to get in. She unlocked her door.

She'd left the lights on inside her small apartment and her balcony doors still stood wide open. She moved toward them quickly to close the doors firmly and locked them for the first time. No one could reach her balcony but she didn't care about logic. She looked down at her arms after she undressed—verifying both were red and bruised from Fury's hands—and then stepped into her bathroom to shower.

Fury survived! That thought kept circling inside her mind. Hot tears spilled down her cheeks. If that day had never happened she would have had a chance to get to know him. *He may have…*Her eyes closed in pain. *What? Fallen in love with me the way I've fallen for him?* It was insane to even consider that possibility. They didn't really know each other but she wanted to change that. *He hates me.* That had been clear when he'd slammed her onto the table and rage had poured off him.

Ellie reached up and wiped at her tears. What she'd done to him couldn't have been avoided. She could only hope that one day he'd forgive her for leaving him inside the cell to take the blame for her crime. *Then maybe...*

"Damn it, don't do this to yourself," she whispered aloud, shaking her head.

Chapter Three

Ellie watched the New Species women with frustration. She knew making friends with them would be a difficult task but she'd had no idea how hard a time they planned to give her. Not one of them had been friendly toward her. They were a tight group but not with Ellie. She hoped she hid her hurt feelings. Helping them had become her mission in life, her sole purpose, and they had refused to allow it so far.

"Would any of you like to learn how to cook? I can teach you or I've acquired a ton of cooking DVD's to show you." She glanced from one face to another. "I'm sure some of you are tired of the meals provided by the main NSO cafeteria. I enjoy cooking. It's good to learn and everyone loves food."

No one spoke as three dozen pairs of eyes watched her. Ellie sighed. "I swear, I'm not the enemy. I'm here to help you learn living skills and to help you integrate into society. I want to help you in any way you need. I really wish you would allow me to do that."

Their silence stretched to an uncomfortable length. Ellie's shoulders slumped in momentary defeat. "Fine. Maybe you need more time to get to know me. If you need anything, please just let me know. That's why I'm here. Oh, I baked a few cakes I put inside the fridge so please eat them."

Ellie fled the room before she allowed them to see her depression. As soon as she moved out of sight she heard female voices, reinforcing her urge to cry. Everyone became silent when she walked into a room but conversation returned as soon as she left. She couldn't ignore the possibility they might hate her. They refused to talk with her except when they had to and they didn't seem to want her help. She'd had to hold mandatory class sessions just to teach them basics such as how to use the appliances in the house. The questions were few but then again, she'd noticed that some of them had amazing memories. They would retain the information and then help the other women who struggled.

She'd considered quitting but she'd been assured by one of the council members that the women would shun anyone holding the position. She was an outsider, it was that simple, and being just plain ole human made the New Species not trust her. She'd been advised to give it time and reminded that it had only been two weeks.

Two weeks of hell, she silently grumbled, and headed for her apartment. If she left though, she had nowhere to go, no life to go back to, after cutting all ties with her past. The very idea of asking her parents to live with one of them until she got back on her feet threatened to give her a migraine.

Her parents argued about everything, regardless of living apart, and then asked her to referee their asinine fights. Both of them had been bitterly opposed to Ellie's own divorce, the *only* thing they agreed on, and they remained in contact with her ex-husband. They'd make her spend time with him with their misguided and annoying attempts to get them back together. She'd rather jump into a pit of snakes than ever return to the life she'd once had. She didn't call home for a reason and she sure didn't want to go back to it. Both her parents were angry at her, which meant they finally gave her peace, something she hadn't had from the pair since their divorce when she was ten.

Her new life consisted of moving forward and helping people with real problems, two things she wanted to do with the New Species. They were important to her and they needed people who cared on their side. She definitely cared.

Ellie changed quickly, put on a pair of sweats, a tank top, and running shoes. She needed fresh air and time away from the dorm, certain she wouldn't be missed. She tried not to feel self-pity. She'd assumed the job would have kept her busier and maybe have been rewarding. Instead she suffered loneliness and depression. She tucked her MP3 player into the front of her bra and shoved her ID card there too since she didn't have pockets. She left her room and started to jog in place while she waited for the elevator.

Ellie glanced at her watch when she left the dorm building and took note of the dark sky outside with only a few stars twinkling above. She turned and faced the windows to peer inside at the women who sat on couches laughing together in the living room area. She couldn't hear what they said but the dozen women she spied on seemed happy.

Happy I'm not there, she thought grimly. She muttered a curse as she turned her back on the sight. She'd never been a jogger until she'd moved into Homeland. Physical activity helped her deal with her boredom. She broke into a slow run along the sidewalk. The park-like area extended for a great distance along the guarded walls.

Ellie reached into her bra to turn up the volume on her MP3 player until music pounded in her ears. She went through phases with types of music and recently she'd been into heavy metal to fit her mood. She traveled steadily along as the path turned away from the walls and toward the park that contained a large pond. She enjoyed running next to the water.

Ellie slowed to a fast walk for a good block when she started to tire until she reached the pond. She stopped to stretch, bent over to touch her toes, and then straightened. She saw movement from the corner of her eye. She turned, expecting to see another jogger appear but she saw no one. She frowned. She could have sworn she'd seen someone.

Ellie shook her head and dismissed it. She figured the wind moving the treetops had drawn her attention. She stretched her arms upward and twisted her body in various positions to loosen muscles. Her body ached when she jogged but she wanted to get into shape. At twenty-nine it seemed to be a good time to do it.

She smirked, knowing her ex-husband would drop from a heart attack if he got an eyeful of her now. She'd once been more than a little overweight. She had almost totally become a different person after her bitter divorce from a cheating, verbally abusive ass who believed her pathetic enough to take whatever he dished out. He'd been wrong. She wasn't a doormat, would never stay with someone who didn't know how to love, and had ended the marriage despite Jeff's protests.

She'd completely turned her life around after she'd witnessed suffering firsthand while working at the testing facility. Forty pounds lighter and free of her ex, she had a much happier outlook. She chuckled. She'd actually lost two hundred forty pounds of unwanted weight since Jeff had accounted for two hundred of them. Her final cut from her past had been escaping her parents after they'd tried to guilt her into taking Jeff back. *Hell hasn't frozen over yet*, she thought with a smirk.

The hair on the back of her neck suddenly prickled. Her limbs froze while just her gaze darted around the park. Landscapers had planted lots of trees, turning the area into a mini forest area surrounding the water. A few park benches had been strategically placed and the buildings were located on the outer edges of the park. She could just make out the tops of them from where she stood. She studied the darkness once more, the sense of being watched growing.

Ellie reached down the front of her shirt to grip her MP3 player and pushed the "off" button as she removed it. She listened intently but didn't hear anything out of place. She started to turn the music back on but a soft growl made her jump. A dog? She looked over her shoulder to scan the surroundings again.

There were a few guard dogs patrolling Homeland but their handlers were always a leash away. Security guards would be in view if one of the canine units were in the vicinity. A sudden urge to return to the dorm gripped her.

Ellie took a few steps but heard another growl, closer this time. Her body tensed with alarm. She scanned the area again to search for the source while she shoved her headphones down to her neck and held her music player in a tightfisted grip. She hoped one of the dogs hadn't gotten loose. They were large, mean animals, and well trained in defending the property. They'd treat her as if she were an intruder.

"Hello?" Her voice rose. She hoped a security guard would answer. "Is anyone there?"

Fury had been watching the women's dorm where Ellie lived and had caught many glimpses of her through the first-floor glass windows. She worked with his women and he'd been proud when they gave the human the cold shoulder until he'd seen the sadness on Ellie's face. It tore at him to witness her pain. He shouldn't care but he did.

He had been stunned when he'd seen her leave the secure building alone, jogging away from safety. Didn't she realize the danger he posed? That he'd be watching her? Didn't her survival instincts scream out that he'd be close?

Obviously not since he'd easily followed her and watched her slowly run into the park where the secluded area nearly begged for him to approach her. Then she stopped as if she were waiting for him. He inhaled her scent on the wind and groaned as his body reacted. He wanted to be closer to her more than his next breath and it really angered him. She was his enemy.

He snarled as he battled the beast that lurked inside him for control. His human side knew she was off limits. She'd been an informant, had helped his people. It was the reason she'd been at his testing facility, but the animal side of him wanted to draw closer to touch and to claim her. That truth startled him.

He balked at following his instincts. She had betrayed him after he'd trusted her to never do anything that would harm him. Regardless of her reasons working for Mercile, it didn't excuse what she'd done to him, or the anger he lived with, knowing the price her actions had cost him.

He trained his males to keep their animal instincts on a tight leash and he needed to do the same, set an example, and stay in control. He had responsibilities to Species to show them life existed outside the testing facilities and that they weren't just animals created by Mercile, who had drilled insults into their heads all their lives. Ellie was living proof, though, that he had a weakness—her.

She peered around her in the darkness, as if she could sense him. His animal howled inside his soul to go to her, to take her, and to touch her. He fought the urge but then he moved toward her regardless of his wishes. Once again he'd lost control when it came to her. He just couldn't resist her scent, the strong desire to look into her eyes and hear her voice.

Rage boiled through his human side while his animal reveled in pure lust at the sound of her sweet, taunting voice. He battled himself once again when he inhaled her fear, wanted to protect her, but also needed to terrify her to send her as far from him as she could get.

Movement once again caught Ellie's attention. She gasped when Fury stepped from behind a tree twenty feet away. Her entire body reacted to the sight of the tall, attractive male, and the sensation of danger radiating off him. She swallowed, her breathing increased and fear jolted through her when the shock wore off. She hadn't heard a dog at all—the growl had come from him. Fury had made that scary sound.

His long silky hair cascaded down over his shoulders and chest, as free and unrestrained as he appeared to be at that moment. The black clothing he wore hugged his broad shoulders, impressive muscular arms, and outlined his trim waist. An air of danger emanated from him when his dark gaze seemed to fasten on her, swept down her entire body slowly, and a soft growl grumbled deep within his throat. His jaw clenched, the muscles tensing, apparent even in the dim light.

He took a step forward, more of a predatory motion than the way a man would move, advancing on her slowly. Her gaze lowered to his muscular thighs, outlined in his tight black pants, all the way down to his black shoes. He radiated strength and sex appeal and she swallowed hard. Her heart speeded up, her breathing increased, and her body became aware of him as a purely male being.

No one had ever affected her the way he did. He advanced another stalking step, the fluid motion nearly seductive and she realized he dressed to blend into the darkness, as if he'd intended to hide, but had allowed her to see him by stepping into just enough light to reveal his presence to her alone.

Fury regarded her silently now, his gaze trained on her face, and as she studied him, she swore she saw a hungry look on his handsome features. His tongue darted out to wet his lower lip, the pink tip a taunt of something forbidden but tempting, and his dark eyes narrowed as if he could read her mind. She wanted to kiss him, longed to know how it would feel to have him touch her again but this time, not in anger. Of course that wouldn't happen. He hated her.

"Oh crap," she whispered but then spoke louder. "Hello, uh, Fury. Nice night for a jog, isn't it?"

He said nothing but took another step closer before he stopped. Her terror built. They were alone and he'd sworn to kill her. She couldn't call to the guards on patrol for help—they weren't within sight.

A low snarl passed his parted lips as he took another step in her direction. The urge to flee increased for Ellie but she held still, having read reports that the New Species were really fast. Their altered DNA, depending on what animal it had been combined with, accounted for that. Fury obviously had been mixed with canine and could certainly run her down if she fled. She wasn't sure if she should scream, attempt to talk her way out of the frightening situation, or just hope he meant no harm. He moved closer.

"Do you know what they trained us to do in order to show us off to their investors?" His voice came out harsh, cold and scary.

She had to clear her throat, which wanted to close with fear. "Not really. Most of the files were destroyed when the testing facilities at Mercile Industries were breached. I wasn't allowed access to that information when I worked there."

"Hunt," he growled. "I excelled at that training. I was the best of the prototypes. They taught us how to do things to sell their drugs, to show living examples of what humans could become if they bought their stupid shots and pills."

Ellie realized her future seemed questionable at that moment. Fury hated her and he spoke in a way she knew could turn deadly. She couldn't find the right words, didn't know how to defuse the situation. He took another step toward her. *Shit, double shit*, she thought frantically. He would reach her with just a few more steps.

"I didn't have a choice that day," she blurted. "I killed Jacob to protect you but if they'd known I did it, they wouldn't have allowed me to leave. I just wanted to save you. I didn't even mean to kill him."

"Did you tell anyone what he did to me or how you allowed me to suffer for what you'd done?"

"No." She shook her head. She had been too afraid to tell her handler that she'd interfered, certain he'd be angry since she'd gone against direct orders to do nothing to make anyone at Mercile suspicious. Killing a technician to protect a New Species would have definitely done that. His words sank in. *Suffered?*

"Were you too ashamed of what you'd done?"

She hesitated. "You have no idea how much so. I—"

"You told the guards I killed him," he snarled, cutting her off. "You smeared his blood on my hands. Don't bother denying it."

Hot tears of regret threatened to spill but she rapidly blinked them back. "I—" She swallowed. "I didn't have a choice. I didn't think they'd kill you or I never would have implied you'd been the one to kill Jacob. You have to bel—"

"Believe you?" His dark gaze narrowed and a dangerous sound emanated from deep within the back of his throat. "It turned you on to see me suffering, to know what kind of cruelty you would cause me."

How does he know I was turned on? She didn't dare ask but she wasn't about to lie to him, considering she owed him far too much to do that. Her lips sealed. She was unsure how to explain to him why she'd responded so strongly to him because she couldn't justify it. Her body's response to him as a man under those circumstances had just been wrong.

"It wasn't because you suffered or that I planned to jab you with that needle. I had to make it look as if he'd died while trying to inject you to make the story believable. I'm so sorry."

"I'm surprised you aren't attempting to lie."

Ellie lifted her chin to meet his angry glower. "You're right. My body did respond to being that close to you. I have no excuse. All I can do is apologize. I know it was immoral and I feel really guilty. You are…" She hesitated, about to tell him how attractive she found him. "You were naked and I couldn't help but notice despite the horrific circumstances. I'm sorry."

Fury's jaw tensed. She could see his features clearly now that only a few feet separated them. "You were working for Mercile Industries. Did you drag your feet on finding incriminating evidence? Did you enjoy what that technician did to me?" He snarled at her, flashed sharp teeth, and inched closer. "Did it turn you on that he harmed me and planned to rape me? Did you earn the trust of other Species males when you walked into their cells until they didn't growl at you either? Did you lure them into a sense of being nonthreatening? Did you allow them to be blamed for things you did?" His nostril's flared and he growled deep in his chest. "Who else did you betray?"

Ellie reeled back at his vicious accusations, as if he'd physically struck her. "No! You were the only one I ever had to do that to. I tried to find enough proof for a judge to issue a warrant. How dare you! I collected samples, wrote reports, but I wasn't given access to any of the older files that showed anything that would prove you existed down there. Every day they strip-searched us before we were allowed to leave. I couldn't smuggle in a camera to prove what the hell they were doing to any of you or that you weren't just a rumor. You have no idea how terrifying it was for me to go through the main door to that elevator every single shift. I always wondered if I'd ever see daylight again if they figured out I spied for the police. They would have killed me. The other employees talked and warned me what happened if Mercile even suspected anyone would turn against them. They cautioned that I'd just disappear and my body would never be found."

"If they stripped you then how did you smuggle evidence out?"

Heat bloomed on her cheeks. "You really want to know?"

"I do." He snarled.

"I swallowed it."

His features blanked for a second and then he frowned. "I don't understand."

"I had to make friends with a few of the doctors and that took time. I didn't have access to anything vital but they did. I carefully gained their trust, became very close to a doctor who looked similar to me, and I switched lab coats with her during lunch. I stole her keycard, started wearing my hair the way she did, I tucked my head when I passed the security cameras and when I marched into her office. I'd seen her punch in her code a few times and remembered it to gain access to her office. I had a tiny computer data drive my handler had given me to copy files. I swallowed it. So many things could have gone wrong."

He stared at her, frowning.

"I was sure they'd catch me and that guards would storm the office and kill me. You have no idea how terrified I felt walking out of there and praying I could switch coats back without her figuring it out. It was *that* day too, you know." She paused. "The last thing I wanted to do was draw attention with that damn thing sitting inside my stomach, knowing how important it was to get to my handler, but I still tried to save you regardless of the risk to myself or the evidence. Do you want to hear how painful it is to throw up something the size of a mini thumb drive? It made it seem easy to swallow it in the first place. I was willing to allow them to operate on me to retrieve it if puking didn't work. They were afraid my stomach acids would damage the thing if much time elapsed."

He continued to frown as seconds ticked by. "You deceived me as well. That's what you do." His mouth pressed into a firm line. "You lie to people and then betray them. You're no better than those monsters who created and enslaved my people."

Pain lanced through her chest at his harsh words, followed quickly by all-consuming anger. She'd killed someone for him and risked her life to free his people. *Damn him.*

"I didn't want to hurt you in any way." She paused. "But I'll tell you one thing. I saved your ass, Fury. You are still alive because of what I did. You would be dead if I hadn't walked into your cell and stopped that asshole. You'd have died chained to a floor being abused by that son of a bitch just mere days before you would have been set free. If that's unforgivable to you then too damn bad. Keeping you alive became my main priority."

"You said you hated me. You called me a worthless bastard and you wanted me to know that. I never forgot what you said."

Ellie gaped at him. "No."

"I lay there on my back helpless and you moved away from me to take blood from the technician to smear on my knuckles. You hissed those hated words at me."

Understanding dawned and she knew the color drained from her face. "I wasn't talking to you. I was saying it to Jacob! I hated him and he was a bastard for what he'd done to you."

"The male was dead. Don't lie to me. You spoke those hated words to me."

"No." She frantically shook her head, her gaze locked with his. "I swear, I was talking to him. I hoped that if he could hear me in hell — I'm sure that's where he went for all his evil deeds — that he'd know how I felt about him."

Fury frowned, studied her features, and remained silent.

"That's the truth."

"Do you want to know the worst part when you walked into my cell?" His deep voice turned ice cold. His entire body tensed visibly.

She just shook her head and her fear returned. Rage emanated from his eyes. They looked darker than she remembered but it was dimmer in the park than it had been inside the conference room weeks before.

"I can still feel your touch on me. You soothed me at first. You saved me and I believed you wouldn't cause me any harm. I actually welcomed your hands on my body. I close my eyes and the memory of you is burned there." He took another step. "I remember you running away after what you'd done, leaving me confused and in pain. The needle you shoved it into my skin hurt less than the pain that pierced my heart."

"I'm so sorry. Not a day goes by when it doesn't haunt me." She paused. "I did it to save your life. You know what Jacob planned to do to you but I stopped him. I had to find a way to smuggle that evidence out. I'm so sorry. The last thing I wanted to do was hurt you more. I didn't want to frame you for his murder or jab you with that needle but I had to make it look convincing enough for them to let me walk out of there."

He took another step. "None of it matters," he growled. "All I remember is what you did. It's all I hold on to. I swore if I saw you again I'd kill you with my bare hands." He nearly touched her as he stopped inches away. "You should run if you have a brain in your head. I'm fighting to keep in control and have no idea which side of me will win. Never forget that I'm part animal."

Fury hoped she would take his advice. He could see Ellie's fear on her expressive, delicate features. He hated noticing the little lines by her mouth that revealed she smiled often. He wondered what it would be like to hear her laughter. *He'd* never had a reason to smile until he'd gained his freedom. Her lower lip pouted out slightly with worry, fuller than her top one, and the urge to suck on it struck him.

Her hair drew his attention next. It was so unlike his, with its near-white appearance and unruly curls. It appeared to have a soft texture, smelled of strawberries, and framed her face, making her bone structure seem fragile.

New Species women are drastically different from my small human. He froze, realizing he'd just called her his. Outrage poured through him. He knew better than to trust any human. They inflicted pain every chance they were given. Especially her. She'd just admitted to being a skilled liar. For all he knew, everything she'd just said could be false to gain his sympathy.

He'd be damned if he gave her a chance to betray him again. And yet the idea of her being his did confusing things to him. His gut tightened, his fingers itched to touch her and he had the crazy urge to say something to alleviate her fear of him. *Hell*, he realized with disgust, *I want to make her laugh just to see her smile.* It was insane and wrong. His conflicting thoughts and emotions when it came to her made his rage burn hotter. Ellie, it seemed, had become a master manipulator and he didn't ever want to be on the receiving end of it again.

Fury tried to focus on the present. He had his enemy within his sights and he had the opportunity to finally give some payback to at least one person who'd harmed him. So far he hadn't been given a single occasion to even up the score. The worst offenders hadn't been arrested to face punishment for what they'd done while others had fled into hiding. That left the woman before him as his only outlet.

His heart hammered erratically and an image filled his mind of the last time she'd run from him after she'd betrayed him. Memory returned so strongly that he staggered back a foot from the blow of emotions washing through him. She'd been so rushed that she'd missed the door and smacked into the wall in her haste to see him punished for what she'd done.

The animal inside him howled out for him to grab her. Chains no longer restrained him and drugs didn't hold his body immobile. He tensed, every muscle rigid, and he saw her move back a step. He inhaled sharply—her fear was so strong he could taste it. It made his instincts scream to cover her, to protect her, even though it enraged him that she had that effect on him. He snarled as conflicting emotions battled.

She was the enemy yet he desperately wanted to touch her. The second she spun around and sprinted away, he lunged forward, charging after the woman he wanted more than anything else he'd ever desired in his life. There wasn't a thing he could do to stop his animal from taking over.

Once again he'd totally lost all control.

Ellie felt the blood drain from her face as she watched raw emotions play over Fury's features. The good intentions that held her in place scattered when she saw his feral look, heard his pained, animalistic snarl. She spun and sprinted away in panic. Fury closed the distance between them. Terror urged her to run faster. Her MP3 player slipped from her terrified fingers to crash onto the sidewalk a second before he grabbed her from behind.

Ellie opened her mouth to scream but slammed into the grass before she could get it out. His heavy body knocked the air from her lungs. He tore her headphones away. The weight on top of her shifted. Ellie sucked in air before he grabbed her again and his weight returned when Fury rolled her onto her back.

His large body pinned hers tightly against the damp grass. She attempted to shove him off but he didn't budge. Her palms futilely pushed against his steely chest. She moaned in fear as she met his furious dark rage. Canine teeth flashed inches above her face in the dim light.

His hands gentled when they gripped her arms, jerked them quickly above her head, and he enclosed her wrists within one of his hands. He clenched his teeth, still showing fang-like canine teeth, and growled deep inside his chest. He vibrated against her body with the very terrifying sound he made.

"Please don't hurt me," she panted.

His chest shifted off her slightly, enough to let her breathe. Ellie gasped in more air. His eyes searched hers for something and she wondered what he wanted to see. Whatever he discovered made him softly curse. He released her wrists and rolled away suddenly to leap to his feet. Ellie remained sprawled on the grass staring up at him in shock that he'd let her go. She ached from his rough treatment and her heart raced.

"Get up," he ordered harshly.

Ellie had to fight to stand. It wasn't graceful, to be sure, but she rose to her feet. She wanted to flee again but didn't have the strength.

"I told you that I'm sorry. What more do you want from me?" She inched closer to peer into his narrowed gaze. "Whatever it takes to make this up to you, just say the words.

I'd do it. I'll do anything to make things right between us. Name it."

Fury watched her as he stepped closer but he remained silent and guarded. His hand shot out suddenly and wrapped slowly around her throat. Confusion turned to panic as Ellie realized that while his grip didn't cause pain, something weird was happening to her. Both of her hands grasped frantically at his wrist. He used his free hand to tear her fingertips away from his skin.

Ellie's knees collapsed under her but Fury didn't allow her to fall, instead he held her up with his grip on her throat. She tried to scream but nothing came out. She stared into his eyes while she silently begged him to stop. Something in his gaze flickered and he suddenly released her fingers to wrap his arm around her waist instead. He tugged her tightly against his taller frame and cradled her as his head lowered to her ear.

"Don't fight it," he rasped.

Don't fight? her mind screamed in terror. She knew she had to be turning blue. Her vision became spotty and his voice sounded far away. Ellie jerked inside his hold but Fury never looked away from her frightened eyes. Blackness threatened to overtake her but she fought it, wanting to live.

He swore he'd kill me and he is. I really didn't believe he'd actually do it.

Fury released her throat the second Ellie's body crumpled against him and pulled her tighter against his body. Now that he had stopped restricting the blood supply to her brain, she relaxed against him, unconscious and breathing easily. He had chosen the safest, quickest method to subdue her. She would have struggled harder and longer if he'd done anything else. This way, she was not harmed, just sleeping peacefully against him. He inhaled deeply, brushed his nose against her throat, and groaned. She smelled so good he wanted to strip them both bare and rub skin to skin against her.

A dog barked in the distance and Fury jerked his head up. His gaze darted around the park, instincts on instant alert. Guard patrols would be along soon. He knew their routine since he kept a close eye on the humans who thought they were in total control of Homeland. They had no idea that Fury and Justice secretly plotted to speed up the process of taking command of their own lives by training their people to do the human's jobs. The humans thought they'd need a lot more time to learn how to be independent but they were wrong.

He stared down at the top of Ellie's head, her face pressed against his chest, and then he lifted her gently into the cradle of his arms, backing up into the darkness to hide. It would be a challenge to get her to his house undetected but he was stealthy enough to pull it off.

He may as well be an assassin. Mercile Industries had trained them to fight but they'd never been able to control them. Species refused to harm other Species males regardless of the orders they'd been given. Mercile wanted recorded proof of their enhanced skills as evidence of what their blood drugs could do. If given the opportunity to attack their male guard captors, they did kill them, though they weren't supposed to. The guards had been vicious, brutal, and Fury had taken a few of them out when they'd been lax enough to make a mistake.

Mercile Industries had spliced animal DNA into their genes and given them countless drugs, changing more than their appearances. His sense of smell heightened as he aged, he'd grown stronger, his reflexes faster than a typical male, and his instincts sometimes ruled his mind.

It had been difficult to manage the rage he sometimes experienced but he'd learned patience over the years. He'd learned control—for the most part. He glanced down at Ellie and frowned. He'd watched and listened to every word spoken between the doctors and staff while they'd run tests on him. Everything he'd heard had taught him the differences between humans and New Species.

Humans didn't have the senses Species possessed. They couldn't see in the dark or smell him if he was upwind of them. They also didn't have his exceptional hearing. Humans didn't possess their speed or strength, either, unless they were given drugs. Species' alterations were permanent, but Mercile's drugs couldn't maintain the same effects in humans, long-term. Sometimes the drugs killed the human volunteers. They'd accidentally made New Species superior but had treated them as inferior.

Fury shifted Ellie's unconscious body in his arms and carried her gently as he stalked through the shadows. He had no idea what to do with her once he reached home but his animal seemed content now that he possessed her. The man inside him plotted revenge. She'd offered to make it up to him and possibilities raced through his thoughts. He wouldn't really harm her, wasn't capable of that, but she could at least learn a lesson or two about what he'd suffered for her crime. A small part of him hoped some time alone with Ellie would cure him of the obsession she'd become.

* * * * *

Ellie woke confused at first, until memories returned with a rush. Her throat felt a little sore. She reached for it but her arms caught on something. Her eyes opened to stare at a white ceiling inside a dimly lit, unfamiliar room. She lifted her head to peer around.

The large bedroom contained dark furniture and a fire blazed in the hearth inside a corner fireplace, the source of the light. A toilet flushed, startling her. With a few tugs she discovered that her arms were stretched wide apart above her head, tied at the wrist with soft, black material that connected to the sides of the headboard.

After a brief blast of running water sounded, a door opened at the side of the room. Fury stepped out of the bathroom. She glanced at his naked chest and the black sweatpants he wore. Ellie's fear increased, seeing his half undressed state. She warily studied his muscular build. He flipped the light off behind him, causing the room to darken again, hiding all the tiny details of his body.

"You're awake." His tone softened. He sounded deceptively calm under the circumstances. He moved toward the bed. "Good."

He'd covered Ellie with a thick, soft blanket. She looked down and realized the top portion of her chest was bare and exposed. She moved her leg, feeling sheets against...bare skin. Her stunned gaze returned to Fury.

He stopped at the edge of the bed. "I removed your clothes." He paused. "All of them."

"Why?" Her voice came out raspy from her dry throat. Her fear level notched higher. Why would he bring her to his home and tie her naked to his bed? She had a really bad feeling and she didn't want to know his answer, positive it would terrify her more.

"You know why." He moved toward the nightstand. "Are you thirsty?"

She nodded. The bed dipped when he sat on the edge, grabbed the bottled water obviously placed there for her, and then twisted to face her. He reached out with one hand to gently slide it under her neck and lift as he brought the mouth of the bottle to her lips. She swallowed as much as she could without choking. He pulled back from her, his touch leaving her as he replaced the water on the nightstand.

"I thought long and hard about what to do to you," he informed her softly. "I once wanted to kill you outright but that was before I knew you were a spy. I didn't understand you were inside that hellish place to save my people." He paused while he adjusted his position to sit sideways to stare at Ellie. "Now I've decided you can live."

Her heart rate slowed and some of the terror eased. "Why am I here? Why did you take me from the park?"

Fury's eyes narrowed. "You said you'd do anything to make it up to me. I decided you deserve some punishment." He paused. "I also don't know if I believe what you say. You are a spy, used to dealing in lies, and telling people what you think they want to hear to avoid danger. You injured my pride, betrayed my trust, and you need to pay for that. Do you know how they made me suffer for killing the technician?"

She gaped at him. "What?" Her mind reeled at his words. *Oh no.* Pain squeezed her heart.

"They were angry that I'd killed that male. They punished me for what you'd done."

Chapter Four

ဢ

Ellie saw the truth in his grim expression. She'd hoped they wouldn't punish Fury for Jacob's death. The technician had assaulted him, had planned to rape, and would have killed him. Tears filled her eyes and she had to blink them back.

"I didn't know." She hated to ask but needed to know. "What did they do to you?"

A soft growl passed his parted lips. "Do you want to hear the details to enjoy the suffering you caused me?"

"No!" It horrified her that he'd accuse her of that. "I didn't think they'd do anything to really harm you. I swear, Fury. They thought you were too valuable to kill, they put so much money into you, and it honestly never crossed my mind that anyone would care about Jacob's death after what that son of a bitch tried to do to you."

"They did." He leaned forward a little, glaring down at her. "They tortured me in retaliation for his death. They caused me great pain. You had to know that. You were a skilled spy and avoided the penalty of his death."

"I just wanted to save you. My handler promised it could be a matter of only days before they attempted to rescue you if I could smuggle out those computer files. I risked it all to rush into that room to stop Jacob from killing you. I lied to everyone at the testing facility but I'm not lying to you. I'm not really a spy either. I was a nurse, Fury." She paused. "I worked at Mercile Industries at their corporate offices handing out aspirins until someone approached me to go undercover. This agent shared the rumors circulating about a secret testing

69

facility with live subjects, human ones, and it outraged me that a company could do that."

"Why?" His tone roughened.

"It's one thing for someone to volunteer to allow a research company to test experimental drugs on them. They know what they are signing up for and I figure some people have nothing to lose if they are sick enough to take those risks. It's entirely something else when people are forced against their will to take whatever is forced upon them. The rumors said they'd locked people up. I worked for them and that meant I had accidentally become a part of what they did. I just wanted to make it right."

"Why would you care what happened to me or my people? Why would you risk your life to save me?"

Ellie carefully debated her words. "I watched you from an observation room I accidentally discovered days after I started working there. All the doors were so similar that I thought it was a supply room. That mirror in your room was two-way. I sometimes sneaked in there to check on you." She didn't mention it had been daily, not wanting him to know she'd been nearly obsessed with making sure he was fine. "I respected your courage and you wouldn't allow them to break your spirit. What they did was a crime. I happened to be in there taking a break when Jacob entered your cell and I overheard him say he planned to kill you. I just couldn't stand by without doing something."

Fury seemed to ponder her explanation. "You never stopped any of the other things they did to me. Did you watch when they forced females into my cell and beat them to make us have sex together? Did you enjoy watching that?"

Horror kept Ellie silent. She'd had no idea the doctors had been doing those kinds of things. Perhaps because she was a recent transfer they had purposely kept her in the dark. Jacob hadn't been the only one to sexually assault Fury. It made her sick inside. She wondered if they would have tried to force her to try to have sex with any of the male Species if she hadn't helped bust the testing facility.

"They made you have sex with women? I didn't know. I never saw any women inside your cell when I came in. Was it the other nurses and technicians? I never heard anything about it, Fury. I swear."

"They were New Species females. They tried for years to breed us. They needed to make more of us but couldn't successfully replicate the procedures they'd used to create us in the first place. I heard enough to know the doctor who had successfully spliced our genetics with animals had left them when we were young, took her research, destroyed what they had, and they wanted more of us. We were growing older and they feared we'd die." Anger changed his voice to a growl. "An infant or a puppy? That was what one of those doctors joked. He laughed over the concept of finding out if our women were impregnated." Fury's voice deepened into a growl. "Did you ever try to save any of them from being forced to have sex?"

He had so many reasons to hate. His rage, directed at her, was even more understandable. "I didn't know about any of that. I never even saw one of your women. I was the lowest-level technician with very limited movement within the facility. It came as a shock later when I heard there were females rescued. I only saw males, Fury."

"You didn't ask. The females were sometimes raped by the technicians. It angers me that you intervened for me but not them."

"I asked plenty of questions but they told me it wasn't any of my business. I had been ordered not to push too hard for answers for fear Mercile would grow suspicious of me. My handler thought they'd kill me if they had any inkling why I wanted to know exactly what they were doing down there and he was right."

Ellie blinked hard to hold back tears. She knew horrors had been committed in the name of science but the things done to Fury and his kind staggered her. They had been treated as though they were guinea pigs, tools, and nothing more. Taking blood samples, forcing drugs into their systems, and keeping them locked up had been horrible but hearing they'd been forced to have sex, used as breeders, sickened her.

"I believed you wouldn't harm me. Were you aware of that? When I didn't growl at you every time you entered my cell, did that amuse you? I didn't want to frighten you. You were kind with your smiles and tender with your needles. When you killed that technician, at first I believed you did it to prevent me from suffering." His features tensed and his voice grew deeper, each word carefully pronounced. "Yet you left me there to be tortured by the guards for your crime. They whipped me and took turns inflicting pain. Some of them were his friends. They weren't allowed to kill me but they caused great harm."

Tears slid down the sides of her face. "I am sorry. I—" She knew nothing she said would erase his hate of her but she had to try. "I'm so sorry. I didn't know they'd do that. I thought only Jacob had it out for you after you'd broken his nose. I knew they valued you too much to kill you. I never thought they were doing breeding experiments either. I thought you'd be safe long enough for me to smuggle the evidence out and help could reach you. I wouldn't have told them you'd killed him if I'd known you'd pay for what I did."

His fangs flashed when his lips parted. "*Thanks*. Is that what you're expecting to hear? You prevented him from raping and killing me. Should I be grateful for the hours they just tormented me?"

"No." *Maybe*. Confusion silenced her. "You're alive and he didn't rape you. Doesn't that count for something? I didn't stand idly by while it happened. I risked my life by going inside that cell to try to save you. I had to make them think you'd killed him in self-defense and I never meant any harm to come to you. I had to do it, Fury. Please try to understand. That evidence I smuggled out ended up being the key factor that swayed a judge to issue the search warrants that located your people. If I'd told those security guards I'd killed Jacob they never would have allowed me to leave. I'd have died and you'd still be locked inside a cell along with all your people. Doesn't that matter at all?"

He took a deep breath. When he spoke, he'd obviously calmed a bit since he didn't snarl anymore. "Sorry doesn't change what happened to me, does it? It doesn't take it back what you did to me or how betrayed I feel. I trusted you, yet I paid for your actions. I am not going to kill you but I plan to make certain you understand humiliation and helplessness."

Fury agonized over how stupid he'd been to trust Ellie. The guards had even teased him before that incident about not snarling at her when she'd come into his cell.

He'd borne their harsh words and accusations that he wanted to mount the human female, their cruel taunts that she'd never want an animal to fuck her, but she'd been his weakness. The sense of betrayal had run deep after that day. He'd spent months hating her, reliving the torture he'd suffered and blaming her for it. She'd left him on the floor, sent guards in to kick him then chain him back to the wall where the abuse had continued.

Humans were deceitful, cruel creatures. He had already misjudged Ellie once. The painful memory of her actions tore at his heart. He would never allow her to fool him again by lulling him into a false sense of trust.

Every human he'd cared about had betrayed him. Memories surfaced from his late childhood. He'd almost thought of Doctor Vela as a mother. She'd given him cookies, a rare treat he'd looked forward to. He would have done anything for her. She'd promised he could earn his freedom if he became a skilled fighter. They had even videotaped him to show off how their drugs worked on his body.

It had been a lie to manipulate him into compliance. When they'd come to take him away to another facility, she'd laughed at him over how incredibly naïve and stupid he'd been.

Hell had begun after that when they'd taught him to endure physical pain. That torture continued into adulthood. The beatings he'd endured as they'd tried to create drugs that would heal humans faster, the sickness and pain he'd suffered on the failed ones that nearly killed him—all those memories surfaced now.

There had been the female guard who promised to help him escape. He had been young, ruled by lust, and still experienced shame at how badly he'd wanted to mount the woman. Her name left a bitter taste in his mouth. Mary had unlocked his chains and he'd followed her out of his cell, down a long corridor, and straight into the trap they'd set up to test his fighting skills against a dozen heavily armed fighters.

They had hit him with clubs and shot him with Taser guns, and Mary had cheered on the guards from the sideline while he'd struggled to survive. Afterward she'd crouched by his bloodied body, shaking her head. Her words had killed something vital inside him.

"You didn't really think I'd want you touching me, did you? You're nothing but an animal, 416." She'd smiled at the men around them and risen to her feet. "Too bad we're not allowed to kill him. Take him back to his cell. Did you catch all that on camera, Mike? That should impress Doctor Trent with how much he endured before he went down. One of the doctors has a new batch of drugs they want to test on him to see if they can speed up the healing process. You did good, guys."

He'd lost consciousness then, but if he hadn't, he would have tried to kill her. He wanted revenge on everyone who had ever hurt him, lied to him, and betrayed him.

Ellie stared up at him with her big, fearful beautiful eyes. If she wasn't face-to-face with him would she laugh at how stupid he'd been to trust her? Had he been a source of amusement to snicker about when he'd allowed her close without snarling at her or fighting his chains? Had she joked with the staff that 416 seemed not to hate her?

"I'll stay away from you if you let me go. That's what you want, right? I'll quit my job and leave Homeland." Hope flared in her blue eyes. "You'll never have to see me again."

Anger surged, hot and fierce, throughout Fury's body. If she were truly regretful of her actions, she'd take whatever punishment he dealt out to make them even. That's what honorable people did. She'd told him she would be willing to do anything to make things right between them but now she asked for mercy. A growl tore from his throat.

Ellie watched as Fury's expression twisted with the anger that burned inside his gaze. She realized that asking him to release her had somehow set him off. She tensed.

He moved then, grabbed the blanket, and jerked. In a heartbeat he'd torn it away from the bed to expose Ellie's nakedness. He stood and stared down at her with a callous expression.

"You should understand how it feels to be naked, unable to move, while someone else has control over what is done to you. That's part of what you did to me. You saw every inch of me exposed. How does it feel to be helpless, Ellie?"

Embarrassment heated her cheeks and she tried to twist away, to roll onto her side, but he'd tied her too tightly. She could only curl her legs up protectively while she tried to use them to cover her breasts. She understood humility without him doing this to her but she didn't say it aloud.

"Then there was touching involved so I'm going to do that to you as well. That's fair, isn't it? Do you know what it is like to have someone's hands sliding along your skin?

Touching your sex? I understand you needed to remove the painful restrictive thing he put on me but your touch lingered. Don't think I didn't notice."

Ellie stiffened with shock and dread but then she took a quick breath. It wasn't easy but she fought down the panic that tried to overtake her. She understood that he needed revenge. He couldn't get back at Jacob because she'd killed him and left Fury to suffer for it. She had touched him, gawked at his body, soaked in every naked inch. She supposed she deserved it. He said he wasn't going to kill her. She could take it if humiliating her was the worst he planned. He'd been beaten and tortured. Some embarrassment seemed tame in comparison.

"Go ahead and look. I do understand." She eased her legs flat on the mattress and kept still. "Just please don't hurt me."

A confused look marred his features as their gazes locked. He glared down at her while he climbed onto the bed to crouch over her body on all fours.

"What?" He sounded as shocked as he looked.

"I understand," she whispered. "Do it."

He clenched his teeth but then lowered his body over hers until he caged her under him. If terrifying her had been his plan, he'd succeeded. The silence stretched between them. Her heart rate slowed.

"Reverse psychology doesn't work on me but I want you to know I won't hurt you," he whispered. "I would never make you suffer what I did. I could never bring myself to punch you or make you bleed. I believe I have come up with something fitting. I'm going to touch you. Do you know what is worse than being tortured with pain?"

She didn't want to know the answer. So far all the responses Fury had given didn't bode well for her. He waited for an answer, though, and she didn't want his rage to return. She had to say something.

"No. I think pain is the worst thing ever."

"It's when your own body betrays you by wanting something you know you shouldn't. You learn to expect being let down by others but never yourself. It is a great, humble lesson to learn. It will also give us both the answer to a question on my mind at this moment."

What does that mean? She frowned. He grinned wolfishly. Her heart raced as his gaze lowered to her breasts. One hand brushed over her stomach so lightly it tickled. His palm slid higher until he cupped one of her breasts with a hot, large hand. Alarm shot through Ellie when he gently squeezed.

"Soft. For a woman your size, these are larger than I expected." He lowered his head when he released his hold on her.

Ellie gasped as his warm breath fanned across her breast a second before Fury's hot, wet mouth latched on to her nipple. His teeth scraped the sensitive skin as he flicked a raspy-textured tongue over the bud of her breast. Ellie jerked under him and tightly squeezed her eyes closed.

Pleasure shot from her nipple straight into her belly that quivered. She bit her lip to silence a moan, shocked that she'd react that strongly to him. He sucked harder, the strong tugs from his mouth sending jolts through Ellie's entire body. He didn't hurt her but she knew he could have. Liquid heat dampened her thighs and she squeezed them together under his body, proof of how turned on she'd become.

This is worse, she decided, as her body responded to Fury's seduction. The arousal he forced her to feel made her stomach clench and with every tug of his mouth, she swore she could feel it on her clit instead. The relentless lips refused to release her breast, the pleasure nearly becoming painful, and her body burned. What he did to her had to be the most incredibly erotic thing she'd ever experienced. She bit her lip but was unable to stop the soft moan that escaped.

His mouth pulled back, drawing her nipple taut until he let go. Ellie swallowed hard as she stared into a pair of intense brown eyes. A soft growl came from the back of his throat. He tore his gaze from hers to lower his attention down her body once more.

"See, Ellie?" He spoke in a raspy, sexy voice. "I am in control of your body. You can't stop me from making you respond this time." He glanced up to lock gazes with her. "Despite what Jacob had done to me that day, I wanted you, and this is the perfect revenge. You made my cock harden after you touched me and your scent of arousal filled my cell. It hurt me more than your abandonment. Now you have a taste of knowing unfulfilled desire put there by someone you tried to resist."

She stared into his eyes as his words sank in. Mortification from her overpowering response to his seduction left her speechless. Ellie's dignity definitely was injured. She'd been betrayed by a body tingling from the touch of a man who hated her. She hoped he'd feel better, think they were even, and he'd let her go. She relaxed under him. *Yeah, this is definitely a perfect way to get revenge,* she concurred. She blinked back tears, waited until she was calm enough to speak again.

"Are we even now?" She hated the way she spoke in a breathless whisper.

Dark eyes lifted to meet hers. "Even? Not yet. I said the perfect revenge."

"But you just—"

He growled softly. "They hurt me for hours. I could torment you for hours with my mouth and hands. There many ways to make someone ache."

Ellie gaped at him. He scooted lower and his hands encircled her thighs to shove them wide apart. His arms slid under her legs and wrapped around them to pin them open with his shoulders pressed against the inside of her thighs.

Ellie tried to slam her knees together after the initial shock but his body was in the way. He tore his attention from her face to where he had her pussy openly displayed under his chin, seemed to study her, and then his head lowered. Shock, dismay, and surprise gripped her. She could feel his hot breath touching her exposed inner folds and clit.

"Wait!" Ellie struggled, wiggled her hips, and bucked to get out of his hold when he turned his face to lick the inside of her thigh. She jerked on the bed, tried to twist away, but he refused to let go. He displayed his strength when he pinned her tighter until she couldn't move at all. His jaw brushed her skin, rubbed her higher on her inner thigh, back and forth, caressing gently.

"Will you hold your legs open so I can touch you with my hands? I'll release your wrists from the headboard if you do as I say."

"I don't do this on a first date or even a fifth one. I'm not comfortable with anyone going down on me." She yanked frantically at the material binding her wrists. She bucked her hips but she couldn't squirm free from his powerful embrace. "Punish me some other way but not that. I angered you but I didn't purposely embarrass you, did I? You want us even but I didn't put my mouth below your waist."

"I didn't think you'd agree. I'll use my hands to hold you still."

"Not like this," she begged.

Fury cocked his head. "Like this?"

"Don't touch me just to get revenge."

"Oh, Ellie," he rasped. "I want you. Don't you know that? This is far beyond something as simple as payback. Tell me yes so I can give us both what we need."

Ellie saw passion burning in his beautiful brown eyes. He looked incredibly sexy and her body ached with need at seeing his handsome face between her thighs, so close to where she hurt the most, and she relaxed. She nodded, realized she'd probably just lost her mind, but Fury's expression of relief validated her agreement.

Ellie gasped when his tongue flickered over the most sensitive spot on her body. His lips sealed over the small bundle of nerves and his tongue applied pressure, teasing up and down over her clit. She froze, tensed, and the sensations of his suckling mouth spread throughout her body.

He's really doing it. He— Oh God. That feels so good.

His tongue had an unusual texture and the response he drew from her with each lick, every suck, almost hurt, but in the best way possible. He kept the pressure on and his tongue moved against her clit without pause, without hesitation. She couldn't stop making the loud moans that filled the room as she threw her head back, her fingers gripping the material around her wrists, just for something to hang on to.

He's going to kill me after all, she thought. It wasn't going to be from him strangling her or breaking her neck. He planned to lick her to death, make her body hurt in delicious ways, and ache painfully to come. She tried to reason with herself, tried to remember that she hated men going down on her, had never enjoyed it, but a growl from Fury sent vibrations against her swollen bud. She lost her train of thought, only able to feel just him, Fury, and his mouth that made her quiver and burn with need.

The climax hit her brutally, an explosion of ecstasy that made her cry out loudly as it rippled through her shaking body. Her muscles trembled, shook, and her mind shut down. She lost all ability to think, to form words, just able to experience the white-hot haze of pleasure until his mouth released her.

Ellie had to catch her breath. Her oversensitive body shivered when his hands released her legs gently and hot skin brushed against her mound, her lower stomach, and then her breasts as he rose up her body until they were face-to-face.

If he killed her now she wouldn't even care. She was a breathing marshmallow. Boneless. *Hell*, she thought, *I've never felt better in my whole life*. She opened her eyes to stare into his beautiful dark ones.

"I should walk away from the room, leaving you here without a single backward glance. That's what you did to me."

I don't care anymore if she is lying to me, Fury thought, licking his lips, the honeyed taste of her passion driving his need to completely possess Ellie to an unbearable painful ache. She was so sweet, so responsive, and he no longer wanted to think the worst of her while staring into her beautiful eyes. He wanted to believe, even for the time he had with her, that every word she uttered would be absolute truth.

Pathetic, he silently berated his line of thinking. He had lost his mind over a small, frail human. He'd sworn to never allow one to get too close to him, but there he lay, on a bed with one — *his* Ellie.

He'd not only lost his temper but his tight rein on his animalist urges and his mind. He'd also lost his heart to her. She was human, not to be trusted, yet he still wanted her. *When did I become a masochist?*

Chapter Five

೮

Ellie opened her mouth to speak but there were no words to take away the bitter expression on his handsome face. She'd helped put it there and no excuse could change the past. She stared at him and closed her mouth. Fury's focus lowered to her chest. The hesitation only slight until he raised his hand to cup her breast again, held it gently, and she arched her back to press tighter against his palm. His gaze returned to hers.

"I want you. I hate it but I hurt to be inside you, to know what it would feel like to have you wrapped around me, and the pleasure I think I could find with you. I've never wanted a woman more. Tell me I can have you or help me remember that I can't ever forgive what you did to me. Say something, anything, to remind me why I shouldn't hurt to be with you so much it makes it hard for me to breathe."

The look in his eyes as they watched each other nearly stopped Ellie's heart. She saw so many emotions there—desire, longing, a little fear, and raw passion. Her tongue came out to wet her lips. A soft growl came from Fury but it wasn't an angry sound, more of a groan. She understood. He wanted her.

She slowly nodded. She wanted him as much as he did her, had from the first moment she'd ever seen him locked inside a cell. He'd been so proud despite his circumstances, the pure masculine beauty of his fit body had tempted her passion, and his powerful presence had strongly drawn her to him.

"Say it," he urged.

"Yes," she whispered.

His eyes closed for long seconds before he looked at her again. "Wrap around me."

She hesitated for only a second before she shifted her legs and her heels brushed the bare, warm skin on the back of his thighs. He lifted more, positioning himself until he pressed against her pussy with the thick tip of his cock. Her body was already wet with need when he nudged against her entrance to penetrate her. He slid easily through her silky folds but missed the mark.

Frustration tightened his features. He braced his arm on the bed, suspended his upper body weight on one arm and reached between their stomachs until he gripped the shaft of his cock to hold it steady and lined them up perfectly. He paused there, hovering.

"You're much smaller than our women. I'll try not to harm you."

Harm me? She was aware of the size difference between them, had never considered herself tiny, but at that moment she realized she was, compared to him. She opened her mouth to ask him what he meant but he lowered his weight to allow gravity to work in his favor before she could say a word. Ellie's eyes widened with shock as the blunt, thick crown of his cock pressed hard against her, breeched her channel, and forced her body to stretch to take him. Panic became the next emotion to leap out when he pushed deeper inside her pussy.

"You're too big," she gasped.

He froze as their gazes met. His eyes narrowed almost to slits and his breathing turned harsh. "You can take me," he snarled. "I want you too bad. I'll be gentle."

He lowered more over her body, sinking into her deeper. Her muscles stretched to accommodate his thick shaft as he continued to penetrate her, giving her body no choice but to take him. He didn't stop until he was fully seated inside her snug channel. He paused to allow her to adjust to his size. Ellie breathed hard but had to admit the sensation of being so full felt incredibly good. He moved, withdrew a few inches, slowly, and then pushed back in.

A moan tore from her lips. He was big and broad enough to rub against every sensitive nerve ending that flared to life. She had nothing to fear from Fury. Her body enjoyed the tight fit of them together. He tensed and a soft groan passed his parted lips, while their gazes remained on each other.

"I knew it would be this incredible," he stated in a raspy voice. "Too good." Anger tightened his features then for a few heartbeats. "Damn you for affecting me this strongly, Ellie."

A snarl tore from his parted lips and then he moved again, withdrew slightly before he again slid deep inside her pussy. She cried out again in pleasure, his amazingly rigid cock creating pure ecstasy that gripped her. She'd never experienced that level of sexual magnificence. He moved again, repeated the slow thrusting but driving into her harder. Ellie cried out in delight of that movement and the way his shaft slid against her swollen clit, his hips angled in a way that kept him from crushing her under his bigger body. Her body became so sexually excited, her pussy so wet, and the pleasure so intense she realized she wouldn't last long. It stunned her to react to a man so powerfully. She'd never even considered it possible to come from just a man fucking her without a lot of other stimulation but then, Fury wasn't just any man.

Fury moved faster, the intense pleasure increasing until Ellie knew she couldn't take it anymore. Her vaginal walls clamped tightly around his driving shaft, she swore that his cock became even harder inside her, and screamed out, her body seizing as the climax gripped her in hot flashes of delight. Her muscles twitched and milked him as he continued to move inside her.

He jerked out of her and turned his hips to the side as he eased down her body a good foot. He roared out his own release loudly and his face dropped to her chest. Sharp teeth softly raked her breast while Fury trembled as warm jets of his semen damped her thigh as he came. He had purposely withdrawn from her at the end.

Ellie admitted being a little disappointed when she could think again after the blissful haze passed. Fury not coming inside her had left her feeling empty and as though he didn't want to share that kind of intimacy with her. She opened her eyes to peer at the top of his dark head, his face still pressed against her breasts, and his hot, heavy breathing fanning her skin. She wished she could wrap her arms around his shoulders and hold him tightly.

Fury had pulled out of her before he could risk harming or horrifying her with the changes made to his body inside the testing facility. He doubted she had knowledge of the sexual differences between his kind and hers. It amazed him that he'd kept enough control to remember he couldn't come inside her since the second he'd entered Ellie's body he'd known pure heaven for the first time in his life. Jerking out of her body had been difficult, almost impossible. He'd wanted to fill her with his essence and mark her with his scent.

Touching her, making love to her and tasting her had been far better than he could have imagined. Hell, he could get addicted to her. *I may already be,* a small part of his mind warned.

She was human, not truly his, and he needed to remember that. As much as he wished he could keep her tied to his bed, make love to her until he had her too tired to attempt to leave, he knew he couldn't do it. At some point someone would look for her when they realized she'd gone missing.

She'd resent being held captive no matter how much pleasure he gave her. He knew all about being locked up and restrained. He may have done it to her to get her into his bed once but to force her to stay there long-term would be unforgivable. She'd grow to hate him. He couldn't bear the thought.

Frustration bloomed inside his chest even as he jerked from another contraction of pleasure. He had marked her with his seed on her thigh and damn it, he thought of her as his already. She'd belonged to him from the moment she'd walked into his cell, touched him, then killed Jacob to protect him. He just couldn't keep her. It infuriated him into a blinding rage now that he believed she hadn't intended to be cruel by blaming the death on him.

He fought it and kept his face against her skin to hide his expression. The rage started to ease and then he smelled her blood. His eyes shot open and he licked his lips, tasting it there. In horror he realized what he'd done.

"Fuck," he growled viciously.

That is exactly what he thinks we just did, Ellie thought. *But it meant more to me than just sex.* His head lifted from her chest, making it easier to catch her breath. His still rigid cock bumped against her pussy and made Ellie aware she'd become very sensitive in that area. It had been a long time since she'd had sex.

Fury pushed up with his hands to lift off her hips and crouched over her, keeping her body pinned between his arms and legs while he hovered there. "Damn it," he sighed. "I'm sorry. I never meant to hurt you, Ellie."

Hurt me? That confused her. What they had shared had been pretty incredible. Mind blowing, extreme climax, the hardest she'd ever come in her life. She followed the path of his gaze to find his attention fixed on her right breast. She had to lift her head to see better and was startled when she saw a tiny amount of blood smeared over the side of her right breast and running into the valley between them. Her gaze flew to his and saw the regret on his handsome face. She wondered what had caused the bleeding and who it had come from.

He opened his mouth but nothing came out. He clamped his lips together, a furious expression etched on his features, and then he nearly leapt from the bed to storm into the bathroom. She was momentarily blinded from the bright light when he flipped a switch but watched him disappear inside the other room.

She carefully closed her legs. *Yeah, I'm going to tender for a while*, she silently admitted, her sex feeling a little swollen and sensitive to any movement. He'd been larger than average and she'd gone without sex since her divorce, having sworn off men after that nightmare.

She experienced slight shame over the fact that she'd so easily been turned on by Fury but she'd wanted him since she'd first laid eyes on him inside that cold testing facility. She'd never imagined the possibility of being with him, tied to a bed, in a different place. *Not the kind of ending after hot sex I hoped for if we ever got together. What a disaster.* The sound of running water came from the other room, pulling her from her thoughts.

Fury reappeared in seconds and she felt proud that she remained so calm under the strange and stressful circumstances. He refused to glance at her face, instead concentrating on her chest. He held a wet hand towel when he perched on the edge of the bed.

"Allow me tend to you. I really didn't mean to inflict pain."

"I'm not hurt." She spoke softly but knew he heard her. "Just release me."

"I'm going to clean you up." He sighed. "You're bleeding. I nicked you with my teeth but I didn't bite into you. It's just a scratch but deep enough to bleed."

Great. My blood. At least it didn't hurt. "Just let me go and I'll tend to it."

"No." He carefully wiped at the skin just under her right breast, tenderly dabbing there. He hesitated and then cleaned her thigh where he'd left his sexual mark, washed away his semen.

Hot sex had turned into a calamity. Her passion cooled to leave a bitter aftertaste. Fury didn't hold her after sex, no tender words came from him unless an apology for making her bleed counted. And he washed away the evidence of passion he'd left on her, as cold as the wet cloth he used to do it with. She suddenly wanted to leave in the worst way and forget what had happened between them.

She attempted to hide how embarrassed it made her feel that she'd come apart under him when Fury probably still hated her. It had all just been an act of revenge regardless of what he'd claimed though it had meant a hell of a lot more to her. She wanted to get away from him before she fell apart. It would happen soon. She hoped he had found the kind of justice he had been looking for.

"We're even now, right?" She fought back the wave of tears that threatened. *Don't cry, damn it.* She kept repeating that a few times. Her emotions were too close to the surface and she felt vulnerable. She also didn't want him to feel worse for the nick he'd given her. He could mistake her tears for physical pain. A remorseful expression marred his grim features. They had enough misunderstandings between them to last a lifetime. She didn't want to add to them.

His dark gaze lifted to hers. He studied her for a long moment and an emotion she couldn't read flickered in his dark eyes. He opened his mouth to say something but he never got the words out. Loud pounding suddenly fractured the silence.

"Damn it," Fury snarled.

He stood from the bed and stormed toward the bathroom door. It shocked Ellie how quickly he could move. He threw the wet hand towel through the open bathroom door. He spun, returned to the bed, and reached down to grab the blanket he'd removed from her earlier. He spread it over her once again to cover her from breast to feet. In the next heartbeat he yanked on his sweats before he lunged out of the room. The bedroom door slammed closed behind him.

Ellie lay there wondering if she should yell for help. If she drew attention by calling out they'd find her tied naked to his bed with the injury from his teeth. It would appear really bad.

They probably would assume he'd sexually assaulted her. She didn't want anyone to arrest him for a crime he hadn't committed.

He'd already paid dearly for a crime he didn't commit. She'd never suffered a moment for killing Jacob. She remained silent so that whoever had come to his home wouldn't hear her. She'd rather take her chances of facing whatever else Fury wanted to dish out than get him into any kind of trouble. *We have to be even now*, she reasoned. *He'll release me after his company leaves.*

The door to the room was suddenly flung wide open. The blood drained from Ellie's face and dread filled her when Justice stomped into the bedroom. He wore a yellow T-shirt and blue jeans and his long hair was pulled back in a ponytail so his features weren't hidden. She couldn't miss the look of shock and horror that transformed them. Ellie flinch from the certainty that he made all kinds of wrong assumptions. After a stunned moment he moved forward, snarled and paused at the side of the bed. Fury filled the bedroom door, pale and silent. He wouldn't meet her gaze but instead had his chin lowered, staring at the carpet.

Justice grabbed the blanket and tore it back. Ellie made a horrified sound, startled at having her body totally exposed to a stranger. Another snarl erupted from Justice's throat. He threw the blanket back over Ellie to shield her nakedness before dropping to sit on the edge of the bed. His outraged glare fixed on Fury while he reached for her arm. He yanked the ties at her wrist, freeing it when he broke the material from the headboard.

"How could you do this?" Justice growled in a very harsh voice.

He stood, rounded the bed and freed Ellie's other arm. He placed his body between her and Fury, his back to her. Ellie sat up, rubbed her wrists, and carefully kept the blanket shielding her body. She couldn't see Fury at all with the big male between them.

"How could you do this, Fury? How? She saved us. She put her life on the line to help us. You are alive regardless of what it was she did to you. You are breathing! We are trying to prove to humans that we are more than animals and you take her by force? You raped her in your bed as if you are a rabid dog? Damn it! They are going to lock you up for this. I don't think I can protect you and I don't know if I want to at this point. How could you do this? You know what is at stake. Our people need guidance and protection! You're my second in command. If I fall, you lead." Justice's voice lowered, calmed. "You are breaking my heart. You hurt this woman. I smell her blood, and because you injured her, it will cause untold problems for us. What the hell do you think you were doing? Have you lost your mind? This just reinforces the belief that we're mindless animals, too dangerous to run free."

Shame burned through Fury while he stared into Justice's shocked gaze. He knew he'd let his people down when he'd kidnapped Ellie. He had taken the responsibility of leadership yet he'd allowed his feelings for the woman to make him do things he knew were wrong. He'd chosen her over them, something he swore he'd never do when he'd taken the job as Justice's second in command.

"I'm sorry," Fury whispered.

Justice softly growled. "What is wrong with you? Have you lost it? Did something make you snap? I can't and won't allow you to get away with this. You must be disciplined harshly to set an example."

"I expect nothing less." Fury took a deep breath. He had known he would be punished before he'd touched Ellie, and he would accept any consequences that came his way. He'd wanted Ellie more than the most important thing in his life — his people.

When New Species had been freed a lot of them had wanted to wage a war on all humans but Justice had been the calm voice of reason. To survive they needed to work with the humans who had freed them. When they'd been told they were being given Homeland, a place to live in peace, a place where they could rebuild their lives, Justice had come to Fury and asked him to help guide them into their new way of life. Fury had agreed quickly, willing to shoulder any burden that came his way as long as he could be of use.

He'd taken over training their security teams and shown them how to control their inner beasts. The irony wasn't lost on him. He hadn't practiced what he preached. He'd gone after something he knew he couldn't have—Ellie. He'd brought her into his home and seduced her regardless of the cost.

He couldn't regret the action. Even the small amount of time with her had been worth whatever pain he'd endure. He had tasted her, touched her, and knew how wonderful it felt to be that close to her. If they locked him up her image would keep him company, her voice committed to memory forever, her beautiful eyes etched into his soul. He could forever close his eyes and hear her, picture her.

"Are you all right?" Justice glanced back at Ellie.

"Yes." She cleared her throat.

Justice's attention snapped back to him. Fury met his stern look with a grim determination. He'd make sure everyone knew the blame rested solely on his shoulders. He'd distance himself from New Species, hope the humans didn't blame others for his actions, and take whatever punishment they meted out to him without complaint or excuses.

Justice's disappointment and shock wounded him deeply. He knew how much rested upon his behavior. He'd let his people down, his best friend, and himself.

"I can't do this alone, Fury," Justice informed him softly, a pained look on his face. "I needed you to hold it together for all of us. Director Boris has fought me every step of the way on us taking control of Homeland. He's trying to tell the President we're not capable of running our own lives. He honestly believes we're more animal than human, little more than trained to speak and mimic them. He hasn't come straight out by saying it but his contempt is so strong it's impossible to ignore."

"I'm sorry."

"This is just going to justify his accusations. We have to work twice as hard to show them we are their equals and we are a race of intelligent, responsible people. You couldn't have totally lost your mind at a worse time."

"I realize it will reflect badly on the NSO. I'll take full responsibility, assure them I'm the only one flawed, and you will need to press for them to deal with me severely."

Justice studied his friend. "You aren't yourself. Why?"

Fury's attention drifted toward the bed but he still couldn't see Ellie around Justice's large frame. He met his friend's curious gaze.

"I think you know why. There's something about her that I can't ignore. It's not just anger. There's more to it than that."

A few Species males had experienced overwhelming urges to mate with certain females, to keep them very close, make them theirs, but none of them had given in to those instincts. Not that they'd been given the chance while they'd been prisoners. They'd been kept separated except for those times that females had been brought to them for breeding.

They were aware of the problem though. It only had happened to a few times inside the testing facilities but they had discussed the potential problem if more Species suffered from what they'd deemed a need to mate. *I have that need*, Fury admitted. He was pretty certain a mating was for life too because of how strongly Ellie affected him. He couldn't see ever wanting to let her go.

Justice started back with worry and understanding etched on his features. "How bad is it?"

"Overwhelming, obviously. I've been fighting it tooth and nail." His shoulders slumped. "I'm sorry for the trouble I've caused but…" He left the rest unsaid.

He still didn't regret it, even knowing how deep was the hole he'd dug. He glanced up to try to see Ellie again but Justice continued to block his view of her. He'd had her once. It would never be enough but at least he'd have the memory to savor.

Ellie spotted her clothes on the floor by the bed. Fury must have stripped her and just dropped them there. Her ID card and her shoes were there too. She moved slowly, definitely tender between her thighs from their bout of hot sex, and slid her butt to the edge of the bed. She kept the blanket around her. She grabbed her clothes and frantically started to put them on. The men seemed to be having a staring contest.

"The human security guards are searching everywhere for the woman." Justice paused. "They found her broken electrical equipment by the pond and suspect something has happened to her. The second I became aware of her identity I came here, hoping you hadn't done something stupid. We need to inform them she is here. She'll need medical attention and you need to face the penalty of your crime. She isn't one of us. I think they will make you face their law punishment. I don't know what those are but you have to stand up for it for all our sakes. Don't fight if they arrest you. I know the urge will be strong if they chain you but don't make this worse."

"I won't struggle," Fury swore softly. "I'll call them now."

Ellie finished dressing. She shoved on her shoes and stood. The movement made her aware of discomfort when her shirt rubbed under her sore breast. She didn't take the time to check on how bad the scratch from his teeth was, promising do that later after she reached home. She took tentative steps toward the door.

"Excuse me." She cleared her throat.

Justice turned his head to meet her gaze, a grim frown twisting his full lips.

Ellie didn't glance at Fury. "I am going to return to the dorm now so please don't call anyone. I'll tell them I've been visiting a friend. Don't get security involved in this. Fury and I are even now. There won't be any more problems between us." She forced herself to look at Fury then, seeing shock slacken his handsome face. "Are we even now?"

He shook his head, frowning.

She swayed on her feet from shock. Her knees collapsed but Justice caught her before she hit the floor. His strong hands gripped her waist to steady her until she regained control and straightened. He released her instantly when she pushed at his hands. She gaped at Fury.

"No? What more do you want from me?" Tears flowed freely down her cheeks. She was no longer able to hold them back. "I'm sorry! I thought you'd be safe, damn it. I'm telling you the truth. I had no other choice. I did everything I could for you. I couldn't tell you what I had to do because I didn't think you'd trust me. I couldn't risk you repeating anything I said to you."

Fury blinked. The look in his eyes definitely appeared pained. "We aren't even because now I'm in your debt. I didn't mean to hurt you with my teeth."

Ellie used the backs of her hands to wipe at her tears. She had her key card fisted in her palm. Fury never ceased to astonish her.

"I know that and I believe you. It's not a big deal about the scratch. We're even then, Fury. You don't ever owe me anything. I have to go." She bit her lip. "Please move out of my way."

Fury stepped away from the door. Ellie darted forward the second she knew she wouldn't touch him. She nearly staggered out of his bedroom, down the hall, and through a large living room. She saw the front door and headed straight for it. She held her head high when she swung it open. Cool night air blew across her damp face.

She glanced down to where her watch should have been to see how much time had elapsed. Her bare wrist made her wince. She wasn't going back into Fury's bedroom to look for it. *No way in hell.* She lurched forward, took in her surroundings, and identified her location. He shoes slipped a little on the damp grass until she reached the sidewalk that would lead her to the dorms.

A hand suddenly gripped her shoulder and spun her around. Ellie stared up at Justice North fearfully. He'd followed her from the house.

"Why don't you want him arrested? What the hell is between you both?" Justice's grip gentled but his confusion was evident in the way he regarded her.

Ellie studied his pretty cat-like eyes. His facial structure wasn't completely human, the bones of his face too pronounced with brawny cheekbones, and his nose was wider and flatter than a human nose. His features were…different, like Fury's, except his traits were feline. She stepped back out of his hold. His hand dropped to his side.

"I need to return to the dorm and let security know I'm okay so they will call off the search. What happened in there isn't what you think. He didn't rape me or hurt me in any way."

"What happened between you and Fury at the testing facility? Tell me now," he demanded.

She peered around him only to see Fury's windows dark and the front door firmly closed. Fury wasn't within sight. Her gaze returned to Justice.

"Why," he growled, "would you allow him to hurt you the way he has and not want retribution? Tell me or I'll beat it out of him myself. He has refused to share any of your history. You are the only thing he won't discuss."

Ellie blinked back tears, hated the idea Fury would suffer if she didn't admit her crime. "It's his story to tell, not mine."

"He won't. I'm his best friend. He is acting insane. Make me understand or I'll have to lock him up, have him evaluated, and force him to tell me what has happened. He won't take being caged well. If you care at all, you'll tell me what he will not."

She hesitated, hated being put in the middle of it, but didn't want Fury to suffer more for what had happened the last day she'd seen him inside his cell. She stared at Justice's shirt. "You won't use it against him?" Her gaze lifted. "Swear it to me."

"I love him like a brother. Family is everything to me. I'd rather cut off my own hand than harm him."

She believed the sincerity she saw in those exotic eyes. "There was this horrible technician named Jacob. He enjoyed hurting New Species but one day Fury elbowed him in the face. It broke his nose. The guy went after Fury the last day I worked at Mercile. I'd just stolen some downloaded files from a doctor's computer and had swallowed it to try to smuggle it past security. I used to check on Fury, um, there was an observation room, and I overheard Jacob saying he was going to kill him. He'd had the camera inside the cell turned off. I got there as quickly as I could." She hesitated.

"Go on."

Her gaze lowered to his shirt, unable to look into the man's eyes as she told him the rest of it. "He'd drugged Fury and had stretched him out, chained down on his stomach. He had started to do vile things to him. I attacked Jacob and he died." Her voice broke.

"Fury should be grateful for this." Justice reached out and gripped her chin, forcing it up until she had to meet his gaze. "What are you not telling me? Why does he feel you did him wrong if you saved him from that fate?"

She cleared her throat. "I had enough evidence sitting inside my stomach on that data drive to get a judge to finally issue a search warrant on Mercile Industries. If anyone realized I'd killed that technician they wouldn't have allowed me to leave after my shift ended. I framed Fury for killing the technician. I smeared that asshole's blood on Fury's hands while he lay helpless on the floor, unable to move, put the needle back into him as if he'd just been drugged to explain how he'd been able to move long enough to do it, and I was too afraid to tell him why I did it."

She waited for the guy to get angry as he stared at her with his narrowed, intelligent eyes.

"There is more you aren't telling me. We often took the blame for things. This is damn personal to Fury."

She clenched her teeth. "I walked in to find that son of a bitch beating and about to rape Fury, okay?" She blinked back tears and lowered her eyes to his shirt again. "He'd already done horrible things to him, started to rape him with a baton, and um, it was traumatic, okay? Fury thought I would never hurt him but instead I framed him for murder. He told me they tortured him after I pinned the killing on him. They beat him up and hurt him because of what I did. He's got reasons to be mad at me. He just wanted some payback and he got it."

Justice said nothing. The breeze stirred. She didn't dare glance up at his face, afraid she'd see disgust or worse, rage. She'd just admitted to doing a horrible thing to his friend.

"He took me from the park to give me a taste of what he had experienced—being restrained, helpless, while someone did whatever they wanted to my body. He suffered that and more for the death of that technician." She paused. "He didn't force me have sex with him. He didn't beat me or anything. He decided seducing me would be more fitting to get his point across. I consented to it. Fury and I are even now, he has his revenge, and I need to go."

"And the blood I smelled? Did you agree to him harming you?"

"He accidently got me with his teeth. It's nothing but a scratch."

Justice sighed loudly. "I see." He released her face and stepped back.

Ellie spun away and fled down the sidewalk. She didn't dare look over her shoulder to check if Justice would come after her again. She didn't stop until a security guard ran into her a few blocks later. She made up a lie, swore she had visited someone, and assured him no harm had come to her. She refused to give him a name but hinted it was of a sexual nature to explain her disarrayed state, which he couldn't miss.

She didn't miss the guard's smirk and the way he leered at her breasts when he'd called in to report that she had been found safe. By the time she entered the dorm building she wanted to collapse from the emotional hell she'd suffered.

Four New Species women were watching television when Ellie passed the living room to go to the elevator. She paused to wait for it to open and studied them only to realize they watched her back. The woman sitting closest to her suddenly stood. Her nose flared as she sniffed the air and frowned.

"Are you all right?"

It surprised Ellie that any of them would care about her emotional state. "I'm fine but thank you for asking. Good night." She faced the elevator doors to break eye contact.

The elevator took a long time to reach the ground floor. Ellie closed her eyes and hugged her chest. She tried to ignore the tenderness where her pants rubbed against her sex and where the underside of her breast slightly burned. She needed a bath, a strong drink, and maybe a good old-fashioned cry.

The elevator dinged as the doors slid open. Ellie opened her eyes when she stepped inside, turned to hit the button for her floor, and gasped. Four New Species women stepped into the small space with her and all four pairs of eyes were narrowed on her. They loudly sniffed, their gazes raked up and down her body, and they inched closer. Ellie backed into the corner.

Their sudden interest in her well-being alarmed Ellie. They were all tall, muscular females, and stronger than average women. She ended up trapped as the women backed her into the corner. One of them turned her head and pushed the button for the third floor. Ellie struggled to remember their names. The woman with red hair appeared as if she'd been altered with cat genes, from the shape of her eyes. She calmly turned her nearly black gaze on Ellie.

"We smell you. Blood, fear and sex. It all has a scent."

"And we smell one of ours on you too," the woman on Ellie's left side stated. She was a strange-looking woman who appeared part calico cat with her multi-colored hair and feline features. She sniffed again. "Dog species, I think. Our sense of smell isn't as great as our males though. Our males could sniff you and identify who harmed you instantly. We have a harder time identifying scents."

"Don't call us that," the redhead snapped, her yellowish eyes showing anger. "I'm not a dog. I'm part canine."

The feline-looking woman shrugged her shoulders and her gaze narrowed at Ellie. "You were attacked." She sniffed.

"I'm fine." Ellie swallowed hard. "Thank you for your concern."

The four women stared at her silently. The elevator dinged as it reached the third floor. Ellie tried to inch around them but the women continued to block her way. She bit her lip hard and glanced at each of them.

"I'd like to go to my room now."

They parted to allow her out of the small space. Ellie squeezed between the women, careful not to touch them, and fled down the hallway. They'd frightened her. She didn't know their sense of smell was strong enough to pick up so much or that they could smell emotions. She jogged the last few steps to her room and pulled out her key card. The light changed to green and she yanked hard at the door handle, shoving it open. She stepped inside and closed the door.

Someone shoved against it instead and the four women entered Ellie's apartment. Fear welled up inside Ellie at their grim expressions. She backed up slowly, alarmed at this turn of events. The door closed firmly behind them.

"Kit, please go run a bath." The tallest, dark-haired woman took charge.

Kit moved toward the bathroom without a word.

"I'm Breeze," the tallest one informed her softly. "There are a lot of us and I don't know if you know our names. Kit is in the bathroom." She then nodded toward the redhead. "This is Rusty and the silent one is Sunshine. Sunshine, go find her something comfortable to wear after her bath."

Sunshine went to Ellie's closet. Ellie stared up at Breeze in shock while the woman frowned back at her.

"I scent blood, sex, and your wrists are red from being restrained. We were forced many times to be with males in our years of captivity." Her eyes darkened. "The human males enjoyed hurting us occasionally. Our males were always careful to never harm us when we were forced to breed with them." She paused. "We were punished or forced to watch them penalize another if we didn't comply when they wanted us to have sex. Our men are incapable of forcing a woman with pain but one of them restrained and hurt you. Why?"

Mute, Ellie stared up at Breeze, feeling horrified over the description of what had been done to them. She silently cursed the ones who'd done it to a very painful hell.

"I'm fine," she swore. "No one forced me."

Breeze growled, her canine traits showing. "Don't lie. Who did this to you? We'll see they suffer greatly for it. There is no reason for a male to force a breeding with a woman. We are free now. Whoever did this to you should pay. He hurt you and that is unforgivable."

Sunshine placed clothes on the bed and moved behind Ellie. Ellie swiveled her head in time to watch the woman bend to sniff at her back. Sunshine suddenly grabbed Ellie's shirt and yanked it up. Ellie remained frozen in stunned silence as the woman's nose brushed along her bare back while she inhaled deeply. The shirt dropped as the woman straightened to her full height, over six feet.

"I don't recognize the scent of him. It's faint enough that I don't believe he took her by mounting. He must have taken her the human way."

Ellie tried to inch out from between the two women, felt trapped between them, but Breeze suddenly grabbed her by the front of her shirt. She crouched down on her knees and yanked Ellie's shirt up to just under her breasts. Breeze pushed her face against Ellie's stomach to sniff before she could protest. The other woman raised her head with a grim expression.

"Like a human, he sweated on her during the attack. I don't know this scent either." She frowned at Ellie as she rose to her feet. "Why are you protecting him? Do you know his name? Describe him to us, we'll find him and make him pay. You are ours and he should have known not to touch you."

Ellie's mouth dropped open. She forced her mind to work. The last minute had been one big stunner after another between the sniffing and their words. They could smell Fury's sweat on her just from his stomach touching hers? She closed her mouth and clenched her thighs. She didn't know what they'd do if they smelled his semen. Then the last sentence sank in.

"I'm yours? I thought you hated me."

Kit stepped out of the bathroom. "We don't hate you. You're our pet."

"Kit!" Rusty shook her head. "Don't say that. You'll offend her."

Kit shrugged. "She is. She's so little and cute. She yaps around trying to please us like...what are they called? A Yorkie?"

Rusty sighed. "We decided she's more similar to a cute little poodle with her long blonde hair." She flashed a smile at Ellie. "Don't take it offensively please. We enjoy having you around and you amuse us to no end. We know you care about us by the way you try to please us."

"I need to sit down," Ellie muttered, dazed, and tried to wrap her head around the idea they thought of her as a pet. She moved over and plopped down on the edge of her bed. She gasped when she sat down too roughly, a reminder of being tender from sex. "Damn." She closed her eyes. *They think of me as a pet.* The comparison to a poodle made her wince.

"You made her sadder," Breeze growled. "Apologize now."

"I'm sorry," Kit said instantly. "It's an endearment. We like you. I mentioned that, didn't I? Is being a pet a bad thing? People love them. We're very fond of you."

Ellie opened her eyes and forced a smiled. "Well, it takes some getting used to but thanks. I'm glad you like me. That's the important part."

"We do," Rusty assured her. "Now tell us which one of our males hurt you and we'll go beat the shit out of him. We can identify the difference between male and female with our noses, even if they are primate, feline, or canine, but telling the difference between individuals is more difficult to determine. You need to tell us everything you can about the male who hurt you so we can figure out who it was."

Breeze cracked her knuckles. "We'll allow you to watch. It will make you feel better to see him bleed." She glanced at the others. "We can't kill him though. We'll just beat him up severely to make sure he is in pain for a good week."

Ellie glanced at each of the women. She wasn't sure if she should be grateful they'd do that to get justice for her or deeply disturbed for the same reason. "I so appreciate the concern. You have no idea how much this means to me. I could almost cry I'm so touched but it's not what you think. He didn't force me."

"Explain why security arrived here checking rooms after they informed us you were missing? They stated there were signs of a struggle in the park." Breeze studied Ellie with a calculated gaze. "We're smart so please don't insult us. You walked in smelling of sex, fear, and blood. Your wrists are red, which tells us you were tied down. I know it is a kinky human thing that we have read about but you had sex with a New Species male. We are not into that kind of sexual play and would never tie anyone down since it reminds us of the testing facilities, yet one of our males restrained you. Tell us his name or tell us what he looks like if you don't know it. We will punish him and make sure that you are safe. You are our pet and we will not have anyone abuse you ever again."

This had to be the weirdest conversation Ellie had ever had, hands down. They thought of her as the house pet, a poodle, not the house mother. She resisted flinching. She had always hated her wild and curly hair but poodles had horrible frizz issues. Perhaps some anti-frizz shampoo could go on her shopping list.

They were being protective and that meant the world to her. She had been certain every woman living inside the dorm hated her. This could be the first step to get to know them and maybe teach them what she could. It had to be a good thing, in her opinion.

"I'm fine. Please just drop it. It's a private matter. I wasn't hurt and the blood you smell is from an accidental scratch."

Kit moved closer to inspect Ellie. "She's too afraid to name him." She leaned down, grabbed Ellie's shirt, and shoved her nose against Ellie's stomach. She sniffed and then jerked away. Horror flashed across her features and she made a soft sound.

"Fury," she gasped. She stumbled back. "Not Fury. He—" She went silent.

Rusty uttered a curse. She lunged at Ellie, grabbed her, and shoved her flat on top of the bed. Fear hit Ellie as hard as a brick smacking her when the big woman yanked her shirt viciously upward to her breasts and pushed her nose tight against her skin. Sniffing sounds were followed by a snarl. Rusty jerked back and spun away. She walked to the corner and her hands slammed against the wall hard enough to make Ellie flinch.

"Fury," Rusty confirmed with a shaky voice. "It was definitely him."

Breeze appeared to be the only one who stayed calm. She regarded Rusty and Kit grimly. "I thought you said he's a protector? Didn't you say that, out of all your men, he took the most punishment to protect you against pain and suffering? Are you sure it's his scent?"

Rusty nodded as she sniffled. She turned suddenly to reveal the tears tracking down her face as she stared at Ellie with confusion.

"Why would he do this to you? Why?"

"We aren't blaming you," Kit added quickly. She sounded miserable, as if she were going to cry too. "We're trying to understand why he would do this. He was always the most careful to make sure we suffered no pain when they ordered us to have sex. When one of us flat-out refused to have sex with him, he took the beatings and wouldn't touch us. He suffered so we didn't have to. He would have died before he drew blood on one of us or hurt us in any way. We are just trying to understand."

Ellie clawed her way to her feet by gripping the bed to get up. "Please, it's not what anyone thinks. I know he didn't mean to hurt me and it's just a scratch. It's a private matter. We, uh…damn. I don't know how to explain this. He doesn't want anyone to know and I already had to tell Justice North tonight when he found me at Fury's house. They did that to you at the testing facilities? God." Ellie sat down again, forgot her tenderness, and winced.

"It won't leave this room," Breeze swore softly. "You have our word, we will never repeat what you tell us. They are upset that this male would hurt you when he means so much to them. You need to tell what happened. We will protect you from him."

Ellie groaned. She studied each woman, noticed Breeze looked sternly at her, her arms crossed, waiting for her to spill the whole story. Kit and Rusty were pale, shaken, and appeared ready to cry. *Pained*. That word fit. Sunshine just looked curious.

She couldn't allow them to think the worst of Fury. Two of them obviously knew him really well. Ellie hated the jealousy that surfaced at the concept that he'd probably had sex with two of these women. They may not have had a choice. That helped a little. She took a deep breath and started from the beginning. She ended up telling them everything right up until the moment they'd followed her into her room. She wiped away tears as she studied each woman. She feared they might hate her now that she had confessed what she'd done.

Kit and Rusty had settled to sit on the floor while Ellie shared her story. Breeze stayed by the door and Sunshine sat on the bed near Ellie. Ellie met Breeze's eyes.

"I just want to take a bath, go to bed, and never talk about this again, okay? He didn't force me and he didn't mean to get me with his teeth."

Breeze nodded, giving Ellie a sad smile. "You are a giving woman, Ellie. Most women wouldn't understand his need for revenge by taking you tonight. They would have..." She sighed. "They would have lied, saying he harmed them without consent. You didn't deserve his anger. You know that, don't you? You saved his life. It is male of him to want payback. He was wrong. I sense your shame at what you had to do by allowing Mercile to believe he killed that technician but I understand the reason. I would have done the same." She took a deep breath. "He won't get near you again. We will take turns guarding you."

"That's not necessary. We're even now and he won't come near me again." Ellie stood. "Thank you for caring and for understanding. I feared you'd hate me for what I had to do. I just wanted to save him from Jacob and I needed to get the evidence to my handler. I never thought they'd beat him for it. I'm really all right and I'll feel a thousand times better tomorrow. I just want to put this behind me."

"Go take your bath and throw your clothes out to us. We'll clean them to remove his scent," Sunshine offered softly. "You did what you had to. Horrible things were done to us — that is the kindest I've heard. You could have been killed by the technician instead."

"I know it doesn't mean much but Fury is a good man." Kit gave her a sad smile. "I know he didn't mean to hurt you in any way. He was always really careful with us."

Ellie nodded, her guess about Fury's sexual history with the two women confirmed, and she tried not to let jealousy eat at her. She walked into the bathroom but left the door cracked open. The full tub of warm water waited. She undressed, handed her clothes through the door, and eased into the bath. She winced as she settled down and the water made her aware of the underside of her breast. She lifted it, tilting her head, and saw two scratches from his sharp teeth. *Damn.*

She closed her eyes, relaxed. At least she wouldn't have to fear Fury plotting to get his hands on her anymore. Of course now she had sexy, erotic memories of them together to live with. She doubted she'd ever get over him.

Her ex-husband had hurt her enough to make her swear off loving anyone again. She'd promised to never allow anyone to matter so much that they filled her thoughts constantly but then she'd seen Fury that first time. Something she thought dead inside her roared to life. He'd become an obsession — first to save him, then to make it up to him for what she'd done. She'd been left with helping his people since she hadn't known what happened to him.

Fury mattered more to her than her ex-husband ever had. She'd been sure once she'd known love, certain nothing could ever hurt her the way her destroyed marriage had when she'd learned she'd married a cheating bastard, but she'd been wrong. Her feelings for her ex were nothing compared to how Fury made her feel.

Nothing at all. Fury's touch would haunt her for the rest of her life. She wished they'd had a real chance of being together. She'd have taken the risk of getting her heart broken again for him but...

"Damn," Ellie muttered aloud. "Wish all you want that things were different but it just isn't meant to be."

* * * * *

"Fury?"

He was a little startled at hearing his name being softly spoken, unaware that anyone had sneaked up on him, and it attested to how obsessed he'd become watching Ellie inside the dorm. He turned his head just enough to stare at Slade.

"What?"

"Your obsession with the human is starting to frighten me. Do I need to report this to Justice?"

"No." Fury's gaze returned to the women's dorm, to Ellie sitting on a couch with some of the women. She smiled at something said and he longed to know what had caused her amusement. "I'm just checking on her."

"You need to let it go. We were told why she worked for Mercile. I understand your need to seek vengeance but she's not our enemy."

Fury held his tongue. It was better if his friend believed that was the reason he lurked behind a tree across the street watching the woman who fascinated him and refused to leave his thoughts. He could think of nothing but her. The sounds of her moans, the sweet taste of her desire and the memory of her tight, heavenly body as he took her replayed inside his mind.

His dick hardened painfully from the memory of possessing her. He'd blown it, drawn blood, and he had no idea how to fix it. He'd been ordered to stay away from her, to have no interaction at all, but it didn't mean he couldn't watch her from a distance. She was unaware and therefore, couldn't feel threatened by his presence.

"Did you hear me?" Slade stepped closer.

"Yes." His focus remained on Ellie. Her hand lifted to brush back her blonde hair from her cheek and he wished he could feel her fingertips graze his face instead. "I heard."

"Are you a danger to her? Be honest with me. We're friends."

That drew his gaze away from her. "I'm not going to hurt her."

They stared at each other for a long moment and then Slade sighed, glancing at the women's dorm and breaking eye contact. "Our women seem to like her."

I like her too, Fury refrained from admitting. *I'm obsessed and can't stop thinking about her. She's all I dream about when I manage to fall asleep.*

"You'll stay away from her, won't you?" Slade glanced at him for confirmation.

"Yes," Fury agreed, hoping intent was the same as telling the truth.

"I'll leave you to it then." Slade spun on his heel and retreated into the darkness.

Fury's gaze returned to Ellie. He knew he needed to stop tormenting himself by spying on her every evening after his shift but he just couldn't seem to do it. He'd even crept closer to the building, trying to find flaws in the security system that would allow him to climb to the third floor where she slept, just to glimpse where she lived. He wanted to know everything about her.

His eyes closed and he took deep breaths. He'd give anything to hold her, to inhale her feminine scent and touch her. A soft growl tore from his parted lips, his dick ached more, and he knew it would be another rough night of tossing and turning. There was no forgetting Ellie.

Chapter Six

❧

Ellie laughed. "Come on, Monarch. You can totally do this."

Monarch, a blonde-haired woman just under six feet tall, examined the vacuum with disgust. "It's too loud and I'm afraid it's going to suck up my toes."

Ellie lifted her hand to cover her mouth, trying to hide her amusement. "We all think that. Trust me. I promise you, though, if you point it away from you, that won't happen. You've mastered the washing machine and your cooking skills with a microwave are wonderful. You can handle this beast."

Monarch sighed. "Fine, but it hurts my ears."

Destiny, a black-haired woman, cheered her on. Monarch flipped on the vacuum and pushed it around the living room carpet without causing injury. Ellie grinned. Whatever the cause, for the past three weeks the women had accepted her. They'd allowed her to talk to them, laugh with them, and teach them household education.

"Ellie?"

Ellie spun to face Breeze with a grin. The tall New Species had really been helpful to Ellie with the other women. Breeze had been appointed leader inside the women's dorm. She and some of the other women were going to classes during the day to obtain the basic education they'd been denied. They'd just arrived back at the dorm.

"What's up?"

Breeze looked grim. "We need to speak privately."

"Oh." Ellie suffered a moment of confusion. "Of course."

She knew something had to be wrong. Breeze led her toward the bathroom, which stumped her more. Rusty and Kit waited by the door. Breeze shoved it open and Ellie followed her inside. Sunshine checked stalls to make sure they weren't in use.

"All clear," Sunshine announced. "We are alone."

Ellie glanced over her shoulder as the door closed to find Rusty and Kit blocked the exit. Ellie shifted her attention to Breeze. "What is going on?"

Breeze sighed. "You can't leave the dorm without one of us with you. I want you to sleep inside my room or one of us will stay inside yours. You are to never be without one of us near you."

"Um…why?" Ellie arched her eyebrows as she glanced at each woman.

Breeze held her attention with a frown. "Fury is outside again. We didn't want to frighten you but we've seen him examining the building on many occasions. Last night he came closer and we suspect he is testing the security to find a way inside."

Shock rolled through Ellie. "Why would he do that?"

A loud alarm suddenly started to blast out sharp warnings, startling all five women. Ellie knew it wasn't the fire alarm, the pitch was too high. It was the lockdown signal. She moved fast, fleeing the bathroom. Kit and Rusty were ahead of her as she ran to the front door but no one stood there attempting to break in. The alarm continued to scream. Ellie turned and saw a dozen New Species women rush toward her.

"Lockdown," Ellie yelled. "Go."

Ellie moved and grabbed the emergency phone from the wall. It rang once before someone at the security building answered. "This is Ellie Brower from the women's dorm. What is going on?" She made sure the door had automatically locked by giving it a tug.

"We have a breach," the security guard yelled over the phone, their fear apparent. "One of those activists groups have broken through the main gate. We have forces headed your way but make sure your women are secure and the doors are closed."

"Son of a bitch," Ellie ground out. She slammed the phone down and spun around to discover some of the women were still there.

"It's those crazy assholes who have been protesting outside the gates about—" She pressed her lips together, finding no polite way to finish that sentence. "Go lock yourselves inside your rooms please. The main gate has been breached but security is on the way. We'll be absolutely safe inside."

Breeze cursed. "It's the humans who think we should be killed, isn't it?"

Ellie couldn't deny it so she didn't try. "They're stupid. They should go home and wait for their alien spaceships to come get their crazy asses because I don't count them as human. They should go back to their own planet and leave ours alone."

Sunshine snorted as she strolled away. "I'll be in my room then."

Breeze showed her anger by wrinkling her nose. "We will wait here with you."

Ellie shook her head. "You know its protocol to go to your rooms. I'll be fine. I need to stand here to man the door in case some of our women need to be let inside. Some are still out there on the way back from school. Those assholes busted through the main gate and they might have guns. I want you safe. My job is to stay here and it's yours to go upstairs."

Breeze hesitated.

"Please? I'm fine," Ellie swore.

Breeze jerked her head toward the women who still stood there, indicating they should go. Ellie blew out the deep breath she'd held, relieved, while she watched them head for the stairs. They avoided the elevators that wouldn't work with the alarms triggered. She faced the door to stare outside, spotting nothing out of the ordinary.

She hated activists who targeted the New Species Organization. Ever since the news outlets had broken the story about the research testing-facility survivors, some hate groups had popped up, claiming the victims were nothing but animals, ones they believed didn't have rights and should be destroyed. Ellie clenched her teeth. The only animals who needed put down, in her opinion, were the ones who threatened the well-being of New Species.

Ellie tensed when she heard an engine race up the street. She saw one of the security cars drive around a corner too fast, another vehicle following it—a large pickup truck that appeared to have been converted into a want-to-be tank. On the side of the truck the word "Hunters" had been spray painted childishly in bright red. Ellie watched in horror as the truck rammed the much smaller security car, causing it to lose control and fishtail. The tires on the smaller vehicle hit the curb, came to an abrupt halt in front of the building, and the truck locked up behind it. Ellie gaped at the sight of guns when two jeans-clad men jumped from the back of the truck. Worse, she saw the back door of the security vehicle thrown open and two women sprinted toward Ellie.

The two security guards who exited the car pulled their weapons and gunfire erupted. The men from the truck dived behind it and returned fire, giving the women time to run to the dorm. Ellie's hands shook badly as she gripped the door and prayed hard for the sisters, Blue and Sky, to reach her safely. Ellie threw her weight against the door she'd opened and pressed her body tight against the glass to get out of the way of the two large women who barreled through the open doorway.

"Go to your rooms," Ellie ordered them. She slammed the door closed and jerked on it to make certain the automatic locks engaged. When the door didn't budge, she released it and lunged for the phone on the wall.

It was dead. *Shit.* More gunfire outside drew Ellie's attention. In horror, she witnessed one of the security guards being struck by a bullet. He flew backward, sprawled on top of the hood of the security car then his body slumped to the street. He didn't get up or move. The second security guard kept firing but he was outnumbered. A cry of anguish came from Ellie when bullets tore through the remaining security guard. His body spun from the impacts, blood bloomed over his face and chest before he fell out of sight behind the car.

Ellie reeled, horrified. The intruders laughed and two of them high-fived each other. They turned to face the building and approached, coming right at her. *Shit.* Ellie grabbed the emergency bar and slammed it down. It had been added as an extra lock in case security cards were stolen or someone managed to torture the code from a guard. They would need both to bypass the lockdown security measures to gain entrance.

"She don't look like no animal," one of the men stated loudly, glaring at her.

Another man, the biggest of the four, pointed his gun directly at Ellie and yelled, "Open up."

Ellie knew the glass would hold. The building had been designed to withstand an assault. She raised her middle finger while pressing down the com button with her other hand to give them the ability to hear her clearly.

"Screw you. It's bulletproof."

"You fucking animal," one of them shouted. He pulled a handgun, aimed at Ellie's face and fired.

She flinched but the glass didn't break. It left a small mark but it didn't even crack. "This is just a meeting building and you can't gain entry," she explained. "You might as well beat your chests, you stupid apes."

She knew she pushed them but as long as they stayed where they were, making threats, they couldn't hurt someone caught outside. She hoped security would show up soon to arrest them before they realized she just wanted to distract them.

"I'm also not an animal. You should go look in the mirror if you want to see one." Ellie gave all four of them a dirty look. "You're a walking zoo, boys."

The one with the shotgun cut loose with his weapon. Ellie winced and flinched from each loud blast. She released the button on the com but it barely muted the sound while the man kept firing. A few marks appeared but the glass held. She hated that she'd gotten an up close and personal test of bulletproof glass effectiveness. The jerk with the shotgun stopped firing.

Ellie remembered the wireless security camera and took a few steps back. The camera hung high on the wall and pointed down at the entryway. She kept her attention trained on it while frantically waving to get someone's attention. She held up four fingers and then mimicked a gun with her fingers, moving her thumb to stimulate firing. She pointed to her watch to indicate it was happening now. She hoped someone at the security office who watched that camera had played charades before since those cameras weren't wired for sound. She touched her arm where the guard patches were and sliced her finger over her neck to tell them two guards were dead, hoping they understood all that.

The men opened fire again at the windows, this time in unison, perhaps thinking multiple-weapon attack would break it. Ellie covered her ears to protect them from the loud noises. She backed farther from the windows and tried again to relay what intruders were doing for the camera.

The gunfire suddenly stopped. Ellie turned her head and watched the men form a huddle to talk. One of them broke away to run toward the vehicles. She wondered why he went to the security guards' car and climbed into the driver's seat. If he thought stealing one of the employee identification cards would help them get in, he would be disappointed.

Ellie had a bad feeling when grins split the men's faces. They looked downright gleeful when they moved out of the way. The man behind the wheel of the security car started it and positioned the car on the street to point at the dorm. Her stomach churned, a sick feeling pitting there. She knew what he planned to do in that moment. The driver stomped on the gas. The car lurched forward, jumped the curb, and barreled up the sidewalk that led right to the double, glass doors.

"Shit!" Ellie screamed as she stumbled back.

The sound hurt her ears when the car crashed into the doors. She ended up flat on her ass on the floor. She watched smoke rise from the damaged front-end of the car as the engine died. The glass doors held but as her gaze lifted upward, to her dismay, she realized the impact had created a good five-inch gap of buckled doorframe at the top.

"Oh God."Ellie muttered, stunned.

The windows hadn't broken but the building holding them in place had. She continued to sit there until the three men pulled their buddy out of the trashed car. He looked dazed but the airbag had saved him from severe injury. The four men studied the damage to the top of the doorframe, grinned, and then started to push the smoking wreckage away from the dorm. They maneuvered the car off the sidewalk and onto the grass, clearing the way for another vehicle assault.

Ellie struggled to her feet and ran for the house intercom system. She knew those men were about to use the truck to push those doors completely down to gain entry. She hit the com button. Her heart threatened to explode from terror but she tried to keep her voice calm.

"Locking down emergency doors," she stated clearly. "I repeat, locking down emergency doors. Get to safety now," she ordered the women. "Go to the third floor. Everyone run, damn it. They are breaking into the building. I won't hit the secondary emergency doors until the last minute but move it."

She released the button and wrenched open the emergency panel box under the com system. On the second and third floors were steel doors for the stairwells, the elevator, and there were also steel shutters that would cover the windows. It was a last-ditch emergency resort in case the lower floor was breached after lockdown. The interior doors that divided the levels were ten inches thick, weighed thousands of pounds, and the exterior shutters were bomb proof. They would also seal off the floors inside the elevator shaft.

Ellie twisted her body enough to view the damaged wall section over the front doors but could still reach the panel. One of the men climbed into the big pickup truck, verifying her worst fear. The men laughed while they talked, having a good time plotting how to kill her. She grimaced and hoped they'd bullshit for a bit longer while her women moved to a higher floor. She knew time was up when the driver's door closed, the truck engine roared to life, and it drove right over the body of a dead security guard. The driver maneuvered the truck to line up with the doors. *Damn.*

"Ellie?" Breeze's voice came from the com speaker. "We're all accounted for on the third floor. Get up here now."

Relief swept through Ellie. "Are you sure you are all there? Are you positive? Sky and Blue ran in last."

"They are here," Breeze assured her. "Get up here with us or I'm coming down there to get you."

"Protect yourselves. I'm safe," Ellie lied.

She wished she could go up there with Breeze but someone had to activate the emergency doors from the panel where she stood. Whoever had designed the building had made that a flaw, in her opinion, as she stood there knowing how vulnerable it left her. They should have installed trigger panels for the blast doors on all the floors.

She punched the three digit code into the emergency panel and twisted the key. A loud siren blasted through the house in fast bursts. She knew steel doors and shutters slammed down on the upper floors of the building. The women would have been safe on the second floor but she wanted them higher up and harder to reach, just in case those men found a way to breach an interior door. She hadn't thought the dorm could be broken into but she'd been wrong. She wasn't taking any chances by making anymore incorrect assumptions.

Ellie slammed the emergency panel closed. She knew the security center had to be getting the signal by now about what she'd done. That system ran on a wireless connection with the cameras. It was a safety backup in case the phones weren't working and the electricity went down so they could still monitor the emergency systems. It reassured her, thinking security had to know she'd just put in the last protocol of protection, which meant the dorm had been breached. They'd come faster to save her.

I hope. Please get us some help right now.

* * * * *

Rage gripped Justice. He found himself locked inside the main security control room watching the screens filled with images around Homeland. Fifteen trucks had driven inside after they'd car bombed the front gate. Shots were being fired, people were dying and he was trapped inside a steel box to watch it go down. His people were in danger and he wanted to help them.

"Calm down," Darren Artino demanded. "The SWAT team and local law enforcement are on their way. The buildings have been locked down, everyone is aware there's a problem, and your council has been secured inside a safe bunker. You've been watching everything just the way we have. It's only my security force being killed out there. Your people are safe."

"Sir," a woman yelled. "Uh, there's a big problem."

"What," Darren Artino snapped. "We have a hundred of them right now."

"It's the woman at the women's dorm. She stopped trying to wave us down and she just put in the last protocol code. She's triggered the Hail Mary doors."

"The what?" Justice growled the words. He wondered if steam came from his ears. He'd never wanted to feel helpless again after he started his new life but he did at that moment. It infuriated him.

"Get me cameras on that building," Darren Artino shouted. "The woman is too green and I bet she's just panicking. I'm going to fire her ass when this is over."

"I've got the East Street camera on line," a man called out. "Screen fourteen."

Darren Artino pointed to the right screen and knew Justice breathing down his neck. Both men focused their attention on the screen. They watched a truck accelerate toward the front entrance of the women's dorm.

"Son of a bitch," Darren spat.

"What are Hail Mary doors?" Justice grabbed Darren by the arm and spun him around.

Darren took a deep breath when he met a pissed-off pair of cat eyes. "Hail Mary is a prayer. It's, 'oh hell, it's bad'. Reinforced doors have been activated inside the dorm and they cut off entire sections of the building." He jerked his arm to break free of Justice's grip. "Get every camera we have inside the dorm on screen and I want heat signatures being tracked on every floor, right now! Priority one to all frontal screens."

Justice reached for his cell phone to place a call. "The women's dorm is under heavy attack." He hung up.

"Thirty-four heat signatures are on the third floor. The Hail Mary doors are down and secure," a woman shouted out. "One heat signature is on the first floor and its moving fast."

"There are thirty-five women living inside the dorms, according to our records," a man called out. "All accounted for."

Cameras normally inactive inside the dorm clicked on. One screen displayed women who sat or leaned against walls inside the hallway of the third floor.

"Those are my women." Justice tensed. "Are they safe where they are?"

Darren nodded. "Very. Nothing can get to them. The steel doors are almost a foot thick. Not even a bomb could dent them. I told you they would be safe."

"We have the front doors on screen ten," a man yelled.

Justice and Darren looked at that camera view and Darren cursed. The glass doors were down on the floor. The damage along the top of the wall where they'd been anchored had been twisted inward.

"Son of a bitch! The glass held but the building didn't." Someone stated the obvious.

"We have movement with four new heat signatures," a woman called out. "We are tracking the original single heat signature. It's inside the kitchen. I've got all cameras on line now."

* * * * *

Ellie ran into the kitchen. She'd heard the doors come down with a loud crash and knew she was trapped. She could either hide while she prayed help reached her before those men found her or she could fight. Her odds of facing off and winning against the four armed men weren't good. Her main concern had been the New Species women and it comforted her, knowing they were safe. She'd understood it would be a dangerous job when she'd taken it but she never thought something this bad could happen.

She yanked open the knife drawer and grabbed the largest one she could find while she watched the open doorway over her shoulder. A she tried to quell her panic, knowing she needed a clear head. *I need a place to hide.*

Her focus immediately landed on the island and she moved to it, ducked down and got out of sight. She cracked open one of the cabinets and started shifting items inside, doing it as quietly as possible.

"Here, kitty, kitty," a male voice yelled.

Are you kidding me? Ellie shook her head. *They can't even tell the difference between a human and a New Species. The idiots don't even know what to shoot at. Hunters, my ass*, she fumed, remembering that word painted on the side of their truck.

"Come out, kitty cat."

The voice sounded closer. Ellie's heart raced while she eased into the small space. There wasn't much room but she managed to wiggle under the counter and get the cupboard door closed. She had her knees pressed to her body and her head bent in a balled position in the darkness. She tried to control her breathing to prevent them from hearing it. Her ears strained for the slightest noise. All she could do at that point was pray they didn't find her until help arrived.

"I'm not going to kill you. I just want to talk."

Ellie clenched her teeth. The guy obviously believed her to be a complete moron if he thought she'd believe him for a second. There was no way she'd attempt to talk to those insane jerks without bulletproof glass separating them. To allow them get close to her would be the fastest way to die and she wanted to live.

* * * * *

Justice continued to glance at different screens to watch what took place inside the women's dorm. He flipped his phone out and hit speed dial. He'd just seen Ellie Brower hide inside a cabinet under the island in the kitchen. His gaze tracked the four intruders who searched the lower section of the house. They'd realized the elevators were out and they were blocked access to the second floor by a large steel door that cut off the stairs. The men split up and moved room to room on the first floor of the dorm, searching for Ellie.

"Our women are secure on the third floor but the human female is hiding inside the kitchen. It's just a matter of time before they find her. She's trapped. There are four heavily armed males inside and they gained entry by breaking down the front doors." He hung up.

Darren Artino spun to frown at Justice. "Who were you talking to?"

"My security team is on their way."

Darren's mouth dropped opened and then slammed shut. "Security is my job. Communications are still down. I can't exactly call my security guards and order them to give anyone permission to enter Homeland. They blocked off the front gates by using employee cars to barricade it to prevent anyone else from coming inside."

"They are already here," Justice growled. "They are my men, my people."

Darren's face reddened with anger. "My job is to protect New Species, not have them leave the safety of where they are to confront these crazy bastards. We almost have it contained. Call them back and order them to return to safety."

"'Almost' won't save that female." Justice jerked his chin toward the screen showing the kitchen. He softly cursed. One of the intruders had just stepped into the kitchen.

Chapter Seven

ဢ

"Kitty, kitty, kitty," a male voice called out, as if she were a cat. He started yanking open cupboards on the other side of the kitchen.

Ellie's entire body trembled and her hand clutched the knife hard enough for the wood handle to dig into her palm. She closed her eyes and listened as he slammed things. Suddenly something hit the counter above her. She bit back a moan of terror. *Maybe he won't think to look inside the lower cabinets,* she feverishly prayed.

Her luck ran out as the cabinet door jerked open next to her. He reached inside and grabbed her left arm. A brutal grasp dragged her out of her hiding spot with one hard yank.

"Got you, you little cat bitch."

"I'm not a cat," she informed him in a shaky voice. "I'm as human as you are."

He jerked her painfully to her feet and glared down at her. He appeared to be in his mid twenties, stood about five foot eight, with a stocky build. A tattoo peeked out from his T-shirt collar.

"I don't care what you are, bitch. Now you're dead. This is our country and you damn two-legged animals need to die." He reached behind him to the waist of his jeans to withdraw a handgun.

Ellie saw the weapon and understood he planned to just shoot her. Pure terror flashed through her as she plunged the knife at his chest. She stared into his eyes when the blade struck him, slid through the shirt, into skin, and watched his green gaze widen with shock. He stumbled back, dragged her by the arm, and she tore her hand from the knife handle imbedded deep in his chest. Blood poured down the front of him and onto her. His arm with the gun rose as he tried to make a last-ditch effort to shoot her. Ellie grabbed his wrist with both hands and struggled to keep him from pointing it at her.

His hold on her arm tightened, caused her pain, but then it eased as he weakened. His knees gave out and he collapsed onto them to the tiled kitchen floor. A horrible moan, along with bright red blood, poured from his mouth. Ellie moaned in horrified distress as the man's gaze locked with hers, his pain, terror and rage clearly displayed there. He lost his hold on her arm. He also released the gun, which crashed to the floor a second before he slumped backward.

Ellie stared down at him mutely. He sprawled on his back with his calves twisted under his thighs in that awkward bent position. His eyes were open wide, blood pooled on the white tile and he took a few more ragged gasps. A slight bubbling noise reached her ears. His hands jerked, twitched, and he blinked before he took his last breath. The knife handle protruded from his chest by his heart where she'd stabbed him. She swallowed the bile that rose up just as glass broke nearby. The sound had come from another room, forcing her attention from the dead guy at her feet.

Instinct took over. She dived for the gun on the floor. She grabbed it with both hands, the weapon cold and heavy, and struggled to her knees behind the island, peering over the counter at the only entries into the kitchen. The open archway to one of the living spaces and the archway to the dining area were her only escape routes. She used the island to shield her body and pointed the gun between those two openings. She planned to shoot anything that moved.

She didn't have long to wait before someone made a noise from the dining area when they knocked over a chair. She trained the gun in that direction, made sure her body remained behind the island, and used the top of the counter to hold her hands steady in the double grip she had on the weapon. She trembled, scared, *and* she'd just stabbed a man to death. She pushed those facts from her mind, knowing she'd fall apart if she dwelled on it. She didn't have time to face repercussions of what she'd had to do to survive.

The guy with the shotgun stepped into the kitchen, just waltzed inside as if he didn't have a care in the world. That changed instantly when he saw her with the gun trained on him. His mouth opened, his eyes widened and then he reacted. He seemed to move in slow motion when he started to lower the muzzle of the shotgun toward her. His mouth compressed into a tight line of determination to shoot but Ellie pulled the trigger first. The sound deafened her when the weapon fired.

He threw himself back into the dining room and disappeared from sight. The shotgun poked around the wall and he fired it but it ended up hitting the ceiling somewhere behind Ellie. Something soft that reminded her of snow rained down over her head. She screamed in reaction and fired at the wall he hid behind, next to the arch.

She wasn't sure if she'd hit the bastard or not but she hoped so. She realized she must not have hurt him when the shotgun barrel extended again. He blindly pointed it her way as he pulled the trigger. The cabinet near Ellie blew to pieces. She threw her body to the floor, almost right on top of the dead guy.

She slipped on thick, wet blood when she tried to push up from the tile. Her knees skated in the slick substance, she gasped, and her hands shot out from under her. She slammed down onto her stomach with a grunt. She had to roll to get away from the blood staining the floor.

She saw movement from the corner of her eye and twisted toward the motion. The guy with the shotgun rushed her, ran right at the island. She pointed the gun and fired while lying on her side. He ducked behind the other side of the counter and slammed into the cabinets with a loud crack as the thin wood took the impact of his body.

"Drop the gun, you bitch," he demanded. "And I won't torture you before I blow your fucking head off."

Ellie's terrified stare fixed on the cabinet he'd hit with his last gunshot blast, proof of its destructive force. The wood had a fist-sized hole in it and bits of it had exploded on impact to scatter across the tile floor. She took a deep breath, realized she had to get away and find somewhere new to hide. What she really needed, she decided, was for the son of a bitch with the shotgun to shoot himself.

"Ellie? We hear gunfire on the coms. Are you all right?"

Shit. She had forgotten to turn off the com system. Breeze's voice sounded worried but Ellie couldn't answer her. She took comfort in knowing Breeze and the other woman were safely locked two floors above. Only the head of security and the director knew the codes to open those steel doors once they'd been activated. Ellie didn't even have that kind of access once the Hail Mary doors were triggered. The men could torture her, but she didn't have the information they needed to reach the women.

"Ellie?" He snickered behind the island but he'd given away his location. "What kind of stupid name is that for an animal to get?"

Ellie eased open the cabinet door. He had to be right behind it on the other side. She peered inside and took aim.

"I'm going to fucking kill you slow for what you did to Eddie."

Ellie pulled the trigger and fired in his general direction until the gun clicked, empty after a few bullets tore through the wood. Ellie spun away in case he returned fire and crawled to the far left. The gun would be useless except as something to pitch at him.

Silence met her ears while she strained to hear anything. She hesitated at the corner to peek around the island, her heart pounding. A groan sounded from the other side of the island.

Had she hit him? She couldn't be that lucky. She crawled forward on her hands and knees. The dead man's sticky blood covered her hands, making it a slippery action. She inched forward, terrified, but knew there were two other men who could show up at any time, drawn by the gunfire. If she stayed put they'd definitely kill her.

The guy with the shotgun had to be messing with her, perhaps playing hurt to get her to stick her head out so he could shoot her. She had a bad feeling until she saw blood flowing across the floor along the grout line.

Ellie held her breath and then took the chance to stick her head out and glance at the side of the island. His body sat leaning against it. The shotgun rested on the floor next to his legs while he stared straight ahead toward the dining room. He blinked. Blood covered his chest and ran down his left arm, revealing that she'd hit him at least once. She continued to watch him.

"Buck?" A man's voice called from the living room. "Eddie?"

She sprang to her feet and sprinted for the dining room. If Buck was the guy with the shotgun, she prayed he wouldn't have the time or the ability, with his injuries, to grab his weapon to shoot her as she dashed away. She made it out of the kitchen without getting shot in the back.

The safest place would be the library. If she could make it there without getting caught she had a chance to barricade herself inside. Heavy furniture filled the large room. She could shove it into place to block the double doors. With that new plan in mind, she made a mad dash for it. A man swore as she darted past an open doorway to one of the rooms. She knew he'd seen her and ran faster. All the other downstairs rooms were too open or had limited ways to seal off sections.

Ellie made it to the library and slammed the door closed. She leaned against the wood, heard the guy following right on her heels. She had no time to grab furniture after all. She panted, totally out of breath, looked down and grimaced at the sight of her hands, arms, and her shirt covered with blood.

"This way," a man yelled. "She's in here."

"Buck and Eddie are dead," a man screamed. "She fucking killed them. That animal bitch killed them both."

One of the men tried to open the door. Ellie screamed and shoved back with all the strength she had. She heard a vicious curse and then someone slammed hard enough into it that the impact shoved her a few inches from the hard surface her back pressed so tightly. She frantically searched for something she could reach with her foot to drag over to help block the door but she had no such luck.

I need a weapon. The large room contained a few couches, some tables, and comfortable chairs. The fireplace sat across the room. Books lined all the shelves surrounding the room. Her desperate attention flew back to the fireplace and the tool set next to it. Her focus zoomed in on the poker.

Both men slammed their combined weight against the door. The force was hard enough to send Ellie flying away from it. She hit one of the couches, slid over the side of it and tumbled to the floor behind it. She clawed frantically at the carpet to find purchase to get back to her feet.

"Get that bitch," one of the men yelled.

Ellie grabbed the fire poker and spun to face her attackers. She struck the man closest to her using the metal rod as if it were a baseball bat. Pain shot through Ellie's hands from the sharp impact when it made contact with the man's body. He howled in pain and jumped back but stared at his torn shirt where blood appeared on the damaged material.

The man glared at Ellie. "You're going to pay for that," he hissed.

The other man unsheathed a hunting knife from his waist as both men moved apart. Ellie kept her back to the fireplace and waved the fire poker between the men, trying to keep them back. They inched apart more to make it harder for Ellie to keep an eye on both of them. Both rushed her. She swung. Ellie managed to hit one of them right before the second one tackled her. She hit the floor hard with a heavy weight crushed down over her. She gasped, tried to scream, but she couldn't even draw breath.

"You bitch," the one she'd hit roared. "I think she broke my fucking hand. You got her, Roy?"

The man on top of her grabbed her hair at the base of her neck and smashed her facedown against the carpet. She tried to fight but couldn't get away from him. He shoved her harder against the carpet and a knee dug painfully against the back of her leg.

"I got the rabid bitch, Chuck."

He adjusted enough for her to turn her head. Ellie inhaled air and instantly regretted it. The man had putrid breath. He kept her pinned down and held her head in place with his fisted grip on her hair. She couldn't get out from under the heavy man. He had to be close to three hundred pounds.

"Let me cut the bitch up," Chuck whined. "I think she really broke my hand. It hurts like hell."

Roy grunted. He shifted and Ellie cried out in pain when his body pressed flush with hers, pushed tighter against her until her ribs threatened to break. Something poked into her ass cheek. The other guy tore the fire poker from her hand.

"Help me get her up," Roy rasped. "I know how to show this bitch her place in society and then I'll let you slice her damn throat like she's a rabbit. We'll watch her twitch until all the blood drains out."

Ellie could only manage to buck and squirm when she tried to fight. The object pressed against her ass wasn't a mystery anymore. Roy was horny. She had a horrible idea what he planned to do to her to show her what her place in his messed-up idea of society would be. Sheep, rabbits, she guessed anything breathing was the asshole's speed.

Hands grabbed her ankles and a second later Roy shifted his weight off her and let go of her hair to grab her other wrist. They hauled her up by her arms and legs, carried her between them, her back inches above floor. Ellie screamed and fought, tried to kick out at the man who held her legs, but they wouldn't let her go. Chuck sure seemed to have no problems holding her ankles in a crushing hold for a guy with a suspected broken hand.

"Toss her over the couch. Then move on the other side of it to grab her hair." Roy panted, out of breath from restraining her while she struggled.

They swung Ellie's body and she hit a coffee table. Sharp pain exploded in her side. She wondered if they'd broken her rib when it hurt to gasp air into her lungs. The men swung her again, this time she hit the couch, and they twisted her body with brutal hands. Roy had her arms and Chuck dropped her legs.

She attempted to kick at Roy when they bent her over the back of the couch. Roy slammed his body down on hers instead, crushed her under him again and pinned her tightly to the couch. She screamed into the cushion when hands grabbed her hair and pressed her face tighter into the material. Sheer panic shot through her when she realized she couldn't breathe. They were suffocating her.

"Hand me the knife." Roy sounded excited and breathless.

One of the hands left Ellie's hair. She twisted her face, gasped air into her starved lungs, and screamed when she exhaled. Roy grabbed the back of her shirt and the knife slid along her spine. Numb with terror, she didn't know if he cut her too. She tried to kick at him but she couldn't get any real force behind the motion.

She blindly reached out, trying to claw Chuck. A brutal hand gripped her hair again but she grasped his arm. She dug her fingernails into skin as he shoved her face back into the cushion, attempting to suffocate her again. She heard his savage curse and Ellie sucked in a large gasp of air when he tore his hand away to stop the pain she inflicted.

Her pants were shoved down her legs, leaving no doubt they planned to rape her. Ellie fought harder, screamed, and then suddenly the weight was torn away from her. She threw her body away from the couch the second Roy's body moved. She tripped and collapsed to the floor on her ass. She sucked in precious air while gaping at the men around her. She instinctively yanked her pants back up.

Roy lay sprawled on his stomach on the floor with a gun pointed at the back of his head. Chuck had his hands up and looked absolutely terrified. Four men dressed in black SWAT-styled outfits with NSO printed in white lettering on their vests stared down at her. Their faces weren't totally human and she identified them immediately as New Species. They held guns and had large knives strapped against their thighs. She heard movement from behind her and jerked her head toward the noise. Fury stood there, bristling with rage far darker than the black outfit he and the other men wore.

Something ugly twisted inside Fury. He'd pushed his men hard to reach the women's dorm the second Justice had called the team and stated Ellie was in danger. He'd been terrified he'd arrive too late and damn near had. When he'd rushed into the room to see the scene before him, those men ready to do horrific things to his Ellie, a murderous impulse hit him. It took everything he had not to roar out in wrath and kill them. His animal wanted to watch them bleed and die.

He breathed hard, his gaze fixed on her face as she gasped for air while attempting to right her pants. Her hair tumbled around her bruised face, her shirt cut apart in the back, and he could see bruises forming on her pale, delicate skin. The scent of her terror clung in the air, making it more difficult for him to gain control of his urges to tear her attackers apart with his bare hands.

He darted a glance toward the cameras and their presence helped him hold his composure. He knew, if they weren't there, he would have murdered the humans without a second thought for daring to touch Ellie. Even now, he was tempted, consequences be damned. They'd gone after his woman and had harmed her.

He took a threatening step toward one of the men but then Ellie softly moaned. His gaze zoned on her instantly and it forced him to rethink his decision. Caring for her became his first priority. He could kill those bastards after he made certain she wasn't acutely injured.

He took breaths through his mouth to help dilute her terrified scent and he fought his animal for control. He glanced at each of his men, acknowledged their rage as well, and knew they were looking to him for guidance on how to handle the situation. That assisted him as well to calm down as he forced his fists to unclench. He gave hand signals to his men to secure the assholes responsible for the attack. He didn't trust his voice.

Fury tried with great difficulty to appear composed, something he definitely wasn't, as he approached Ellie. He wanted to drop to the floor and cradle her in his arms and give comfort. It reassured him that he'd reached her in time but then the male human scents mingled with hers.

It enraged him, smelling them on her. She was his, damn it, and he'd fought hard to stay the hell away from her after Justice's warning. He had, except for a few nightly trips to glimpse her from afar, and now she'd nearly died. Orders be damned, he'd touch her now. He moved with care not to startle her. He needed to make certain she was really all right even if he had to strip her to inspect every inch. He wouldn't settle for less.

Fury knew he had to keep a cool head. Ellie had to be leery of him after the incident at his house and he didn't want to show her how much she meant to him. The last thing he needed would be Ellie understanding how badly she could hurt him.

Keep it cool, he ordered himself. *Act as if I can control myself in her presence.* He hoped he could anyway. She would be safe and he would remain with her since she'd been traumatized. To have her worry that he'd toss her over his shoulder, carry her back to his house, and tie her down on his bed again wasn't something she needed at that moment. No matter how much that was exactly what he wanted to do. He'd keep her safe even if it meant he'd guard her around the clock. He knew he really couldn't do it but it soothed his animal to at least consider doing exactly that.

He needed to be with her right now, to talk to her, to stick close to her until he had no doubt she'd be okay. Otherwise he'd breach the edge of insanity knowing how close she'd come to death and how he could have lost her forever.

Ellie stared up into Fury's intense, dark gaze when he crouched down in front of her. He hesitated a second before his finger curled under her chin. He wore black gloves, leather from the feel of them, and his touch gentled while he examined her. He turned her head to study her neck and face. He released her chin. Without any warning or word, he grabbed Ellie's arms under her elbows, and gently pulled her up, to stand.

She realized the back of her shirt parted and exposed her skin. Fury's hold tightened on her as she nearly collapsed when her legs wobbled. A soft growl came from the back of his throat and rage once again gripped his features. It frightened Ellie's, wondering why he'd made that scary noise directed at her. His hands eased their hold from her arms but in a heartbeat he leaned down, gripped behind her legs and back. He swept her into his arms to secure her tightly against his chest. He didn't look at her.

"I'll clean her up and check for injuries. Hold ground with them outside." Fury snarled the words. "No one comes inside the dorm."

A fierce-looking man with long black hair nodded. "Understood."

Fury strode forward. Ellie hesitated a second before wrapping her arm around his neck. She was tired, hurting, and too traumatized to care where he took her. She rested her cheek against his shoulder and closed her eyes. For whatever reason, he and his men had come to save her from a horrible death at the hands of the two assailants. *Another few minutes…* She shivered at the thought of what would have happened to her. She burrowed closer against Fury and didn't miss it when his body tensed. He kept walking though.

Ellie opened her eyes when he paused and kicked something. He pushed open the door to carry her inside the women's bathroom. He frowned, glanced around, and then headed for the long counter of sinks. He gently set her down so she perched on the edge, facing him. She had to let him go when he slowly backed away.

Fury spun and glanced around the room. She followed where he searched and realized he looked up into the corners. She immediately knew what he searched for.

"There are no cameras in here," Ellie informed him softly. "Security wanted to install them but I argued about the women's privacy."

Fury nodded and turned his attention to the sink next to her. He stripped off his gloves and tossed them onto the counter. He waved his hands under the faucet, activating it to turn on. As water started to flow he washed his hands then moved away to a paper napkin dispenser. Ellie watched him with raised eyebrows as he yanked fistfuls of brown paper towels out and piled them next to her on the counter. He completely emptied the dispenser and moved to the next one.

"I think that's plenty."

Fury frowned at her. He put the rest of the napkins down and stalked toward her in a graceful way that reminded her of a cat about to pounce. "Take your clothes off now."

A gasp tore from her lips and she had to close her gaping mouth from the shock of his demand. "I won't."

He growled softly at her. "You're covered in their stink and blood. I can't tell what is yours and what is theirs. I'm going to wash you and find your injuries. If you can't undress I'll do it for you."

Ellie relaxed, understanding why he made insane demands now. "You want to clean me up to treat my injuries? That's all?"

His eyes narrowed. "Would you prefer I send one of my males inside here to strip you down? Your security is still trying to retain order." He snorted. "We might be here for a while. One of us is going to remove your clothes and clean you to see if you are hurt and how badly. Decide now if it will be me or one of my men. I don't want to waste time and that's what you're doing."

Ellie clenched her teeth. He could be such a rude bastard at times. She'd just gone through the worst trauma of her life and he didn't need to be so abrupt. "I think I can manage."

"I caught you before you fell. You can't even walk."

"I just killed two men, could have been brutally raped, and they were going to murder me. Excuse the hell out of me for being a bit weak-kneed."

He moved closer to her. "You killed two? I didn't search the house since I heard you struggling and knew where to find you. I just rushed to your side."

"They didn't trip and kill each other." She trembled still. The reality of what she'd done to survive sank in. The blood drained from her face and a wave of dizziness made her sway where she sat. "I killed them. I really killed them."

Fury growled out a soft curse. "It was self defense. Don't go there, sweetness. You had no other choice and they had it coming. You did the world a favor by taking them out. They would have killed you without a second thought." He closed the remaining distance until only inches separated them. He grabbed the front of her shirt and yanked it up until her shirt peeled from her body. It made it easy for him to do with the back already sliced open. "Do you understand? They aren't worth that haunted look in your eyes. Argue with me, talk to me, but think about something else. Don't fall apart because I can't stand to see your tears. Call me names instead and get angry."

She blinked her tears back. He was being kind and it only served to draw her emotions closer to the surface. He had the most beautiful eyes in the world. The urge to throw herself into his arms and cling to him became almost overwhelming. He tore his gaze from hers before she could act on it.

"I need to get you cleaned up now. I really can't stand smelling their stench on you. It's a New Species thing but it makes me have to fight my rage." He paused, glancing at her. "I have instincts that were a side effect from what they did to me and sometimes I have to fight those urges. It's worse when I'm angry, agitated, or afraid. If that stink isn't gone from you soon I'll be obligated to go out there to rip their heads off."

"Okay." She nodded. "As much as I wouldn't protest someone doing that to those jerks, I don't want it to be you. You'd get into trouble."

Ellie realized her bra had been sliced along with the back of her shirt and made a grab with both hands to cup and cover her bare breasts. Fury grabbed her wrists before she could hide them from him and yanked her arms out wide. He didn't look at her chest but instead inspected her bloody hands.

"Don't touch yourself with their blood. Get down and face the sink. I will clean you."

Fury's soft, husky tone made her relax and not fight with him when their gazes met again. She inched off the edge of the counter, not wanting to argue with him. He tried to distract her from the pain of reality and she realized it was almost sweet. She also hadn't missed the fact that he'd used an endearment by calling her "sweetness". It warmed her a bit from the shock she suffered.

Her feet touched the floor and her legs wobbled. Fury turned her until he hovered at her back and released her arms. He reached around her waist and waved his hands under the faucet, activating it to turn on again. He gripped her wrists gently and shoved them under the cool water. Ellie looked down to watch the water change color as blood washed from her wrists and hands. She closed her eyes tightly to fight the sick feeling that gripped her at seeing the water turning red.

"Why the hell don't they have showers down here?" Fury growled.

"We have our own private bathrooms with showers inside our apartments. No one ever thought the dorm could be breached."

He sighed. "Well, you need one now and all I have are these sinks."

Ellie kept her eyes closed, grateful that he kept her mind busy by asking questions. Fury leaned against her bare back, his clothes a bit scratchy, and his arms brushed against the side of her ribs while he rubbed the blood from her skin. He ordered her to bend forward and she didn't hesitate. He kept cleaning her by spreading water up her arms all the way to her shoulders. Water trickled down her body and soaked her pants. There was nothing to be done about it, nor did it matter since her clothes were already soaked with blood.

"Kick off your shoes." His voice whispered near her ear.

Ellie complied, toeing off her slip-on flats that had once been white but were now bloodstained. She'd slid in blood in the kitchen, crawled through it, and knew her shoes were destroyed. She forced those thoughts away. Fury's hands eased her cotton pants down a few inches but then hesitated.

"I'm just cleaning you. Be strong for just a while longer. You're safe and no one will hurt you, Ellie. I won't allow it.

They'd have to go through me to reach you and it wouldn't happen."

She believed him. "Okay."

She kept her eyes closed to prevent seeing if Fury stared at her body. His hands were gentle when he tugged her pants the rest of the way down and hooked her panties with his thumbs to remove those too. She lifted one leg and then the other to help him when she realized he wanted them totally off her body until she stood naked. Fury turned the water back on and dumped water over her body with cupped hands. When every inch of her from the neck down dripped with water, he used wet paper towels to softly scrub at her skin while Ellie held unnaturally still.

"That's the best I can do," Fury said in a deep, tight voice. "You'll need a shower but I can't see any more blood. You managed not to get it in your hair from what I can see and smell."

Ellie opened her eyes finally when he didn't touch her in any way again. Her gaze instantly found his image reflected on the mirror and her mouth opened in shock. Fury had his back to her while he removed his vest and unbuttoned his shirt to peel it from his broad shoulders.

"What are you doing?" Surprise sounded in her voice and she hated it.

"You need something dry and clean to wear. I thought I'd give you my shirt and briefs." He glanced over his shoulder and met her gaze in the mirror. "Do you want to leave this bathroom naked?" Dark eyes narrowed. "I won't allow it so don't even think about it. If you'd told me to send in another male to help you get undressed that wouldn't have happened either."

She shook her head and crossed her arms over her breasts to hide them from his view. "Please lend me the shirt and your briefs. I'd appreciate it."

He turned his head away. "You don't have to watch me strip."

Ellie realized she stared as he unbuttoned his shirt and removed it to expose a tan, muscular back. She squeezed her eyes closed, her only choice since she faced a mirror and turning around would just be facing him in the flesh. She listened as he undressed and it seemed like forever before he finished and spoke.

"I'm decent. Here."

Ellie opened her eyes to find Fury closer, nearly touching her back. He faced away and held his shirt and a pair of blue boxer briefs over his shoulder toward her. Ellie turned and reached up to take them from him. She noticed again how much taller he stood than her.

"Thank you."

"I owed you." He growled the words.

Anger flared over his gruff taunt about their strained relationship. She clenched her teeth to avoid snapping out a rude response. She didn't need to be reminded of that now. She dressed quickly instead. The boxer briefs were soft cotton, still warm from his body, and hung baggy, low on her hips. *I have a fly now.* She smirked at that thought while she put on his shirt. It smelled of him, held his warmth, and she was happy to be covered up again.

"You can turn around now." She finished buttoning the borrowed shirt.

He slowly faced her. He looked sexy with just the vest on with his form-fitting pants. His arms were totally exposed, big, thick muscles showcased by the tight vest that looked too small for his impressive frame. She tore her gaze away from those biceps and rolled up the sleeves of the shirt until they didn't fall past her hands. Fury stepped forward to help her by brushing away her fingers to do the task. She stared at his vest where NSO had been printed in large letters across it.

"I didn't know you guys had your own security team."

He inhaled deeply. "Yeah, well, we can't trust humans to totally protect us. We've been training in secret and none of your people knew until now. Look what an incompetent job they did today. Mercile gave us strength, reflexes, and the ability to take a beating but remain fighting beyond normal endurance. The ones of us with any skills are teaching the others. We're fast learners."

"Why do it in secret? It's your Homeland. You can do whatever you want."

"Tell that to your people." He hesitated. "They denied our requests when we asked for a space to train just for such a purpose or to have their instructors train our males in fighting skills. Now we do it ourselves in the men's dorm out of their sight. We have removed all cameras inside. We tore them out when security refused to comply."

She frowned. "Mike doesn't tell on you to the director?"

"The dorm father?" Fury shook his head. "He drinks smelly alcohol every evening. After nine, a bomb could go off inside his apartment and he wouldn't move. He has no idea what we do at night."

"I'm sorry you have to do that." She didn't know what else to say. "If your women want to train here, I won't tell on them. They won't have to hide it from me."

He shrugged. "We work around the roadblocks they throw in our path but thank you for the offer to the women. I'll pass it along. One way or another, we're going to become self-sufficient."

"I know you will."

He reached up but then froze midair, his fingers inches from her face.

Ellie couldn't resist inching closer until the tips of his fingers brushed her cheek. Fingers curled around the curve of her face, slid into her hair, and she pressed her face against his palm. His touch soothed her. She wouldn't say it aloud but she'd been happy to see him even under horrific circumstances.

Ellie raised her gaze to his. "Thank you for saving me."

His dark eyes were beautiful and some unknown emotion flickered inside them for a heartbeat. "I told you I don't want you dead anymore." He caressed her face. "I was worried about you."

She hesitated. "I've been told by a few of your women that they've seen you outside watching the dorm. Why are you out there?"

His cheeks flushed as if it embarrassed him but then his features blanked. His hand pulled away, dropping to his side. "I like to know where my enemies are. Come," he growled. "The blood wasn't yours. You have bruising and some scratches but you will live. I have a job to do. I need to see what is happening."

It felt as though he'd slapped her with his out-of-the-blue harsh words, letting her know they weren't even friends. She tore her gaze from his. "I'll put on my shoes."

"Don't. They have blood on them and I just cleaned you. I can't do that again. I'm not that strong," he muttered.

What does that mean? Ellie wasn't sure as she walked toward the bathroom door. Fury stayed at her side but didn't touch her as he slid his gloves back on as they crossed the room. He opened the bathroom door for her and then walked away, leaving her to follow him. She stared up at the back of his head, wondering what his thoughts were. He had been nice to her up until the enemy comment.

The four NSO officers guarded the damaged entrance. Darren Artino and a dozen of his security guards waited. He glared at Fury.

"Your men wouldn't allow me to go inside."

Fury gave a smile that didn't reach his eyes. He showed sharp canine fangs. "You may enter now."

Artino uttered a foul curse and waved his men into the dorm. His angry gaze traveled down Ellie's body and he visibly tensed. His focus zoomed in on the men's briefs she wore, just an inch or so of them displayed at the bottom of the shirt, and his mouth gaped. He spun to glare at Fury.

Fury shrugged. "She needed clothes. You should put showers and towels inside the bathrooms on the lower floor if you have shitty security. When the people you fail to protect need to clean up the blood that was spilled, they can do it in comfort after they save their own asses. Paper towels weren't going to cover her modesty afterward but my underclothing was much preferable to walking around naked."

Ellie put her hand over her mouth to hide the smile. Artino's face reddened as the words sank in. The head of security could be a real self-righteous prick sometimes and she enjoyed him getting a good verbal kick. She let her hand drop as she watched Fury nod at his men. They walked out of the women's dorm without a backward glance.

Artino faced her. "Can you believe he said that to me?" He glared at Ellie in outrage.

She hesitated, choosing her words carefully. She wasn't in a position to tell him his security had failed big time. "You really should put in at least one shower and real towels on the first floor bathroom. It would have come in handy."

Ellie tore her gaze from his stunned expression to head over to one of the couches. She collapsed onto the soft material. Exhaustion and the need for a good cry set in. *Or a stiff drink. Maybe all of the above.*

* * * * *

Fury paused outside on the sidewalk to face his men and to stare over their shoulders at Ellie. She sat on the couch looking tired and pale from her traumatic ordeal. It had taken every ounce of his willpower to leave her when he really wanted to wrap his arms around her to give comfort. If she burst into tears he knew he'd go back inside regardless of how stupid it would be to cuddle her until her fear eased.

His phone rang and he snatched it up. "Yes, Justice?"

"What did you do with the human female while you were inside the bathroom? The cameras followed you when you carried her there but there is no footage inside. Are things well?"

"Yes." Fury tensed.

"You should have sent one of our men with her if she needed assistance. We've had long talks about her, my friend. Are you all right?"

He lowered his voice. "They touched her and hurt her but I kept my cool."

"Good." Justice paused. "You did a damn good job, Fury. I'm proud of you. The humans are a tad upset that our team saved the woman. They weren't happy when they realized we have our own security now."

"It's our Homeland. We were told by the President of the United States that this is our home and, when we're able, we can run it ourselves."

"I know. They feel guilty for funding Mercile Industries without knowing exactly what they paid for. They want to make it right with us and it would be very bad publicity worldwide if we pointed a finger at them. We need to tread lightly still until we're in a position to govern ourselves. The conversation with Darren Artino appeared unfriendly. What was said?"

"He wasn't happy we succeeded where his security failed. It displeased him that I ordered my team not to allow anyone access to the dorm until I made sure of Ellie's safety and well-being."

Justice hesitated. "Are you in control? I need you to be. Our people need leadership and guidance the most right now while we learn to thrive in the world outside captivity. I chose you to be my second in command because you're respected, you usually keep your emotions on a tight leash, and you want what is best for our people as much as I do."

"You have nothing to worry about," Fury swore, his gaze still locked on Ellie. "I know I can't have her."

"I wish you could." Justice sighed softly. "You deserve happiness. Return to the male dorm. I'll be there soon to address our men."

Chapter Eight

80

Director Boris glowered at Ellie. "I want an explanation for your refusal right now."

She glared back at him, furious, and beyond ready to tell the man off in a rude way. "What is to explain? Don't make me go over this again. I already have a hundred times and nothing is going to change just because you have a problem with them having their own security officers. Officer Fury helped me clean up inside that bathroom. I shook too badly to walk from being that upset. I had to kill two men, I'm not military, and I don't have that kind of background."

"I know that," he snapped.

"I was shaken up that day those crazy freaks broke into Homeland and I couldn't even walk. If you saw the videos of what happened then you know Officer Fury had to carry me. My clothes were bloody and he just lent me his briefs and a shirt. He did the decent, kind thing. What is your problem?" She rose to her feet and resisted the urge to smack the offensive asshole.

"He inappropriately touched you and I want a formal complaint filed by six o'clock today. We need to show them they can't do whatever the hell they want. They didn't get authorization to do what they did."

Unbelievable. Ellie gaped at him. "I won't do it. He didn't inappropriately touch me. If you want to have a pissing contest with someone to show who's in control, don't pull me into it. I don't even have the right equipment."

He ignored her sarcastic comment. "That man carried you into a bathroom where you stripped naked in front of him and he stripped naked in front of you, obviously, to give you his damn boxers. That is totally unacceptable. Write that report now. That is an order."

"There are no cameras inside that bathroom. You don't know what went on in there!" Ellie yelled, beyond furious.

"I can guess. Is that it, Ms. Brower? Do you have the hots for Officer Fury? Did you two do more than exchange clothing? Did he fuck you?"

She took a step back and her hands balled into fists. She wanted to deck him so bad she had to struggle to get hold of her temper. She couldn't. He'd gone too far.

"You're a dirty-minded asshole, Director Boris. That man and his team saved my life. Where the hell was your security when those men were using vehicles to ram down the front doors of the dorm? Where were they when they chased me through the first floor and I was forced to kill two men? Where were they while those jerks manhandled me and planned to brutally rape me in front of your cameras before they killed me? Let me tell you where they were. They were watching from their safe control room. The NSO security officers saved my life and Officer Fury, for your information, stepped into a stall while I cleaned myself, kept his back to me the entire time, and his eyes closed. He never saw me naked," she lied. "And I never saw so much of an inch of his skin except his arms," she lied again. "Don't tell me to commit perjury on some bogus report because you're pissed they saved the day when your shitty security measures were a joke."

Director Boris rose to his feet. "You're fired. Get your shit and get off Homeland immediately. I'll personally have you arrested for trespassing in one hour if you are still here and let my shitty security toss you onto your ass out the front gates. I'll have the local police waiting to give you a new home inside the city jail."

She nodded. "You're a spineless prick." She spun and stormed out of his office.

Ellie choked on tears as she headed for the outer door. She only had one hour to gather everything she owned and leave the only home she had. She'd have to call security to ask them to bring her car to the dorm to load her belongings. All personal vehicles were stored inside a secure parking lot at the back of Homeland. It was a standard security measure to prevent their cars from being messed with. She had no home anymore, only a few thousand dollars in her savings account, and no job. What hurt most would be that she'd miss the women she'd grown closer to. She reached the security guard at the door that lead outside and he moved suddenly to block her path with a grim demeanor.

"Director Boris ordered me to take your security card and escort you directly off Homeland. He stated your personal possessions would be packed into your vehicle and brought to you within the hour at the front gate."

Shock tore through her that she wouldn't even be allowed to say goodbye to the women or pack her own things. *My prick comment has probably driven Director Boris to a new level of asshole. Shit.* Her next thought centered on Fury. *I'll never see him again.* Pain lanced through her. She might not be his favorite person but to never lay eyes on him again left her feeling miserable.

She nodded grimly as the security guard put his hand on his gun in case she argued the point. It would only make the impossible situation worse. She unclipped her security card to hand over. He released his gun but grabbed her arm instead.

"I can walk myself, thank you." She tugged to break his grip but he didn't let go.

"I've been told if you put up any kind of resistance to arrest you and have you transferred to civilian officers of the law when we reach the gate."

She didn't struggle but she wanted to. She lifted her chin instead. She fought back more tears as the man yanked on her arm roughly and pulled her out into the bright sunshine. Two more security guards waited outside, one of whom snatched her security card from her hand.

Director Boris had really rolled out the angry red carpet for her, it seemed, since she'd been assigned three security guards. *Asshole.* The two new men took front and back positions while the guard still gripping her arm stormed to one of the security cars. He practically shoved her into the back seat. She closed her eyes when the car moved, knowing they drove her to the gate, and out of Fury's life forever.

Ellie was shoved outside the gate into a group of protesters. Nervousness ate at her as she stood there to wait for her car. She glanced at the anti-New Species group and looked away quickly when she met suspicious glowers aimed at her. The protestors didn't know her association with the New Species but they'd seen security escort her out. She inched closer to the gates when a few of the protesters approached.

"Back away," one of the guards demanded, reaching for his weapon.

Ellie froze. "I'm waiting for my car. They don't like me." She jerked her head toward the people behind her. "Can't I wait here so I'm safe until my car comes? Is that too much to ask?"

The security guard smirked. "Move back to the line now or I'm going to have to make you."

He looked totally sincere. She spun away and moved ten feet back to the line painted on the ground. Some of the protesters were within a yard of her now. One of the men glared at her and walked closer. He was a burly thug sort and he appeared to be a reject from prison with badly inked tattoos on his bare arms.

"Who are you? You came from inside. Are you one of those bleeding-heart animal lovers?"

She swallowed. "Please leave me alone."

A woman protester glared at her and turned to face one of the guards. "Who is this woman?"

The guard didn't even glance at Ellie. "She worked inside but just got canned."

Ellie gaped at the guard for ratting her out and instantly sensed the hostility that came from the people around her. She again moved closer to the gate, fearful. Some of them belonged to the same group who'd stormed Homeland. The guard with the shotgun shook his head at her.

"I ordered you to get back."

"Yeah," one of the protesters yelled at Ellie. "Why don't you come over here, bitch? We'd love to have a chat with you."

Ellie studied the crowd. They weren't walking around anymore, carrying their hate signs. They watched her and drew closer together, mob style. Their signs were gripped as if they were baseball bats and terror filled Ellie. She faced the gates again and grabbed at the bars.

"I will sue every one of you if you let them harm me and you will be canned right along with me."

"So leave," one of the security guards snorted at her. "They can't attack you if you aren't here."

"I can't. My car and my personal belongings are being brought to the gate. I don't even have my purse."

He shrugged and smiled coldly. "It's not our job to protect you anymore. You're an ex-employee so fend for yourself and back away before we have to force you." He paused. "And roughing you up would be my pleasure. We heard you want us all fired so those New Species can take our jobs."

"What is going on here?" An angry male voice came from above, from the catwalk.

Ellie peered upward. She didn't know the New Species by name or by face. His features revealed him to be one though and he also wore a black SWAT-type outfit with the letters NSO across his chest.

"Nothing," the security guard called up.

The New Species frowned as he met Ellie's gaze. "I'm an NSO officer and I'm in charge. Why are you out there?"

"I'd been fired." Ellie glanced over her shoulder at the crowd behind her. "I have to wait for my car to be brought to me before I can leave. Security refuses to allow me to wait inside and I'm really kind of in a jam here." She looked back up at him. "I'd really like to be safe while I wait."

Someone threw something and hit Ellie on the side of her arm. She winced and spun around to see what had nailed her. A soda can lay on the ground and dark liquid sprayed from where it had ruptured. Ellie backed away from the protesters, inched along the gate as someone else threw something. She barely ducked out of the way as a full water bottle bounced off the metal bar next to her head.

"Get her inside," the NSO officer ordered. "Now!"

"She's been fired," the security guard explained. "She's not our damn problem."

"I am ordering you to do it now," the NSO officer snarled. "Secure her to safety. Don't make me say it again."

Relief flooded Ellie as one of the security guards glared at her but pointed to the entry section of the gate. Something else flew and hit her shoulder. She didn't see the object but it hurt. The gate opened as the crowd pitched something else but it missed this time, barely, as she lunged to get on the other side of the fence. She rubbed her shoulder where she'd been struck and looked up, intending to thank the NSO officer, but he'd disappeared.

"Stay by the gate," the security guard closest to her ordered.

She nodded. She'd happily wait there for her car while she watched the protesters from safety. They glared at her and still hadn't resumed their circling protest. *Assholes*, she thought, and turned her back on them. She wished she could sit down but the ground didn't appeal to her. She closed her eyes, hugged her body, and hoped she wouldn't have long to wait.

"Ms. Brower?"

Ellie opened her eyes, surprised to see Fury approaching with the NSO officer who'd ordered the security guards to allow her back inside the gate. Fury wore jeans, a black long-sleeved shirt, and a pair of boots. His hair had been pulled back into a ponytail and he looked furious. Her heart immediately started to race at the mere sight of him. Despite his angry, tight expression, he looked sexy in his casual outfit that displayed his broad shoulders and trim waist. He stopped about four feet in front of her with the NSO officer on his immediate right.

"What is going on? Slade here informed me what happened outside." His gaze ran up and down her body, examining her. "Were you hurt by anything they threw at you?"

She shook her head, deciding not to mention her throbbing shoulder. She forced her gaze away from Fury to glance at Slade. The NSO officer who'd saved her just peered at her curiously.

"Thank you for making them allow me to wait here for my car. It was getting ugly out there."

He nodded. Ellie's attention returned to Fury. She bit her lip, indecisive for seconds, and then made a decision. He needed to be warned and she wanted him to know what had gone down inside the director's office. She also wanted to say goodbye to him.

"Can we speak privately?" She glanced at the security guard standing very close to them who obviously listened to every word.

Fury frowned but nodded. "Is this a private matter between you and I or can Slade be included?"

Ellie smiled at Slade. "He's more than welcome to be a part of this conversation."

Fury spun around. "Follow me."

The security guard next to Ellie suddenly grabbed her arm. "She stays right here. I'm under orders from Director Boris that she is to be kept outside. I'm already in violation of those instructions by allowing her on this side of the perimeter. She goes no further."

Fury spun back around. "Get your hand off her." Fury growled the words. His irritation showed. "I give the orders above your director. The woman walks with us and you stay put. Understand? Don't touch her again."

The security guard looked stunned but he released Ellie to step back. Fury waved her to walk in front of him and Slade. She took about twenty steps before she faced both men who were right behind her. She darted a glance around the area to make certain no guards were close enough to eavesdrop.

"What is it you wanted to say privately?" Fury's gaze met hers, softened, and his tense, angry features relaxed.

"I wanted to warn you that Director Boris has it out for your new security teams. He tried to make me file a bogus complaint today against you and your men. I'm sure if he did that with me, he'll try to do it with other people. He's really pissed that you are taking control of your own community. I just wanted to let you know." She paused. "You guys saved me the other day and I think you're better than the present security. I believe you were dead-on right about how he's going to try to keep command of Homeland. I just wanted to give you a heads-up."

Fury studied her but nodded after a few long moments. Slade's expression turned stony. He didn't reveal what he thought. She may as well have been talking about the weather. Fury took a deep breath.

"What kind of report did he want you to file against my team?"

The ground suddenly became really interesting to Ellie. She was unable to look at him. "He tried to make a big deal about you helping me clean up inside the dorm bathroom. He implied some pretty messed-up things." She glanced up at him before focusing on the ground again. "I refused to write the complaint and told him he couldn't make me commit perjury. I just wanted to warn you what he attempted."

She could sense Fury watching her as the silence stretched. She finally looked up at him to see a few frown lines around his mouth. "Is that why you were fired? I was just informed that happened."

Word sure travels fast. "That and it may have had something to do with me calling him some not-so-nice names when he got really angry about my refusal." She smiled sadly. "He probably would have let me pack up my own belongs before I made some choice insults."

Fury's lips twitched but he didn't smile. "I see." He paused. "I need your address and your home phone number in case Justice wants to have a word with you. Just tell me and I'll remember the information."

Ellie's shoulders slumped, hating to admit her situation to him. "I'm going to get a motel room in town and go job hunting. I moved from another state when I relocated here to work. I'm homeless right now. I can give you my cell phone number though if they pack it with my things. Otherwise I could always call the office to leave my motel number for Justice if you really think he'll want to speak to me. I have no idea what motel I'll be staying at yet."

Dark eyes blinked and Fury's mouth tightened into a firm line. He stared down at her, seemed to be studying her for some reason she couldn't fathom. She forced her gaze from Fury's when Slade spoke.

"I'm sure that will be fine, Ms. Brower. Please don't forget to call the office with your contact information."

Ellie nodded. "Well, again, thank you for making them let me back inside." Her gaze returned to Fury. She realized it would be the last time she'd ever speak to him and sadness filled her over that fact. He stared down at her mutely. She wanted to say so much to him but could only think of one thing that summed it all up.

"Please be happy and thank you for deciding I shouldn't die." She gave him a sad smile before she returned to the waiting security guard by the gate. She sensed his gaze on her the entire way but she kept her back turned. She didn't want to watch him walk away for the last time. He had his freedom now and they were even.

Half an hour later her car arrived at the gate. She took the keys, noticed they'd put her purse on the front seat, and climbed in. Depression hit her hard. She'd never return to Homeland or Fury. She had no idea where to go or what to do with her life at that moment.

The guards opened the gates and pushed back the protesters to give her access to the street. Someone threw something and it hit the side of her car. She flinched but drove away without checking to see if they'd caused any damage. That was the least of her problems.

* * * * *

"You did the right thing." Justice put his hand on Fury's shoulder. He stared at the gate his friend had been watching for nearly forty minutes. "I know it was difficult for you to let her go."

Fury fought his emotions, a complex thing to do, and met his friend's concerned gaze when he turned his head to end his vigil. "I did as you asked when you informed me she'd been fired. I allowed her to walk away. She'll be safer now that she's not at Homeland, in case more assholes attack us."

"Our enemies could have killed her," Justice reminded him. "I know this is difficult for you."

"I can't imagine never seeing her again," Fury admitted. "I feel pain."

Regret tightened Justice's features and he squeezed the shoulder he gripped once more. "I didn't know it was that strong."

"It is."

"I'm sorry."

"I realize she's better off in her world than here. She said she has no home though. What will she do? Maybe I should have asked her to stay. We could have forced the director to keep her on at the dorm."

"We can't make waves right now, Fury. There's a time and a place for everything. You did the best thing for our people. I'm sorry that it comes at such a price since she means so much to you. The only thing I can say is you can offer her a job again when we're ready to totally take control of Homeland."

Some of the pain eased inside Fury's chest. "I want her to come back." He needed her. To never see her smile again or hear her voice—that concept left a bitter taste in his mouth. A bleak future loomed in his mind's eye. "I believe she was fired for standing up for us. It doesn't feel right not to do the same for her."

"Then definitely offer her the job she held as soon as you're able to. It won't be too much longer. We just need to learn enough to do things right. There's so much though that we don't know yet. Every day brings us one step closer to controlling our own destiny."

"What if she doesn't want the job? What if she never wishes to return? She could find another job out in her world." A flash of grief sliced through Fury. "I might never see her again."

"Then you let her go, Fury. You try to get over your feelings."

Fury said nothing but the burning pain inside his chest spread. He didn't want to let Ellie go and he sure didn't believe he could ever get over the emotions he experienced when it came to her. She was in his blood, a part of him, but now she would no longer be a part of his life.

"Come," Justice urged softly. "We'll take a walk together. You shouldn't be alone right now."

Fury hesitated, glanced at the gate, but knew she wouldn't be back. He nodded.

"Thanks."

* * * * *

Ellie cursed viciously while staring at the spray-paint job on her car, knowing that one of the protesters must have followed her to the motel. She'd looked for a tail but hadn't seen one after she'd left Homeland four hours before. *Those assholes are sneaky, damn it. And obsessed jerks.* They knew what motel she'd checked into and had vandalized her car because of her association with the NSO. She really hated bigoted idiots.

Ellie stomped to her room, angry that she'd have to call the police, file a report, and contact her insurance carrier. She sure couldn't drive a car around town with those bad words sprayed in large letters along the side of it. It would make for a really bad impression when she showed up at job interviews. She snorted and gripped the bag of fast food tighter as she fished for the motel-room key in her back jeans pocket.

Ellie pulled the key out and tried to shove it into the lock but something prevented it from going inside. She bent to peer at the small keyhole, her eyes narrowed as she examined what appeared to be green gum crammed where the hole should be, and wondered what kind of troublesome kid would go around screwing up doors that way. The door next to her room suddenly banged open.

She turned her head in time to watch three big, mean-looking men step out onto the walkway to glare at her. Fear slammed her when she realized they were totally focused on her. She released the handle of her door and stumbled back.

Ten feet of space separated her room from the next one, not nearly far enough, in her opinion, from those guys, and it was confirmed when the lead man lunged fast.

"We got you," he gasped and grabbed Ellie when she tried to run.

"Drag her in here, Bernie," one of the men muttered urgently.

"What the hell is your problem?" Ellie latched onto the railing with both hands while panic gripped her as tightly as the cruel hands on her hips. "Let me go!"

"My problem," the man hissed against her ear as he slid his arm around her waist and jerked, attempting to yank her free from the rail, "is we got word you're screwing one of those animal things and we're going to save you. You've been brainwashed."

Save me? At least they weren't trying to kill her. *That's something,* she thought. The idiots believed she'd been forced to change her way of thinking. She screamed and kicked hard at the bigger man. Her gaze frantically darted around, seeking help. She saw a few people lingering in the parking lot below and they gaped up at her. Someone yelled from the distance for the guy to let her go.

"Damn," a man yelled from the next room. "People are seeing!" He sounded panicked. "Run."

The arm around Ellie suddenly released her waist. All three of them bolted the opposite way. She panted, hurting from the struggle, and sagged against the railing. The big crazy jerk who'd assaulted her had been strong. She twisted her head and watched while the three men reached the far corridor, nearly fell down the stairs in their haste, and fled from the parking lot to disappear around the building. She nearly crumpled to the walkway but managed to lock her knees to keep upright. She trembled all over. A door opened and she spun toward the noise, expecting another threat. A woman holding a baby stood there looking pale.

"Were they muggers?"

Ellie relaxed. "No."

"The police are on their way," a man shouted from the parking lot. "Are you all right?"

Ellie had to clear her throat. "I'm fine. Thank you!" She saw her fast food bag on the ground where she'd dropped it when she'd grabbed the railing. She leaned down to pick it up and winced at the ache the movement caused around her sore middle. She cursed under her breath, hoped the jerk hadn't left bruises with his little tug of war with her body, and staggered back to the stairs. She sat down hard, darted glances at the people staring at her, and noticed a crowd gathered to gawk at her. Her heart pounded still from her scary ordeal but she was safe and hungry. She reached inside the bag. She might as well eat while she waited for the police.

Ellie munched on her burger and twisted the lid off her flavored water, glad she hadn't bought a soda since it wouldn't have survived being dropped. She wiggled her fingers into her back pocket to dig out her cell phone. She'd already left a message just an hour before with Homeland to let Justice know her cell number but his secretary had insisted on her leaving an address as well. She could no longer stay at the motel since the nut jobs knew where she'd rented a room. She hit redial to connect her to Justice's office. She wanted to reach someone before they left for the night and her watch stated she only had minutes before five o'clock.

"Hi," Ellie said after finally getting transferred to a woman who claimed to be Justice's secretary. "I think we spoke before. I'm Ellie Brower. I left my motel information in case Mr. North wanted to contact me but I'm afraid that information isn't any good anymore. I have to switch motels. I guess I'll call you tomorrow morning with the new information. You have my cell number so you can reach me still, right?"

The woman on the other end of the line went silent for a moment. "Why would you change motels?"

"Uh..." Ellie spotted a cop car turn into the parking lot. "I had some problems. I promise I'll call in the morning with my new address. I really need to be going now. The police have arrived and I need to pack quickly to get a safe escort out of here when I leave. I'll talk to you tomorrow." Ellie hung up.

* * * * *

Fury paced his office. Ellie wouldn't ever come back, he'd never see her again, and he needed to get a grip on that painful bit of reality. A knock sounded on his door. He took a deep breath, schooled his features, and cleared his throat.

"Enter."

Brass, his friend, and the man he'd placed in charge of scheduling classes for the Species to learn different skills, walked in. He closed the door behind him and leaned against the wood.

"We have a problem."

"What else is new? What is it this time?"

"Some of the human guards have been flirting with our females. Our males are very protective of them."

A grin curved Fury's mouth. "Our women can handle a human. I've yet to meet a human who could take down a Species, male or female, when they are angry." The smile died. "Is it harassment or just typical flirting?"

"Typical flirting but our males may start fights over it. None of the women feel threatened or have filed a complaint. I wish to avoid conflict between the humans and us. If our males start busting the heads of humans who wink at our women it may cause a lot of tension."

"I'll talk to them. Call a meeting." He glanced at his watch. "Let's say in two hours?"

"Sounds good." Brass flashed a grin. "You realize you've become a father figure to everyone. You give advice and deal out harsh threats when we misbehave. Justice is our mother figure—protective, nurturing, and nesting to make our new Homeland a home."

Fury's hand lifted and his middle finger extended. "There's your lesson today, son."

A bark of laugher filled the room. "I decline if that is an offer. You aren't my type."

"No one is." Fury chuckled. "Our women are too smart to choose to mate with you."

Brass pushed away from the wall and took a few steps closer, his smile fading. His eyes narrowed as he studied Fury.

"Speaking of women, I heard the little human you saved has left Homeland."

All humor fled. Fury nodded. "The director fired her and Justice asked me not to get involved. I wanted to overstep the director's authority, give her job back, and keep her here. I saw the danger it placed her in to be associated with us after the attack we suffered. Justice made me understand she'd have a better life without me in it."

"If you'd pulled rank on that pompous asshole, he would realize we're aware of the power we yield."

"That's what Justice said. I felt conflicted, Brass. I didn't want her to go but I have responsibilities to our people as well. I'm torn in half. The only way to have her stay was to take on the director. That action would have undermined our plan for our community."

"You really care for this female?" His eyebrows arched. "I saw her plenty of times and she's very unlike our women. She's small."

"I am aware of our size difference."

"And she's human." Brass frowned. "She also worked for Mercile. I'm aware of why she did, everyone has been briefed that she worked there undercover to gather evidence, but I also heard you had a personal issue with her. I was in that conference room, Fury. I feared you'd kill her in front of a room full of humans."

Fury sat down hard on the edge of his desk, crossed his arms over his chest, and sighed loudly. "Something happened between us and I felt betrayed by her. I completely lost my control."

"No shit. I've never seen you so feral. What did she do to you?"

He paused. "She is the one I told you about when we were freed and detained inside those motels while we waited to be moved here. She's the human who came into my cell and killed Jacob."

"Shit," Brass muttered, at a loss for more words.

"I have never reacted to anyone as strongly as I do to her. I'm..." He searched for a way to express his emotions. "I'm obsessed with her. She smiles and I melt. I want to hear her voice and just be close to her."

"Shit," Brass repeated.

"I want her back. I couldn't be with her but I drove by the dorms nightly and at least got to watch her interact with our women from a distance. Now I don't even have that. It...hurts me."

The silence stretched. Brass finally spoke.

"When we take over Homeland you could invite her back. You'll be in control of security. We won't have to worry about how the humans react. Can you just hold off until then?"

"I don't know," he admitted. "I just want her back. I want her near me." He paused. "I need her close even if I can't truly be with her. All I can think about is what she is doing right now, where she will go, and..." His voice deepened into a snarl. "If human males are attempting to touch what is mine."

Brass' eyebrows shot up. "Yours?"

"Mine." Fury nodded. "It is how I feel when I think of her."

"Hang in there. Our people learn quickly and we'll be able to completely run Homeland soon. You'll be able to invite her back. I hope for your sake she accepts your offer."

"I do as well." Fury stood. "Make those calls and set up the meeting. I'll talk to our males and schedule extra training sessions to give them an outlet for their anger. The humans within our walls aren't our enemies, for the most part."

Chapter Nine

&

Ellie finished packing her bag after the motel clerk had jimmied her door open to allow her to retrieve her things. She was grateful she hadn't unpacked yet. She studied the policeman at her door, watching her every move. "Thank you. I'm done and ready to go now. I appreciate you babysitting me."

The policeman shrugged. "It's my job."

Ellie gripped her purse and her suitcase. The policeman moved out of her way and closed the motel door for her. She walked down the stairs, trying not to notice that some of the guests of the motel were still outside, gawking at her as though she were the evening's entertainment. She sighed. She didn't like being the main source of morbid amusement for strangers.

She winced at the words on her car. The police had made a report of the damage, had taken pictures, and given her a card with the police report number. The policeman unlocked her trunk while she lifted in her suitcase. She closed it and forced a smile when he handed the keys back.

"Would you like some advice?"

She nodded. "Sure."

He glanced at the car and then at her. "Go get a rental car and leave this inside the parking lot of the rental company. This is a small town. If these morons are set to harass you all they have to do is drive around to motels and hotels looking for this. You'd be pretty easy to find until your insurance company has it painted."

Great, Ellie thought. Her finances were going to be tight until she found another job. She could almost mentally see money burning but he made a valid point. "Thank you. I think that's a great plan and I will do that."

"I can't wait for these morons to leave this area. Ever since the protestors showed up it's been like this. The locals were happy about accepting Homeland, for the most part, and we welcome those poor people out there into our community. It beat having a military base as a neighbor. I lived next to one as a kid and they were always tearing up the town when they drank in their off hours. The New Species don't do that. Then these Humans for Pure Humans jerks showed up on the scene. You'd think they'd have something better to do."

Ellie gave him a grateful smile, the tension easing from her body. It was nice to hear someone agree with her views after her ordeal. "Yes. The New Species have been through enough without those racist morons."

"I'll drive behind you for a few blocks to make sure you aren't followed."

"Thanks."

Ellie stepped to the driver's door of her car but paused when a large, black SUV pulled into the parking lot. She froze, staring. It looked very similar to the ones Homeland used, with all the windows tinted black. It stopped right behind Ellie's car. Ellie tensed while the cop beside her reached for his gun with one hand, his radio with the other.

The driver's door opened and Ellie stared warily at the man who circled around the front of the SUV. He wore a business suit and dark glasses. He stopped, his head turned toward the cop, and then he seemed to be looking at Ellie by the way his face lowered in her direction. His hands were open at his sides and he spread his fingers, moving his hands away from his body to show the cop he wasn't armed.

"Ms. Brower? I'm Dean Hoskins. Mr. Fury sent me. You called Mr. North's office and he has been made aware that you were having some kind of situation."

Fury? Ellie relaxed. "It's okay," she assured the policeman.

Dean Hoskins let his hands drop as soon as the policeman released the butt of his gun. He reached up, removed his sunglasses, and it revealed he had green eyes in a nice face.

"Mr. Fury asked me to collect you and your things. I've been asked to give you a message. I'm not sure what it means but Mr. Fury assured me you would understand it. He told me to say that after saving your life, you owe him this time. He requests you follow me back to Homeland to talk to him in person. He would have come himself but regrettably, because of the situation outside Homeland, it wouldn't be advisable for him to leave."

No shit, Ellie thought. Fury wanted to talk to her. She wondered what he wanted to discuss. He may have regretted not really saying goodbye to her. He might even want to say he'd forgiven her for what she'd done to him. Of course he might just want to know what had happened. She didn't want to get her hopes up that he just wanted to see her again. She'd never know unless she spoke to him. It would bother her, wondering, if she didn't go.

She nodded at Hoskins. She had no doubt he was on the level. Only Fury would talk about who owed who. "All right."

He placed his sunglasses back onto his face. Ellie turned to the policeman.

"Thank you so much for everything. I'll go to the car rental place as soon as my meeting with Mr. Fury is over."

Ellie climbed into her car and waited while Hoskins turned the large SUV around inside the parking lot. Ellie backed out of the space to follow the SUV back to Homeland. She hated the stares she received from other drivers and dreaded when the protesters got a load of what had been spray painted on her car.

The hateful words humiliated and embarrassed her. The guard who let her inside the gate gaped at her with raised eyebrows. Ellie softly cursed and resisted flipping him off. She had no choice but to drive her vandalized vehicle. She followed the black SUV to the main office to park next to him in the visitor section.

Ellie grabbed her purse as she exited the car. She wasn't about to let her wallet out of her sight after already being tossed out of Homeland. She needed to have options if they kicked her out again without a car. Dean Hoskins studied her vehicle with a frown.

"Was this the trouble you ran into?"

"Partly. It seems some idiots think I've been brainwashed and three jerks were set on trying to supposedly save me. God only knows what they thought they were going to do if they'd gotten away with kidnapping me." She shook her head. "Some of them are just insane."

* * * * *

Fury paced while Justice watched him closely, studied everything about him, and it annoyed him. He stopped, shooting a glare at Justice. "What? She was in trouble. She mentioned police to your secretary and needed an escort out of there. Do you have a problem with my sending Dean to collect her? He works for us. What good are having humans help us if they don't do anything?"

"I'm not disputing your reasoning. I believed she'd be safer in her world but I freely admit when I'm wrong if she's experienced trouble so soon. I'm just wondering if you're going to explode when she arrives. You look about ready to totally lose control again."

Fury snarled, fought his rage, and met his friend's worried gaze. "Every protective instinct inside me is battling. My first impulse was to jump into a Jeep and go out there to track her down. I am in control since I sent Dean."

"Good to know." Justice inched closer. "If it means so much, you can keep her here. I'll smooth things out somehow with the director and if that doesn't work, I'll outright order him to allow her to stay. Under the circumstances it may not arouse too much suspicion from him that I'd go over his head. He's very paranoid about how much power we flex and he's attempting to retain absolute command of Homeland. He is being an ass by treating us as if we are children but the bottom line is, he works for us. I'm sure there is housing available at the visiting-human section. I'll make some calls."

Fury's eyes narrowed. "And have the director go behind our backs again? You put me in charge of security. I won't allow her out of my sight."

Justice's mouth dropped open. "Where will you assign her then?"

"I have two bedrooms. She'll be safe inside my house. No one would be stupid enough to go after her there, and I can guard her."

"You mean protect her."

"It's the same thing."

"It's a bad idea." Justice shrugged. "But you are in charge. I have enough headaches trying to figure out the business side of Homeland, how to afford to pay for everything and where to find more funds for us to use after we start running it ourselves. While the president is generous, we're bleeding out a lot of money with the construction costs for all the extra preventative measures we need in place after the attack. Don't forget that you have a meeting in the morning with the architect. I want you to go over the plans carefully and it's your call on whether what they have come up with will prevent another breach at our front gates."

"I'll be there."

Justice moved forward, gripped Fury's shoulder, and stared deeply into his eyes. "I know you will do your job. I'm more worried about your emotional state when it comes to this woman. It's the only chink in your armor I've ever seen. Emotions can play hell on our kind."

"I can separate my responsibilities to our people from my personal matters."

"I know you can." Justice released him. "Good luck with your human." A grin split his lips. "I don't envy you. Of course, they've got to be easier than attempting to handle our women."

Fury snorted. "Not really. She's very hard to understand since we come from two different worlds." He hesitated. "I feel rage that she may have been harmed."

"Try to keep it under wraps. They spook easily when we snarl and show teeth." Justice chuckled, walking away.

Fury growled softly. He'd try to hear what happened to Ellie without letting his anger show. Dean had called to tell him she was following him to Homeland now but refused to tell him what had happened. Ellie hadn't been harmed if she could drive and that was all that mattered. He strode from the office toward the parking lot where she'd arrive. He'd wanted to be there waiting but Justice had delayed him.

* * * * *

"They what?"

The deep voice behind Ellie startled her. She spun and dropped her purse. Fury had stalked right up behind her without her knowing it. He'd moved so stealthily he hadn't made a sound to warn her of his approach. She clutched her chest as she faced him.

"Don't sneak up on someone that way. I had no idea you were there. You almost gave me a heart attack." Her arms dropped to her sides.

Fury moved closer. "Someone tried to kidnap you?" He bent down, lifted her purse from the pavement, and held it with his big hand while he straightened to his full height again. "How?"

Ellie's racing heart started to calm. "I'm guessing one of the protestors followed me to my motel and they rented a room beside mine. They were waiting to ambush me when I returned to my room after grabbing some food. I screamed when one of the three men grabbed me. There were people around who started to yell and they ran away."

The look on Fury's matched his name. *The name sure does fit him*, Ellie decided. He became silent while he continued to stare down at her but then he softly growled. His canine teeth peeked out from his slightly parted full lips. She backed away, leery of his anger. *What did I do? It wasn't my fault*. He looked as if he wanted to tear out her throat again.

"You aren't safe out there," he stated in a harsh tone. "From now on you stay here. Don't argue with me."

Dean Hoskins cleared his throat and pulled out his cell phone. "I'll call guest housing to make sure they have a room for her."

"Hang it up," Fury demanded. "She is staying with me."

Ellie gawked at him, trying to make sense of his offer. "With you?" she gasped.

He took a step closer. "You seem to know how to find trouble, sweetness. Or maybe it just seems to know how to find you. I have a guest bedroom and you are staying with me. That way I can keep an eye on you."

Uh-oh. She watched as Fury tore his gaze from hers to turn his attention on her car. He paced all the way around it, examined every inch of damage, only stopping when he stood in front of Ellie again. He snagged her hand, holding it firmly inside his hot-skinned but gentle grip.

"Let's go. My house isn't far so we'll walk there. I'll have someone remove your things from *that* and tell them to fix what they did to it."

"But my suitcase—" Ellie tried to stall.

"Not now," he snarled, tugging sharply on her hand, forcing her to move when she hadn't meant to.

He pulled Ellie alongside him, giving her no choice but to accompany him. She noticed Dean Hoskins' alarmed expression. She didn't want to cause a scene or for Fury to get into any kind of trouble. She knew he was protecting her for some reason and she hated the idea of leaving Homeland more than living inside his house.

"Thanks for coming to get me," she called out.

"Not a problem," Hoskins mumbled.

Ellie glanced at Fury's handsome but grim profile while she all but jogged along beside him as his long legs ate up ground. He still clutched her purse in a fisted hand. She gave her purse a worried look and hoped nothing inside it got crushed in his white-knuckled hold. Ellie didn't protest as Fury kept going until they arrived at his house. He released her at the front door, reached into his back pocket, and used his key card to open it. His dark gaze fixed on her.

"Inside, now."

Ellie hesitated. "Why are you so mad at me?"

"I'm not," he growled. "Get inside."

Ellie entered the dim interior, darting glances around to take in the room. The door slammed behind her loudly. She spun to face him. Fury leaned against the door, just dropped her purse onto the floor, and she flinched, hoping her cell phone she'd shoved in there survived the hard hit to the entry tile. Her attention returned to Fury only to find him staring at her with his dark, intense gaze. His sharp teeth peeked out between his slightly parted lips again.

"For someone not mad at me," she stated softly, "you're doing a hell of an impression of it. Could you please, at least," she pointed to her own mouth, "put away the fangs?"

He growled.

She backed away a few feet. "Fine. Don't. It's just that when you show fangs and have that angry look, you tend to give people the impression, well, me at least, that you're pissed at them." She took a breath. "And the growling…" She shrugged. "Kind of implies you're mad."

"I'm furious," he snarled.

"What did I do?" She took another step back.

"Nothing. It's not directed at you. You were fired for protecting me. You were tossed out there into your world and because of us, you have been targeted as though you were one of us."

"Well," she relaxed, secretly thrilled she hadn't ticked him off. "I worked at Homeland and knew I wouldn't make friends with dim-witted people when I took the job. If I agreed with those jackasses I wouldn't have been here at all and they know I'm pro New Species. It's just a fact of life that they are jerks. Everyone has hate groups."

"No one hates you because of where you come from."

She smiled. "I'm originally from California before my family moved to Ohio. Half the country is sure every freak and weirdo in America lives or is born here in Southern Cali."

Fury blinked. "How pro New Species are you?"

She wondered if he questioned whether she secretly didn't like his people. "If you're asking if I'm prejudiced, I'm not. When I heard the rumors about Mercile Industries and their kind of testing and the subjects they used, I was outraged. I instantly agreed to help bust them. It horrified me that I might somehow be a part of anything to do with a company that cruel." She paused. "New Species are people to me, period, just like everyone else. You have the right to do anything humans do. Is that what you mean? I hate to even make the distinction."

He pushed away from the door and took a step toward Ellie. He paused. "Have you heard the latest outcry against us? They are afraid we'll start wanting to date humans. What do you think about that?"

"Did you not hear me when I stated that I think you're just people? You have as much right to date or be with whoever you want to be with as I do."

He nodded. "Would you be with one of my males? Slade is quite taken with you."

Slade? Ellie blinked, remembering the guy who'd saved her ass at the gate. It came as a surprise that he might be attracted to her. "I don't know him." She couldn't think of anything else to say.

"You met him this morning."

"Well, I know who he is but I don't know him personally. I don't know if I'd like to spend time with him or not."

"But if you did like him, would you date him? Even knowing what he is?"

She watched Fury intently enough to spot his anger. She couldn't figure the man out. "Sure. I guess. I don't see why not. I haven't really thought about it."

"Our species aren't totally compatible." Fury took another step closer.

Ellie took a step in the opposite direction. He advanced while she backed away. She felt stalked. His anger radiated off him, making her certain that coming to his home had been a mistake. *Is he still angry about what happened at the testing facility? Does he still want to punish me for it?* She'd forgiven him and he'd done worse. She hadn't terrified him, cut off his air, or kidnapped him from a park to tie him to a bed.

"Why are you backing me into the wall?" She glanced over her shoulder. She only had a few more feet of space and then she had nowhere else to go. She jerked her head around and stared up at Fury. "Could you please stop? You're starting to scare me."

"Would you be afraid of me if I were Darren Artino or a man like him? Human?"

She frowned. "If someone were angry and coming at me, yes, I would be afraid. Will you stop it?"

"I noticed you didn't deny our species aren't compatible." He advanced.

Ellie took another step back and bumped the wall. She'd run out of space to put between them. "What do you want me to say? I don't even know what to tell you. I know you're mostly human DNA and I don't understand your point. We're both people."

"I spent my entire life inside a testing facility." His hands flattened over the wall on both sides of Ellie's shoulders. He pinned her there between his chest and arms, not touching her.

"I assumed." She couldn't look away from his handsome face, hovering so close to hers. She inhaled that wonderful masculine scent of his and held still to avoid brushing against his body.

"We were constantly experimented on, changed, and tested," he growled. "We are still learning new things about our bodies, what has been done to us, and we aren't human enough to ever fool ourselves into believing we could be. There are too many animal traits present. You can see some of the changes by looking at us but they also are inside our bodies, in our DNA. I'm worried that if you knew how much of me isn't human it would terrify you." He paused. "It would scare most humans if they realized what we hid in the hopes of fitting in with them. We want to live together in peace, we hope for acceptance, and to just be left alone by the hate groups."

Ellie peered up at him curiously. "What kind of animal traits do you hide?" *It sure wasn't growling. He does that often or maybe it's just at me.*

He hesitated. "I'm just not completely human. I won't go into details. We are very different from your people though. We don't even have parents and if we ever had them, we will never get to meet them. Those records weren't recovered, leading us to believe they were destroyed. Our childhoods were completely different. So much so that we have very little common ground."

"What was your childhood like?"

His jaw clenched. "I remember being afraid and being locked up. I remember the darkness that terrified me and then the pain. They would strap me down and inject me with all those damn needles. I remember," he hissed, "pain and terror were my only childhood companions."

Tears filled Ellie's eyes. She reached up without thinking and put her open palm on his arm. "I'm so sorry." She wanted to comfort him.

He closed his eyes, took long, deep breaths, and then opened them. "They changed me. I remember my shock when my baby teeth fell out and my new teeth were longer and sharper. I didn't have a mirror but I could feel the difference. I could feel my face, knew I didn't look like the technicians or the doctors. By the time I hit puberty I'd grown muscular because they were filling me with drugs to alter my body. I knew I wasn't right, my body changed, and they were making me different with the drugs but they didn't stop giving them to me."

"I'm so very sorry, Fury." She trailed her hand a little higher, then lower, rubbing him. "They were so wrong for doing that."

"I know this. It's little comfort to be told some of the research they did created drugs to help sick humans when a lifetime of painful memories haunt me. Now there are groups of people, thousands of them, who wish me dead just because someone tossed me into hell as a kid and forced me to endure that nightmare. We suffered for the benefit of humans and for Mercile to make money." He cleared his throat. "I am tired of always feeling on the outside of life peering in. Being different," he rasped. "I knew something made me unique for as long as I can remember. I'd look at them, feel my teeth and face, notice my body's differences, and then I started to pay attention to what they would say. In time I was able to learn enough to figure out what had been done to us and why. I felt so alone and only saw humans until—" He clamped his mouth closed.

"I don't blame you for hating everyone at Mercile. Doesn't it help at all though to hear some good came from it?"

"No," he snarled softly. "Maybe. I don't know. I hate what was done to us."

"I do too. What were you going to say about only seeing humans until? You stopped."

His dark gaze narrowed, watched her, and he cleared his throat. "Until they brought a female into my cell. She was New Species and it was the first time I ever saw someone who looked similar to me. They wanted to see if we could breed." He glanced at the wall next to her face, stared there. "They forced us to be together sometimes but it never worked. We weren't able to produce children." His jaw tensed before he met her gaze again. "I'm glad. We didn't want them to succeed and bring new life into that hell."

Ellie bit her lip and her hand stilled. "I heard something about that from the women," she admitted. "It's not fair what was done to you. They were wrong and just evil to do that, Fury. I call people like that total morons without a speck of intelligence or compassion."

Fury searched her eyes, looking deep into them. "Are you afraid of me, Ellie?"

She hesitated. "I am when you're angry, though you'd scare me if you had animal DNA or not, to be honest. You're a big man."

His whole body slumped, his tension eased. "I didn't mean to hurt you on my bed by drawing blood."

She hadn't expected him to say that. She blew out the air she'd gasped in. Her heart raced and then she forced herself to calm down. Fury silently watched her.

"I believe you."

"I don't think I would have hurt you if it wasn't for what they did to me. I wouldn't have sharp teeth."

Ellie didn't know what to say. She just swallowed the lump that formed inside her throat. The attraction she held for Fury was strong, she admitted that, always had, since the day she'd laid eyes on him. She'd thought about what he'd done to her in his bed many a night, her mind filled with erotic memories while dreaming. It had been fantastic until that last part when he'd suddenly withdrawn from her and Justice had arrived.

"I just thank your God that I didn't do the things I wanted to do to you."

Ellie warmed all over suddenly. "What...?" She had to swallow. Her voice had broken. "What did you want to do?" The question came out a whisper.

His eyes flashed some emotion she couldn't quite identify. "I really would have scared you. We aren't sexually compatible in all ways."

Ellie stared up at him. She opened her mouth to ask him what he meant by that. Fury suddenly pushed away from the wall and turned his back to her. He stalked away until a good eight feet separated them.

"Your room will be the first door on the right down the hallway. Make yourself at home. I'll run by the security office and have a temporary pass made for you but for now you should stay inside. I'll make sure your things from your car are on the way. There's lots of food to eat in the kitchen if you're hungry." He stormed out of the house and slammed the door.

Ellie leaned against the wall for a long time staring at the door he'd disappeared through. *What did he want to do to me that night?* She closed her eyes, hugging her body. *And why do I suddenly wish I knew really, really bad? Damn!*

* * * * *

Fury left the house before he totally made a fool of himself by grabbing Ellie, burying his nose against her throat, and inhaling her wonderful scent. The urge to hold her, put his arms around her, and cradle her was so strong he physically ached.

He regretted telling her they weren't sexually compatible. He'd just said it to shock her. She had been too close, they'd been alone, and he'd wanted to do a hundred things to her. That's why he walked at a brisk pace to put distance between them.

He focused on his anger instead. She could have been kidnapped, taken for just being associated with New Species, and it infuriated him. She cared about his people, had risked her life to save his kind, first by working undercover inside the testing facility and again by protecting his women when the dorm had been breached. She'd stayed alone to face those violent intruders in order to activate the steel doors to secure the women.

That had been the first thing he'd ordered changed. Humans had screwed up that design by not installing enforced walls to slam down on the first floor as well as the upper floors. The main control panel also should have been installed where she would have been protected as well.

Her eyes haunted him, so blue and pretty, he could gaze into them all day and never get weary of the sight. His fingers ached to touch her soft, pale skin, and run through her soft blonde tresses. Her voice sounded as sweet as pure honey to him, soft and slightly husky. If he knew he could keep a handle on his desire to touch her, he would have stayed, and grilled her for more personal information. He needed to know everything about her but the urge to be closer to her had become too strong.

Now that she'd returned, would live under his roof, he wasn't about to let her go. He could keep her and look out for his people at the same time. He wouldn't let Justice down by not doing his job but Ellie would be there when he returned home. A small smile curved his lips.

She was inside his house. His speed increased. The faster he dealt with everything he needed to do, the sooner he'd be able to see her again. He just needed to go slow and avoid spooking her into running away. He could be patient. It wasn't his best trait but he'd learn for her.

177

Chapter Ten

᥅

Ellie smiled at Breeze. "I'm so glad you came to visit me. I really miss all of you. I wanted to visit the dorm but Fury told me it wasn't a good idea." She glanced around the living room. "I'm kind of stuck inside." Her attention returned to Breeze. "You're saving me from going stir crazy. I've been here for three days and Fury has refused to allow me to leave."

Breeze smiled back. "Think how difficult a time I had talking him in to allowing me to see you. I wanted to bring more women with me but he refused to give permission for anyone else to come." She studied Ellie and cocked her head. "He must really be concerned for your safety."

Ellie shrugged. "Why? Those crazy jerks outside the gate holding signs can't hurt me while I'm safe inside Homeland."

A strange look passed over Breeze's face but Ellie caught it. She sat back on the couch and crossed her arms over her chest. "What am I missing?"

Breeze hesitated. "There are rumors."

"What kind?"

"I know it isn't true. I can't smell Fury on you besides the faint, lingering scent that comes with living inside the same home with someone. It's just that since he brought you to his house, some have presumed you and Fury are breeding."

"Breeding?" Ellie's eyebrows shot up. "You mean the gossips think we're doing it?"

A chuckle escaped Breeze. "Yes. That's the term. Doing it."

"But we aren't. I mean, we talk and then he avoids me as if I'm the plague."

"The plague? Is that a religious fanatic group member?"

Ellie laughed. "It's a deadly disease."

"Oh." Breeze grinned. "We're still learning some English we weren't exposed to inside the testing facilities. I hadn't heard that word yet." Breeze's smile faded. "It is...gossip...that you and Fury are breeding. Doing it," she corrected. "Not everyone is happy about that. There have been some problems with humans who work at Homeland over it. I think Fury is afraid for you."

"He's heard that crap being rumored about us?"

Breeze nodded. "Everyone has heard." Her gaze flicked around the living room to the TV. "Is your television broken?"

"Television?" Ellie gasped. "It's on the news?"

"Yes. Some of the employees must have heard and told some of the...what did you call them? Media vultures? They don't know your names but there are media vultures saying a New Species and a human are living together."

Oh crap! Ellie's shoulders slumped. "No wonder he has refused to allow me out of the house when I mentioned leaving Homeland to go job hunting. I mean, how long can I live in the guy's guest bedroom and mooch off him?"

"Mooch? What does that word mean?"

Ellie smiled. "It's a term when you live with someone and take something freely from the person who has to work for it. It's not a good thing. It's hard to explain that one. I guess I could describe it as I'm a burden to him."

"How? He already had a room you could have."

Ellie struggled with her thoughts. Some words were hard to explain. "Yes. He did but usually you don't live with someone unless you are a couple. Then it is acceptable if you share food and a home. If you aren't, then both parties are supposed to work, similar to a partnership, be equal. I am not his girlfriend or his partner. He provides a home and food for me while I give him nothing in return. I'm a mooch."

"I think I understand." Breeze smiled. "And you are not a mooch. He doesn't know what one is so therefore you can't be what he doesn't know exists."

Ellie laughed. "I guess you got me there."

"You should do it with him and you will feel better. You'll give him something in return to avoid being a mooch."

Ellie was glad she hadn't taken a sip of the soda clasped in her hand or she would have choked. She gaped at Breeze. "Uh, you shouldn't do it with someone unless you are in a relationship and care about them in a special way. If you do it with someone for food, money, or a roof over your head, that's called prostitution. That's bad."

"Your world is too complicated."

"Yeah," Ellie agreed, taking a sip of her soda. "It is."

"You should still do it with him. He likes you and I think you like him. He is very manly and sexually appealing. We all think we should do it with each other if we are mutually attracted. We had meetings about it."

Ellie put down her drink. "You had meetings about sex?"

"Of course. We once didn't have choices. We had to do it with whomever we were forced to be with. We hold all kinds of meetings where we discuss things. Doing it was one of those topics. We can do it with anyone we desire to do it with if they want to do it back."

Ellie rubbed her hand over her mouth, trying to hide her smile. "That's acceptable too."

"We thought so. We even discussed doing it with you after the rumors started."

"Fury and I were the topic of a meeting?" Shocked, Ellie knew her voice had risen. A blush warmed her cheeks. *The NSO discussed me and Fury having sex? Dear God!*

"Not you and Fury exactly but it was brought up about doing it with your people and ours."

"Oh." She relaxed as relief washed through her. *Thank God.* "How did that go?"

Breeze shrugged. "We don't know if it will work. We have watched your people doing it on DVD's and we do it different."

Ellie tried not to laugh. She had to compose her features to hide her amusement. "You watched pornos? Is that what you are saying? Pornos are videos of my people having sex together."

"Yes." Breeze smiled. "We watched those."

"Uh…" Ellie eyed Breeze. "Those videos are kind of…" She was at a loss. "Well, they don't really, well, they aren't really…" She sighed. "I don't have sex that way."

"You don't? What is different?"

Where do I begin? This may be embarrassing but I'm here to help these women. Ellie kicked off her shoes to sit cross-legged on the couch. "The way they talk for starters. I never speak that way and if a man spoke to me the way they do in those films, I would probably get pretty upset."

"Calling females offensive bad words and demanding they do sexual acts even though they don't look that pleasurable for females?"

"Yes. Exactly."

"We thought it kind of shocking. Some believe it's downright rude."

"Yeah, well, if a guy said some lines in those movies to a woman in real life, well, he'd end up being slapped or worse."

"Understood. What else is different?"

Ellie shrugged. "I don't know what you've seen. Most people don't have sex with multiple partners to start with. We're monogamous in general."

"So I don't have to invite a female friend to our bed if I want to do it with a fully human man or sleep with two of them at once? I had decided to never touch a human because of that. We don't share well and I figure a capable male should be able to please a woman without needing help from a friend."

"No!" Ellie closed her mouth, which had fallen open. "Stop watching those. Watch love stories. Porn movies are…well, they just…" She softly cursed. "Tell them to stop watching them and forget what they've seen. Please. Those are actors and actresses who are paid to have sex on film. They are given a script that someone wrote. Do you understand? They are made to be entertainment but not a 'how to' guide on sex unless you want to see how something is done without actually doing it."

"Okay."

"What is your version of sex? Maybe we can start there. It might be the same."

"Well, we enjoy kissing. We love to kiss. That is new to us but we picked that up after we were freed. We love to touch. We say soft, appealing words, and growl to show our level of arousal. Is that all right?"

"Perfect," Ellie admitted. The growling… She let that slide.

"We fight for dominance and whoever is tougher gets to decide the position we have sex. The male usually wins unless he is tired or weak from injury."

"Uh…" Ellie's mind blanked with that shocking news.

Breeze stopped talking. "Is that different from you?"

"Explain 'fight for dominance'."

She blinked. "It's just the way it sounds."

"Like wrestling?"

She nodded. "Very similar."

Ellie shrugged. "That would be okay but we don't usually enjoy pain during sex. You know that, right?"

"Okay. I'll share that. So no fighting?"

"I'd skip that part. I'm sure some people would be into it but it's not something you'd want to generally assume as okay to do."

"So who gets to decide the positioning?"

Her mouth opened and then closed. *Who indeed?* Ellie smiled. "We talk and try to mutually agree on that. Sometimes we mix it up."

"Mix it up? Explain."

Ellie hesitated. "Well, let's say I'm on top straddling a man and then after a while he could flip me over to be on top of me. Mixing it up. Is that clear enough?"

Breeze nodded. "Yes. We don't do that. We get into a position and stay with it to the end." She hesitated. "Why would you be on top? What man would lie there for that? Isn't his pride injured being dominated that way?"

Ellie knew her eyes widened. "It's…" *Damn. I'm so glad I never had children if this is the kind of discussion I'd have to face.* She was at a loss for words yet again but Breeze expected an answer. "It's not about dominance with us. It's about pleasure. Have you ever been on top during sex?"

Breeze appeared horrified by the question. "No. I refused to take a man when he was tied down and helpless. Even when the technicians threatened to punish me I would not do it. I would rather have taken the beating than harm the male's pride."

"Oh boy. Human guys don't think that way. He would be thrilled for a female do that to him."

"Oh. Our males wouldn't be. They would get very angry. Fury would feel insulted if you even asked him to lay meek under you. Our men are dominant."

She had nothing to say to that. Ellie just nodded. "I wouldn't ask it of him," she finally got out.

"Good. He would be very insulted. Our men would rather die than be submissive. That's why, inside the testing facility, I took a beating before I would do what they wanted when they bound one of our men down."

An image of Fury restrained against the floor while Jacob hurt him flashed in Ellie's memory. She'd never forget seeing that sight or the horror she experienced at knowing what kind of hellish nightmare she'd walked into. *God*, she thought, hugging her chest tightly with both arms.

"Ellie? Are you cold?"

"I'm fine. So what positions do you like for sex?"

"We enjoy facing the men to keep eye contact but our men prefer taking us from behind. That is what we fight about." She hesitated. "I'm quite shocked that Fury took you face-to-face. He must have been in a hurry or otherwise he would have set you free to mount you from behind. That is what our men do."

An image of that flashed through Ellie's mind. Fury naked, caging her under his big, sexy body, and maybe his arm wrapped around her waist when he entered her body from behind. *Mounting. Wow.* She bit her lip. "And what if a woman doesn't want to be mounted?"

"Our men don't touch us unless we are willing to do it with them."

"I meant what happens if you want to have sex but not in that position?"

Breeze smiled widely, revealing sharp teeth. "Best sex ever."

Ellie didn't ask. She just nodded. "Well, that cleared up some things, didn't it?"

Breeze agreed. "Yes. I shall share this information at the next meeting. Thank you, Ellie. You have told me many things I will pass along."

"Could you leave my name out of it?"

Breeze laughed. "Yes. I understand. Your face is pink. You are shy about your sex." Breeze stood. "I must go. The new dorm mother," she spat that word as though it were a curse word, "has demanded we be inside to take attendance four times a day. She is a bitch."

"I'm sorry."

"If she doesn't grow on us soon, which I can tell you now she won't, she will be gone. We have a meeting planned in a few days about her." Breeze smiled. "We have final say if she stays and we can replace her if it's not working out."

Ellie escorted Breeze to the front door and hugged the taller woman. Breeze laughed as she left. Ellie sighed loudly when she was left alone. Rumors were being spread about a couple shacking up. *Damn.* If they released Ellie's name to the press she'd never be able to leave Homeland without fear of some moron harassing her or worse, making her a target of violence.

She headed for the kitchen after a quick glance at her watch. She noticed Fury usually came home to change his uniform around six in the evening. He tended to change into comfortable clothing, ask her questions about her day, and then disappeared out the door again as quickly as possible.

She had no clue where he spent his evenings after that. He just wasn't staying at home with her. She opened the fridge to remove the package of chicken breasts she'd thawed. She hummed under her breath as she started to cook.

* * * * *

The smell of food made Fury's stomach rumble as he stepped inside the front door. He'd missed lunch when meetings had run too long. Ellie knew how to cook, obviously, and he followed the tantalizing smell into the small dining area to find a nice dinner for two spread out on the table. He turned and froze in front of the archway as she stepped from the kitchen.

He wanted to groan over the sight of her smile directed at him. She appeared genuinely happy to see him. His hunger for food instantly changed into a desire to touch her. Her scent tempted him more than the smell of food, called to his animal side, and the urge to take her into his arms nearly overpowered him, weakening his will to resist. Lust roared alive inside his entire body.

Every smile she gave him melted his heart and every word she spoke fascinated him. The night before she'd sat down with him on the couch, just a few feet away from him, and he'd asked about her family. The sad expression on her features had made him happy not to have parents for the first time in his life.

She'd told him about her parents' bitter divorce, putting her in the middle of it at the tender age of ten. He didn't like her parents already and he'd never met them. He didn't want Ellie around them after she stated they tried repeatedly to talk her in to reconciling with her ex-husband.

If he ever met Jeff, he'd beat the stupid human. Ellie had avoided his gaze when he'd asked her questions about her marriage. The idea of another male touching her had nearly sent him into a rage but he'd kept calm. The conversation remained inside his thoughts…

~ ~ ~ ~ ~

"How long were you with him?"

"It doesn't matter. We made a mistake when we married. He had affairs and I didn't know."

"Affairs?" Fury had frowned, not understanding. "He went to events? What kind?"

A grin had spread across her beautiful, tempting lips and she'd turned to face him on the couch. "The event he went to was spending time with other women." Her smile faded and anger glinted, changing her eyes to a darker blue. "He told me it was my fault when I found out about his cheating with other women." Her chin rose, showing him the stubborn streak he admired. "What bullshit. I may have been overweight but he wasn't thin either."

Fury's gaze had wandered over her body slowly, taking in every inch he found delectable. "You are not overweight. I think your curves are perfect."

She'd reached over to place her hand over the top of his, rewarding him with a smile. "Thank you. I lost weight."

"Even if you gained weight I would find you perfect."

She'd stared at him for a long moment and he'd wondered if he'd said the wrong thing. She was Ellie. He'd want her regardless of her size. He actually wished she were bigger. *Maybe, if I put more food inside the house she could gain back the weight she lost,* he thought. She was too tiny in his opinion and he always worried that if she did allow him to touch her again he might accidentally harm her in some way.

"I know you don't really mean that but it was great to hear."

"I mean it." He'd growled at her softly, slightly insulted that she'd question his word. Her eyes had widened in reaction. He cleared his throat. "I don't lie."

"There are lies and there's saying things to be polite."

He'd chuckled. "Haven't you learned yet that I don't say things just to soothe someone?"

His beautiful Ellie had laughed with him. "That's so true. You're blunt. All New Species are."

"Is that a bad thing?"

She shook her head. "No. It's a wonderful trait."

"I'm glad. So he spent time with other women?"

"He had sex with them."

Shock tore through Fury. "Why? What is wrong with him? He had you and needed no other."

Little delicate fingers had wrapped around the curve of the back of his hand. "I believe you really mean that. Thank you, Fury."

"I don't like your ex-husband." He growled. "I will change his mind quickly if he ever comes here and tries to get you to go back to being married to him. I wouldn't mind using my fists a few times to make sure he left you alone."

He instantly worried that his threat to the man she'd once married would upset her but he hadn't censored his thoughts before it popped out of his mouth. She'd reacted with a laugh instead.

"Will you call me first if he does show up here? I want to watch if you punch him." Ellie released him then, stood, and gave him a warm smile. "Good night, Fury. Sweet dreams."

Her hips swayed when she left the room and he waited until he heard her bedroom door close before he released a pent-up, frustrated groan. It grew more difficult for him to resist his impulses to take her to his bed instead of allowing her to go to hers alone. He didn't want to frighten her. She'd need time to learn he would never harm her in any way and he'd be certain that feat had been accomplished before he tried to get her back into his bed.

He smelled desire on her, which gave him hope that the memory of them together lingered inside her mind the way it did in his. He wanted to take her back to his room, spread her out naked over his sheets and touch every inch of her skin. He just needed a sign from her when she reached the point that she wanted to take their relationship farther…

~ ~ ~ ~ ~

He drew his thoughts to the present when she placed more food on the table. His fingers itched to touch her. He inhaled when she inched closer to him and had to force his body not to move at all or he'd close the distance and do exactly that.

Just give me a hint that you're ready, he silently begged. He'd talked to some of the human security guards he'd become friends with. They told him that some women needed a man to make the first move. Some women enjoyed a strong male who took charge, and if Ellie were that type, Fury would be that man for her.

He glanced at both filled plates, realized that her making a meal for the two of them might be her subtle way of hinting she might be ready to deepen their relationship. Of course, he had given Breeze permission to visit Ellie. Perhaps that second plate of food wasn't intended for him. He tried not to get his hopes up. If she planned to share dinner with him, he'd take it as a signal.

If he could get Ellie into his bed he might be able to seduce her into staying there. New Species females were strong-willed females with a preference to keep males at arm's length except during sex. He needed to find a way to soften Ellie's defenses and push for more, something deeper than just sex. He'd show her everything could be great between them and they could have that out of bed as well.

Chapter Eleven

&

Fury studied the table. "Is that for me?"

Ellie smiled. "Yes. I swear I'm a good cook. It's safe to eat."

His dark gaze fixed on her. "That was nice. What is the reason?"

"There isn't one. I just wanted to do something nice for you. I love to cook. They delivered groceries yesterday. I cooked last night but you didn't show up until late. Tonight you arrived on time."

He studied her closely. "You wish to do something nice for me?"

"Yes."

"Why?"

"I wanted to do something special for you. You have taken me into your home and you—"

Fury moved so suddenly Ellie didn't have time to react before he grabbed her. Strong arms lifted her into his arms and carried her toward the hallway before she realized where they headed.

"Fury?" Alarm jolted through her and she clutched at him.

He walked into his bedroom and dropped her onto his bed gently. Ellie gawked at him while he grabbed the front of his shirt, tearing it wide open. Buttons flew. She lowered her shocked gaze to his bare chest. Tan, muscled skin beaconed in the dim light from the fading sunshine through the thinly curtained windows.

"What are you doing?" Her voice trembled.

He reached for his belt as he toed off his boots. "I won't hurt you this time. I have it worked out."

Fury yanked open the front of his pants and threw the belt he tore from the loops behind him. The sound of it hitting the carpet tore her focus away from his tight abs and sexy black boxer briefs peeking from the vee of the pants that hugged lean hips. Her gaze lifted to his, watched him bend closer to shove his pants down, and her heart hammered. Fury tugged and stepped out of the pants to straighten in front of her again in nothing but his briefs. Her gaze lowered to take in that sight but he lunged suddenly.

Ellie gasped again when he bent over her, his hands gripped both sides of her shirt, and material tore. Air met skin. Surprise held her still as she stared into his eyes. He growled softly at her, his dark gaze taking in the view he'd bared—her stomach and bra.

"Fury?"

He shoved the shirt wider apart and his hands released it to grip her skirt. He didn't bother tugging it down her body. Instead he gripped the waistband, his biceps bunched, and more material tore. He shredded it down the center to spread it completely open. Ellie couldn't move, didn't even breathe, until she gasped when his fingers slid into the front of her panties. The back of his hand was warm on her lower stomach. One good tug and he threw the destroyed silky material over his shoulder.

"Fury!" She tried to roll away from him. He'd nearly stripped her naked. Only her bra remained. "What—"

His hands gripped her hips and flipped her back onto the bed on her backside. He dropped to his knees next to the bed, his body between her thighs, and yanked her toward him.

"I won't hurt you this time. I'll be more aware of my teeth."

"Stop it," Ellie panted. Her heart pounded but she wasn't afraid, just shocked, and confused. She breathed as if she'd just run a mile.

His dark gaze locked with hers. "You enjoyed this part." His rough-feeling palms caressed her inner thighs, pushed them farther apart, and he licked his full lips. "I brought you pleasure with my mouth."

She swallowed with difficulty. His gaze lowered to his hands holding her thighs firmly apart. Ellie remembered. She shivered. *Yeah*, she'd loved the first part last time once she'd gotten over the shock of what he was doing to her. Temptation to urge him on gripped her but she tried to be reasonable.

"Let me go. We can't do this again."

His gaze jerked up to narrow on her. "Why not? I desire your taste, the sounds you make as my tongue teases your little bud and it swells with pleasure."

She stared into his eyes. *Yeah, Ellie*, she asked herself, *why not?* Her belly quivered. She didn't want to think about how else her body responded to what he wanted to do to her but she guessed he wouldn't have to coax her with his mouth to make her wet. Just staring at him did that to her. She opened her mouth.

"Um…" Her mind blanked.

"I will not hurt you. I give my word. I'll make you scream but it won't be from pain."

She bit her lip hard. Fury turned her on. She couldn't lie about that. Even having him that close to repeating what he'd done to her last time had her stomach clenching and an ache started just above where his hands played on her inner thighs. Her nipples puckered.

"I know you want me, sweetness."

She loved it when he used endearments with that soft growly tone of his. "You hope I want you," she corrected.

He showed teeth. "Sense of smell. I know you want me. Your scent is so sweet when you are aroused. I want to lick you and feast on your desire. You've been torturing me for days."

She knew the color drained from her face. Looking at him and being close to him always affected her but she'd thought he'd been oblivious. "Is that true?"

He growled. "Yes. I have lived with it taunting me. I've just been waiting for you to stop hiding it and give me some sign you were ready to be with me."

"But—"

"I won't have an affair on you. I am not the stupid male you once chose poorly to allow the honor of being with you."

Ellie smiled, amused despite the tense moment. "Chose poorly is an understatement."

He shrugged. "You are the only one I want or need, Ellie. I give you my word, I won't touch another female. You are it for me. This isn't a one-time thing."

Sincerity shone in his intense gaze. Ellie hesitated and then nodded. "I do want you, Fury. I've wanted you since the day I first saw you. That's never changed. It's just that it's so complicated between us."

"It's only complicated if we allow it to be." A glint of determination flashed in his dark gaze. "Just feel." His hands released her thighs to grip her hips.

He growled again, softly, as he pulled her ass down the bed to the very edge. Ellie gasped when he let his hands slide from her hips back to her thighs. He shoved them wider apart. His head lowered and in the next heartbeat he licked her. His hot, wet tongue zoomed directly for her clit. She tensed while she grabbed for the bedspread. Her fingers clawed the material.

He growled again as his mouth pressed tighter against her pussy. He lapped at the sensitive bud rapidly in a near frenzy. The pleasure shot straight to her brain and made her spread her thighs wider to give him better access.

"Dear God," she panted. "You're like a vibrator with a tongue when you do that."

He chuckled against her and then he growled louder against her, drawing out the vibrations he created while his tongue applied pressure and slid along her sensitive bundle of nerves. He teased without mercy. She moaned and thrashed her head. Fury shifted her legs to hook loosely around his shoulders then changed positions from his knees to hovering over her pussy, pushing her knees higher, holding her wide open.

Ellie worried he'd kill her with raw pleasure. She couldn't take the intense feelings he created. They were too strong to withstand. The man knew how to hit her "on switch" so hard she didn't think anything could turn her off. She knew her fingers tore at his bedspread, her nails digging into the fabric. It took everything she had not to clutch at him, too afraid she'd scratch his skin.

"Fury!" she screamed. Her body jerked under his mouth as ecstasy tore through her, wave after wave. The climax hit so strongly that she screamed out again.

Fury released her with his mouth. He nuzzled his cheek against the inside of her thigh as he withdrew his face from between her legs and removed them from his shoulders to place her heels on the bed.

She lay there panting as she tried to pull her thoughts back together but couldn't. He'd made her feel as though he'd blown her mind apart. The bed moved. Her eyes opened to watch Fury climb onto the edge of the bed to crouch over her on his hands and knees. When they were face-to-face he stopped to hover over her. Their gazes met.

"I won't lose control this time and I will make sure I don't draw blood with my kisses. Scoot up."

Her attention roamed down his beautifully sculptured chest as she did as he instructed to reach the middle of his big bed. He still wore his briefs but they couldn't hold down the proof of how aroused he'd become. She reached for the thick erection tenting the material. She felt the soft cotton under her palm when she slid it across the hard length of his trapped cock and then her hand closed over him gently, curving around the width of his shaft.

Memories were instant of the last time she'd seen him naked. He wasn't freakishly large but definitely impressive and he'd brought her a lot of pleasure with his size. Her gaze lifted to his as she swallowed. Her hands worked his briefs down his thighs. He maneuvered enough to kick them away.

"You're bigger than anyone…" She sealed her lips together when she saw his instant anger.

"I don't want to hear about someone else who has touched you," he growled.

She nodded. She could honestly say she wouldn't want to hear about any women Fury had been with before either. Her intent had been to give him a compliment but he wasn't a human guy, not fully, and she needed to remember that. She licked her dry lips. He growled softly.

"Roll over for me. Hands and knees. Just like me."

She hesitated but rolled over under his body, onto her stomach. He helped her toss the remnants of her destroyed skirt out from under her and remove her bra. She didn't want anything between them. He crouched over her. One of his hands slid under her hips to lift them up. She put her hands down to brace her upper weight. She had a good idea he wanted to mount her. That term fit. She remembered everything Breeze had shared about New Species men. When she positioned on her hands and knees, her body pressed up against his, she noted his hot body temperature. She inhaled that soft, wonderful scent he carried.

"Frightened?" His mouth brushed her ear. It tickled and she shivered in response, too turned on to laugh. His voice deepened into a very sexy tone. "Don't be. I'm killing myself to be gentle with you. It isn't a bad way to die."

She turned her head to peer into his incredible eyes. His mouth moved next to hers, just a breath away. The urge to kiss him grew stronger. She pushed her back against his chest. He hesitated and then moved. He let her inch up against him, moving back as she did until he sat up and she leaned against his chest, nearly sitting on his lap.

"Kiss me," she urged softly.

One of his hands flattened on her stomach. His hand opened wide and he slid his palm down her stomach and then lower, between her slightly parted thighs. His fingers teased her clit, rubbing her, and she moaned. Her mouth opened and Fury's lips covered hers. His other hand cupped one of her breasts firmly. Their tongues met softly and then entwined.

Ellie moaned into his mouth while his fingertips traced the line of her sex, teasing her when his finger came close to entering her pussy. She pushed back against his body more, angling her hips to urge him to do just that. Fury growled into her mouth in response. His canine teeth slid against her tongue gently but Fury broke off the kiss. He breathed harsher when their gazes locked.

"I am going to lose control soon." He lifted his hips against hers. He'd grown so hard his erection rubbed up against Ellie where his fingers were tracing the seam of her labia. He growled deeper, almost viciously. "Am I doing this right for you, the way you want?"

She nodded.

"I think you are so beautiful."

"So are you," she breathed. She thought of him as perfection.

He snarled, a scary sound.

She looked up at him to see his frown.

"What?"

"I'm not beautiful."

She smiled. "I think you are. It's a good thing."

"Women are beautiful."

"Men are too when they look the way you do."

His frown deepened.

Ellie smiled. "Communication breakdown?"

He softly sighed. "Agreed."

She laughed softly.

"You're laughing during sex?"

"That's a great thing. I'm having a good time."

"I'm not. I want inside you so much it hurts."

She bit her lip to avoid laughing again. "Breeze and I talked. She mentioned something about mounting." She dropped forward to her hands to bend in front of him and turned her head to give him a sexy look over her shoulder. Her legs spread, her back arched, and she pushed her ass up. "Is this right?"

He draped his body over hers in a heartbeat, caging her inside his arms. His chest pressed tightly against her back. "Yes."

"Go ahead." Her gaze held his. "Mount me, Fury. I want you to."

"I will be gentle."

"I hope so. You're pretty big. Go slow to give me time to adjust to you."

He reached between them. Ellie closed her eyes to concentrate on the wondrous sensation of the crown of his cock sliding, teasing the length of her slick folds. It brushed her swollen clit, drew a moan from her, and then pressed against the entrance of her vagina. She was wet and ready for him, soaked with desire. He growled deep. His chest against her back rumbled from the sound as he started to press inside.

"Relax."

She swallowed. "I am."

His cock had appeared pretty thick and memory of their first time verified that. When he started to breach her pussy it resisted the broad tip, not wanting to admit something that size. Another growl tore from Fury's throat. He pushed inside her more, made her body stretch to fit him, and Ellie fought a loud moan at the immediate satisfaction of him filling the ache there. She feared he'd mistake it for pain if she made a sound. Fury froze and withdrew a little. He pushed forward again, delved deeper into her pussy. He groaned.

"Talk to me," he suddenly urged in a frantic tone.

Ellie's eyes flew open and she twisted her head to see a pained expression on his face. "What do you want me to say? I can't think when you're doing that. Don't stop. It feels good. I can take you."

He bit his lip. "Tell me not to hurt you. Tell me not to lose control and not to force my way into you so hard and deep that I make you scream. You're so tight I'm afraid I'll tear you up by being too rough. I want to fuck you hard and fast."

It stunned Ellie. "Is that what you want to do?"

He growled.

"Sit back."

His entire body tensed. "Why?"

"Please?"

He cursed viciously and withdrew totally from her body. Ellie straightened up when Fury collapsed to sit on his legs. He gripped his thighs hard enough that his knuckles turned white. His eyes were nearly black in color and filled with a look of frustrated passion.

Ellie eased back and curled her fingers around his cock. He closed his eyes, groaned, and his big frame quivered. It amazed her that just her touch created such a strong reaction from his body. She shifted closer to him and positioned her hips over his cock with her bent legs between his, her back to him, nearly sitting on his lap. Their gazes locked when his eyes snapped open.

"Can you hold really still?"

"If it kills me," he swore.

"Don't go that far."

Ellie lowered her hips until the head of his cock pressed against her entrance again. She wiggled until his cock slid into her pussy with less resistance but he still felt too big, the fit too snug. The feeling became nearly painful but pleasurable too. She rose up and lowered herself. She kept doing it, each time she'd press down, Fury's cock filled her more. Soft noises rumbled from him as a fine sheen of sweat broke out over his skin from the way he fought to control that big body of his.

He kept his hands locked on his thighs. Ellie moaned, moved against him a little faster, adjusted to him, until she completely sat on his lap, taking all of him. The sensation was amazingly good with him buried there, a part of her, and she loved that connected feeling she experienced. Every steely inch of him inside her pussy caressed sensitive nerves.

"Ellie," he rasped.

Ellie experienced a moment of shock when Fury suddenly moved. He pushed both of them forward until he positioned her on her hands and knees under him. He took control by thrusting into her faster. She moaned every time his hips hit her ass. He was incredible, powerful, and raw ecstasy bloomed with each thrust. His lips brushed her shoulder with a kiss. He lifted a hand from the bed, wrapped it tightly around her waist to hold her in place, and seemed to let go of what little control he'd kept.

Moans tore from Ellie. He hammered against her ass, rocking against her with powerful strokes and his cock seemed to grow larger. Her body tensed and she screamed Fury's name. Heat tore through her as she climaxed and she swore she could feel him actually getting thicker inside her until the pressure became nearly unbearable. Fury's body tensed, bowing hers under him, and a sound she'd never heard filled the room as Fury made a loud, animalistic noise that resembled a half shout, half howl. Fury stilled completely, except they were both breathing heavily. The pressure eased against her vaginal walls but she could feel his cock quiver deep within her pussy, little tremors that teased her.

"Did I hurt you?" he panted. "I didn't attempt to bite you this time."

"You definitely didn't hurt me," she chuckled. "That was amazing."

He chuckled too as he forced her body lower until he pinned flat onto her stomach. His cock remained inside her, his chest and hips pressed against her backside, and his legs rested on the outside of hers. He used his arms to brace his upper chest to keep his weight from crushing her.

"Um, Fury?"

He brushed a gentle kiss onto her cheek. "Yes?"

She opened her eyes and turned her head enough to see him. "What just happened?"

His eyebrows arched. "We had great sex."

Ellie nodded her agreement. "The best but I happened to be talking about the pressure at the end. It felt as though..." She had no words to describe it.

"Oh...that." His grin faded. "Your doctors found that interesting when we were examined. Our cocks swell right as we ejaculate. It's nature's way of locking a male inside a female at the end of sex with some species. We were assured by the doctors that it wouldn't harm a woman. We can't swell past what we're contained inside. I pulled out of you last time before that happened but this time I wanted to come inside you."

She let that information sink in, trying to grasp the concept of it. "Contained in? You mean me?"

"Yes. You are so tight it almost caused me pain. I could have swelled more but your body wouldn't allow me to. It's also why I didn't pull out right after I came. I love being where

I am but I think I'd hurt you if I tried to leave your body. Give it a minute or two more before I try to ease out of you."

She blinked up at him. "You're wider now than you were in the beginning?"

His expression grim, he gave a sharp nod. "You feel like a tight fist around me and it's almost painful. That's why I'm not moving. It's at the base of my cock only."

Ellie wiggled her hips and instantly stopped. She felt fused to him in the best way. She wiggled again under him and Fury groaned.

"Stop it."

She studied him. "Move out a tiny bit."

"Am I hurting you?"

"No. I'm curious."

He watched her intently when he used his arms to push back in an attempt to withdraw slowly.

"Stop!"

He froze.

Ellie stared up at him. "Let's not do that again. The pressure..."

"Hurts when I try to pull out?"

She hesitated. "It just feels weird but not painful."

He sighed. "Does this turn you off?"

She hesitated but smiled. "I guess this means if we do this again I can turn you into a cuddler."

"A what?" A confused look transformed his handsome features.

She laughed. "You know. Cuddle. Hold me. You'll have to talk to me after sex."

His teeth flashed when he grinned. "You can definitely turn me into a cuddler. And we will do this again. Many, many times."

"Oh boy," Ellie laughed. "Lucky me."

Fury's amusement died. "I am the lucky one, Ellie. Thank you for trusting me. This means more to me than the sexual pleasure we just shared."

She stared into his beautiful eyes and fought the urge to cry. He really meant what he said. She decided to change the subject before she turned into a blubbering mess. No guy wanted a woman to get all emotional after hot sex. It would make him regret what they'd done and she wasn't willing to risk that.

"How come you didn't tell me that would happen—about the swelling?"

"I didn't know how you would react."

Another unmentioned part of them having sex together suddenly came into her thoughts. "We didn't use a condom. I don't have any diseases but I'm not on anything. The Pill or any contraceptives," she clarified. "I need to see a doctor if we are going to start having sex. We took a big risk."

"I don't use condoms and I'm certain I can't get you pregnant."

She searched his eyes. His voice held a sad tone but that emotion didn't show on his face. "Why not?"

He slowly withdrew from her body and watched her features for any sign of discomfort. It didn't hurt Ellie. He rolled to the side to stretch out on his back. Ellie turned her head and stayed on her stomach. Their gazes met.

"Ellie, inside the testing facility they spent years doing breeding experiments to make more of us but it never happened. They kept coming up with new drugs to make it possible for us to be fertile but they always failed. By the time they believed they had found a way around all the changes they'd made to our bodies with the DNA they added, we were rescued before they could test them out. The drugs they gave us have worn off. We will die out as a race when old age claims the last New Species that Mercile created."

The reminder of what had been done to them haunted her. She had no words of comfort to give him.

Fury sat up suddenly. "Let's shower. I'm starving and what you cooked for dinner smells really delicious. I'm glad you took it out of the oven when I walked in the door. It smells too tasty to have been wasted if it burned." He refused to look at Ellie.

Fury walked into the bathroom and left the door open. Ellie softly cursed. She'd reminded him of his time in the testing facility. Maybe it reminded him of what she'd done, how he should hate her, and made him regret what they'd just shared. That left her cold inside. Water turned on inside the bathroom.

"Ellie? I'm waiting for you."

She climbed off the bed to follow him into the bathroom. Fury stood holding the shower door open. His dark eyes met hers and he smiled.

"Allow me to wash your hair."

Surprised and relieved that he welcomed her company, she smiled back at him. "No one has ever done for me before. At least not since I was a little kid."

His smile widened. "Then you are in for a treat."

* * * * *

Ellie finished loading the dishwasher. She listened to the quiet house. Fury had informed her that he needed to make phone calls after dinner when she'd started rinsing the dishes. She wondered who he had to call after eight o'clock at night but hadn't wanted to be nosy.

Ellie flipped off the kitchen light and strolled into the living room. Fury stood in front of the wide-open front door and soft male voices greeted her. She spun away to head down the hallway to the guest bedroom, not wanting to eavesdrop on his conversation with whoever had come to see him.

She flipped on the television and sat on the bed. The local news station wasn't hard to find. She wanted to know what they were saying about a New Species and a human hooking up. It certainly concerned her.

Fury walked into the bedroom a few minutes later. She turned her head to give him a tentative smile. He didn't smile back, looking grim instead.

"I have to go out. There are some matters my people need me to attend."

Ellie nodded, curious, but didn't ask when he didn't offer up the information readily. "All right."

He hesitated. "I don't want you to be here when I come home."

Shock tore through Ellie as she mutely stared at him. He'd had sex with her, they'd showered together, laughed during dinner, and now he wanted to throw her out of his home? She couldn't even form words. She felt physically and emotionally gut-punched.

Fury moved suddenly, charged at her, gripped her upper arms and jerked her to a standing position. "You have an expressive face. I meant I don't want you staying in this room. You belong in my bedroom where I want you from now on. Do you really think I would ask you to leave our home? I meant I don't want you sleeping away from me. You belong in my bed, sleeping in my room, with me."

She could breathe again. She knew it bordered on pathetic, being so intensely relieved at the misunderstanding.

Fury growled at her. "Move your things into my room. I will hunt you down and tie you to my bed if you leave my house. I will mount you until you are too tired to even think about crawling away from me. Is that clear enough for you?"

She mutely nodded. The image of him wearing her out until she couldn't even crawl turned her on. That was a whole lot of sex. She bit her lip and grinned at him.

Fury shook his head. "Women."

"Communication breakdown."

Fury's hold on her arms eased and his gaze softened. "You think I'm beautiful."

"I do."

"Understand I mean it about tying you to my bed. Don't leave me. I don't want to lose you. I won't."

"I want to stay with you."

Chapter Twelve

✆

"No," Fury roared.

Ellie heard the commotion after the doorbell rang. They had planned to spend Saturday together watching movies. Ellie had just finished a load of laundry while Fury made popcorn. At Fury's outburst, Ellie ran from the bedroom where she'd started folding clothes.

Justice, two NSO security officers, and Fury faced off inside the living room. Ellie came to an abrupt halt when she realized how tense the situation appeared to be. She worried a brawl might break out between the men and stayed frozen by the doorway.

Justice crossed his arms over his chest. He wore jeans and a T-shirt. His dark gaze slid to Ellie. The enraged expression on his face surprised her. His features were tense and his lips pressed together to form a grim line.

"I said no." Fury growled deeply. He backed up toward Ellie but he didn't glance her way. "Ellie, come here now and get behind me."

Fear inched up Ellie's spine immediately at the tone of Fury's voice. She did as he demanded without thinking about it. One of his arms curved back and pulled her snugly against his back until she nearly hugged him from behind. His body felt rigid. Ellie didn't know what had made him angry but when she moved her head enough to peer around Fury's body, the fear rose. The NSO officers had their hands on their Taser weapons.

"Fury," Justice growled. "Her people are concerned. I am just saying they need to see and talk to her. We will bring her back. No one will harm her."

"I go with her or she doesn't leave." Fury snarled deep within his chest.

Justice snarled back. "The humans are being unreasonable but once they see her, are assured you haven't hurt her, they will let the matter drop."

"No!"

Ellie cleared her throat. "What is going on?" She looked to Justice for the answer.

"You aren't leaving with them," Fury ordered harshly as he glanced over his shoulder at her. "They won't allow me come with them to protect you and I won't let them to take you from me." His dark gaze tore from hers and he glared at the men inside the living room. Fury took another step back, forcing Ellie into a corner with his body in front of hers.

Ellie's heart raced from adrenaline. She realized Fury protected her by sealing her into a corner to prevent anyone from reaching her without going through him first. She rubbed his back with her hands, trying to silently calm him. She had to wiggle to see around Fury and her attention returned to Justice.

"Who wants to see me and why? What is going on?"

Justice flashed sharp teeth as his upper lip curled with disgust and then his shoulders straightened. He took a deep breath as he met Ellie's questioning stare. "Some of your people think Fury is forcing you to stay here like some kind of…" He shrugged. "They are afraid he is raping and beating you, and whatever else they can think up that would be monstrous."

"That's not true." Ellie huffed in outrage. "Who is saying that bullshit?"

Justice growled. "Your boss made those charges. Director Boris has everyone in an uproar over your supposed mistreatment."

"Hey, he's not my boss anymore. God, he's an asshole." Ellie stopped rubbing Fury's back. She kept her body against his though and she curled a hand around his waist loosely. "Fury, it's all right. No one is going to hurt me."

"They aren't taking you away from me," Fury snarled. He backed up more, pushing Ellie into the corner tighter.

"She has to come with us," Justice growled. "Look at how you are acting. What is wrong with you? She's not a chew toy, Fury. You're behaving the way they are accusing us of being. Calm down."

"No one is going to hurt my Ellie."

Justice's eyebrows rose as surprise transformed his features. "*Your* Ellie? You're breeding with her, aren't you?" His voice softened. "You won't let us get close enough to her to smell her. Is that why?"

"She's mine," Fury snarled.

Justice's normally tan skin tone paled slightly. His gaze swung to Ellie. "Did he force you? Are you all right?"

Ellie flinched over the memory of Justice discovering her tied to Fury's bed. "I'm great except for being crammed into a corner. Fury, you're crushing me. Could you please stop pushing back? This isn't a good way for you to pin me against a wall." She relaxed when he gave her a few inches of breathing room. She locked her gaze with Justice's surprised ones. "Fury hasn't forced me to do anything—he never has. We're great. We're fine."

"He didn't just breed you. He mated you." It was a grim-sounding statement Justice made.

Ellie hesitated. "We're sleeping together if that's what you mean. Yes. We're great. Everything is fine and I want to be here. Fury wouldn't hurt me. You know him so you should know that."

Justice's eyes narrowed. "What about last time? What he did wasn't rational."

A blush warmed Ellie's cheeks. "We were working things out. He didn't mean to hurt me. He accidentally scratched me with his teeth."

Eyebrows rose. "How does one accidentally kidnap a woman from a park and tie her naked to a bed?"

"That part wasn't an accident but you know that. I told you why he took me from the park."

Fury stiffened against her and turned his head to stare at her with shock. She glanced at him, inwardly winced, and returned her full attention to Justice. She had a sinking feeling she and Fury were going to have a tense conversation in the very near future.

Ellie refused to acknowledge the two NSO officers. She wished a hole would open up under her. She didn't want to discuss this but she knew Justice was concerned for her safety. He'd brought men with him who looked ready to possibly hurt Fury to get her away from him.

"You know we had some issues. He might have gotten me into his bed without my agreement but once there, it turned consensual. I told you he didn't rape me and I wasn't being dishonest or covering for him, damn it. He asked my permission before he entered me."

Justice watched her closely, studying her for a long moment. He finally nodded. "I see. You were seduced until you couldn't refuse him."

She took a deep breath. "I've always been very attracted to Fury. He didn't have to try real hard. Can we please drop this now? I'm here with Fury because I really want to be."

Justice turned to the two NSO officers. "Go outside and guard the door."

The two men closed the door behind them as they left. Justice ran his fingers through his hair and let his hands drop to his sides. A thumb hooked inside the front pocket of his jeans. He focused on Fury.

Fury hated to feel fear but he experienced it now. He knew he alarmed Justice with his gruff behavior and possessiveness of Ellie. Panic still coursed through him that somehow the humans would whisk her away from Homeland, out of his reach. He didn't trust Director Boris. The human had beady eyes and failed to hide his dislike for New Species.

Some of the human employees weren't happy over Ellie living with him and they resented a human being with his kind. Ellie had become his, making her a New Species, and humans had no claim on her anymore in his opinion. It was that simple. If he were allowed to go with her to see Director Boris, he'd feel more secure that nothing would happen but they refused to allow him to be present. That triggered every alarm inside him.

He'd assigned a New Species guard outside to protect Ellie from being taken while he worked. He'd go to any lengths to keep her safe. He met Justice's gaze and didn't look away. His friend knew how deeply his feelings for Ellie ran.

Justice watched him with curiosity. "I'm concerned because you act so differently when it comes to the female."

"I am aware but I would never hurt her. Trust me."

Justice's cat eyes narrowed. "I do. I'm sorry for implying otherwise but you have to admit you're not always yourself when it comes to your female."

"I'm aware of that as well."

The two men studied each other. Justice spoke first. "They are pressuring me to bring her to see them, to verify that she is fine. I have no choice and you know that we must appease their concerns."

It was difficult to be reasonable when it came to Ellie but he knew Justice had a good point. The humans were still wary of New Species and they had to be concerned with her well-being. To be honest, if it were any other New Species male with a human female, he'd be closely monitoring the situation too. Fury sighed, calmed, and knew Ellie wouldn't leave him willingly. He needed to allow the humans to see her.

"They want a doctor to examine her. They are worried. Hell, I'm worried. We've talked about crossing this line but I know of no one who has so far, except you and her." Justice paused. "So we're compatible sexually?"

Fury nodded. "A little different as we suspected but it works out extremely well. She doesn't need a doctor. I would not hurt her."

Justice frowned. "What about biting?" His gaze roamed her bared skin around her throat and shoulders. His gaze swung back to Fury. "They are more fragile than our women and they don't heal as fast."

"I don't bite her."

"You actually bite during sex?" That surprised Ellie. The discussion about her sex life with Fury embarrassed her but curiosity won out. "I didn't know that."

Fury looked at her and flashed his fangs for a split second when he lifted his upper lip. "I don't think you would enjoy it."

She studied his canine teeth. "Probably not."

Fury snorted, amusement flickered in his brown eyes, before he faced Justice. "I will allow her to go but I stay at her side. Those hate groups have already attacked her for working here. I won't risk her life now that it's rumored she lives with me. It's made her a bigger target."

"I understand but Director Boris is adamant that you not be present. He is afraid you've dealt out severe enough abuse to her that she'd be too terrified to be truthful in your presence."

"I don't give a damn what Boris wants," Fury growled. "She's mine and not his. She is none of his concern anymore."

Ellie shifted her weight, eased her body out of the corner, and wiggled around Fury. He let her move until she tried to step away from him. One arm snagged around her waist to prevent her from leaving his reach. He pulled her back against the front of him until she leaned back against his body. Ellie relaxed. She loved him holding her regardless of the circumstances. She curled her fingers around his forearm to assure him she didn't plan to move.

Justice watched them with interest. "Did you mate her the first day you brought her into your home?"

"We mated last night." Fury's body relaxed. "I don't trust Boris. I don't trust anyone with her life. She's mine, Justice. I won't allow anyone to harm her. Not even you with your concerns."

"I'd never harm her," Justice swore softly. "I give you my word nothing will happen to her and I would defend her with my life. I need to take her with me to see the director. We're close to taking over and he will be gone soon but for now we must work with him. I'll bring her right back. They want a doctor to examine her first but I won't leave her side. We need to set their minds at ease, Fury. They are concerned about our breeding habits combining with theirs. They are sure you bred with her and they will not leave this alone."

"They don't know for sure if Fury and I have been intimate, right?" Ellie spoke.

Justice nodded. "All it will take is one whiff to tell them the truth. Now that you are close to me I can smell Fury's scent. You are covered in it."

Ellie hesitated. "Guess what? We can't smell as good as you guys do. All we can do is study things with our eyes and speculate."

Justice slowly smiled. "I forget about that. We take it for granted."

She nodded. "They can only hypothesize about what Fury and I have done together."

The smile faded from Justice's face. "You are living with him."

"She's mine," Fury stated softly with a threatening tone. "She will continue to live with me. That isn't up for debate."

Justice studied Fury very closely. "Are you all right? You're very possessive."

"I'm fine. I admit I feel possessive. She is mine and it is that simple."

Justice hesitated. "You definitely mated her. This is far beyond breeding with a female. I will take her to see Boris and then bring her back to you. I won't leave her side."

"You will protect her as if she is one of ours," Fury demanded.

Justice nodded. "She is yours and that means she is one of ours."

Fury's arm eased its tight hold around her waist and both hands gripped her hips. He spun her to face him until their gazes met.

"I will get you back if they try to make you leave Homeland. No one will keep you from me."

It startled Ellie at how fierce he sounded but she nodded. "I'll be home really soon. I…" She wanted say she loved him but resisted. The level of emotion she felt toward him didn't come as a surprise to her. "I will miss you," she finally settled on saying.

Fury cupped her face with both hands and leaned down until their noses nearly touched. "You will be missed too." His passionate gaze lifted from hers to stare pointedly over her head. "Bring her back soon and protect her at all costs."

"I will," Justice swore. "With my very life if need be. Let's go, Ellie. You will want to put on shoes."

* * * * *

Ellie darted glances at the intimidating big men who surrounded her and fought a claustrophobic feeling from too many bodies pressed tightly together. No one touched her but she knew if she lifted her arm she'd brush against an NSO officer. Justice acted as though her life were in extreme danger. It made her more than a little terrified until they entered the conference room. The shock at seeing the room packed to full capacity overwhelmed the fear. She clenched her teeth to prevent her jaw from dropping open as her glance darted around the room filled with at least sixty-plus people. It had to set a new record for attendance for a meeting.

Director Boris stood behind a table in the back. "Ms. Brower."

Ellie's gaze met his and anger surged. She glanced at Darren Artino, who stood next to the director. Other familiar faces were present but most of the people weren't ones she recognized. Their seemed solely focused on her. It left her feeling as though she were a bug under a microscope. Justice motioned his NSO officers to spread out with a flick of his hand but he stayed at her side to address Director Boris.

"Here is Ellie Brower and you can see she is fine." Justice's irritation sounded in his voice.

Darren Artino cleared his throat while he studied Ellie. "It has been brought to our attention you might want to leave Mr. Fury's home. We're concerned about you."

Ellie crossed her arms over her chest and thrust her chin out, really uncomfortable with everyone staring at her. "I'm fine. Mr. Fury has been nice enough to let me crash in his guestroom." She paused, glaring openly at Director Boris, not bothering to hide her dislike of him. "I was nearly kidnapped by a few members of the hate groups who picket outside after I left Homeland. Mr. Fury is concerned about my safety. I'm much better off here than outside those gates."

A blonde woman with her hair pulled into a tight bun stood. She wore a trim, black business suit. "I'm Doctor Trisha Norbit."

The woman appeared too young to be a doctor but Ellie didn't share her opinion aloud. "It's nice to meet you." She wasn't sure what else to say.

"We were told you and Mr. Fury have become very close. I'd like to examine you to make sure you are in good health and we could discuss some things." The woman glanced around the room and then gave Ellie a meaningful look. "In private, of course."

"There's nothing to talk about and I don't need a medical exam." Ellie sighed loudly, not wanting to spend the day there. "Look, I'll get to the point. I heard the reports on the news. I know you believe Mr. Fury has hurt me or some other bullshit but that's not true." She shot another dirty look toward Director Boris and then turned her attention to the doctor. "I'm his guest who sleeps in the spare bedroom. I hardly see him and there's nothing dirty going on. I don't even know why I'm here but Mr. North said I had to show up so everyone can see I'm all right. My day was going great until I had to come here for everyone to gawk at me, imagining the worst."

"Are you and Mr. Fury involved in a physical relationship?" A stranger spoke.

Ellie glared at him. "That is rude to ask a person, way out of line, but the answer is no. Didn't I just say that? Mr. Fury is a perfect gentleman. I sleep in his guestroom."

"But you are living with him." The man glared at Ellie, his hostility clear. "We know you both are sexually active together."

Ellie lost her temper. She took a step toward the rude man but stopped. "We're roommates. Did you miss that part? Are you one of those stupid people who believe a man and woman can't share a home without jumping into bed together?"

An older man sighed. "We didn't mean any disrespect, Ms. Brower. It's just that we need to know about it if you and Mr. Fury are having sexual relations. You would be the first couple between the two species who have had sexual intercourse that we're aware of. We need to run tests and study this." He shoved his glasses higher up the bridge of his nose. "There could be dangerous side effects. We're looking out for your best interest and Mr. Fury's. You wouldn't want to harm him in some way, would you?"

Ellie frowned. "I understand what you're saying but understand this. I am not with Mr. Fury in the way you're implying. We aren't having intercourse, as you put it. He's just a really nice guy who allows me to live with him until I can find another job. I went outside the gates and my association with New Species nearly got me kidnapped by fanatical freaks. I'm safer here, living at Homeland."

"Fine." Director Boris sighed loudly. "You can have your job back at the women's dorm immediately. We'll send security with you to Mr. Fury's home to collect your belongings."

The floor may as well have opened up under Ellie. She gaped at Director Boris. *That evil bastard.* She had to calm down before she responded by shaking her head no, refusing to allow him to force her away from Fury. All eyes inside the room were scrutinizing her for a reaction and she knew it. *Damn it.* She forced her mind to work as she cocked her head to glare at the jerk.

"I would love my old job back, believe me, but the reason I lost it in the first place is because you were trying to force me to commit perjury. You didn't like the new NSO security team who rescued me when Homeland guards couldn't handle the attack. You ordered me to file a false complaint saying horrible things against them that weren't true. They saved my life while your security guards couldn't even get to me."

She saw the color leave his face and many of the gazes turned from staring at her to fix on Director Boris. He appeared too shocked to do much but dart his gaze around the room.

"I don't work for people who tell me to make up false accusations, nasty ones at that, and then fire me because I won't do it. I would have quit if you hadn't canned me. I refuse to work for you, Director Boris. I'll find my own job where I'm not ordered to lie."

"That's not true," Director Boris finally sputtered. He pointed a finger at Ellie. "Have her escorted out of here now and I want her removed from Homeland permanently!"

Justice glared at one of the security guards who stepped toward Ellie. She nearly backed into an NSO officer who'd inched closer to her. She realized all the NSO officers had surrounded her again protectively. Ellie froze in place and so did the security guard intent on removing her from the room.

"That is a good point," Justice's coldly stated. "Do you have a problem with my teams, Director? Unless someone lied to me, this place has been set up so we may structure our own community, create a real home for New Species, and that includes training our own security teams. Ms. Brower informed me about the conversation that took place between the two of you the day you fired her. Speaking of which, you had no right to do that in the first place without my consent. You really overstepped your bounds and here you are repeating that offense. This woman is under New Species protection yet you dare order her removed by force?"

An older man sporting a suit stood suddenly and moved around a table. He walked toward Director Boris, a deep frown creasing his face. "Jerry?" He obviously knew the director on a first-name basis.

"It's not true," Director Boris sputtered. "One of his men, that Fury she's living with now, carried Ms. Brower into a bathroom and stripped her naked. He gave her his underwear to put on. She washed up at the sinks and he had to have watched her strip and bathe. I just tried to protect the woman by making her tell the truth and come forward about the abuse she suffered. We can't have security forcing women into bathrooms to take advantage of them."

The older man arched his eyebrow at Ellie. "Is this true?"

"No," she ground out. "Yes, Fury took me into the bathroom since blood covered me. He stepped into a stall, removed his underclothing to lend me something to wear, while I washed myself privately. I had blood caked on my skin. The only other option involved walking around naked or putting my wet, bloody clothing on again. We were in lockdown and no other clothes were available. I told the director this clearly but instead he made horrible accusations that I'd been sexually molested or was some kind of mega slut who would do a guy inside a bathroom after the most traumatic experience of my life. Director Boris ordered me to write the report accusing Mr. Fury of horrible things but that's not what happened. I refused to make up sick things like that just because it really angered him when the NSO security team saved my life."

The older man studied Ellie silently with icy blue eyes. He finally nodded and turned to face Director Boris. "Jerry, I hate to do this but I'm replacing you immediately. There seems to be a conflict and this is too important a project to allow for any kind of misunderstandings." The man addressed Justice. "I apologize. Obviously we've been given some incorrect information. I am the new director." He paused. "Of course, only if that is acceptable to you."

Justice nodded. "Fine, Tom. I have a telephone conference call with the president in ten minutes. I'll be leaving now." Justice nodded to his men. He held out his arm to Ellie. "Shall we, Ms. Brower?"

Ellie shot one last glare at Director Boris. *Ex-director*, she reminded herself, and linked her arm with Justice's. The NSO security team surrounded them as they left the building.

"Remind me to never piss you off, Ms. Brower," Justice softly chuckled as they walked outside.

She glanced up at him. "That wasn't about being pissed off. I admit I've been a little angry but I was mostly scared."

He stopped and peered at her with curiosity. "Of what? We wouldn't have allowed any harm to come to you. They weren't going to allow you to be tossed outside the gates again."

She didn't say a word. She couldn't be sure if she could trust him.

He watched her for a long moment. "You thought they were going to take you from Fury? That was the source of your fear?"

Hell, she thought. *Am I that transparent?* She looked away from him to glance around the parking lot. Cars were jammed along the street that usually didn't allow parking. She nodded.

Fury had been such an important part of her life since she'd first laid eyes on him. She'd have done anything for him. She'd dreamed about him, continued working undercover at Mercile despite her terror of being killed, and even taken a job working for the New Species in an attempt to right the wrong she'd done to him. She'd walked away from her family and her friends after the life-altering event of seeing Fury. Now her world centered on him and his people. They were together, a couple, and she didn't want to lose him. It would tear her apart inside.

"Let's take you back to him then," Justice stated softly.

Ellie met his gaze. "Thank you."

They'd made it a few steps when a snarl of warning sounded behind them. Justice spun, grabbed Ellie, and put her out of harm's way. She stared at Justice's wide back when he shielded her with his body. She peered around him.

Ellie recognized Slade, the NSO officer, and he had the woman doctor from inside blocked from getting any closer with his outstretched arms corralling her. The doctor had a frightened expression on her pale face due to being snarled at. Slade looked tense and a softer growl rumbled from his lips. Justice relaxed his stance.

"What do you want, Doctor Norbit?"

Slade glanced back at Justice. "You know her? She ran after us."

Justice nodded. "Slade, it's all right. Let her pass. She's no threat."

Trisha Norbit edged around Slade when his arms dropped. Her gaze locked on Ellie. "I just wanted a private word with Ms. Brower."

Justice shoved his thumbs into the front pockets of his jeans. "What is it you wanted to say, Doctor?"

The doctor still looked frightened. "I wanted to give her my card." She pulled one from her skirt pocket to offer it with a trembling hand.

Ellie hesitated to take it. "Why would I need it?"

"In case you need me. You have to know how important this is. I would be your doctor. It would be strictly confidential if we spoke. If you and Mr. Fury are being intimate please think of what this could mean if you allow me to examine you and be in charge of your medical care."

"That you're nosy? That's what it would mean." Slade snorted. "Leave her alone, Doctor. She would have mentioned it inside if she wanted your help."

Trisha Norbit ignored Slade, keeping her focus on Ellie. "I've seen the medical reports on their physiology and they are slightly different from us. There is so much that is unknown."

"What is different?" Slade frowned but then a grin split his full lips. "You mean we're bigger than your men."

Doctor Norbit flashed an irritated look at Slade but her attention refocused on Ellie. "Don't you want to know if you could get pregnant? Wouldn't you like to know if it's possible if the right treatments are applied?"

Justice frowned. "I've had many talks with doctors and they've assumed it's not. We're incapable of breeding children."

Doctor Norbit cocked her head at Justice. "We don't know anything for certain but we've never had a mixed species couple to do a case study on either. If this woman and one of your men are engaging in intercourse, don't you think it would be a good idea to see what could result from it? It's not just pregnancy that concerns me. Think about it, Mr. North.

More of your people might want to get involved with mine. Wouldn't you want to know if there are any adverse affects? Your men weren't able to get your women pregnant but she's totally human."

"What kind of adverse affects? Penis envy?" Slade chuckled. "I've been to the men's room with humans, Doc. The only thing your women should be afraid of is realizing how small your men's dicks are compared to ours."

Trisha Norbit shot Slade a dirty look. "You're a pig."

Slade's smile died and a low growl issued from his throat. "I'm canine, not pig."

"It's a slang term, not a species call," Ellie managed to say without laughing. "She thinks what you said is dirty and offensive."

Slade nodded at Ellie before he grinned at the doctor. "But honest."

"Enough." Justice chuckled. "As amusing as this conversation is getting, I have a call to take from the president. That wasn't just an excuse to get us out of there."

"Please," Doctor Norbit pleaded softly. "Ms. Brower, Ellie, please take my card. I'm the New Species doctor. I understand the need for discretion and can visit Mr. Fury's home privately. No one needs to know. Just consider letting me in on this. You have no idea how important it is for us to understand how we relate to each other sexually."

Ellie debated but took the card, shoving it into in her jeans pocket. "I'm not having sex with Mr. Fury. I stated that inside and I know if I were it would turn into a circus."

Slade's nostrils flared and he shifted his gaze to Ellie. She glanced at him. He inhaled slowly and smiled. She looked away from him. He knew she lied, could smell Fury's scent on her, but she was relieved when he didn't say anything.

"It's imperative I know how our species interact during sex," Doctor Norbit explained softly. "I'm in charge of the health and well-being of not only New Species but humans too. Between the New Species and the human employees, I really have to know what I'm dealing with. It's just a matter of time before it may become an important issue."

"I'll tell you what," Ellie lied. "If I ever consider having sex with Mr. Fury, I'll let him know, and on the off chance he's interested, you'll be the second person I tell."

Ellie spun away and stared to walk. Justice immediately matched her steps while they headed toward Fury's home. He chuckled.

"You handled that nicely." He hesitated. "You might want to give her a call tomorrow. According to the files I reviewed, she's one of the best doctors in the country. I personally handpicked her. She's young but brilliant and she's New Species friendly. If she says she'll keep a lid on it, I would tend to believe her."

Ellie nodded. "I won't hesitate if I think I need a doctor."

Chapter Thirteen

ဢ

Fury paced the entire time that Ellie was gone, certain something would go wrong. He had refrained from rushing to the control room to spy on the meeting with the cameras set up around Homeland. He had access to those feeds as head of security and second-in-command. He hadn't left though, wanting to be at home awaiting her return.

He trusted Justice and their men to protect Ellie. He'd trained all their security officers personally, each and every one, and his people knew how much she mattered to him. He missed her scent, hearing her musical voice, and when he closed his eyes, her face appeared, burned into his memory.

To sleep with Ellie, feel her skin against his, while they talked late into the night had been wonderful before falling asleep. He wanted to do it every night and hear every detail of her life—minus any mention of men she'd known. He didn't want to imagine anyone ever touching his Ellie. He'd have to track them down and take them out. If her husband ever did show up at Homeland wanting Ellie back as his wife, he hadn't been kidding about beating the man until he changed his mind. She was his, now and forever.

The thought of her ex-husband reminded him of her deficient parents. Fury paused his pacing and stared hard at the door. She would never be alone again. She had him and all his people as her family. He would assure her of that and make it known that she belonged with him. He'd fight tooth and nail with Justice if that's what it took to make it a New Species law that any humans who were with New Species were considered one of them. He wanted her to have the same rights he had, knowing she made no distinction between them so none would be made against her when it came to his people. She should be considered New Species.

He nodded, deciding to push that new law at Justice while they made new ones to govern their people. Soon they'd manage their own Homeland and he'd talk Ellie into making their relationship permanent. It already was, to him.

She just needed to come home.

Forever seemed to pass before he spotted her through the window. He fought the instinct to rush outside, run to her, and hold her but he kept calm, as much as he could. No one had tried to take Ellie since she didn't look afraid. Justice and the team members appeared completely at ease. He jerked open the front door.

Fury stepped outside and strode toward Ellie, his relief evident on his face.

"We are being watched," Justice warned softly. "Ellie, walk into the house as though you don't give a damn. Fury, don't look so happy to see her. She just lied to a roomful of people. Don't make her effort meaningless by kissing her in full view of anyone within sight. Let's talk for a minute so it seems you rushed out the door to interact with me."

Ellie kept walking. She wanted to touch Fury when they passed but she managed not to, refused to even glance his way until she entered the house. She closed the door, kicked off her shoes, and paced the room. A minute later Fury walked into the room and locked the door behind him. Their gazes met for a split second before she lunged at him. Strong arms caught her up and hugged her tightly.

Ellie's feet didn't touch the floor when she found her face buried against Fury's neck. He clutched her so tightly it nearly hurt. "I can't breathe," she gasped.

Fury's hold on her eased. "You're back."

"I'm back."

Fury swung her into his arms and strode through the house, carrying her into the bedroom to set her on the edge of the bed. He reached for his shirt and pulled it over his head. Ellie smiled at him.

"When you came home last night you thought I'd be too tender to do anything but let you hold me while we slept. This morning when we woke you refused to shower with me because you said I needed a few days more to adjust to you. Why are you undressing?"

Fury kicked off his shoes and shoved his pants down. His dark, sexy gaze fixed on hers. "That was before they took you from me. I have to have you now."

Ellie stood and started to undress. A naked Fury waited and watched her silently until she finished removing her clothes. She took a step closer to him.

Ellie gasped when Fury lunged, grabbed her and spun her around. She found herself bent over the bed on her knees before she could catch her breath. His body curved over hers, pinning her under him.

"Fury?"

He growled then buried his nose against her neck. He inhaled deeply and softly groaned.

"You're just going to mount me?" It startled her. "No foreplay? Nothing?"

"You're mine."

A little fear eased into Ellie. "You're scaring me. My body isn't ready for you."

"I don't mean to." He nibbled her earlobe. "I just want you. I paced the entire time you were gone, imagining the worst. I just want inside you. I want you screaming my name and your scent filling my head. I need to feel your wet heat, to bury myself in you deep and hold you there for as long as I can keep us connected."

"Forget foreplay," Ellie said in a shaky voice, turned on by his words.

His hands gripped Ellie's hips but moved on to slide up her ribs until he cupped her breasts and used his hold to tug her more firmly against his chest. His mouth opened on her shoulder to allow his tongue to trace the skin there. His firm hands squeezed her breasts, his thumbs teasing her nipples until they responded by hardening.

Ellie reached down between their bodies until her palms rested on his thighs. She hesitated for only seconds before she moved them and cupped his firm buttocks. She pulled him tighter against her body and frantically wiggled her ass against his stiff cock.

Ellie released his ass and squirmed her hand between their bodies until her fingers curled around the hot, hard flesh of his thick shaft.

Fury moved against her fingers, allowing her to stroke him. Ellie shifted her hips and lowered her chest to the mattress. She positioned him until the head of his cock was just where she wanted and then he pushed forward. She was wet and ready for him as he slowly started to press into her pussy. A loud moan from her welcomed him. He filled the aching need she suffered. Her body stretched to accommodate his broad erection. It felt wonderful. She moaned, moving her hips to push back against him.

Fury withdrew a little and then his hands released her breasts to slide across her skin to her hips. Firm hands curved around her there, got a good grip, and he thrust into her more quickly, deeper. Ellie moaned louder at the wondrous pleasure of his pounding cock.

"You're so tight and hot. So wet for me," he growled. "I don't want to hurt you though."

"You can't," she panted. "God. It feels like there's only you. When you move inside me it's all that exists."

Fury withdrew and then thrust into her hard and fast. Ellie whimpered. Fury froze, his hips locking into place, his cock buried deep inside Ellie.

"Don't stop," she begged.

"I hurt you."

"No. God no. You feel so good. Don't stop, Fury."

He growled and nibbled on her neck. His tongue worked the sensitive flesh on the side of her neck, teeth scraped skin, making her aware of them, and it notched up her passion. Ellie tried to push back against him but Fury held her hips firmly in place, holding her still.

He started to move again, driving in and out of her slick channel faster and faster. Ellie's body tensed in anticipation of her pending climax and her fingers clawed the edge of the bed. Fury's teeth sank into her shoulder, gripped her firmly, but he didn't break the skin. She didn't give a damn if he did at that point. Only the driving pleasure building inside her existed as he growled and hammered her firmly, rubbing against nerve endings that were aching for release.

Fury shifted and drove into her over and over at a new angle, hitting the spot that drove her into a mindless splash of gripping ecstasy. Her body seized around Fury. She shook as she climaxed. Fury's body nearly crushed her against the bed as he released her shoulder from the grip of his teeth. He threw his head back and a loud sound tore from his lips as he started to swell inside her.

Ellie threw her head back against his shoulder when more waves of pleasure hit her. She screamed out Fury's name again.

They were both breathless and lying across the bed with Ellie pinned under him when calm settled over them from the aftermath of sex.

I love Fury. I never knew something this strong could exist between two people. I never want to leave him and never want to be without him. That was why she had walked away from my previous life. She was certain, once and for all, that she'd done the right thing.

Fury recovered faster than Ellie. He lifted some of his weight off her back and chuckled. "I really missed you."

She opened her eyes and craned her neck to stare at him over her shoulder. "I've only been gone for an hour."

"It was a long one."

Ellie laughed. "Remind me to leave the house more if this is what I get to come home to."

He chuckled. "Forget it. I think I should just tie you to my bed and keep you here. I don't need you to leave to want to be right where I am."

Their bodies were relaxed and seemed to have melted together. To Ellie, it was a heavenly feeling. Fury touched her, his hands caressing her where he could reach. Ellie made soft little sounds of pleasure. His palms felt amazing on her skin. Fury gently eased his cock out of her after the pressure from the swelling created by his release eased.

"How flexible are you?"

Ellie shrugged. "I don't know."

Fury stood. Ellie shifted around to get to her feet but Fury suddenly bent to scoop her into his arms. He smiled as he rounded the bed to gently lay her head on his pillow at the top of the bed and adjusted her comfortably until she was stretched out on her back.

"You're going to break something if you keep carrying me around," Ellie teased. "I could have just crawled up here if you'd just told me this is where you wanted me."

"You aren't heavy enough to hurt me. I'm a hell of a lot stronger than you. I could carry you around for hours and not break a sweat."

He gripped her calf and lifted her leg upward. Ellie watched silently as Fury climbed onto the bed with her, pushed her leg to bend it, and settled his hips into the cradle of her thighs. Ellie reached up to touch his chest, letting her fingertips explore every ridge of muscle there, finding a lot of them on his very fit body. Her gaze roamed his shoulders,

Fury

enjoying looking at him. He was beautiful. Her fingertips brushed his nipples and he inhaled sharply as they instantly responded and beaded. Ellie sat up until her mouth closed over one of his taut nubs.

Her tongue traced a circle around the hardened bud and his body tensed above hers. Fury groaned. Ellie smiled around his skin and then sucked his nipple into her mouth. Her teeth lightly nipped the tip. Fury's body jerked and he growled. His cock instantly responded against the cradle of her lap, growing hard against her, trapped between their bodies. She hadn't expected him to recover from sex so soon. Most men needed time to recuperate. *Fury*, she thought, *isn't anything like most men. I love that about him too.*

Ellie released his nipple and let her hands surf over his ribs to his back. Her nails raked his skin lightly from his shoulder blades down his spine. Fury arched against her chest, reminding her of a really big kitten. She smiled and licked the skin between his nipples. She wished she had honey. She would love to drip it onto his skin and lick it off. Her fingernails traced up and down his back from his shoulders to the curve of his sculptured ass again, loving the way he arched and quivered.

"You are sweating."

Fury smiled. "I said you weren't heavy enough to make me break a sweat but you are definitely hot enough to make me sweat with need."

She laughed. "I see."

Fury's mouth lowered and Ellie lifted hers to meet his. Ellie loved the way he kissed her. There was nothing tentative about him. He dominated her mouth, his full lips strong and sure. His tongue teased, exploring her mouth with licks and thrusts, a silent promise of what his body would do to her. She was barely aware of his sharp teeth when the side of her tongue rasped against them. She moaned into his mouth, arching her body against his, wanting him. Her body burned for him to make love to her again.

Fury's hand slid around her thigh. He gripped her behind the knee and shoved her leg higher to wrap around his waist while he came down on top of her, pressing her flat onto the mattress. Ellie tried to break from the kiss but Fury's other hand cupped her cheek and under her chin to hold her still. He kept kissing her, refusing to stop, and groaned into her mouth as he shifted his hips. His cock stretched her vaginal walls as he slid into her slowly, fully, to bury his sex deep inside hers. Ellie moaned against his tongue.

Fury finally broke the kiss. He opened his eyes and Ellie stared into them. "Don't look away from me, sweetness. Your eyes are the most amazing thing to me and watching how you respond when I touch you is the most beautiful thing I've ever seen."

Ellie wanted to cry at hearing such wonderful, touching words. No man had ever spoken such remarkable things to her as he did. He really meant it. She believed that with her whole heart.

"That's the sweetest thing anyone has ever said to me."

Their gazes held while Fury stared to move inside her. She clutched his shoulders, clung to him as he thrust inside her body slowly, deeply, creating ecstasy with every movement. She had the urge to throw her head back and her eyes nearly closed from the pleasure. Fury's hand cupping her face tensed, holding her in place.

"Keep looking at me," he ordered. "I want to see your eyes when you come."

Ellie stopped thinking, only able to feel and do as he commanded. It became near torture as Fury slowly thrust in and out of her. The feeling intensifying but she wanted him to move faster. Her eyes nearly closed again but Fury growled as his hips plowed into hers hard.

"Look at me."

"Faster," she begged. "I can't take this. It feels too good. I ache. I need…"

Fury thrust into her faster, kept eye contact with her the entire time, and Ellie clutched him tighter as he pounded into her. She tensed, feeling something akin to pain slide through her abdomen before rapture exploded when the climax struck. She never looked away from his gorgeous eyes.

She watched his eyes narrow and then his face twisted into savage satisfaction. The brown of his eyes seemed to turn black as his mouth opened to growl her name. She could feel his cock swell inside her as heated semen poured into her from his release. Fury smiled.

"Tell me that didn't feel better."

She realized her fingernails had dug into his shoulders. Horrified, she released him. There were indents where her nails had been and blood welled inside the tiny marks the second her fingernails were gone.

"I'm so sorry!"

Fury laughed. He twisted his head to glance at the damage to one shoulder. His gaze met hers. "I'm glad."

"You like scratch marks?"

"Wait until you see the back of your shoulder. I don't feel so guilty now."

She tried to look at her shoulders but Fury collapsed on top of her. He didn't crush her but he definitely pinned her down. He kissed her quickly and then he lifted his head to grin down at her.

"I bit you, Ellie." He winked. "I kind of broke the skin a little. Ready for a shower?"

He actually bit into me? Ellie knew she probably should be upset, maybe horrified, but she didn't feel that way at all. It hadn't hurt when he'd gripped her with his teeth, thinking at the time that's all he'd done, so she had no complaints if he'd drawn blood. She smiled instead. *No harm, no foul,* she decided. *It can't be worse than my nail marks.* "Yes. And I'm hungry too. We missed lunch."

Chapter Fourteen

Ellie studied Director Tom Quish with suspicion. The blue-eyed man had a handsome face for someone his age. She guessed him to be in his mid-sixties and in remarkably good shape. She could see that clearly since he wore a tank top and a pair of sweatpants. He'd been jogging before he stopped at Fury's house. It had come as a surprise to find him on the doorstep when the bell had rung. She recognized him from the conference room, could never forget the man who fired Director Boris. It had been a satisfying thing to see.

"May I come in?"

Ellie stepped out of the house and onto the porch next to him. She spotted two New Species officers across the street, knew Fury had them watching the house, but as she met their gazes, she didn't see alarm. They obviously didn't believe the new director was a threat to her safety. They'd have stopped him from reaching the front door otherwise. She relaxed a little.

"It's not really my house, as you know, and I wouldn't feel comfortable inviting you inside." She took a deep breath. "May I help you?"

"I hope so. I'm here to offer your job back at the women's dorm. The women highly respect and like you, Ms. Brower. They decided to replace the current house mother and your name came up."

Ellie tried to hide the dismay his statement caused. The man's eyes were cold and blue, reminding her of chunks of ice. He had laugh lines around his mouth though, which deflected his chilly, disconcerting look. He seemed nice enough and she believed his motives were honest, but didn't know how to respond. If she took the job she'd have to move out of Fury's home and didn't want to do that.

"Can I think about it?" *Stall*, she ordered herself. "It was quite traumatic for me when I was fired. It left me homeless and jobless at the same time."

He swept his gaze up and down her. His eyes were intelligent, maybe too much so. "Of course you may think about it. The job is yours if you want it. I would just request that you decide soon. We need a new house mother inside the dorm as soon as possible. As you know, we have more women arriving within the next few weeks."

"I didn't know that," Ellie admitted. "I thought they were only going to send in a few dozen women at first to make sure it would be a good environment."

"They've decided it is." He smiled. "You helped them make that decision. Every woman at the dorm highly endorsed you as a positive role model. I heard your cooking classes were a favorite."

Ellie smiled back. "I tried to make it fun."

"And you succeeded. They are very fond of you."

"I do miss them," she admitted. "I am fond of them too."

"I heard they needed help learning how to do almost everything."

Ellie shrugged. "They were locked inside sterile cells inside the testing facilities. Learning how to dust, make coffee, and cook pancakes wasn't exactly something they had the opportunity to learn where they were raised. I remembered how daunting a washing machine could be when I became a teen and my mom told me I had to wash my own clothes. When you are raised with all of that stuff, you learn it a little at a time. They've had all this technology shoved at them suddenly. It's all the things we took for granted. Imagine facing an answering machine when you didn't even know what a telephone was a year before."

Interest sparked in his gaze. "Did they talk to you about their lives before they were freed?"

Ellie studied the man warily. She refused to share private details she'd been given in friendship. "Some. Why?"

His expression softened. "I've read the reports and talked to a lot of them. It's horrible what they had to deal with all their lives. I swore to Justice North that I'd do my damnedest to make sure the rest of their lives were nothing similar to the past. It's very important to me that the New Species be happy and safe. I want what is best for them and I think that's you, for their women."

It touched her. Ellie would have taken the job back in a heartbeat if it weren't for having to leave Fury. She caught a glint of satisfaction flash inside Tom Quish's eyes and opened her mouth.

"You're really good at manipulation. You know that, right?"

A grin curved his lips. "It's my job. How else do you think I've been able to get all the funding for Homeland so quickly and talk the military into giving it up? The reason it's nearly completely built and we could move into it so fast is because it had been slated for a new Army base. Charm and good friends in high places have their advantages. Will you take the job, Ms. Brower?"

She wanted to but couldn't. "I have to think about it still."

"You look as though I've held out candy to you that you want really bad but you're afraid to take it because you were taught to never trust strangers."

She grinned. "I couldn't have put it better myself."

"I'm good with words too."

"What is going on?" Fury stormed up the sidewalk glaring at the new Homeland director. He moved to Ellie's side, tense and angry.

Ellie glanced up at him and wanted to flinch. He looked as if he were a jealous boyfriend, which she guessed he was. If he didn't get a leash on his emotions the director would be an idiot not to see they were involved. She peered up at him and gave him a warning look but he refused to glance at her. He was too busy glaring threateningly at the director.

Tom Quish took a few steps back. "I've been just talking to Ms. Brower. It's good to see you again, Mr. Fury."

"What do you want with her? She stays here. You have no power to make her leave."

Quish's gaze darted from Fury to Ellie and back. Ellie could almost see the man's mind taking in the scene, his thoughts going where she feared they would, and it just confirmed it when he took another step back. A wary, "oh shit" expression paled his tan features.

"I came to offer Ms. Brower her job back. Your women really miss her and they fired the last woman who held Ms. Brower's position. They've stated they wish Ms. Brower to return to the dorm. I've been told by Justice that the women could choose their own house mother. I came here to let her know the job is open and available for her if she's interested."

"She doesn't want it," Fury stated firmly in an angry snarl.

Shit, Ellie thought. *Fury isn't keeping his cool at all.* Her gaze flew to Tom Quish. He studied her and then he looked at Fury again. "She could remain living inside your home if you are worried about her safety. She could work at the dorm during your working hours. It's not exactly what the job hours entailed but I'm sure everyone would be able to work around a schedule that you would find suitable."

Fury finally glanced down at Ellie. "What do you think?"

It amazed her that he'd thought to ask her for her opinion at all after how he'd first reacted by refusing her job offer. She nodded. She knew Tom Quish watched both of them with fascination. Fury nodded back. His focus returned to Tom Quish.

"She will take the job on the condition that she lives with me."

Tom looked amused suddenly. "Great, Ms Brower. Can you start tomorrow at nine?"

"Yes," she answered before Fury could open his mouth and speak for her again.

The director seemed pleased. "Terrific. I'll make the calls and have everything set up. Someone from security will drop by later with your new badge."

"Thank you," Ellie called out as she watched the new director jog away and out of sight before she dared face Fury. She shot him an annoyed look. "Damn it. You should have kept your cool. He knows we're a couple. You acted like my boyfriend."

Fury's gaze darkened as his mouth tensed into a line. "I am."

"Well, no one is supposed to know that. Remember? And thanks for letting *me* make a decision finally." She stormed inside the house.

"Why are you angry?" Fury followed her and closed the door.

Ellie spun and put her hands on her hips. "We are supposed to hide our relationship, remember? Do you want those doctors bugging us to do tests and have people in our faces demanding we tell them how we have sex? I don't. What if they want to video it? And you told him I didn't want the job without even asking me first. I miss the dorm but I want to live here with you too."

Fury knew he'd messed up. He'd been instantly alarmed when he'd gotten word from his men that Tom Quish, the new director, had come to his door. There could be no reason for a human to be in that section of Homeland except for Ellie. He'd quickened his pace knowing that everyone on the human side preferred Ellie not live with him. He'd heard their concerns and ignored each one.

Ellie loved working with New Species women, he knew how much they meant to her, so when he heard Tom offer her job back, he'd instantly said no without thinking. It had to be a lure to get her to leave him but one look at Ellie's face told him that he'd messed up by answering for her. Human women could be as stubborn as New Species ones. They demanded the right to make their own decisions, and while they appreciated some protection, they were by no means weak enough not to be able to fend for themselves if the need arose.

He'd backed off when he received the assurance that Ellie could live with him and the job wasn't a bribe for her to leave his house. He'd relaxed when the new director walked away but Ellie's anger remained. He studied her features and knew she was still ticked off at him. He'd overreacted but he just wanted to protect and keep her with him.

He'd grown tired of hiding their relationship. He was proud to be with Ellie, even if some of his people didn't understand. Some of them were still a bit bitter toward humans. That was their problem to deal with and as long as they didn't take it out on Ellie, they could slowly release that bias in their own time frame.

He knew he needed to defuse Ellie's anger. She had a quick wit, a great sense of humor, and she didn't hold grudges for long. All things he'd learned about her. Sex also worked to soften her up and get her to forgive him.

A smile curved Fury's lips. "Do you know how appealing you are to me when you're angry? Videos, huh? I could buy a camera and tape us having sex."

"No!" Ellie glared at him. "You better be teasing about that last part."

He laughed. "I am. I don't want to video our sex. I just want to have it." He stepped toward her. "You are sexy when you're mad at me, sweetness. I'm not kidding about that. I'm hot for you."

Ellie backed up and let her hands drop from her hips. "I'm mad at you. Don't you 'sweetness' me, Fury. I want to yell at you. You didn't hide the fact that we're together and you told that man I wouldn't take my job back. That's my choice."

"You are right, I am wrong, and I'm sorry." He grinned as he inched closer to her.

Ellie backed up more. "You're humoring me, aren't you?"

"Yes." He winked. "Now let's have sex." He lunged, opening his arms, and tried to grab her.

Ellie spun toward the kitchen, amused at his playful demeanor. It was great to see the usually serious man so lighthearted. *Damn, how can I stay mad at him when he acts this way?* She couldn't. She entered the kitchen and dodged around the small island. She grabbed it and her gaze narrowed when Fury stopped on the other side.

"We're talking. Stop it."

"We'll talk during sex." He edged to the left.

Ellie shook her head and moved to keep him on the other side of the island. "Damn it, Fury. I'm trying to be mad at you. Wipe that grin off your face."

He paused and his smile faded. "I won't grin."

Her gaze narrowed and watched his lips twitch. Amusement sparked inside her. She almost laughed. She had to struggle to remember why he'd made her mad in the first place. *Oh yeah.*

"You can't go around making decisions for me and you know we're supposed to hide that we're a couple."

"You are really turning me on right now. You're breathing hard and if you don't watch it, your breasts are going to break the buttons on that shirt." His gaze riveted to her chest. "Breathe harder. Please?"

Ellie glanced down at her shirt but saw movement from the corner of her eye when she did. Her head jerked up too late. Fury grabbed her. His arms wrapped around her waist and swung her up until she sat on the island, bringing their faces almost level. Fury shoved her legs open and stepped between her parted thighs. His arms wrapped tighter around her waist, pulling her against his body in a tight hug.

"I am sorry I made you angry." He gave her a sincere look. "Now let's have make-up sex. I heard it's the best."

Ellie cupped his face with her palms and grinned. "You're bad. Do you know that?"

"I'm good. Do you know that or should I remind you?" He dipped his head and nuzzled Ellie's face aside until his lips brushed her throat. His tongue darted out and licked the sensitive spot under her ear. His hot breath fanning her tickled. "I could take you right here."

Ellie laughed. "Bedroom."

Fury straightened his head and his voice deepened. "Here."

"Bedroom. We prepare food on the island, Fury."

His eyebrows rose as he released her and inched back. He reached for her shirt and unbuttoned it. Ellie held her breath as Fury opened it and tore it off her. He unfastened her pants next and moved his body out of the way. He pulled her down from the island until her feet were back on the floor and then bent in front of her, going to his knees, and helped her out of them.

"I guess the kitchen is good," Ellie whispered, totally getting turned on.

Her heart raced as she kicked her pants away and reached for the front snaps of Fury's pants when he rose. He yanked his shirt over his head, just tossing it aside.

"Very good," Ellie muttered as she brushed against his body. Her tongue traced his nipple.

Fury groaned and he shoved down his pants, kicking them down his legs. Ellie's hands ran across his flat stomach and surfed lower, slipping her fingers into the waistband of his briefs. She raked his hips with her fingernails. Fury pushed his hips forward against Ellie's body. His arousal pressed into her stomach where he became trapped between their bodies.

"Honey," Ellie whispered as she moved her mouth to his other nipple.

"Sweetness," he growled.

Ellie smiled and pulled back from his chest. "I want honey from the cupboard behind you. It's up to the left. My left."

Dark eyebrows rose slightly. "Honey? You want to eat right now?"

She grinned. "I want to lick it off you."

His fangs dented his bottom lip when he groaned softly. He twisted his body and stretched to retrieve the honey from the cupboard in record time to hand it over to her. Ellie twisted off the cap. She glanced at him once, assured he was into it, and turned the plastic container upside down above one of his nipples. She let the golden treat drip onto his chest and over the other nipple. She heard Fury take a sharp breath but he didn't say a word. She set the container on top of the island next to them.

Ellie arched up on her tiptoes and started to lick his skin where the honey droplets stuck to him, following each one with her tongue. Fury groaned deeply. Ellie moved lower, to his nipple, and lapped at the honey there, teasing the hardening bud. She covered his nipple with her mouth and started to suckle him. Fury's hands tangled in her hair but he didn't try to tug her from her task.

"That feels amazing," he growled.

Ellie nipped him with her teeth. He jerked from the shock of the sudden jolt it created. His cock thumped against her stomach and it had grown more rigid when he ground his hips against her softer belly. She released his nipple and slowly moved across his chest. Her tongue and teeth cleaned away the sweet drops slowly, teasingly. Then she pushed him back against the counter. Fury moved to lean against it.

His black, passion-filled gaze met Ellie's when she looked up at him. She'd noticed when he had become really turned on, his eyes darkened. She loved it and him. She moved forward and started to go for the drops of honey that had rained down on his stomach. One by one she found them and licked them off. She paused at the waistband of his briefs when she realized she'd run out of drops. She smiled up at him and then slipped her fingers into the band to tug them down. Fury's cock had grown so hard that she had to actually put the elastic of his briefs to the test to free it from them.

Fury made a groaning sound when she kissed his hipbone and turned her face, studying his impressive erection up close. She couldn't avoid a turned-on Fury. She smiled and ran her tongue along the side of the hard, hot flesh that stood at full attention for her — trailing up his shaft to the head.

Fury snarled and then grabbed her upper arms, jerking her up to her feet. Shock tore through Ellie as she stared into his face. He looked angry. She frowned.

"Don't you want me to keep going? I was just getting to the good part."

He hoisted her up until Ellie found her ass planted on top of the island again. Fury turned away from her and yanked open drawers, looking for something.

"Fury? Did I make you angry? What—"

"I can't let you do that. I'm frustrated as hell but not mad at you."

"Why not? I want to."

Fury turned, revealing he had a roll of silver duct tape in his hand. He walked over and gently flattened his palm over her chest. He pushed until she ended up flat on her back on the cool surface. He leaned over her.

"My cock swells. Remember? I'm so damn ready to come right now that I wouldn't last a minute. Can you imagine if I swelled inside your mouth?"

She stared at him with dawning comprehension. "Oh. That probably wouldn't be good, considering you're already pretty big. I think it would be okay though as long as I stick to the top. You swell near the base."

His features relaxed as some of the tension melted away. "Yeah. I'd love for you to do that but don't turn me on so much next time, the first time we try something. I'm a shooter, Ellie. You can feel me inside you when my semen releases, can't you? I'd shoot so hard and so much, I'd choke you. You can do that to me later if you're up for a second round. Now I need to calm or it won't be good for you."

She stared at the tape with confusion. "What is that for?"

He grinned. "Give me your wrists."

"Why?"

He grabbed a dishtowel. "Now."

She hesitated but she trusted him enough to lift her arms. Fury smiled and wrapped the dishtowel around them and then used his teeth to pull tape free from the roll. It astonished Ellie when he wound tape over the dishtowel and bound her wrists together. She lay there and watched him pull more tape, leaving it still connected to the roll and her wrists.

He rounded the island to stand at her head. She looked up at him until he squatted down out of her line of sight. She heard more tape being pulled and then he slowly tugged her wrists above her head with the tape until her arms stretched. She heard him doing something at the side of the island before he stood. He'd gotten rid of the roll.

Ellie pulled on her wrists but couldn't bring them back down. Her gaze flew to Fury. He looked damn amused. "What are you doing?"

He lifted up the honey and shifted her legs, bent over the island until his hips wedged between her thighs. "I want to eat some honey too."

Ellie bit her lip and shivered. Fury turned the bottle over and dripped honey over her lower stomach and lower still, until drops hit the inside of her thighs. Fury moved his hips, pushing hers farther apart, and Ellie closed her eyes when more drips landed on her spread pussy.

Fury sat the honey bottle on the edge and then bent over her. His hot mouth and tongue licked her as he lapped up each sweet drop. Ellie wanted to touch him but her hands were secured over her head. By the time he reached the inside of her thigh she burned with raw need.

"Fury," she begged.

"Easy. I'm getting there."

"Now, Fury. Please? Do that later but I need you. Please? Take me."

He growled. Ellie opened her eyes and met his. He rose and gripped her inner thighs, moving his hips closer to hers. Ellie wrapped her legs around his waist as he pulled her a few inches down the island to the edge a heartbeat before he entered her body. Ellie threw her head back and cried out in pleasure.

"Let me go," she moaned. "I want to touch you." She pulled on her wrists but the tape and dishtowel wouldn't break. He'd tied the tape too tightly around the material.

Fury's hands gripped her hips as he started to thrust into her at a steady, deep pace. Ellie thrashed on the countertop. She moaned, whimpered, and wondered if she'd survive how good the sensations were to have him awakening her body, bringing her to the edge of ecstasy. He moved faster, feeling even better. Ellie tightened her legs around his waist, moving them higher to give him freer access with his hammering hips.

She heard him growl and then pressure registered against her vaginal walls as he started swelling inside her. The pressure increased while he continued to fuck her. One of his hands spread where he held her and his thumb brushed against her clit, rubbing it. Ellie screamed, climaxing hard, and Fury roared out her name as he buried his cock deep, his body trembling as hot semen poured into her as he came hard within her.

"Fury!" A male voice roared.

Ellie's eyes flew open. She was dazed, shocked, and horrified when Justice rushed into the kitchen with two NSO officers on his heels. Justice threw himself at Fury, tackled him, and threw him away from Ellie.

Ellie screamed in fear and shock at what happened as Justice and Fury locked in battle in the corner of the kitchen. Justice punched Fury and Fury tried to throw the other man out of the way to get to her. The two NSO officers rushed to help Justice restrain Fury, grabbed his arms, and slammed him into the counter. Fury roared, tossed one of the men hard into the nearby counter. Glass broke.

Ellie twisted hard to her side, trying to roll off the countertop where she lay stretched naked, her wrists still restrained above her head, but too upset, too shocked, and too full of adrenaline to be graceful.

Her movement was too violent and she ended up misjudging the edge. She fell and pure panic struck when she couldn't even grab for something to stop her fall. Pain exploded inside her head as she slammed into the side of the island, the tile edge of it making contact with her temple. Blackness rushed at her along with intense pain. She heard one thing before she lost consciousness.

"Ellie!" Fury yelled.

* * * * *

Fury hated being restrained inside a cell when he awoke in the security office. Justice paced the floor. Fury's memory returned at that point.

"Where is Ellie? Is she all right?" He'd sprang to his feet to grab at the bars that contained him.

"She's at the doctor's." Justice faced the bars, looking grim. "You forced her?"

"No," Fury snarled. "I would have explained that to you if you hadn't attacked and knocked me out."

"You had her tied down and she screamed." Justice's normally tan face appeared unusually pale. "I never would have believed you'd harm her now that I know how strongly you feel about her if I hadn't seen it with my own eyes."

"I didn't force her."

Justice snarled. "This is the kind of shit we feared when some of us started to show stronger animal traits with our honed instincts. You were aware of them though, we've discussed it at length, but you didn't control yourself."

Anger rolled through Fury. "I'm aware that I am unreasonable when it comes to Ellie and that I have mated her. It goes beyond sex. I've claimed her as mine but I would never hurt her, Justice. You have the entire situation wrong."

"You're out of control!" Justice moved fast, grabbed the bars inches from Fury's fingers, and barred his teeth in a vicious snarl. "We know all about force, don't we? You love her? Then you shouldn't have tied her down and made her take your cock."

"I didn't," Fury snarled.

Justice released the bars and backed away. "I want to trust you but…" He shook his head. "You're the first one of us to take a mate. You've allowed your animal instincts to rule you enough to take it to that level. We aren't fully human, no matter how much we pretend to be for the sake of peace between them and us, and there are no cameras here. Is it that bad, Fury? The need to take her so strong you would force her?"

"I didn't!" Fury tried to calm down by releasing his death grip on the cell bars and retreated a few steps. "I won't lie. I'm obsessed with her. I breathe and live Ellie. My heart beats for her, Justice. She is everything to me. I think I'm addicted to her scent. Without it around it's all I can think about. Despite all of that I'd never do anything to cause her pain. You have the situation wrong."

"I need to hear it from her. Until we see how this mating takes and what side effects you suffer from it, I'm sorry but I can't allow you to speak to her."

Fury moved forward quickly, gripped the cell door, jerked on it, but it was locked. "Let me out. Is she hurt? I need to get to her."

"You are going nowhere until I talk to her. Securing a woman and tying her down is force. Have you lost your mind?" Justice softly growled. "You're insane when it comes to the human, damn it. I'm stunned and —" He cleared his throat. "How could you do this?"

"I wasn't hurting her. You know me. You know she's everything to me. I would never harm her. We were making love."

"The years inside the testing facility have driven you to insanity if you believe forcing a female by tying her down and her screaming from pain is making love. You've become twisted inside your mind, Fury. I have to leave. My heart is breaking."

Justice spun away, quickly moving toward the door.

"Justice? Come back! Release me. It's not what you think. I'm not insane and I would never hurt my Ellie." He violently shook the cell bars but they held.

He spun and howled out in rage. Ellie had gotten hurt and he couldn't go to her. His best friend believed he'd gone insane from mating.

Chapter Fifteen

ဆ

Ellie knew something was wrong even before she fully awoke. Her head throbbed with dull pain. She opened her eyes only to stare at a light and study a ceiling she didn't recognize. Confusion hit her. *Where am I? What happened?* Someone leaned over her, getting between her and the light source from above.

Ellie recognized Doctor Trisha Norbit instantly and frowned. *Why is that woman standing over me?* The Doctor's hair had been pulled back into a messy ponytail and her neat appearance was gone. She looked worried as her blue eyes blinked down at Ellie.

"You're okay. I gave you some pain medication. Would you like to sip some water?"

Ellie frowned. "What happened?"

Trisha frowned back at her. "You don't remember?"

*Remember what? The last thing I remember is…*memory slowly returned. Ellie struggled to sit up. She frantically searched the room for Fury. She had somehow ended up inside a small bedroom but he wasn't there with her.

"Where is Fury?"

"They have him in lockup."

"Why?"

Trisha took a seat on the edge of the bed. "Someone informed Justice that the new director had gone to your home." She took a deep breath. "Justice went to see you and Fury to ask what Tom Quish wanted. He knocked but when no one answered, he and his security officers let themselves inside after they heard you scream and they heard Fury yell out. They ran into the kitchen and saw him hurting you. They believe he tied you down to prevent you from fighting him off."

"Hurting me?" Ellie's mouth fell open. She was so astounded it took her seconds to respond. "We were having sex."

Trisha bit her lip. "You hit your head hard on the edge of the island you were secured to. I had to give you a few stitches at your temple." She paused. "I can have a rape councilor here within an hour if you want to speak to someone. Your head is going to be fine. You might have a slight concussion but I'm sure you'll be physically fine. Emotionally..." Trisha reached over and took Ellie's hand. "I'm here for you. I think you should talk to a rape counselor. No one will know. Justice North is waiting in the other room to talk to you when you're ready. He promised they will punish Fury severely for what he's done but if you want to contact your outside police he will do that for you. It's your call."

Ellie yanked her hand away from the doctors. "Justice!" She yelled his name.

The bedroom door was thrown open in seconds. Justice looked like hell. His shirt had been torn, he had a busted lip, and sported a bruise over one eye on his forehead. He stepped into the bedroom and froze.

"Let him go now." Ellie's voice shook with anger and horror. "He didn't hurt me. You did. Let Fury out right now, damn it!" She started to yell but didn't care. "What the hell is wrong with everyone? Fury wasn't raping me!"

Shock blanked Justice's face. He opened his mouth but nothing came out.

Ellie grabbed the blankets covering her, threw them back, and felt grateful she wasn't naked. She hadn't been sure until she swung her legs over the edge of the bed. Someone had dressed her in a two-piece light-pink, baggy pajama set. She put her feet on the floor. Her head ached enough that she nearly regretted leaving the bed as she used it to push up to stand.

"Don't get up," the doctor demanded as she grabbed for Ellie. "You're drugged. You need to stay down."

Ellie slapped at the woman's hands and turned her anger on Justice. She managed a step before her knees gave way. The doctor grabbed her but they were both heading for a crash onto the floor when Justice suddenly lunged forward to wrap his arms around both women. His strength showed when he gently positioned them to angle their fall to the bed. Ellie hit it and the doctor came down next to her on the soft mattress. Ellie lay there glaring up at him as she fought tears.

"He wasn't hurting me. How could you think that?"

He hesitated. "You were tied down and screaming. He's the reason you're injured."

Tears spilled down her cheeks. "We were having sex and it was great until you tackled him and threw him away from me, you son of a bitch. We were having fun, laughing, and then..." Her voice broke as she just stared at him. "You hurt me, not him. *You* did. Everything would have been fine if you hadn't run in there, attacked Fury, and I wouldn't have taken a header off that island."

Justice backed up a step and grew paler. "But I heard you scream when we walked up to the front door. You were tied down when we rushed inside."

Ellie looked at the doctor. "Don't their women get loud sometimes at the end of sex?"

The doctor shrugged. "I don't know. Some of our females have loud sex. That's true."

"He tied you down," Justice reminded her softly. "That's force."

"It wasn't. Are you deaf? We were playing and having a great time. Didn't you notice he put a dishtowel around my wrists to keep the tape from touching my skin? Do you think if he tried to hurt me that he would have cared if I got red marks from the tape?" More hot tears tracked down Ellie's face. "Where is he? Did you hurt him? Let him go. I want Fury right now."

Justice turned away. "I'll get him." He walked out of the bedroom and slammed the door closed behind him.

Ellie turned onto her side on the bed and covered her face. She couldn't stop crying. A hand brushed her back, the doctor trying to comfort her, and Ellie sniffed.

"Did they hurt Fury?"

"I don't know," Trisha admitted. "I treated one of the officers who came in with you. Fury did some damage before they took him down."

Alarm at that news shot through Ellie and motivated her to sit up, wiping at her face. She stared at the doctor. "But you didn't have to treat Fury? That means he's okay, right?"

The doctor hesitated. "I don't know. I'm sorry. If he'd really been hurt you would think they would have brought him here too or called an ambulance to treat him."

"God!" Ellie rasped. "Why the hell did this happen? We were laughing and making love. Then this." She shook her head and regretted it instantly when it made her dizzy from the movement. "Why can't everyone leave us alone?"

Trisha's look softened. "No one knows what to expect. I'm sure Mr. North and those two officers thought they were saving you."

"From Fury?" Ellie ignored them as more tears slid down her cheeks. "Fury wouldn't hurt me."

Trisha reached over and took Ellie's hand. "I'm sorry."

The bedroom door almost exploded inward and Ellie and Trisha both jumped as Tom Quish entered the bedroom. His gaze jerked from Ellie to the doctor. "What the hell happened? I just received word that there's a big problem here. Security informed me one Species is locked up and Ms. Brower had to be carried into your home unconscious by two Species men who looked as if they'd been involved in a brawl."

Great, Ellie thought. *Just fucking great.* She couldn't even speak. Now the director was involved in her worst nightmare too.

Trisha released Ellie's hand. "How dare you come bursting into my house? This is my bedroom, Director Quish. As for what you heard, an unfortunate accident happened and that's all."

She moved forward, putting her body between Ellie and the director. He looked confused.

"What happened?" He sounded calmer.

Trisha straightened her shoulders and glared at the director. "What happened is that someone got past your security and scared Ms. Brower. She screamed. Mr. Fury, Mr. North, and the security officers were at the house," the doctor lied. "I told you I saw some idiot with a camera today sneaking around by the clinic. It could have been the same guy." She twisted her head to stare at Ellie with wide eyes. "Was the guy you saw peering into the window a short blond man wearing jeans and a green shirt?"

Ellie stared at the doctor, trying to hide her stunned surprise that this stranger would tell lies to protect her secrets but managed to nod. "That sounds like the guy who startled me."

A frown marred the director's face. "Then why is Mr. Fury in lockup?"

Relief flashed over the doctor's face before she faced the director again. "Because he wanted to hunt the son of a bitch down and kill him. Ms. Brower was startled, fell back, and hit her head. It knocked her out cold when she struck the edge of the counter. You know how protective of women these guys are. She's a guest in his home and some flash-happy jerk scared her, she got hurt, and he lost his temper. You know they can hunt and track with those animal instincts. Mr. North thought it would be a bad idea to allow Mr. Fury to kill the man since he's a human. They didn't see eye to eye in the heat of the moment. Mr. Fury is being detained until he can cool down."

"That's true," Slade agreed from the doorway he leaned against. He wasn't wearing the NSO uniform this time, instead he sported jeans and a black tank top. "I came over here to take a statement from Ms. Brower about the man she saw at the window. If you'll excuse us, Director, I'm off duty but I'd like to get her statement as fast as I can. Maybe you could get your security guards to search for this guy before he causes more problems?"

Ellie watched Tom Quish's face, seeing anger there. "Fine. If that's the story you want to tell, I'll run with it." He gave Ellie a grim frown. "Are you all right, Ms. Brower? Is there anything I can do for you?"

"I'm fine now," she promised softly. "But thank you for caring."

He spun on his heel to march out of the room. Ellie stared at the doctor, still surprised that the woman would help her by lying. The doctor shrugged.

"I told you that you can trust me."

Slade blew out a heavy breath. "I think I'll go have a seat in the living room to prevent anyone else from barging in." His gaze slid to Ellie. "They are bringing Fury to you and he should arrive real soon. He's pissed as hell but fine." His gaze swung to the doctor and he grinned. "You lie good, Doc." Slade winked at her and softly closed the door behind him.

Trisha's shoulders sagged. She sat down next Ellie on the bed. "I'm not the best liar. Was that at least passably good?"

"Pretty good. He left, didn't he?"

Trisha studied Ellie. "You need to take it easy for a few weeks. You really whacked your head good on that counter. If you suffer headaches, dizzy spells, or just don't feel right, you need to call me immediately. I want you to take it easy and try not to have sex for at least a week. You need to remain calm with no physical activity. Keep the area where I stitched you as dry as possible. I used dissolvable stitches and I won't need to remove them. I doubt you'll see much of a scar."

"Great." Ellie couldn't hide the anger that flared or her sarcasm at that bit of news.

"Could I ask you just a few questions?"

"Like what?"

"Well," Trisha scooted to face her, adjusting her body on the edge of the mattress. "I read some of the medical records on New Species and realize Fury is canine. It says their penises swell during sex." She paused. "Does the swelling hurt?"

"No," Ellie shook her head. "I can't believe this happened."

"How long do you usually have to wait until the swelling goes down?"

Ellie frowned at the doctor.

"Please? I want to know."

"So you can help other people if a woman decides to sleep with one of them?"

Trisha hesitated. "For my own benefit. I'm attracted to one of them."

Ellie relaxed. "Oh. Well, in that case, it's not painful. The swelling only lasts a few minutes. Maybe three."

"Thank you. Any surprises?"

"I love him more than my own life."

Trisha stood. "You can go home with him tonight. Just remember what I warned about your head and Mr. Fury is going to need to wake you every few hours to make sure you're okay. If he has any trouble rousing you, he is to call me immediately. I'll get you pain pills to help with the headache you're going to have after the medication wears off."

"Thanks, Doctor Norbit."

"Just call me Trisha." She left the room.

Ellie heard voices a few minutes later. The bedroom door swung open and Fury stalked inside. Ellie gasped. Bruises marred his face and someone had given him a shirt that looked as though it had been shredded in places. He crossed the room in just a few strides, leaving the bedroom door ajar. He sat down carefully and reached for her, his arms wrapping gently around her. He picked her up and lifted her carefully onto his lap to hug her tightly against his chest.

"Are you all right?"

She wound her arm around his neck. He had a bad black eye but it wasn't swollen closed. She studied the damage to him. One of her hands trembled as she touched his face, pressing her palm to the only area of his skin that didn't seem injured.

"I needed some stitches on my head. Are you all right? What happened to you?"

He growled. "They tried to stop me from reaching you." His gaze lingered on her forehead. "There are stitches under the bandage?"

"Just a few. I'm fine though." Her hand left his face and she reached for the shirt he wore. She pulled the neck of it away from his skin and peered down the front of it, spotting red marks on his chest. Her horrified gaze flew up to stare into his eyes.

"I'm fine. Major communication breakdown."

Ellie fought a sob. "This was more than that."

Fury held her a little tighter. "Yeah but it's cleared up now. I've learned an important lesson from this."

"What's that?"

"We're going to barricade the doors next time."

A smile tugged at Ellie's lips for his sake, appreciating his attempt at humor. "I want to go home. Trisha said I can leave. She's getting me some pain pills right now. We're banned from sex for a week and you're supposed to wake me up every few hours to make sure I'm okay."

Fury flinched. "A week, huh?" His brown eyes softened. "I'm just glad you are all right. I heard you scream. It terrified me when you fell, you weren't moving, and I smelled your blood."

"I'm fine."

Fury stood, shifting Ellie inside the cradle of his arms. "Let's go home."

Ellie rested her cheek against his shoulder and wrapped her other arm around his neck. She left wearing borrowed pajamas but she didn't care who saw her. Fury walked toward the bedroom door, using his foot to pull it completely open. Justice, Slade and Trisha waited for them in the living room.

"I'm sorry," Justice apologized softly. "I didn't know or I never would have rushed into that kitchen." He met Fury glare. "I didn't think you would hurt her but after the last time, I wasn't sure."

Trisha frowned. "What last time? What happened before?"

Ellie sighed. "It's just another mix up, Trisha. I'll tell you about it another time."

Trisha held out a pill bottle toward Ellie and Fury.

"I'll take those," Slade offered, plucking them from her hand. "I'll drive them home. It would look strange to see Fury carrying a woman wearing night clothes."

"Just take one pill as needed for pain," Trisha instructed.

Slade hesitated at the door. "Do you want me to take her for you, Fury? Those Taser guns hurt like a son of a bitch."

"I've got her," Fury growled.

Slade opened the door and stepped out of the way. Fury carried Ellie out of the house to the waiting car at the curb. Slade opened the back door for them. Fury shifted Ellie inside his hold and climbed into the car with her on his lap. He sat down hard enough to jar her and made pain shoot through her head. She groaned softly.

Fury

Fury growled.

Ellie rubbed him where her hands touched. "I'm fine. It's just a headache."

Fury hugged her tighter, obviously upset. Ellie was shocked at how bad their evening had turned out. She had to blink back tears for fear that Fury would grow even more upset if he saw them.

* * * * *

Ellie smiled at the women who shared the dorm kitchen with her. The eight women were new, having just arrived early that morning. Ellie had been shocked when the eight women had been brought to the door with their suitcases. Breeze had stood at her side to welcome the new dorm roomies.

"They are so small," Ellie gasped.

"Yes," Breeze acknowledged grimly. "They are."

Ellie glanced up at her. "I just assumed you were all tall since so far that's all I've seen."

Breeze hesitated. "We're the experimental prototypes, Ellie. We were changed for strength and endurance to test out drugs that would make humans stronger. Justice sent us here first because we are more durable. We're tough. Those," Breeze's attention focused on the women entering the house. "Those are the truly unfortunate ones."

"What does that mean?"

Breeze shot Ellie a warning look. "Later."

Ellie had assigned them rooms and now they had assembled inside the kitchen for their first lessons. It had been an odd feeling, being around women her own size and even smaller after getting accustomed to the much larger New Species women. The new women ranged from around five-foot to about five-foot-five. They had smaller body frames, similar to frail humans except their facial features revealed them as New Species. They also seemed timid and shy, unlike

257

the larger New Species women. Ellie smiled in an attempt to put them at ease.

"I know this all seems like a lot but trust me, by the end of the week you will be cooking and you will know how to handle everything inside this kitchen."

A blonde with big gray eyes raised her hand.

Ellie kept her smile in place. "Yes?"

The blonde bit her lip. "Are you one of us?"

Ellie shook her head. "I'm not New Species." Ellie glanced at Breeze. She'd stayed close to the group of women as if she were their shadow since they'd walked into the dorm a few hours before.

"She's pure human but she's a good one," Breeze assured softly. "She's our house pet." Breeze winked at Ellie. "We call her a poodle. That's those cute dogs that are small and have puffy hair."

The blonde looked shocked as her wide gaze turned to Ellie. "Aren't you angry, being called a pet?"

Ellie chuckled. "I know it's meant with love. What is your name?"

The blonde hesitated. "They call me Halfpint."

Ellie glanced at Breeze. Breeze shrugged. Ellie had a ton of unanswered questions but pushed the one she really wanted to ask back for later. "Well, do you have any other questions?"

Halfpint addressed Breeze. "May I?"

Breeze sighed. "You don't need permission anymore. You're free. There's no fear here, Halfpint. You can ask anything you want."

Halfpint straightened her shoulders. She looked frightened when she faced Ellie. "Are you training us to go back to be better at what we were meant for?"

"No," Breeze snapped. "That's done and over. You are free. Do you understand? You are here so you can learn to run your home like any other human. They all learn how to cook meals and operate appliances." Breeze stood suddenly from the chair. "I need some air." She fled the kitchen.

Confused, Ellie stood there. She didn't know what was going on. Halfpint's gray eyes filled with tears. Ellie moved to stand in front of her.

"It's okay. This is all new to you. Are you all right?"

Halfpint wiped at her tears. "I made her angry."

Ellie glanced at the empty doorway knowing she couldn't disagree with that. "What did you mean by going back to what you were before?"

Halfpint looked even more fearful. She turned suddenly and threw herself into the arms of another woman, hugging her tightly. Ellie realized they were all suddenly afraid for some reason. No other New Species women had ever been afraid of her. Ellie stepped back, hoping it would alleviate their fear.

"Why don't you go and unpack you clothes? We'll just take today really slow and you can meet the other women. I put notes on the backs of your doors to let you know when meals are served. If you have any questions I'll be here until five. The other women will help you if I'm not around."

Ellie watched the women flee then went in search of Breeze. She spotted her through the living room window and let herself out of the building. Breeze sat on a bench under a tree on the front yard of the dorm. Ellie sat next to her.

"What was that about?"

Breeze used her foot to rub the grass. "What was done to them pisses me off. The doctors created them weak on purpose. Those women are afraid to even ask you a question and did you hear that comment about before? No matter how many times they are told that shit is over, they are still terrified they are being lied to, and being sent back."

"I don't understand."

Breeze lifted her head and revealed the tears in her eyes. "They spliced their DNA with domestic animals to make them weak and small. They didn't create them to run tests on. They weren't combined with different species for medical research. They made them to be used and abused."

Ellie crossed her arms. "For what?"

Breeze wiped at a tear that slid down one cheek and let her head drop. "Gifts. The doctors made them to be sex slaves to the bastards who funded the testing facilities. They were passed over to whatever asshole had enough money and was perverted enough to want to fuck an animal that was human looking enough to be appealing. They made them small enough to be helpless and unable to defend themselves."

"Oh God." Ellie knew the blood drained from her face. "Please tell me you are kidding."

Breeze shook her head. "We found some of them but Justice is still searching with the help of your government. We were too late to save most of the ones we've traced the money transactions on so far. The men who were arrested confessed to abusing them to death. These were the ones who were tougher and bigger, who survived the worst."

"I think I'm going to be sick."

Breeze met her eyes. "Me too. Not only did those bastards hand out gifts to sickos with animal fetishes but they gave them to the worst of humanity. Murderers who have admitted to beating the life from them or starved them to death."

Ellie was glad she'd missed breakfast or she might have thrown it up on the grass at her feet. "So when they said before, they meant that? They think I'm trying to train them to be better..." She clamped her mouth shut as bile rose.

"Gifts," Breeze growled.

"Those sons of bitches."

Breeze nodded. "I shouldn't have lost my temper but I get enraged. I had it bad, Ellie. Trust me. We all had hellish lives but they had it so much worse. I had a few guards try to sexually assault me. I fought back and even killed one of them. Most of the staff inside the testing facility was willing to protect us against that and it didn't happen often. They said we were too expensive to damage. The testing facility only made us have sex with our own people but we didn't hurt each other. We shared dignity and respect and kindness. They didn't have that when males touched them."

Ellie rose to her feet on unsteady legs. "I guess I'm going to have to really reach out to them and hopefully they can learn to trust us."

Breeze stood and smiled down at Ellie sadly. "You are small the way they are and maybe that will help them. Halfpint thought you were one of them."

She and Breeze returned to the dorm. Depression coursed through Ellie. Every time she thought she had a handle on the kind of horrors the New Species had suffered, a new one was exposed.

* * * * *

Ellie smiled at Fury. He hadn't wanted her go to work but she'd argued with him that morning. Now he was going out of his way to make it up to her. Makeup sex couldn't happen since Fury feared he'd hurt her somehow. Ellie's smile died. She wished he'd realize she wasn't as fragile as he believed her to be.

"I feel so bad for them," she admitted.

"You're softhearted." Fury rubbed her cheek with his thumb. "They are free now. We'll find more of them soon."

"I wish I could do something nice for them."

"What do you have in mind?" Fury pulled Ellie down on the couch to sit next to him.

Ellie curled against his side, loving to cuddle with him. "I don't know. Breeze mentioned they were kept away from anyone except their abusers."

"Yes. They call us animals but those men were truly the beasts. Some of those women were found locked inside basements. They were kept far from any other person to avoid their presence being discovered. They were never taken anywhere and never even owned clothing in some cases."

Ellie shivered from the horrible images that tidbit created inside her mind. "They thought I'd tried to teach them how to use the kitchen so they'd have a new skills to take back with them to their former owners."

Fury flinched. "I heard it was bad. Justice keeps them far away from all the men. He wants them to grow stronger emotionally before they are introduced to us."

"But you protect your women. I've seen it."

"We do but they've never had that, Ellie. They've been hurt and abused by men. It's all they know."

"Where have they been kept after they were rescued if they haven't been around men? Were all of them discovered at once and brought directly here?"

"No. Justice contacted a church. They have a few secluded retreats without any males. They accepted the women with open arms to give them some time and peace to recover from what they have been through. They are to be sent here when the therapists believe they are strong enough. The first batch is a test to see how they do. Hopefully they are able to overcome their pasts and find a future."

"And if they aren't?"

"Justice has thought about making our own female-only community to protect them."

"Those poor women." Ellie snuggled tighter against Fury's side and glanced at the television. Fury enjoyed watching baseball and a game would be on soon. "I wish I could think of something to do to help them."

"You'll come up with something."

"Yeah. I hope so."

The news came on before the game. Ellie sat up straight and stared in shock at the reporter who opened with the evening's top story about the New Species. They flashed an image of Fury carrying Ellie to a car. He appeared furious in the photo and Ellie looked to be in pain.

"Son of a bitch," Fury growled. He moved, stretching for the phone.

"Shush," Ellie ordered him. "I want to hear this."

"How the hell did they get a picture of that?"

"I don't know."

They both listened to the story. Fury finally clicked off the television and lunged to his feet. He dialed the phone as he stormed toward the kitchen. Ellie heard his furious undertones from the other room. She sat there, trembling.

The public now knew about her and Fury. The reporter stated she and Fury were the first New Species and human couple. They'd hinted that Ellie—they'd mentioned both of their names—had somehow been injured. The reporter claimed it may have been Fury who'd harmed her.

She closed her eyes and fought angry tears. Worse, she hurt for Fury. Why did people think he would hurt her automatically just because he happened to be a New Species? They even knew he'd been mixed with canine DNA, had mentioned that during the report. It obvious that someone inside Homeland had leaked that information to the press.

Ellie still trembled when she rose to her feet. She found Fury pacing inside the kitchen, talking on phone. Their gazes met. Fury paused, looking furious and pale. Ellie walked directly into him. One of his arms circled her waist and he rested his chin on the top of her head.

Ellie just held Fury until he ended his call. He hung up the phone and slammed it down on the counter. His other arm wrapped around her waist, holding her, while he rubbed her back.

"Justice is on it. He has to call a news conference, Ellie. He has no choice. They were hinting that you're being hurt. We need the support of the public."

She nodded against his chest. "I know."

"There has to be a leak somewhere. They knew I'm canine. That's not publically known. They cited our first names."

Ellie winced. "Do you think it was Doctor Norbit? I'd hate to think she did this."

"I don't know but we will find out. I hate to say it but I'm betting it was her or someone inside the human security force. They have access to our files too. Someone informed me that Tom showed up at the doc's house. Human security alerted him and that means they knew something had happened."

Ellie pulled back from him far enough to peer up at his face. "I'm sorry they implied you hurt me. They are idiots."

Some of the anger eased from his features. "It's not your fault. People always assume the worst. Hell, my own people thought me capable of it."

"What do we do now?"

His lips twitched and he gave her a slight smile. "Look on the bright side. We don't have to hide our relationship anymore."

She snorted. "Yeah. They had it on the news. I guess I should probably call my family soon before they hear about it and freak out."

His smile died. "What if they are upset about you being with me?" His gaze searched hers. "Will you leave me?"

Ellie hugged him tighter. "Never. I swear. I don't care what they think."

He couldn't hide his relief. "I checked something out."

"What?"

He hesitated. "Have I told you that I love you?"

Ellie's heart soared. "No. You haven't. Are you telling me now?"

His lips twitched before he spoke and amusement sparked his gaze. "That depends. Do you love me?"

Ellie laughed and nodded. "I do."

"I love you, sweetness."

"I love you too." Tears blinded her until she blinked them away. "I've loved you for a while but I refrained from telling you."

"Why?"

She shrugged. "I guess I was being stupid. Human guys tend to flinch a little when a woman declares she's fallen in love quickly."

His eyebrows arched. "I'm not one of them, not fully, and I'm filled with joy that you love me. Never say you are stupid again. You're cautious because you have been hurt by a man in your past. That will never happen with us because this time you chose well." A smile curved his lips, a teasing sparkle in his beautiful eyes.

Ellie had to fight her emotions not to become overwhelmed. She did laugh at his joke. *He loves me!* More tears blinded her. She had to blink them back. It wasn't just sex to him, he shared her feelings. Suddenly their problems seemed irrelevant. *He loves me!*

"Good. I love you more than words can say and I'm so happy you love me too."

Fury chuckled. "I checked into marriage." His smile died. "They don't have a special marriage clause for us but it isn't exactly against the law either since there's nothing regarding New Species."

Marriage? Ellie stared up at him in shock. She'd never once expected Fury to think about that kind of commitment but he obviously had. Did she want to be married to him? She stared up into his eyes. He had become a huge part of her soul since that first haunting day she'd seen him inside his sterile cell.

"You want to talk about getting married? Really?"

"Would you mind being married to me? I love you and I want to commit to you, Ellie. That's the deepest one humans have."

"I love you for that even more."

He lifted her and carried her into the living room. He sat back down on the couch with her on his lap. She put her arms around him and they smiled at each other.

"Would you seriously consider saying yes if I were to ask you to marry me in the near future?"

Ellie laughed. "I would but you aren't supposed to ask if I will consider it. Just ask me."

"I would but I haven't had a chance to buy you a ring yet." He reached up and gripped Ellie's hand behind his neck. He brought it to his lips to press a kiss on her palm. Then he turned her hand to study her fingers. "I don't know what size your finger is unless they just come in small."

"I'm a size six."

"Six." His gaze met hers as he held her hand inside his. "I'm having the legal department look into whether we can get married. All they have found so far is that it isn't on the books but there's nothing against us marrying either. We're what they called a landmark case. It sounds like we are real estate."

Chuckling, Ellie nodded. "Yeah. It kind of does."

"They believe it shouldn't be a problem. They were hoping no one would find out until after we were married if you agreed to be my wife. Now I'm afraid someone will think of it and try to protest our right to do that."

"I don't think they can. You have rights, Fury. They can't give New Species the right to live as all citizens live then tell you that you don't have the same rights as other people. It would just be too wrong for words."

The phone rang and Fury lifted Ellie off his lap and gently placed her onto the couch next to him. He got to his feet to get the phone. Ellie leaned back and tried to relax. She could hear Fury's voice but not the words.

He wants to marry me. She grinned.

* * * * *

"The calls are already coming in, Fury." Justice swore softly. "I just got off the phone with the president. He fully backs us but I hear the worry in his voice. I assured him things are fine and that the news reports were purposely grim."

"Good. I called our teams and they are on standby to assist the human forces at the gates in case we get an influx of protesters. I'm expecting that to happen. It's going to drive those nut jobs insane that their worst fear has come true and that a New Species officially lives with a human woman." Fury paused. "I'm sorry for the trouble but I wouldn't change it. She's worth it to me, Justice."

"You have made that clear and as I said, we are happy for you both. We back you." Justice paused. "I know we need to address this issue with the press. They are imagining the worst—that she was injured by abuse from one of ours, and we need to clear this matter up."

"Agreed but I refuse to put Ellie in front of them to answer questions. They will verbally attack her and say mean things that will hurt her feelings. I won't allow that. It's my job to protect her. We need to allow the humans to deal with their own kind. They are getting paid to handle the press. Let them do it."

"It's also your job to protect Species and our image. We may have to allow them to see Ellie to assure all humans she is fine. We need the public on our side, Fury. The last thing we need is more humans hating us and showing up outside the gates. The president can't back us if he's getting slammed by everyone for doing so."

"I can do my job and Ellie *is* New Species. She's mine to protect as well. I won't risk one for the other because it won't come to that."

"Good. I will call a meeting with Tom next and he's the best public relations person we have. He's heavily into politics and has a vast amount of experience in dealing with the public. He'll tell us the best way to handle this." Justice sighed. "I wish these anti-New Species humans would just go away."

"I wish it as well but we're free. This seems to be the price of it. We realized it wouldn't be easy from the start. We'll get through this. Our security teams are prepared for the worst and you'll handle the humans. You're much better at dealing with them than I am." A chuckle escaped Fury. "I don't envy you that job today."

"Is there any way you'll allow the press access to Ellie?"'

"No. She's waiting for me to end this call and I'm going to her. She's worried. I need to soothe her."

"Did you just say you needed to soothe her?" Justice laughed.

A flash of irritation tore through Fury. "What? She gets upset and I can't stand to see her that way."

"Soothe?"

"I get to run my hands all over her." Fury chuckled. "I distract her and as her mate it is my job to keep her mind on more pleasant things. Are you really going to give me shit about doing that? If you had a woman waiting for you, you would want to soothe her as well."

"Go. I envy you right now. I have no one waiting for me." Justice hung up.

* * * * *

"Justice is going to hold a press conference tomorrow. He's decided we don't have to talk to them unless we want to.

I told him we won't." Fury said when he walked out of the kitchen without the phone.

Ellie arched an eyebrow. "You might have asked me."

Dark eyes narrowed. "I am not going to put you up on display and allow humans to say hurtful words to you."

"Don't get angry. I'm trying not to get mad myself. You need to ask me things though. It's just the right thing to do."

Fury growled. "You're mine to protect."

Ellie sighed. She loved him. He was naturally dominant, it being his nature, and he wanted to protect her. She could either fight him every step of the way or just accept that he was prone to that behavior. She knew he loved her as deeply as she loved him. She nodded and his anger eased.

"I just want to shelter you."

"I know, Fury. I just like to be asked. All right?"

"I'll try. Do you want me to call Justice back and tell him that we will be there for the reporters to question?"

"You'd do that for me? Go with me if I wanted to?"

He sat down next to her. "If you go, I go."

She loved him even more for saying that. "Don't call him back. There's no way I want to be there."

"Women," Fury growled but he smiled.

Ellie leaned toward him and softly brushed a kiss on his lips before pulling back. "Get used to it if you want to marry one."

"I do."

The phone rang again. Fury cursed. "Damn it. It's not going to stop."

Ellie silently agreed. "I guess I should call my family on my cell phone while you take that call. It would be rude not to give them a heads up before they see it on the evening news."

Fury's expression darkened.

"I don't care if they aren't happy about us. You're my life now, Fury. You're all that matters. I should call them though so they hear it from me."

"Maybe I should just tear the phones out of the walls."

Ellie was tempted to let him but then reality set in. "Then they'd come to the door."

"Good point."

Chapter Sixteen

ත

"I'm really sorry that I had to make you be here." Director Tom Quish appeared sincere as he glanced between Ellie and Fury. "Justice is furious with me but I have more experience handling the press and the public than he does. Most people love a good romance. We need those people on our side. They want to see you together and it will squash all the nasty rumors circulating in the tabloids."

"Do we want to ask what those rumors are?" Fury arched his eyebrow.

Tom shook his head. "Not really, unless you really do have Ellie locked up, living inside a doghouse and chained with a collar to get revenge on humans for what was done to you. It's crap like that."

Ellie turned her head to smile up Fury. "That sounds kind of kinky."

He laughed. "Maybe I'll build a doghouse."

"That's what I need," Tom encouraged them. "You are both taking all this really well."

Fury shrugged. "I got angry but Ellie told me it only made it worse. She cried when I swore I would kill them all."

Tom's smile faded instantly. His eyes widened in horror.

Ellie chuckled. "He's kidding."

"Thank God." Tom smiled again.

"I didn't cry when he said that. I told him I didn't like seeing blood."

Fury chuckled. Ellie winked at him. Tom groaned.

"You two are going to kill me out there if you act this way. People won't know what to think of you. I'm hoping that was a joke."

"They think I'm a savage animal who is forcing Ellie to be my sex slave." Fury's teeth clenched. "Am I wrong?"

"Calm down." Ellie moved closer to him and touched his chest to caress him with her hand. "Anger isn't our friend. Remember our talk this morning? I know how mad you are but that's what they want to see. You need to keep control of it. Laugh at them. If you get accused of crap like that by some reporter, just think of this." She moved closer to him. "I would love to be your sex slave any day."

Fury smiled wide enough that his canine teeth showed. "That won't stop me from being angry. That will make me want to take you home."

"One hour, Fury. That's as long as you have to keep your cool. You can control your temper. You need to do this," Ellie assured him. "You can yell later and be angry then if it gets hairy out there."

He cupped her face. "I promise to try, Ellie. I would do anything for you."

"Thank you."

"But if they insult you, I might get angry. You know my temper is short when it comes to someone harming you or saying bad things about you."

Ellie groaned. "They will insult me. I'm pretty sure of that. I can handle it so just keep calm."

"What kind of male would I be to sit there while they say bad things about you?"

"A smart one," Tom snapped. "The world is going to be watching this, Fury. You two are huge worldwide news. You have no idea how much coverage will be out there. If you charm the press they will love you. They will totally back you having a relationship. If this goes bad then it could get ugly. We really need the incoming money, Fury. Think of all the

New Species and Ellie even. What would happen if support got pulled and the funds stopped coming in that keep Homeland open? It would close down and then where would everyone be? Our legal staff is working hard on those lawsuits to get cash inflowing but I've been assured it won't be too much longer before Mercile Industries is going to pay for what they've done."

"Fine," Fury sighed. "I understand. I will sit there and be calm no matter how much I want to hurt someone."

"Thank you." Tom sighed. He shot Ellie a grim look and crossed his fingers. The man walked around his desk and yanked his jacket on. "Let's go."

Fury took Ellie's hand. She tried to fight down her nervousness. She'd never had to talk in front of a bunch of cameras and reporters before. For security purposes the press conference would be held in front of the main gates. That way it kept everyone out of Homeland but next to the security walls to help them control the area.

"I'm here," Fury assured her. "I won't allow anyone to harm you."

Ellie flashed him a weak smile. "I just hate being around a bunch of people but I'm going to be fine with you at my side."

Fury kept a firm grip on her hand and pulled her closer against his body when they walked outside the gates. Ellie realized immediately it had turned in to a media circus of the worst proportions. Flashing cameras blinded them when they drew closer to the area set up for them.

Justice and Tom walked ahead of Ellie and Fury. Fury released her hand and put his arm around her waist. His body shielded her from a lot of the cameras. The press shouted out questions they purposely ignored since Tom had prepared them well.

Ellie took a seat between Fury and Trisha Norbit. Ellie was grateful to be next to the woman. Trisha squeezed Ellie's hand under the table and flashed a brave smile. Ellie squeezed

Fury's hand. His other hand covered hers so he held it between both of his. He rubbed her skin gently to assure her. Tom stood and tried to quiet the press. *Good luck,* Ellie thought. A shouting madhouse had broken out.

Tom was able to silence the crowd after a few minutes. Ellie listened while Tom spoke to the press.

"The rumors circulating about Fury harming Ellie Brower aren't true." His voice rang out clearly. "They are a couple who live together inside Homeland. The video you saw on television happened after Ellie had a simple accident. She was treated by our doctor. This is Doctor Trisha Norbit. She will verify that for you."

Trisha leaned forward to the microphone, introduced herself, and immediately a volley of questions were shouted out by reporters. She had to wait until their voices died down to speak.

"Of course the rumors aren't true," Trisha shook her head and looked angry as she glanced around at reporters. "It was a simple accident while Ellie cleaned the kitchen," she lied. "She hit her head on the edge of the kitchen island when she stood from sweeping the floor. She had a bump to her head. Mr. Fury wasn't even home at the time of the incident. He came home and found Ellie. All you saw was him carrying Ellie out to the car after I treated her. It was that simple."

"Ms. Brower," one of the reporters rose to his feet. "Is that true?"

Ellie forced a smile and tried to slow her erratic heart rate, caused from being in the spotlight. "Unfortunately. Trust me." *Just smile and lie,* she told herself. *I can do this.* "Imagine how mortified I am. I bumped my head and it's on the eleven o'clock news."

"Are you and Mr. Fury having sex?" Someone else rose and asked.

Ellie hesitated. "Are you having sex? That's kind of a personal question, isn't it?"

"I'm not." The male reporter smiled. "But I would be if I were dating someone. Come on, Ms. Brower. Are you and Mr. Fury having sex?"

Ellie squeezed Fury's hand to assure him she was fine when he tensed. "My sex life is not up for public discussion but I will say that Fury and I are living together, as Tom let you know, and we are involved in a serious relationship."

The man nodded and sat down. Another man popped up. "Mr. Fury, do you bite Ms. Brower? We heard rumors that there is biting during sex."

Fury's hold on her became intense enough that she had to hide a flinch. Ellie used her thumb to rub the back of his hand. Fury relaxed and shook his head.

"I would never hurt Ellie." He suddenly pulled back his upper lip to show his teeth quickly. "It would hurt if I bit her."

Questions started flying. Ellie fought back a laugh at the absurdity of some of them. Tom yelled for order. He repeated his instructions of one question at a time or the interview would end. Silence reigned again and one person stood.

"How do you two kiss with his sharp teeth?"

Fury opened his mouth. Ellie bumped him with her shoulder and answered. "How do you kiss someone with an overbite? Or someone with buck teeth? Or someone with missing teeth? You just do. That's a silly question."

"So you two do kiss?"

"Of course I kiss him. Look at him." Ellie turned her head and smiled at Fury. She looked back at the reporter. "Teeth aren't a problem."

A female reporter rose next. "How do you feel about being with a man when you know he can't have children with you?"

"Doctor Norbit," a male reporter shouted out of turn. "Are you doing research on them?"

"No," Trisha denied. "They are people, not lab rats."

"How do you feel about being with someone that you may never be able to have children with, Ellie?"

Ellie stared at the same female reporter who asked again about kids. She hesitated. "There's never a guarantee, no matter who you are with, that you can have children. There are plenty of couples in this world who are together and then discover for whatever reason they can't have them. That's why we have surrogate mothers, sperm banks, and adoption available for those couples. I don't think anyone meets someone and judges if they like them or not on the basis of how well their reproductive system works and how many children they can get out of that person. That's just unreasonable and stupid. I'm not concerned in the least about that. I don't even think about it."

The reporter sat. The next one popped up and it went on. Ellie tried to keep her calm. They were asking stupid questions for the most part. They wanted to know if Fury helped with household chores and if Ellie treated him as if he were a regular person. Fury kept his cool, laughed at a lot of the questions, and never lost his temper. Ellie watched him, really proud of how he took it all. He could be charming when he wanted to be. He met her gaze and smiled back at her.

"Ellie?" A man in the back suddenly yelled.

Ellie turned her head, trying to find the source. "Yes?"

"How does it feel to betray your own race by allowing an animal fuck you?"

Shock tore through Ellie at the sudden verbal attack. Just as she found the jerk who'd asked that question, a thin, tall man in a business suit suddenly shoved at the people in front of him, flashing a gun clutched in his hand. Screams erupted around them and gunfire exploded. Ellie froze in horror before someone slammed her into the ground and something heavy crushed down on top of her.

Ellie's eyes flew open. Fury sprawled over her, covering her body with his. Shots continued to ring out along with panicked screams and shouts from the crowd. Fury crawled higher to cover her better, twisting his body to put himself between her and the source of the attack.

His arms dug underneath her and then he lifted her, shoved her knees into her chest to force her into a tight ball inside his arms, and staggered to his feet. He sprinted for the gates with Ellie clutched in his arms, hunched over her, still shielding her body with his.

Fury jerked hard, his hold on her slackened, but then tightened again. He kept moving and yelled out words she didn't catch. Ellie was too shocked to understand him and she couldn't breathe. He had her crushed within his arms and her knees and legs were shoved against her chest, compressing her lungs. The pounding impact of his body as he ran didn't help either. Ellie couldn't see much with him wrapped around her and the way he held her so tightly.

She knew they cleared the gate, saw a section of the wall flash past them just as Fury collapsed onto his knees. He groaned loudly but somehow kept hold of her inside the cradle of his arms. Then his grip eased. Ellie moved in his arms, lifted her head, and she saw pain twisting his handsome features.

"Fury?"

He shifted her and put her on the ground in front of him. She looked up at him and watched his eyes roll back in his head. He just crumpled sideways, crashing onto the grass next to her. Ellie ignored the shouting, the screams, and all the other sounds going on around them. She frantically crawled to huddle over his still form. That's when she saw the blood.

"FURY!" She screamed his name. Her hands frantically grabbed for his side where the red stickiness spread. Her terrified, panicked mind understood he'd been shot. She pressed both palms over the wound, trying to slow the bleeding. Her terrified gaze locked on Fury's face. He breathed but wasn't conscious.

"Someone help me!" Ellie screamed.

Trisha Norbit suddenly dropped to her knees on the other side of Fury's body. Trisha shoved Ellie's hands away and tore at Fury's shirt to get a look at the wound. Ellie ignored her hands, covered with Fury's blood. She inched up to his face while the doctor and a few other people started to work on him.

Ellie trembled. "Fury?" She touched his face, not caring that her fingertips brushing his skin were bloody. Tears streamed down her face. "Fury? Please wake up." Her voice broke with a sob.

"Get me a med kit," Trisha demanded loudly. "Now!"

He didn't move. Ellie frantically looked at the doctor. "Trisha? Is he going to be okay?"

Trisha met Ellie's eyes and then turned her head away. "We need to get him to the hospital immediately. Call the trauma center and tell them we need an operating room prepared and—" She cursed. "Justice? I need a few of your canine people to come with us. He's going to need blood and hopefully one of them will match his close enough."

Justice stood behind Ellie gripping his cell phone. "I'll get them all."

"Trisha?" Ellie continued to shake.

Trisha met her gaze then, her expression grim. "He's been shot twice, Ellie. It's really bad. I promise I'm going to do everything I can to save him."

Ellie totally fell apart in that instant. She knew he wasn't going to make it. She saw all the blood soaking her hands, his clothes, and Trisha's hands. She caressed his face and whispered his name. Someone grabbed her from behind and yanked her away from the man she loved. She fought whoever held her, screaming Fury's name, but he didn't move. The man holding her held on tighter and spun away.

"They need to work on him, Ellie. I'm going to drive you to where they are taking him. You need to calm down," the man yelled in her ear. "This isn't helping him."

Ellie sobbed. She stopped screaming and struggling, admitted the futility of it. Slade held her and he was as big as Fury. Her feet weren't even touching the ground. He kept hold of her, saying soothing things in her ear, as Ellie watched the doctor and the emergency medical staff work on Fury, trying to stabilize him. Someone brought a stretcher and they quickly loaded him onto it. She looked up when she heard a news helicopter circling.

Slade turned with her, still kept a good hold on her in case she tried to run after Fury, and quickly strode toward the parking lot. He gently dumped her into the back seat of one of the SUV's when he got there and grabbed his radio.

"Canines, meet me at the parking lot. We're ready to roll. I have Ellie secured."

Slade got behind the wheel, turned in his seat and studied Ellie. She cried, curled into a ball on one of the back seats, but had overheard enough to piece together most of what had happened from the car radio. Slade was obviously torn up too by what had happened. It was obvious by his grim expression and the pained look in his eyes as they stared at each other.

"I was patrolling the wall when it happened. There were three shooters in all. I took out one of them but I couldn't get the other two without risking hitting innocents. I'm sorry I wasn't able to take them all out before they shot him." His gruff voice paused. "Fury will be fine," Slade promised in a firm voice. "We are stronger than humans and we heal faster. We can take more punishment."

Ellie wiped at her tears. "I can't lose him."

Slade nodded. "You won't."

Men opened doors and climbed inside the SUV. Ellie noticed they were armed to the teeth with weapons secured from ankle to chest on their big bodies. They were also canine, judging from the shape of their solemn eyes. Slade started the engine and backed out of the parking space. He punched the gas and headed for the gate. He turned his radio up to hear it clearer over the sound of the engine.

"Clear the way. We're just about there."

He didn't even slow as they came to the opened gate. The crowd normally present had been evacuated from the area. Gunfire and bloodshed had scattered the protesters and the reporters.

* * * * *

Ellie paced and kept glancing at the men surrounding her. There were at least seven NSO officers guarding the private waiting room. The hospital had offered one to them as soon as they realized the NSO officers were armed and determined to guard Ellie. More officers were outside the operating room where Fury fought for his life.

"He's still alive," Justice assured Ellie.

She nodded, knowing Justice spoke on his cell phone with one of the NSO officers who guarded the operating room. The officer could see inside to give detailed information. Ellie was grateful for the relay system Justice had thought of, to keep tabs on how Fury faired. Ellie didn't know how people could stand just waiting without any kind of word when a loved one underwent surgery.

Slade entered the room, moved directly to Ellie, and offered her a large, white, covered Styrofoam cup. A straw stuck out of it. Ellie forced a smile.

"Coffee doesn't come with a straw but thank you."

"It is iced coffee." Slade smiled. "You're shaking. I didn't want to hand you something hot that could spill. Fury would kick my ass if I allowed you to get burned."

Tears filled Ellie's eyes and she smiled for real at him. "Thank you."

He nodded before turning away to approach Justice next. Justice kept the cell phone against his ear but shifted it away from his mouth.

"Report."

Slade sighed. "All three shooters are accounted for. One survived, unfortunately. The police informed me the man is an idiot who can't stop talking. He's claiming to be a member of the Pure Humans terrorist group."

Justice snorted. "We aren't supposed to call them terrorists but go ahead."

"They heard about the press interview and infiltrated it by using photographer credentials. We didn't cover security." Slade growled the words. "It seems, if they had a press pass, they weren't searched."

"From now on we handle all the security where any of our people are concerned."

Slade nodded. "Any word on Fury?"

"He's fighting and has survived this long. We have two blood matches. Searcher and Darkness are inside the room donating blood as needed."

Ellie sipped her iced coffee while she listened to them. She had to admit that everyone had really been great to her. They were guarding her and Fury. The New Species had made sure plenty of their men came to the hospital to be blood donors for Fury. Just regular human blood might have worked but matching their altered chemistry worked better. Justice had explained it to her.

Ellie remembered when they'd reached the hospital. Justice had taken her into one of the bathrooms, talked calmly to her, and promised everything would be done for Fury. He'd led her to a sink while he'd talked. She'd still been in shock as he'd washed her bloody hands as if she were a child and then handed her clothing someone had brought for her with the tags still attached. He'd left her inside the room to change out of her stained, bloody clothes. He hadn't left her side after she'd stepped out of the bathroom. Her attention returned to him.

He shifted the phone back to his mouth. "Yes. I'm still here. What is going on?"

Ellie's heart fluttered when she saw Justice close his eyes. Fear gripped her hard when Justice snapped his phone closed. Ellie continued to stare at him until his eyes opened. His gaze turned her way.

"He's alive, Ellie. They removed both bullets and closed him up. They stopped the bleeding and his vitals are good. Trisha is sure, barring unforeseen circumstances, that he will make it."

Tears slipped down her cheeks when she realized Fury would live. She nodded but was afraid to really believe it until she saw him. Hours passed before they took Fury from recovery to a private room in the ICU. They allowed the NSO to guard him and watch from the observation room next door.

Ellie rubbed her neck, tired, but she didn't want to go to sleep. She watched Fury through a wall of glass, from the same room as the officers. They only allowed her to sit with him at his bedside for a few minutes at a time. A doctor, not Trisha, monitored Fury.

It brought back memories of other times she'd regarded Fury through glass when he'd still been locked inside the testing facility. It made her want to cry once again. It broke her heart to see such a strong, vital man helpless.

Justice sat in the corner. Someone had brought him a laptop computer and he had his earpiece for his cell phone clipped to his ear. He spoke softly to someone every once in a while. Ellie glanced at him. The man never seemed to stop working. Ellie's focus returned to the glass. Fury slept on. The doctor checked Fury's vitals and then left through another door.

"Ellie?" Justice spoke softly.

Ellie turned. "Yes?"

Justice gave a small smile. "He's going to be fine. I told you that Trisha ordered that he stay sedated. New Species don't do well laying flat on a bed because we like to be mobile. It's best to keep him out of it while he heals more or he'll try to get up no matter how bad it hurts him. We're annoyingly stubborn that way, unfortunately."

"I know. I just don't think I'm going to feel better until I hear his voice and look into his eyes."

"I understand. I know Fury requested marriage information. Were you aware of that? He told me he planned to ask you."

"Yes." She sat down. "We talked about it last night actually."

"He loves you. Do you know that?"

"I love him too. He's everything to me."

"You didn't have to tell me that. I see it every time you look at him." He paused. "We never had anything that belonged to us while growing up. Did he tell you that? We never dared care about much either. The staff and doctors always took it away from us or used any perceived weakness against us as a punishment. Marriage means security to him, that he can keep you until he dies. It means that you belong to him and that you won't ever be taken away from him. I wanted you to be clear about. If you do marry him he will expect that to mean forever. Don't agree unless you are sure."

"I am."

His eyes narrowed. "He won't let you divorce him. That's what I'm saying. It would kill him. Marriage is permanent to him. It is vowing that he never has to fear losing you. He will die or kill to protect you and will love you with everything he has to give. I have heard about your human marriages. We're not similar to humans at all in this matter. He would be loyal and Fury would kill another man if you allowed one touch you. We are possessive as hell. It's been forced into us like the DNA they put into our cells. Not only did it physically change us but we carry some of the characteristics. We are protective and aggressive. We are possessive of what is ours. I don't know if Fury explained that to you but I wanted to. We call it mating and it's for life. He already has mated you but part of him has held back because he had to accept that you might leave him. He's committed to you already."

"Thank you but you can save it if you are trying to scare me. I love him. I don't plan on divorce and I sure as hell wouldn't cheat on him." Ellie wasn't offended. She knew Justice just wanted to make sure she understood what she was facing as Fury's wife. "I'm looking forward to spending my life with him. Every second of it."

"He will scare you sometimes. We snarl, growl and dominate. We try to restrain it but it is worse since we found our freedom. We struggle with the animal and the humanity inside us, Ellie. I know how independent women are. Our own females are that way up to a point but they also understand our males. They're able to work around us better. I just wanted to you be aware of it. He won't mean to insult you or your pride. It is just our nature to be aggressive and take control of situations."

"Like when he turned down a job for me without asking?" Ellie smiled at the memory.

"He did that? You took the job anyway."

"He finally asked me if I wanted it. It did irritate me at first."

A smile flicked across Justice's mouth. "I'm sure it did. He wanted to look out for you though."

"I know."

"So you are already aware of the differences."

"Yes."

Justice hesitated. "May I ask you a very personal question?"

"Sure. Go ahead."

"Why did he bind you?"

Bind me? Her mind blanked for a second and then she understood what he meant. *Oh.* Ellie blushed. "You mean with the dishtowel and the tape?"

"Yes."

"He got a bit overexcited and wanted to calm down. He bound my hands so I couldn't touch him."

"He was angry?"

Ellie shook her head, blushing more. "He got overly sexually excited. He wanted it to be good for both of us and he wanted to touch me until I became as aroused as he was. I love to touch him so he bound my hands."

Justice's eyes sparkled with amusement. "I understand now. You don't mind being bound? Our people hate to be restrained. We fear it."

"Nobody ever hurt me the way your people were. I don't have nightmares about being tested and prodded. I'm sure some people would find it frightening to be tied up but I don't. I trust Fury and know he wouldn't hurt me, nor do I have a problem with being dominated. It appeals to me when Fury does it. Is that a good way to put it?"

"Perfect. Thanks, Ellie. I am sorry for my reaction and the resulting harm I caused you. I thought he had lost his mind and had hurt you. Ever since the day he grabbed you in that conference room he hasn't been sane where you are concerned. I believed he really wanted to do you harm."

"He actually did want to kill me that day." Ellie chuckled. "I'm glad he changed his mind."

"I do have some good news."

"What is that?" Ellie leaned back against her chair, relaxing. "I could really use some."

"Something good has come out of all this." Justice motioned toward Fury. "I just concluded a meeting with our public relations director. She informed me the press has backed us a hundred percent. Phone calls and emails have been pouring in supporting us. Your people are horrified over what happened. The cameras were still rolling and a lot of the news stations carried the broadcast live. Did you know that?"

Horror washed through Ellie. "They were broadcasting it live on the news when Fury was shot?"

"It's all right," Justice said, to reassure her. "It's actually a good thing, it seems. Good opinion for New Species has jumped phenomenally. How much do you remember of it? I know you aren't trained to retrain details or react calmly under extreme conditions the way we are."

"Not much. All hell broke loose and then Fury carried me to the safety inside the gates where we couldn't be shot at anymore. Then he collapsed on the ground."

"When the men opened fire," Justice informed her calmly, "Fury reacted. He kicked over the table to shield everyone sitting there from the incoming bullets. He threw himself over your body to make certain the bullets would strike him instead of you. He was shot once and must have realized the table wasn't thick enough to stop them. At that point he lifted you up and ran to get you to safety. He took another bullet while running." Justice paused. "You were the target. They wanted to kill you. He got you to safety before anyone accomplished that."

Tears blinded Ellie and she had to wipe them away. Fury had saved her. She knew he had but hearing exactly what he'd done to protect her broke her heart. He'd taken two bullets for her.

"They did harm me. They shot Fury."

"I know. The good news is, our public relations director believes the general consensus is that every father is wishing right now his daughter grows up to marry a New Species since Fury risked his life to save yours. Women think we are natural heroes." He shrugged and gave her a confused look. "I've been assured that's a good thing for fathers to feel that way."

Ellie couldn't help herself. She laughed. "It's a good thing women tend to be very attracted to those kinds of men."

"I see. Thank you." He winked at her. "I'm supposed to know these things but the truth is, I'm still learning about humans."

"I'm glad the response was favorable toward New Species."

He nodded. "The bottom line is, this turned out to be a positive thing for us. Fury risked his life to save you and that seems to have gone over really well for the general public. We even got word that a lot of your people are pressuring the government and local law authorities to do something against the extremist groups who have targeted us. They are putting pressure on anyone who has supported the protestors to stop. This really could be the best thing that happened, as horrible as that sounds. It gave the world a real view of our situation and made us a bit more human to them."

Ellie's gaze returned to the glass to watch Fury's sleeping face. "I'm glad something good came out of this."

"Me too. He's going to be fine, Ellie."

She nodded. "I know."

* * * * *

The pain tore through Fury when he woke but he thought of Ellie first. He struggled to sit up, to find her. Strong hands held him down.

"Fury?" Ellie's sweet, soft voice called to him.

His eyes opened and there she stood, pale, tired, and hovering just inches above his face. He breathed in her scent to assure she wasn't an apparition. The smell of medicine, cleaners and something foreign nearly overpowered hers though.

"Don't move, Fury," she ordered him. "You were shot." Big tears welled in her beautiful blue eyes. "You saved me and you're going to be fine. You need to stay very still to help you heal."

He studied her face carefully. "You are unhurt?" Fear jolted through him at the thought of what could have happened to his Ellie. "I just wanted to get you out of the line of fire. I couldn't allow anything to happen to you."

"You got me to safety."

He relaxed and the strong hands holding him down released. "Where is Justice?"

"I'm here."

Fury turned his head to stare at his best friend. "Protect my Ellie while I can't. I want a full team guarding her. Only New Species. I only trust our people to make sure no one hurts her. She's priority, Justice. Swear."

"You know it's being done without you having to ask. Heal and don't think about anything but getting better. She'll have around-the-clock New Species officers guarding her and no one will get near her. I give you my word."

Fury's gaze drifted back to Ellie and he moved his arm, reaching up to caress her cheek. His thumb brushed at the tears that slipped down her face. "I love you."

"I love you too, Fury. I was so afraid you'd die on me."

"You won't get rid of me that easily. You're stuck with me forever."

He loved seeing her smile through her tears. She was safe, he'd taken the bullets instead of them striking her, and that's all that mattered to him.

"Good. They gave you some heavy medication to help you sleep but I'm right here, okay?"

"I love you. Did I tell you that?" His voice slurred and he fought to keep his eyes open.

"I love you too and you did tell me. Just get better. I'm fine."

He relaxed, let the pain take him, and blackness came quickly.

Chapter Seventeen

🕹

Ellie watched Tiny, the small brunette, scrub the hallway floor as she laughed. Ellie had to hide her own smile. She glanced at Breeze.

"You'd think washing the floor is cool, to see her do it."

Breeze chuckled. "You should see the joy some of them get scrubbing a toilet. Kind of crazy. I hate to clean them. The chemicals smell bad."

"You guys do tend to have oversensitive noses."

"No kidding. How is Fury doing?"

"Great. He's angry that they are keeping him so drugged up. They had to. He kept trying to get out of bed, demanding his clothes. You should have seen the poor nurse who walked in on that one. Imagine Fury butt naked and snarling for his clothes. She screamed when confronted with that. I think they finally got her to stop running by the time she reached the parking lot."

"Why would that send a woman screaming?" Breeze looked confused.

Ellie chuckled. "He's a big guy, Breeze. He was angry and all that blood of his pumped everywhere. I mean everywhere. Now imagine being some timid woman who walks into a room with a big, muscular naked guy with a major erection and he's snarling at you."

A grin spread across Breeze's face. "Our men are impressive that way."

"Yes, they are," Ellie agreed with a matching grin.

"She wasn't turned on?"

"She was scared for her life."

"What a dumbass."

Ellie laughed. "Where did you pick that one up?"

"I've been watching more television. I'm down these days. What a dumbass. A twit. A brainless floosy."

Laughing harder, Ellie shook her head. "You still need work. You were doing well until you called her a brainless floosy. A floosy is a woman who sleeps with a lot of men. This woman saw a naked one and bolted from terror."

"Got ya." Breeze winked. "I'll watch more television."

"Oh boy. I do have a question."

"Hit me," Breeze smiled. "That is slang." The smile died. "Don't really hit me though. You couldn't hurt me but I might hit you back and that would injure you."

"I understood." Ellie tried to hide her amusement. "I'm sure you could hurt me if you did. My question is, where do you guys come up with your names? They are great but what do you have against regular names like Mary or Tina?"

"That's simple. We aren't regular people. Some of us are named for our best skill and some of us are named for our favorite thing. Some of us go with names we think describe us best. I picked Breeze because I enjoyed the breeze upon my face most of all after I knew freedom."

"My name was picked for me," Halfpint said as she walked to the couch and sat down by Ellie. "When they took me to the medical hospital where they were treating New Species, one of the doctors looked right at me and said that the other women could make two of me. They started calling me Halfpint while I recovered and it stuck."

Ellie fought a laugh but managed to smile instead.

"The doctors who treated us had only seen our experimental prototype females. Halfpint was one of the first of her kind to be treated," Breeze explained.

"Tiny is smaller than I am so when they brought her in, the doctors called her that name." Halfpint beamed.

"Justice picked his name because he wanted it for our people," Breeze informed Ellie. "He is from a testing facility up north and he chose that as his last name."

"I thought most of you didn't have last names." Ellie glanced at Breeze for an answer.

"No. We don't. We'll work on that eventually. When we need one, we'll pick something. Justice has offered to share his last name with anyone who wants it. What do you think of Breeze North?"

"It's catchy," Ellie admitted.

"I like it too. It has meaning and I'm from the same testing facility as Justice."

"I didn't know that."

"Yes. They used to try to breed Justice and me often. He is a good man."

"I know he is," Ellie agreed. The image of Justice and Breeze together shocked her. She was unable to picture them being intimate.

"When you have females and males from the same testing facility chances are we were forced together. The scientists wanted to see if we could have offspring. They thought if one male and female didn't produce, if they switched us, maybe we could conceive with another male."

"We were never given to any of our males," Halfpint whispered in a soft, sad voice. "I wish we had been."

Breeze reached over to pat Halfpint on the arm. "I am sorry. They were always kind and gentle with us. We shared respect and dignity. I wish you had known that as well but if you are ever ready, you will know it one day."

Ellie wanted to ask but didn't. Halfpint looked at Ellie. "I've been one of the luckier ones. They only gave me to an older man who didn't share me. Tiny…" Halfpint blinked back tears. "The man they gave her to happened to be young, strong, and hurt her more. He also made her available to some of his friends. The one who had me was frailer and his strikes weren't very painful. The last few years he wasn't able to use his man part. It failed with age. He became angry when he tried and hit me but he didn't hurt me much. He mostly yelled near the end."

"I'm so sorry." Ellie resisted the urge to try to hug the other woman, to give comfort. "Do you know how they found you?"

"The financial records were traced," Breeze answered. "Anyone who made really large deposits into the Mercile Industries accounts had warrants served on them when we realized some of our women were given away. They found Halfpint. That's how most of the gift females were retrieved."

"It was terrifying," Halfpint whispered, almost seeming afraid someone would overhear. "I heard loud noises and then all these men with guns broke down the door. I thought they'd come to kill me. That's when I saw a woman behind them and she told the men to leave us alone. She talked to me while she removed my chains and led me safely out of where I'd been kept. She promised to take me somewhere I wouldn't be hurt anymore."

"A New Species woman?" Curiosity filled Ellie.

"No," Breeze shook her head. "She's a full human. I forgot her name but she goes on all the raids when a new warrant gets issued. She is the one who takes charge of our females when they are found and brings them to us for care and treatment."

"Her name is Jessie." Halfpint smiled. "She has fire-red hair and really blue eyes. She is small like us. She has the softest voice."

"Ellie?" One of the New Species women drew her attention.

"Yeah?" Ellie stood.

"You might want to go home. I just got a call on the dorm phone saying that Fury left the hospital. He's heading there."

"But he shouldn't to do that until the day after tomorrow."

Breeze snorted from behind Ellie. "Our men don't always do what they are supposed to."

"Oh hell," Ellie sighed. "I'll see you guys tomorrow. I hope he didn't hurt anyone," she muttered under her breath.

* * * * *

Ellie pushed and pulled Fury toward the bed even though he didn't want to go there. She shot a dirty look at Tiger, the NSO officer who smiled, highly amused at the situation. His arms crossed over his chest and he refused to help Ellie make Fury get into bed. He did back up, making his intention to leave clear.

"I don't want to lie down. I've been doing that for a week," Fury growled.

Ellie shook her head. "You are going to rest or I swear I'll borrow a Taser gun, shoot your ass, and tie you to the bed."

Fury growled viciously at her and his dark eyes narrowed. Ellie growled back at him and tugged harder. "Don't snarl at me. I will do it right back. Now let's get you undressed." She glared up at him. "You are supposed to be in the hospital still. Don't give me any shit, Fury. I love you to death but if you don't lie down, I will borrow his Taser gun. I mean it."

Fury stopped fighting. He suddenly showed his sharp teeth as he grinned. "If I get into bed naked will you take off your clothes with me?"

Ellie gasped at him. "There won't be any of that. You just had surgery a week ago, were at death's door, and you're not cleared for that yet. Now behave."

"I'll be in the next room." Tiger laughed.

Ellie spun to watch the security officer leave. Her gaze flew back to Fury. "You knew he hadn't left and said that on purpose."

He chuckled. "He's gone now. Take off your clothes and I'll strip too. We'll both go to bed. I can look and touch at least." He turned and wrapped his arm around her. "I want to feel you against my skin. That will make me heal faster."

"I didn't know touching skin to skin helped your healing process."

"It doesn't but I'd feel better."

Ellie laughed. "I'll make a deal with you. You get undressed willingly, climb into bed, and I'll make you some lunch. After you eat, I'll come lie down with you."

"Naked?"

"No. You're supposed to be resting but I might scratch your back and play with your hair. You'll enjoy that."

He softly growled. "Sweetness, I'd lie down on a bed of nails if you wanted to touch me and play with me but it's not my back or my hair I want you to put your hands on."

Ellie licked her lips, thinking, and decided it might not hurt him if she just rubbed him with lotion if he held real still. Fury growled, pressing his body closer to hers. She nodded.

"I'll get lunch. You get into that bed. I'll be back in a few minutes."

He released her. Ellie moved toward the door. She heard material tear and turned her head to look over her shoulder to discover Fury watching her. He'd torn his shirt open instead of taking the time to carefully pull it over his head and the bandage on his side. She laughed.

"In a hurry?"

"Run to the kitchen and back."

Ellie opened the bedroom door with a laugh and nearly walked into Tiger. The man inched back, grinning. He looked highly amused.

"Don't tell me. Great sense of smell and keen hearing?"

"I'll guard him from the living room. That way, I have enough rooms between us not to hear what he wants you to play with."

Ellie fixed Fury a turkey sandwich and grabbed a soda. She also took him a bag of chips when she headed for the bedroom. Even if he arrived home days early Ellie was thrilled to have him with her. She'd wanted to stay at the hospital full time but the hospital staff didn't want her there. The media had become a circus and it made it worse when she was with him.

She closed the bedroom door firmly. There wasn't a lock but she didn't worry about it since Tiger knew not to come in. Fury was on the bed, obviously naked under the sheet, a happy grin on his handsome face, and he had pushed pillows behind his back to comfortably wait. The sheet tented over his lap. Ellie saw that and laughed.

"A little excited to see me with lunch?" She teased. "I know you like turkey but geez, Fury."

His dark gaze sparkled. "Are you really going to make me eat that first?"

She perched on the edge of the mattress and handed him the plate. Her attention lowered back to the impressive pole keeping up the "tent". "I'd put this on your lap but there's no room." She chuckled. "Eat up, sweetheart."

With a groan, Fury grabbed the sandwich and took a huge bite. He barely chewed. Ellie laughed and opened his soda to hold out to him. He took a drink but kept his gaze fixed on her. Ellie stood and headed toward the bathroom.

"Where are you going?" Fury growled at her as his smile faded.

"I'm coming back. Patience."

"I have none."

Ellie opened the cupboard inside the bathroom and found lotion. She grabbed a hand towel. She returned to the bedroom brandishing both for him to see. "How does a massage sound?"

"Don't tease me. It's been a long, lonely week."

Ellie sat on the edge of the bed and uncapped the bottle. She poured lotion into her hands and used her elbow to shove the sheet away from his lap. Fury groaned and arched against her palms the second she touched his hard, aroused cock. Ellie leaned forward, licking at his chest. She had to avoid the tape that kept his bandage in place. He'd taken one shot to the back near his side and another shot to the back near his shoulder. He had been lucky his shoulder blade hadn't been shattered by the bullet.

"I love you," he groaned.

Ellie stroked him slowly, loving every second of touching the velvety skin that wrapped around his steel-hard shaft. She teased him with her mouth from one nipple to the next while her hands massaged him from the crown to the base of his cock. Fury growled and swelled to a substantial size. She looked down. This time she wanted to see him come.

Fury snarled her name as he tensed against her. His entire body quivered when he started to come. A lump formed on the underside of his cock just above his balls at the base of his shaft. That's what she felt when he was buried deep in her pussy at the end of sex. The sight fascinated her as it continued to bulge.

She remembered his claim of being a hard shooter. She curved one of her hands over the top of his cock head while she stroked his shaft faster, fisting him a little tighter. Hot jets of his white semen blasted hard against her palm and she realized he hadn't been kidding about choking her if he was really excited. She lifted her gaze to watch his face.

He threw his head back and shouted her name as she milked him of every drop of semen. Ellie smiled as she continued touching his oversensitive flesh until Fury grabbed her hands to make her stop.

Ellie kissed Fury on his lips. Her tongue teased his bottom lip. He groaned her name as his hands reached for her breasts.

"Do you feel better? More relaxed?"

He growled in response.

Ellie pulled away from his exploring hands to clean him up with the towel and threw it toward the bathroom. She put a little distance between them. Fury's gaze locked with hers.

"I want you," he growled.

Ellie squealed in surprise when Fury lunged suddenly, grabbed her arm and gave her a hard yank that sent her sprawling on top of the bed. Her back hit the mattress and Fury came down over her to cage her to the bed under him. Ellie stared up at him.

"You're going to open up your wounds, Fury."

"I won't." He reached down to grab hold of Ellie's skirt, fisting it with his hand. He pulled hard to jerk the material up Ellie's body to her waist.

"Fury, stop."

His dark gaze met hers. "I'm still having lunch. You're on the menu."

Desire seeped right through to Ellie's bones. "But your stitches—"

"I'll be careful not to pull on them." He smiled. "I'll keep to the high ground so I don't move much. What is that you call it? Your button? I'm in the mood to lick a button, Ellie."

"I should say no but I can't," Ellie rasped, her entire body coming alive with the promise of what he wanted to do. She pressed against Fury's hand as he wiggled his fingers into the edge of her panties. He hooked the center section of them and yanked hard. He threw the torn material away from the bed.

"You know you should stop wearing those things," he growled. "They just annoy me."

"Okay."

He chuckled. "No argument?"

She shook her head. Fury's fingers massaged her clit, teasing her, and driving her passion higher. He shifted lower on her body. She opened her thighs wider so he could settle between them. "I'll burn all of them if it makes you happy as long as you don't stop touching me."

"Burn them," he urged softly, sliding down the bed even lower over Ellie. He used his free hand and jerked her shirt up to her breasts. His mouth brushed her lower stomach and his tongue traced her bellybutton. "Burn the bras too."

"Anything," Ellie moaned, ablaze with passion. She'd missed his touch so much she already hurt to come though he'd barely started. She moaned. "I love your thumb and the way you torment me."

Fury inched lower, his mouth sweeping over the material bunched over her hips to find skin again. He pushed her thighs apart wider. Fury growled and then lowered his face. Ellie clawed at the bedding and moaned his name, arching into his mouth when he licked her pussy.

"I missed your taste," he rasped. "I'm addicted to you."

His tongue wiggled, found the exact spot that drove her mindless, and she moaned to let him know how amazing it felt. He pressed tighter against her, keeping the flat of his tongue there to rub back and forth over her clit.

"Fury," she moaned.

"I said 'stop', damn it!" Tiger yelled.

The bedroom door flew open. Fury's head jerked up but his fist grabbed hold of the material bunched at her waist to yank Ellie's skirt down enough to fill the space between his chin and her body to hide the view of her exposed pussy. Confused and in a daze, Ellie twisted her head. A woman and Tiger jerked to a halt just inside the door. The woman stood open-mouthed in shock. Tiger laughed before he spun around to present his back.

"I tried to stop her." Tiger chuckled. "Sorry, Fury. Sorry, Ellie. This is the home-healthcare nurse."

Fury growled. Ellie frantically pushed at her skirt to lower it down her legs more but Fury's body prevented her from managing it. She wiggled away from Fury's shoulders until she could sit up all the way. Her gaze ran down Fury's body, sprawled on his stomach over the bed. Most of the sheet had twisted across his hips covering his ass, barely. Ellie then looked at the twenty-something brunette nurse who gawked at both of them. The nurse snapped her mouth closed but then it opened again just as quickly.

"You shouldn't be doing that," the woman preached. "Mr. Fury, you're going to open your wounds. Ms. Brower, shame on you!"

"Get out," Fury growled. He grabbed Ellie's ankle when she tried to climb off the bed. "Now."

The nurse had a pretty face but her expression was stern at the moment. "I will not. It's a good thing I got here when I did."

"I don't think they agree with you," Tiger snorted with a laugh. "I think you have really bad timing. Right, Fury and Ellie?"

"Get her out of here," Fury demanded.

"I can't." Tiger turned back around and shrugged. "She's your nurse. She's going to be living here for the next week. That was the condition Justice set, since Ellie is gone every day, at work. You agreed so you could come home early to recover with Ellie. Sorry, Fury. It's out of my hands."

The nurse shook her head. "You know he was shot twice to protect you. Wasn't that enough for you, Ms. Brower? He needs to sleep and not move around." The woman bent down to the floor. She straightened, holding Ellie's torn panties between her finger and thumb. She glared at Ellie. "This kind of thing is not acceptable."

Tiger leaned against the wall, clutched his stomach, and started laughing again. Ellie knew her face must be bright red while Fury looked ready to kill something. The nurse tossed Ellie's torn panties into the wastebasket by the door.

"Everyone but Mr. Fury needs to leave this room right now. I need to make sure he didn't tear his stitches and he needs his pain medication."

Ellie jerked her ankle, which was still in Fury's grip. The second he released her, she climbed off the other side of the bed. She walked to the dresser and yanked open the drawer containing her panties. She knew her face continued to flame red when she marched into the bathroom and closed the door behind her. She hurried but could hear everything going on in the next room.

"And I thought this would be a boring job," Tiger said and chuckled loudly.

"Shut up," Fury growled. "Don't ever come into our bedroom again when that door is closed. Ever."

Ellie walked out wearing panties again. She marched back to the dresser and opened another drawer to pull out a pair of sweatpants for Fury. She met the glare of the nurse. "You need to leave or turn your back while I help Fury dress."

The nurse snorted at her. "No need. I just plan to give him a sponge bath."

"I'll give him a sponge bath. You can give him his pills. You need to leave so he can put these on."

The nurse and Ellie squared off. "It's my job to care for Mr. Fury."

Ellie's mouth tightened. "It's my job to take care of him. I also happen to be a nurse."

"Uh-oh," Tiger groaned softly. "Territory fight."

Fury frowned, incensed he'd been interrupted from enjoying his Ellie—again! All he'd thought about was getting home to her so they could be alone without the watchful looks of security and hospital staff. He'd missed holding her in his arms, hearing her laugh and talking to her late into the night while they cuddled. He'd also missed her taste and having her hands on his body. He had recovered well enough to make love to her.

The nurse shouldn't have arrived until much later and he wasn't happy with the one they'd sent. She glared at Ellie in a way that had him fighting back a snarl. No one should look at his woman with anger, and if he hadn't promised to allow a nurse into his home, he'd make Tiger escort her to the main gate immediately.

New Species women were protective of their possessions. As he watched Ellie, saw how her shoulders were set and her mouth tense, he realized that Tiger wasn't far off the mark. The two women were about to fight for dominance.

No way would he allow his woman to fight another. Ellie could be harmed. He forced himself to relax, hoping that his calmness would also soothe her, show her that she should feel secure being his female and that the other one posed no threat. He would never allow any woman except Ellie to touch him. He'd make it clear who bathed him, who dressed him if he needed help and that the female nurse took Ellie's commands. He took a deep breath.

"Ellie gives me baths," Fury stated clearly. "Only Ellie."

The nurse glared at Fury. "She isn't your nurse. I am."

"I don't give a damn," Fury snarled, his temper rising toward this rude human. "Ellie is the only woman I want touching me. Ellie?" Ellie turned her head and her gaze met his. "Calm down. I belong to you." He kept eye contact with her to make sure she'd know he meant it. "I don't have affairs. You are the only woman I want." *The only woman I'll ever want for the rest of my life*, he silently amended. He was certain that mating was definitely forever. Every second with Ellie only tightened the bond he had with her. "You're it for me."

"I know that." Her tense expression softened.

"Don't tear out her throat." He decided to use humor to grab Ellie's attention and if it frightened the nurse, so be it. He hid his chuckle. "No matter how much she deserves it for walking in on us."

The nurse gasped and jumped back from Ellie. "They told me you were human. You're New Species?" Panic laced her voice.

Amusement sparked inside Fury at the annoying human's fear. "She's New Species all right. She's with me."

Ellie sighed. "I'm as human as you are. Not exactly a great thing in my opinion." She approached Fury. "I wasn't going to tear out her throat. Geez. I just don't like the idea of her touching you all over."

He smiled. "Jealous?"

She gave a slight nod. Her anger seeped out of her expression completely. "I give the sponge baths."

Fury reached out to clasp Ellie's hand. "Only you. Now, can I have another sandwich? I'm hungry still." He fought back frustration. "My meal was interrupted."

A smile touched Ellie's lips. She dropped the folded sweatpants over his sheet-covered lap. "Since we're not alone, put those on." Ellie faced the nurse. "You follow me. I'll show you to the guestroom while Fury gets dressed." She shot Tiger a dirty look. "You...stop grinning. It's not funny. Can you stick around for a minute and make sure he doesn't fall over when he puts those on?"

"Sure thing." Tiger chuckled. "This is definitely not a boring assignment."

"Bite me," Ellie muttered as she passed him.

"That's my job," Fury called out, laughing. Tiger laughed with him.

* * * * *

Ellie wanted to murder Belinda Thomas. She unclenched her hands and tried to take deep breaths but it didn't help. She counted to ten slowly. *Nope, I'm still pissed.* Ellie unclenched her teeth. The last thing she needed was to have to visit a dentist for broken teeth. Her temper boiled.

The nurse was with Fury again. The woman currently sported a pair of cut-off jeans that should have gotten her arrested for indecent exposure and had topped off her bad fashion choice with a bra-like top. With her tan, flat stomach revealed, she bent over in front of Fury while pretending to vacuum the already clean floor. Fury's gaze seemed riveted on the inches of bare butt the woman flaunted.

"Fury?"

His attention instantly shifted to Ellie and he smiled. "Hi."

Belinda jerked with surprise, shot Ellie an unfriendly frown as she straightened and turned off the vacuum. "You're home from work early today." It sounded close to an accusation.

Ellie nodded. "Is that the new nursing outfit? Someone should talk to your boss."

Anger flashed in the nurse's eyes. "It's hot. I'm not required to wear a nursing outfit while doing home care."

"Well, you should be. I vacuumed this floor yesterday. You didn't need to do it again."

Dark eyebrows arched. "Maybe you should learn how to vacuum better," the woman replied snottily. "I do a lot of things really well. I guess I'm just better at these kinds of things than you are." The nurse winked at Fury.

Ellie took a step toward her. "You little—"

"Ellie!" Fury's voice rose. "Come here. I missed you."

Ellie walked to Fury instead of decking the bitchy nurse the way she wanted to. Her anger remained as she sat on the bed. Fury had the nerve to look amused and that made her madder. He seemed to enjoy her jealousy and she felt green with it. Belinda Thomas had been flirting outrageously with him for days.

"I'm going to go heat up some oil," Belinda called out. "I need to rub your shoulder. It will get stiff if I don't." She walked out of the bedroom carrying the vacuum.

"Don't let her get to you," Fury urged softly.

"I just walked into our bedroom to catch you staring at her ass," Ellie ground out. "And if she touches you with hot oil, I swear to God I'm moving out, Fury."

His amusement vanished instantly. "I am not attracted to her, Ellie. I've been looking at her ass but it is because her skin is weird. Your ass doesn't look that way."

"Weird?" Ellie tried hard not to blow up.

"She has folds of skin lining the bottom of her ass and there are dents. Your ass is full and smooth. I love your ass."

"You're staring at her ass because she has cellulite?"

"I've got nothing else to do. She took my remote and stated that television was bad for my recovery. I wanted to make her give it back but Tiger said I'm not allowed to torture its location from her to find out where she hid it."

Ellie stared at him. "I can't live like this. She's flirting with you. Maybe you don't know it but she is. She's driving me crazy. I'm a nurse. I can take care of you and I don't care if you promised Justice he could send one here for you."

"You're jealous."

"Yes, damn it. I am."

Fury grinned. "I love you too. Don't feel that way. You're the only one I want. Don't let her get to you. I know she is flirting. She can do that all she wants to but it doesn't matter. I feel nothing for her." He pulled Ellie into his lap.

"You're the one I'm hard for. Feel that? All for you. Only for you."

"Time for that shoulder massage," Belinda called out.

Ellie closed her eyes. Fury pulled her tighter into his arms until her head rested on his good shoulder.

"Go away," Fury growled at Belinda. "Ellie will massage me."

"Now, Fury," Belinda huffed. "I'm a professional. You should tell your little friend there to go do something while I tend to that shoulder."

Ellie tensed. Fury snarled, obviously enraged.

"Ellie is not my little friend. She's going to be my wife. Never talk about her as if she matters so little when she is everything to me. I also told you not to call me by my name. It is Mr. Fury to you. I ordered you to get out and damn it," he roared, "get out!"

Ellie's ears rang. She heard Belinda gasp and then the door slammed closed behind her. Fury's hands rubbed her back.

"She's gone."

Ellie lifted her head. "Thank you. I trust you. I do. It's just that…" She shook her head. "I know it will be better once you're all healed up and that bitch is gone."

"We're under a lot of stress with other people inside our home and we don't get much alone time." He paused and cupped Ellie's face in his hands. "I can't wait to be alone with you again. There's nothing I want more than for us to just be together."

"I know. She just pushes all my buttons, Fury. I honestly can't think of anyone I dislike more and she just throws herself at you. Can you imagine how you'd feel if I had a male nurse who hit on me as hard as she does you?"

"I can't imagine." He grinned. "No male would dare. It would be tough for him to come onto you with broken hands to prevent him from touching you and a broken jaw to prevent him from speaking to you."

She laughed. "Oh, don't give me ideas on what to do that that woman. I can't wait until she leaves. Thank God it's going to be soon."

He laughed. "Yes. Thank your God for that." His eyes sparkled. "I've been promised a hot oil massage. Want to give me one?"

"I'd love to."

"Not my shoulder," he growled softly. "And get out of those jeans. I hope you kept your word and aren't wearing panties."

"Hey, I promised to burn all of them if you didn't stop touching me but you stopped that day when Nurse Witch walked in." Ellie climbed off his lap and took a few steps from the bed. She unzipped her jeans and spread them open. "But I'm not wearing them anyway."

Fury's gaze locked on the skin she exposed. He growled and grabbed the bedding, shoving it off. He rose to his feet quickly. Ellie licked her lips as she glanced nervously at the door.

"We need to put a lock on that."

Fury growled. "She wouldn't dare."

Ellie put up a finger. "Hold that thought." She turned and ran to the small desk. She grabbed the chair and carried it to the door to wedge it under the doorknob. She spun and grabbed her shirt, yanked it over her head, and tossed it to the floor.

"You didn't burn the bras." Fury gripped the waist of his sweatpants, shoved them down and kicked them away.

"I had to work. You don't want me bouncing around in front of other men, do you?"

"I'd have to kill someone who stared at *my* breasts."

Ellie laughed, stepping out of her jeans. "Your breasts, huh?"

Fury reached her. "Mine." His hands cupped them. Ellie wrapped her arms around his neck.

"Massage first?"

"No. I got to be first last time. Lie down for me, Ellie. You owe me a meal."

Ellie slipped out of his arms and climbed on the bed. She flipped onto her back and smiled at Fury as he came after her. "If someone interrupts this time, I'm going to have to kill someone." Fury growled as his hands gripped her thighs, his hands caressing her skin. "I have a gun inside the nightstand drawer."

Ellie laughed. "You shouldn't have told me that. I might use it on that nurse."

Fury winked at her. "I'll teach you how to fire it later."

Chapter Eighteen

ဢ

"No." Fury growled the words. His dark eyes flashed rage.

Ellie watched him grimly. "Justice stated it was important. The public wants to see me and make sure that we're fine now. I could tell them you're doing well and healing."

"No." Fury crossed his arms over his chest.

Ellie took her hand off the lower portion of the phone. "He won't allow it, Justice. I'm sorry."

Ellie listened and then hung up. She sat down on the edge of the bed. "He understands and he'll just release a press statement from us. He said someone would bring it by later for our approval, before tonight when it's released."

"I don't care what it says. Call him back and tell him to say whatever he thinks needs to be said. I trust his judgment."

"Fine." Ellie hesitated. "Why don't you want me to talk to reporters?"

"You aren't going anywhere out there. Someone shot at you. I am not going to allow you to be a target again."

Her anger eased. "You're worried about me."

"I always worry about you. It's my job to protect you and that means I won't allow anyone to make target practice out of you again."

"Okay."

"Okay? You are complying? No argument?" He didn't look completely convinced. "You won't go behind my back to talk to the reporters, will you?"

"I already told Justice no. I'd never do that anyway." Ellie frowned at him.

"You don't like me telling you what to do."

She shrugged. "I know it's because you are worried about me and you have reason for it since you were shot twice the last time we were in front of reporters."

Fury relaxed on the bed. "Thank you." His tone roughened.

"It's time to change your bandages and give you your medications," Belinda said as she walked into the bedroom carrying her medical bag.

Annoyance rolled through Ellie. She made a face at Fury to show him her thoughts but then stood. "I think I'll go take a shower."

"Hurry back."

Ellie shot a dirty look at the nurse as she walked into the bathroom. Belinda ignored the fact Ellie existed. It had been that way since Fury had yelled at the nurse. No one had walked into their bedroom again once the door closed though. Ellie stripped out of her clothes and adjusted the water. She was tired and it had been a long day at work.

A loud sigh passed her lips when she stepped under the hot spray of water. She closed her eyes, tried to relax and just enjoy the moment.

Her mind drifted to work, though, immediately. One of the human security guards had done a walkthrough of the dorm and had surprised one of the small New Species women. She'd had a screaming fit the second she'd encountered him inside the kitchen.

It had taken Ellie an hour to calm the woman. Afterward, Ellie had to make phone calls to the security office, to Darren Artino, and to Justice. She had requested that no male security guards be allowed in the dorms unless an emergency took place until the new group of women adjusted to being around men. It had been an ordeal to get security to agree but Ellie had won that battle with Justice's help. To make it worse, she had come home to face Nurse Bitch and all the stress that came with her.

The bathroom door suddenly jerked open. The door hit the wall so hard Ellie jumped. She grabbed for the shower door and yanked it open. Fury stood inside the room, anger darkening his features. Ellie grabbed for a towel and then flinched, pain shooting through her hand, and looked down. She saw a scratch from hitting the top of the corner of the metal, it had sliced her palm slightly. Blood rose up but she ignored it. It was tiny and her concern fixed on Fury.

"What is it? What's wrong?"

Fury slammed the bathroom door closed, sealing them inside together. "That woman has to leave!"

Ellie wrapped the towel around her body and stepped out of the shower. Water dripped everywhere but she ignored it. "Nurse Bitch? You're preaching to the choir."

"That one, yes!" Fury trembled and had paled as he stared at Ellie. "I did not kiss her. She grabbed me and put her lips on mine. She tried to push her tongue inside my mouth." He snarled. "I shoved her off me and she started to undress." He snarled, enraged. "I came in here. I want her out of my house."

Now Ellie was angrier than Fury. "She kissed you?"

"She gave me a shot and changed my bandage. She suddenly tried to kiss me when she threw herself on my lap. Get her out of here or I will hurt her, Ellie."

"Stand in line."

Ellie dropped her towel and yanked her nightgown off the hook by the door. She didn't want to take the time to go in the other room to get fresh clothes and she didn't want to put her dirty ones back on. She studied Fury, taking note of his tense features. He watched her silently.

"I'll take care of it."

"I did not flirt with her to provoke that."

Ellie nodded. "I believe you."

Fury suddenly grabbed Ellie as she tried to storm past him. He pulled her into his arms and cupped her face. "Kiss me."

"Let me take care of her first."

"Kiss me," he snarled. "I have her scent on me and I can't stand it."

Understanding dawned. She knew how sensitive Fury's sense of smell could be and he liked her scent a hell of a lot, always rubbing against her just to get it on his clothes. It was a little strange but great to know he wanted to smell her wherever he went.

She turned into his arms and kissed him. She rubbed her body against his. He didn't seem to care that she was damp and it seeped through her nightgown to his clothes. She ran her hands along his face and neck. She made sure to rub anywhere that she thought Belinda might have grabbed him.

Her feet left the floor and the wall pressed against her back suddenly. Fury's hands slid down to her hips. He lifted her higher, spreading her legs, until they were wrapped around his waist. Reality intruded and Ellie struggled inside Fury's arms. She released his face and let her legs drop.

She tore her mouth from his. She instantly saw a smear of blood on his jaw and cheek from her forgotten injury. "Let me go. I bled on you."

Fury instantly looked worried. "You're bleeding? Are you hurt? I was too distracted to notice and was trying not to inhale that woman's scent clinging to me."

She blushed. "I just scratched my hand on the shower door. I guess I caught a rough edge. I just need a bandage and then I'll deal with Belinda. I also have PMS so she's going to be sorry she screwed with you today."

Something in Fury's eyes changed. Fury inhaled. "I don't smell that it's your time."

"That is so freaky. Breeze warned me that you guys can smell a woman on her period from half a mile away. She told me how to deal with that when it happens."

Fury softly growled. "She needed to."

"She said otherwise I'd never make it home without being sniffed after." Ellie suddenly smiled. "She was joking, right?"

"It's a turn-on," Fury growled, passion darkening his gaze.

"Why?"

"Have you ever let a man touch you at that time?"

Ellie shook her head. She hadn't. Her ex-husband had been disgusted by it and Ellie hadn't really had a desire to press the issue. She didn't exactly feel sexy at that time of the month, between the bloating and cramps.

"You're hotter and wetter inside." He moved closer to Ellie, pressing her tighter against the wall. "Did I mention it's a turn-on?" He growled at her and then firmly pinned her against the wall again.

"Fury, back off." Ellie laughed and gently pushed at his shoulders to put some space between them. "I haven't started it yet. My palm is still bleeding and I need to go talk to that nurse. Hold that thought. It shouldn't take long and we can resume this."

Fury growled deeper, refused to back away and kept her pinned tightly. Unease inched up her spine. She shoved at him harder.

"Fury? Please? You're crushing me. You need to let me go."

He backed off but looked as though he didn't want to. Ellie inched her body between his and the wall until she broke free.

Ellie shook her head at him. "Back off, big guy. I mean it. I have some nurse ass to kick out of this house and then we'll get you back into bed." She rubbed him. "I'll take care of you then. You're still not completely healed. You heard Trisha. If you took me standing up you might open up your stitches. Just a few more days and we can have sex any way we want but for now we still have to take it real easy, on a bed."

Heat boiled through Fury's system, and he fought hard to control it. He frowned, fighting the urge to howl. He breathed hard, watching Ellie move around the bathroom. It wasn't directed at her but he got really angry all of a sudden.

He wanted her so much it actually hurt. His body burned with the need to grab her, pin her to the wall again, and take her. His hands fisted at his sides as he fought the urge. She'd said no and he'd never hurt Ellie, never force her, but he battled his desire to grab her.

What the hell is wrong with me? No answer came to him as he breathed in and out. The hot flash grew stronger and as he inhaled Ellie's scent his dick hardened until it throbbed painfully.

It has to be a reaction to that woman coming on to me and touching me. He knew he'd become seriously addicted to Ellie's scent, needing it around him, or he longed for it. He just didn't realize how strong that compulsion had grown until another woman had touched him.

This has to be one of those animal traits rearing its ugly head. He needed to get a grip on it for Ellie's sake but the longer he stood there the harder it was to even try to conceal his need to fuck Ellie. He wanted his cock inside her.

The urge to taste her blood made him drool a little as the scent of it teased his nose. It shocked him, left him a little scared—horrified even. He backed up, his breathing increasing to pants and tried to get control of his mind.

The urges built until he couldn't contain them any longer. Fury spun suddenly and punched the wall. The agony of pain shooting up his arm helped. The anger receded enough for him to think again.

Surprise froze Ellie for a second at Fury's violent outburst but she understood how upset the hellish nurse could make someone. She could easily relate to his reaction. "Still mad about what she did? Did nailing the wall help?"

He turned, shaking out the hand he'd just slammed into the drywall. "No. I'm mad that I can't touch you the way I want."

"I know but we don't want you to have to go back to the hospital, Fury. Now go back to bed and I'll handle Nurse Kissy Force. We'll have sex after, on the bed, real slow so you don't strain anything." She shoved a adhesive bandage over her palm. "I'm getting rid of her once and for all."

Fury snorted and then yanked the bathroom door open. Ellie followed him into the bedroom, left him there, and went in search of the nurse. She didn't take the time to put on panties since her nightshirt fell to her knees. It wouldn't take her long to tell Belinda Thomas to pack her shit and get out. She'd never seen Fury so agitated.

Ellie found the nurse sitting on the couch looking irritated, holding the remote control to the television. Tiger reclined on a chair by the door, flipping through a magazine. His eyebrows rose as Ellie walked into the living room wearing her nightgown.

"Little early for bed, isn't it?" Tiger glanced at his watch. "It's only four."

"You," Ellie pointed at Belinda, "are no longer needed. You're fired. You're done. Call it whatever you want but go pack your things and get out." She faced Tiger. "Get her off Homeland grounds pronto or I swear she's going to the medical center on a stretcher. She's not to come back here ever again."

"You can't tell me what to do." Belinda glared at Ellie. "I've been hired by Justice North to take care of Fury. He's the only one who can fire me."

"Fine." She stomped to the phone. She knew Justice's number by heart now. She dialed quickly.

"Justice North here," his calm voice announced.

"Belinda Thomas just threw herself at Fury. He's killing mad and I'm worse. I just told her to pack her shit and leave but she informed me that you're the only one who can fire her."

He paused. "She what?"

"She threw herself at Fury. I took a shower and she mauled him on the bed. He came into the bathroom in a rage. I'm lucky he didn't crush me trying to get her scent off him. He is beyond angry, Justice. I've never seen him so mad. We both want her gone and don't need her anymore. I'll take the next few days off work to care for him myself. Just please get her out of here."

Justice's voice deepened. "Are you all right? Did he hurt you?"

"I'm fine. He is just enraged that she hit on him and was really aggressive, trying to get her scent off him to get mine back."

"Did he hurt you? Did he have rough sex with you? Do I need to send the doctor?"

"We didn't have sex. He just rubbed against me and almost crushed me against a wall. Who cares about that? I want this woman gone, Justice. He wants her gone. Will you fire her or do I have to break her arms to make certain she can't work here anymore? Trust me, I'll do it."

"I'm on my way. Hand the phone to Tiger now."

Ellie marched the phone over to Tiger. He appeared alarmed when he accepted it. Ellie glared at Belinda. Flames should have been shooting from her nostrils from the level of burning rage she experienced.

"Pack your shit. He's on his way to fire you."

Belinda stood. "You—"

"What?" Ellie shouted, totally pissed off.

Green eyes glittered with anger. "You're going to get yours." Belinda stormed down the hallway.

Ellie tried to force back her temper. She glanced at Tiger. He leaned against the front door, away from her, and the tense expression on his face made her frown. She stared at him as he hung up.

"Are you all right?" Ellie was concerned since Tiger actually appeared a bit pale.

"Ellie, come with me now." He opened the front door wide.

She glanced down. "I'm not going outside in my nightgown. Why would you want to talk to me out there? That woman is packing and can't overhear us from her room."

Tiger stalked toward Ellie quickly. "Damn it, woman. Don't argue with me. You need to get out of the house now."

Ellie retreated a few feet. Tiger stopped and sniffed at her with a frown. "I smell blood on you. You told Justice that Fury didn't harm you."

"He didn't." She held up her palm to show off the pink bandage wrapped around the curve of her hand. "I sliced it a little getting out of the shower. Fury would never hurt me."

He sniffed again. "I don't smell much of your blood."

"That's because it was just a scratch. It didn't bleed much."

"We need to leave right now."

She backed up more. "I'm not going anywhere with you. I'm not even dressed and if you think I'm leaving Nurse Bitch alone with Fury, think again."

"Ellie," Tiger hissed, "they pumped Fury full of our healing drugs to help him recover faster. We have been assessing him for signs of threat but now he's acting hostile. You're in danger here and need to go to safety." He glanced at his watch. "He was given his medication about fifteen minutes ago, correct?"

Ellie glared at him. "Belinda told me she would give him his meds when I headed for the shower. Fury did say she gave him a shot. Why would I be in danger?"

Tiger moved quickly and grabbed Ellie around her waist, spun her, and clamped his hand over her mouth. Her feet left the floor. Tiger strode quickly toward the front door with her struggling, caught inside his arms. They were outside in seconds.

"Quiet," Tiger growled next to her ear. "And don't be afraid. He'll smell it. You said he took your scent. Just take some deep breaths and I'll explain it all to you, okay? You have to keep your voice down. Promise me?"

Ellie was furious, not afraid, when she nodded against his hand. The body holding hers relaxed as he lowered her to the ground and released her. His hand left her mouth. Ellie spun to glare up at him.

"What was that for?" She hissed.

"Don't you realize how injured Fury was?" Tiger frowned. "A human would have died. It's been just over a week but he's walking around. He's been healing really fast. Didn't you wonder about that?"

"You guys just do that faster. Fury told me it's normal for New Species."

"We do to a certain degree but not as fast as Fury has, without help. This is classified but as Fury's mate, you're considered New Species. You need to be told. Not all of the records were destroyed when we were discovered. Some of the doctors hadn't kept all their notes and research on the computer systems they destroyed when the testing facilities were breached. In some cases we were even able to get the formulas and exact chemical compositions of some of the drugs they used on us."

The news surprised her. "Why keep it a secret?"

Fury

He hesitated. "Did you ever wonder why the President and the United States was so eager to hand over a military base to us for our home? To be so agreeable with whatever demands we made? We had some humans who were very sympathetic, very happy to give Justice advice. They told him about sovereignty. We demanded equal human rights and were given them as well. New Species govern themselves on American soil, on the land we were given. We were also extended diplomatic immunity in many ways for New Species. We're considered American citizens but given special concessions."

"Of course you're Americans. You were born here. It's only right you are given a safe place to live. There are so many hate groups out there that it wouldn't be safe for any of you to try to merge with regular society right off the bat."

"Mercile Industries were given billions of dollars to help fund drug studies and research for decades. The President signed off on the last six years of the money given to Mercile. It came from military funds."

Ellie stared at him, confused. "How does this apply to Fury right now?"

"Mercile promised to create drugs that would make the armed forces stronger, better fighters, heal faster after battle, and even heighten their senses. A pharmaceutical advantage that other countries wouldn't have. They vaccinate our fighting forces to prevent them from catching diseases when they send them to other countries. Imagine giving them a shot that would make them stronger, faster, and harder to kill in battle situations. It would win wars easier, quicker, with a lot less casualties. No one knew Mercile had crossed moral and legal boundaries to gain the advancements they were promising to develop. Every dollar they were given helped enslave us and paid for blood, sweat, and torture."

People would be outraged if they discovered their tax dollars had been sunk into something so vile. Every human rights organization on the planet would be up in arms and

319

some countries might accuse the government of horrific crimes.

"That's awful," she whispered. "I'm so sorry. What does this have to do with Fury and why you believe he could be dangerous? I want to get back inside, Tiger. Just get to the point."

"They created a lot of drugs and a few of the recovered reports stated that some humans who volunteered to take them died. One batch of the drugs increased healing in New Species at a phenomenal rate." He cleared his throat. "It also drove a small percentage of New Species temporarily insane when tested on us. The doctors didn't drop the study. According to the few notes on it, they believed an insane, injured person on the mend was worth the temporary insanity. New Species who had that adverse effect of rage-driven insanity always recovered fully. The humans in that study weren't so lucky. Either they died, or if their bodies healed, their minds were permanently destroyed."

Her mind clicked. "You were worried Fury would go insane?"

"Yes. The notes weren't complete. We don't know a time frame on when the insanity strikes or how long it lasts if he's one of the unfortunate ones. Aggression and murderous rages are part of those side effects."

"And you believe he's exhibiting them?"

"You said he was enraged and very aggressive, that he forced you against the wall when he scented you, Ellie. Tell me the truth. Is he acting normal for him? You know him well."

She hesitated, remembering the scene inside the bathroom. "He didn't hurt me and I don't believe he will. Maybe he's just mad because that nurse could piss anyone off. I'm not on experimental drugs but I still want to strangle her."

"It's best to be safe than sorry. You need to be taken away from him until we are certain he's not a danger. The human side of Species seem to fade during the reaction and our animal instincts take total control. We're natural predators and he may have scented you as prey, Ellie."

"Don't be ridicules," Ellie sputtered. "Fury loves me. He was just upset that Nurse Bitch in there threw herself at him. He didn't hurt me and he wouldn't."

Tiger watched her face closely. "We can't take any chances."

She hesitated. "I understand but I'm not leaving him. Let's just go talk to him and you'll see that he's fine."

A car pulled up in front of the house. Ellie turned as Slade opened the driver's door of the car and Justice climbed out of the passenger side. Trisha and a stranger got out of the back.

"You're safe." Justice looked relieved. "You need to leave. Tiger will drive you to Doctor Norbit's house."

Trisha held out keys to the tall New Species. "These are to my house. I have a guestroom." She visually scanned Ellie from head to foot. "Help yourself to my clothes and anything else you need. My closet is your closet."

"Where is the nurse?" Slade glanced around the area.

"Inside still." Tiger shrugged. "She's packing her things."

"Damn it," Justice growled. "He might attack her. She started this. Get Ellie out of here."

Slade jerked open the front door and stormed into the house, Justice right behind him. Trisha and the stranger stood outside. Ellie studied the man with curiosity.

"This is Doctor Ted Treadmont. He's the leading scientist on New Species," Trisha said. "You need to go, Ellie. You can come back when it's safe."

"How many times do I have to say that Fury isn't going to hurt me before someone listens? I'm not leaving."

Tiger cursed. "He's going to kill me for this." He suddenly lunged, grabbed Ellie around her waist, and clamped his hand over her mouth. He jerked his head at Trisha. "Don't stand there, Doctor Norbit. Could you please go open the trunk of the car for me? There's a release pull for it on the dash. I need to get her away from him in case he goes nuts."

Trisha ran for the car. Ellie struggled and clawed at Tiger's arms but he wouldn't put her down and she couldn't do more than make soft sounds with his palm cupped firmly over her mouth. She kicked at his legs but no matter how many times she nailed him with her bare feet, it didn't slow him down. The trunk opened and Tiger dumped Ellie inside.

"Don't," Ellie screamed. The trunk slammed closed, leaving her in the dark. Ellie kicked at it and shouted. "Let me out!"

The car started. Ellie kicked again but the trunk lid above her wouldn't open. She screamed, still shocked that she'd been locked inside the trunk of a car by Tiger. She'd trusted him. She stopped screaming as the car speeded away.

She hated small, cramped places. She fought a panic attack. The car turned suddenly and Ellie rolled to bang into something hard. Pain slammed into her knee. She screamed again. She'd take a beating inside the trunk from being thrown around if he made a lot of sharp turns at that speed. The car turned sharply again and Ellie slammed against the back of the trunk against the passenger compartment. Pain shot up her arm.

Ellie curled into a ball and struggled to breathe normally until the car finally stopped. She knew there was plenty of air but it didn't stop her from suffering. Her claustrophobia had never been this bad. The trunk opened and Ellie tried to frantically claw her way out. She gasped in gulps of fresh air as Tiger reached for her.

Ellie smacked at his hands. He jumped back when Ellie practically threw her body from the trunk. She stared at him wildly.

Tiger frowned. "What is wrong with you? We're at the Doctor's house."

"Don't you ever lock me inside a small space again!" Ellie shouted. She stumbled back a few steps. Hot tears slid down her cheeks. "I hate small, dark places!"

"Stop shouting," Tiger ordered. "I'm sorry. Calm down, Ellie. Just take some deep breaths. You're fine. Breathe in and out. That's it. I didn't know you had hole sickness."

"I don't have hole sickness!" She stopped shouting. "What is hole sickness?"

"You panic when you are put inside dark, small places. That's what we call it. I'm sorry. Are you all right now? We should go inside. That nightgown is thin and I am afraid we will draw unwanted attention here. This is the human area of Homeland."

His words sank in, she realized she was nearly nude and wanted clothes immediately. *Then, I'll find my way home.* Ellie nodded and followed Tiger to the front door. He unlocked the door. Ellie walked in and then turned, kicking Tiger in the shin hard enough to hurt her foot.

Tiger cursed and growled at her. "What was that for?"

"Everything. I don't suffer from hole sickness. I have claustrophobia."

He frowned. "Doesn't that mean the same thing?"

"Go to hell." Ellie stormed away from him into Trisha's bedroom, remembering where it was from her last visit. She slammed the door between them and headed to the doctor's dresser.

Ellie borrowed a pair of sweatpants, an exercise bra, and an oversized T-shirt from a rock concert Trisha must have attended. She tried on a pair of the doctor's shoes but they didn't wear the same size. She had to remain barefoot. Ellie grabbed up the phone from the bedside table and called home, wanting to talk to Fury. She shot a nervous look at the door, afraid Tiger would walk into the room and stop her.

"Ellie?" Fury sounded pissed.

"Hi, Fury. They made me leave. Are you all right?"

"Where are you?" He growled.

"Don't tell him!" Tiger yelled, nearly exploding into the room.

"Where are you?" Fury repeated, roaring the words.

Tiger tore the phone from her fingers and slammed it down into the cradle. He glared at Ellie. "Did you not hear the whole scent and prey talk we had?"

"I just wanted him to know I'm safe and ask him how he is doing. You guys are seriously overreacting if you think Fury is a danger to me."

Tiger arched an eyebrow. "Really?" He picked up the phone. "Let's see how off the mark we are."

"Who are you calling?"

"Justice."

Ellie sat on the edge of Trisha's bed, glowering up at Tiger. He listened and a frown marred his features. He hung up. "Something is really wrong. Justice didn't pick up his phone. It connected to his voice mail after six rings."

"So he's busy."

"He always answers." Tiger dialed another number. He listened and his face grew pale before he hung up.

"Slade didn't pick up either and he always answers by the third ring. They both entered the house and they aren't answering their phones. Shit." He dialed another number. He cursed after a minute and hung up. He waved the phone at Ellie. "Doctor Norbit isn't answering either."

"Maybe they are talking to him right now and don't want to be rude by answering their cells."

"Call home, talk to him for a few minutes to see how he is, but don't tell him where you are. Can you do that?"

Ellie accepted the phone. "This is just moronic."

"Just talk to him. You know Fury. See if he's your male or if he's not quite himself. Ask him where Justice and Slade are."

"You're going to feel stupid."

"I'll risk it. Just don't tell him where you are. Promise?"

"Sure," she muttered, glad to speak to Fury. Tiger was being paranoid.

Fury answered on the first ring by snarling her name. He sounded so mad she barely recognized her own name coming from his lips.

"It's me. Are you all right?"

"Where are you?"

"They were afraid you were reacting to one of the medications they've been giving you and think you're dangerous to me. I'm fine. Are Justice and Slade still there?"

"Where are you?" He ground out the words harshly. "Tell me right now, Ellie."

Ellie met Tiger's concerned gaze, having to admit that Fury was acting weird. "I'll be home soon. Are Justice and Slade still there?"

"They are outside," Fury growled. "I will come find you if you won't tell me where you are. Come home right now to me. You don't want to make me have to search for you."

"You need to calm down. The doctors just wanted to check you out and I'll be right home after they are sure everything is fine."

"I'm coming for you," he snarled. He slammed the phone down.

"Fury?" She shook her head, stunned. "He's really angry. He said he's coming for me and hung up. It sounded like...a threat."

"Damn it," Tiger groaned. "He's in total hunt mode, just as I feared. We need to get you the hell out of here." He hung up the phone and then snatched his cell phone from his back pocket. He dialed.

"This is Tiger. Justice and Slade have lost contact. They were at Fury's. He's gone feral from the medication and he's hunting his mate. I'm at Doctor Norbit's house with Ellie. I need one team sent to Fury's now and I need a second team sent here to extract her from the kill zone." He hung up.

"Kill zone?" Ellie gasped. "Have you all gone crazy? If Fury is mad it's because you took me from the house and he's worried."

Tiger reached down and gripped Ellie's arm firmly. "He's not worried. He's nuts. Move your ass. Your mate is one of the best trackers we have. We need to get you out of his reach." He yanked her to her feet.

"Stop it!" Ellie yelled. She jerked out of his hold.

"Let me remind you what I already said if you didn't catch it the first time. The drug he's been given can override his human side and let the animal loose. Your mate is mainly animal right now, and if I'm right, and he scented you, that means he's hunting you as if you're prey. Being prey means he will probably harm you if he finds you."

"Fury loves me. He's just mad that—"

"He could kill you. Imagine how he's going to feel when the drugs are gone from his system and he has to live with something he had no control over. He'll have to withstand the painful knowledge that he killed the one thing he loves. Now if you give a damn about him, move your ass, Ellie. Let me get you somewhere safe to make certain he doesn't do something that will destroy both of you."

Ellie stared at Tiger. There was a lot about New Species that wasn't known. *Is it possible he's right? Fury did act kind of crazy from the moment he burst into the bathroom.* Of course leaving him wasn't an option to her if he needed her.

"I need some spare clothes and I have to use the bathroom. Where are we going?"

"We need to get you away from Homeland. That's a certainty. Homeland isn't big enough to hide you and we don't need a scene with human witnesses."

Ellie entered the bathroom and yanked open cupboards, searching for aspirin, feeling a stress headache coming on. The doctor didn't seem to keep any medicines inside her bathroom. Ellie turned, startled a bit at seeing Tiger hovering at the doorway.

"I need to use the bathroom and that isn't going to happen with you watching me," she warned. "Have you ever heard of privacy?"

"Hurry," Tiger demanded. "He might not have to track you if he guesses we brought you here."

* * * * *

Breeze climbed out of the car and grimly assessed both males. Justice and Slade waited outside Fury's home. She'd expected the worst when she'd gotten the call but Fury hadn't hurt either of them. She'd been informed of the situation, of their only plan to save the Species male, and she'd agreed. She approached them with dread.

Justice spoke first. "Breeze, I'm sorry to ask this of you." His gaze dropped to her feet, where it stayed. "He could really hurt his female. She's so much frailer than our women. He could break her bones just by holding her and she would probably die if he's as aggressive as we fear."

Breeze winced inwardly. "I understand. She might hate me for this later but I won't allow her to be killed. I'll go inside and deal with the situation."

Justice finally raised his sad gaze. "I'm so sorry."

Breeze nodded. "I am very fond of Ellie. I would do this for you because you asked but I *need* to do this for her."

"She'll understand once it is explained."

Breeze snorted at Justice. "Males know nothing."

That response drew a frown from him. "If we go in and attempt to restrain him, he will try to kill us, or we will have to kill him," Justice explained softly. "Until we can assess him, it's too dangerous to tranquilize him. The added drugs could cause an overdose or heart failure. Sending you in to calm him is the only thing we could think to attempt. Scream for help if he won't allow you to help him. I won't allow you to die. We'll have to put him out regardless of the consequences if he attacks."

Breeze opened the front door and stepped inside the house. She closed the door firmly behind her and paused there, fighting down fear. She'd only seen this situation once before and she'd barely survived it. She straightened her shoulders. Ellie had become her friend and this happened to be a Species problem. She only hoped he didn't kill her outright since she wasn't the female he wanted.

Breeze froze a few feet inside the living room, inhaled deeply, and then backed up. She yanked open the door to speak to Justice. "Who has been inside this house?"

"Why?"

"Tell me," Breeze growled.

"Me, Tiger, Slade, Fury, Ellie and the nurse were here. Why?"

Breeze glared at him. "Is the nurse a short female with green eyes?"

Justice nodded. "That describes the nurse, Belinda Thomas. What is wrong?"

"I know this scent. She worked inside my section of the testing facility. Didn't you ever meet her? Her name isn't Belinda Thomas. It's Beatrice Thorton."

"Are you sure?" A deadly cold glint entered Justice's angry eyes.

Breeze showed her own anger by barring her teeth. "I would never forget the stench of someone so evil. She took care of Fury?"

Justice paled. "She's in charge of his medications."

Breeze growled deeper. "She was one of the cruelest of them. This is no coincidence. She was in charge of test drugs given to us."

They heard something break from the back of the house. Breeze clenched her hands into fists. "Where is she?"

"I had her taken to security while they process her out of Homeland. We couldn't retrieve her things yet so she's waiting for them to be delivered." Justice reached for his cell phone and then realized in the rush to flee Fury's rage, he'd left it inside the bedroom. When he'd been thrown into a wall, it had fallen from his pocket. "I'll have her taken into custody." He spun and walked to the car to use the radio.

Breeze closed the door, worried by the sounds coming from the back of the house. If their enemy had been giving Fury the wrong drugs, they could be dealing with something really bad. Breeze trembled slightly and then she straightened her shoulders. Maybe he could be reasoned with and it wouldn't be as bad as she feared. She heard more things breaking. It sounded as if Fury had started to destroy at least one room of his home.

* * * * *

"I'm coming," Ellie snapped, glaring at Tiger who waved her toward the front door. "Let me put on socks first though. I don't want to be walking around barefoot wherever we go."

"Hurry up. The team will be here at any moment and I want us ready to go when they arrive." He strode toward the front door. "I just hope Breeze can stop him before he leaves the house in search of you."

Ellie heard what he said and she took a step toward him. "Breeze? Why would Breeze go to Fury's house?"

Tiger turned. "She's going to attempt to get him to scent her instead. She knows he would kill you in the state he's in and she wants to save your life. Out of all of our females, she is the strongest. We wanted one of Fury's testing facility females since he'd be familiar with them but they were too frightened. They've seen this happen before inside the testing facilities when they overmedicated one of our males. Only Breeze was brave enough and willing to risk her life for yours. Now, hurry, Ellie. If Fury won't scent Breeze he will come for you."

"She's going to allow him smell her? Why would that be risking her life?"

Tiger cursed. "Sometimes if we're in hunt mode and crazy, the rage can be turned into sexual desire." He paused. "It's not something a female would enjoy, Ellie. If he accepts Breeze in your place, let me assure you, it will be hell for her. He could still kill her."

Ellie felt punched in the gut, hard. "You mean she's…he's…they'll…"

"It would be down to basics animal sex and violent, Ellie. Now do what you need to and let's get out of here. There's no telling if he'll accept her or not. He could just kill her and she might only be able to slow him down. They think if they try to drug him more after whatever has been given to him, it could kill him outright. We're trying to save you both." Tiger turned his back to peer out a window, watching for his team to arrive.

Her heart pounded. She closed her eyes and let everything slam into her. *Son of a bitch.*

"I think I'm going to be sick."

She fled to bathroom, slammed the door, and flipped the lock. Ellie turned on the water full blast in the sink to cover the noise and yanked open the bathroom window.

Chapter Nineteen

ဆ

Ellie had gotten lucky. Tiger had left the car keys in the ignition when he'd taken her into Trisha's house. He probably had assumed she remained inside the bathroom until he spotted her streaking across the yard for the street. He'd yelled as she'd thrown open the driver's door but by the time he'd made it outside, she had the engine started and left tire tread along the street in her haste to prevent him from stopping her.

She parked the car at the back of Fury's house, glanced around and made sure no one waited to stop her. She shut the engine off and jumped out of the car. She studied the backyard fence, deeming it wasn't too high to climb. Ellie cursed and grabbed hold of the top of it. She hadn't sneaked over a wall since she was a teenager.

It turned out to be harder than she remembered but she made it over. She limped as she headed toward the back bedroom. She'd cut her foot when she'd jumped from the top of the fence to the patio below. She cursed not having shoes. Her palms burned and, as she glanced down, she saw a few scratches she'd received from the rough textured wall. The sound of furious growls and breaking glass made her hobble faster toward the back of Fury's house and the sliding glass door of their bedroom.

"No," Fury snarled.

Ellie didn't think or pause before she grabbed the sliding-door handle and just yanked it open. She stepped through the drapes and stared in shock at the scene before her.

The bedroom had been trashed. The dresser lay on its side, the nightstand was broken and the mirror that had been over the dresser was smashed into pieces that littered most of one corner of the room. Breeze huddled in that same corner between the closet and the bathroom door, trapped there against the wall. A red mark showed on the side of her face. Blood smeared from her mouth on that side as well and dripped down her chin to the front of her shirt.

Breeze appeared frightened and Fury had her trapped in place with his body mere feet from hers. He growled viciously. He'd torn off his shirt and crouched down as if he were going to launch himself at Breeze. His hands were fisted.

"Fury?" Ellie's voice trembled from shock and fear.

Fury snapped his head in her direction. The cold look in his eyes made Ellie actually take a step back. He snarled at her, a deep, vicious sound, and barred his sharp teeth.

"I'm home," Ellie whispered.

"Run," Breeze hissed. "Run now."

Ellie glanced at Breeze and took notice again of her injuries. That meant Fury had done it. It stunned Ellie that he'd actually hit a woman. It escalated her fear, knowing he really had lost his control. The man she knew and loved would never have struck Breeze. Her gaze returned to Fury, unsure if he recognized her in the state he was in. He growled again and straightened, taking a step in her direction.

"Flee," Breeze growled. "Get out of here."

Ellie tensed but didn't break eye contact with him. "Fury? Can you hear me?"

He lunged toward Ellie. She stumbled back, terrified at the scary look on his face. Breeze leaped on Fury's back and both of them crashed to the floor almost at Ellie's feet.

"Get out of here," Breeze panted, fighting to keep Fury down. "He'll kill us both. Run!"

Fury threw Breeze away from him and she slammed into the nearby wall. Ellie heard the thump when Breeze hit the plaster. Broken glass from the mirror crunched under Breeze's body when she landed. Fury rose up to a crouch and his wild eyes were locked on Ellie. He growled again viciously, deep within his throat. She saw a stranger staring at her, someone who wasn't all there, totally insane. She took a step back and then another as Fury rose to his full height.

"Drop to your knees," Breeze groaned, pushing up from the glass-littered floor. "Don't look into his eyes. Put your head down."

Ellie was so terrified she didn't hesitate to follow Breeze's orders. She dropped to her knees and curled into a ball. Her eyes squeezed tightly closed and she was afraid to look up at her seriously drugged-out boyfriend. She knew Fury hovered over her now, stood very close, because she could hear him breathing heavily.

"Fury?" Breeze growled when she spoke. "Listen to me. You don't want to hurt Ellie. You love her. Remember?" Material tore. "Look at me, Fury. Here."

Ellie lifted her head and opened her eyes. Breeze had torn her shirt wide open to expose her breasts. She rubbed her hand across some of the cuts on her arm from the broken glass she'd fallen into and wiped the blood across her breasts. She held her hands out to Fury slowly, as if to make certain the blood there drew his attention. He sniffed, growled, turned away from Ellie to face Breeze.

"That's it," Breeze crooned softly. "Come to me."

Fury took a few hesitant steps toward her. He started growling again. Breeze shook with fear and paled more but she didn't back away. She did drop her offered hand slowly to her side where it fisted.

"Get out of here now," Breeze ordered her softly.

Ellie knew Breeze spoke to her as she struggled to stand. "What's wrong with him?"

"That nurse worked for Mercile. I think she gave him something that's made him totally violent," Breeze whispered. She slowly eased back into the corner until her back pressed flat to the wall and turned her head cautiously until she could glance at Ellie. "Get out of here while he's focused on me and the blood. I don't know if he will breed me or kill me." She gave Fury a worried stare.

Breed her? Ellie shook her head. "I'm going to distract him. Get out of here, Breeze. Tell everyone to stay out. He won't kill me."

Breeze's head snapped back in her direction to give her a shocked look. Fury stood mere inches from the other woman now. He sniffed at the blood on Breeze's chest and growled. He gripped one of Breeze's hands suddenly and yanked it to his mouth. Horrified, Ellie watched Fury sniff at the blood smeared on her palm. She guessed it was better than biting her hand off.

"Get out of here, Ellie," Breeze whispered.

"You go!" Ellie quickly removed her clothes. If Fury wanted a woman, he would get one—her. "Leave, Breeze. He won't kill me. Tell them to stay out of the house. Fury?" Ellie walked slowly toward him. She raised her voice. "Fury! Let that woman go, damn it!"

Fury's head snapped in Ellie's direction. For one instant panic set in when his dark look hungrily fastened on her bare body. She still didn't see Fury in those eyes.

"Hey, big guy. Remember me? I'm Ellie. I love you and you love me. Let her go and come to me if you want to touch a woman."

He released Breeze's hand and turned. His gaze ran down her body again and his nostrils flared as he sniffed. Ellie's heart beat erratically. Breeze grabbed at Fury, trying to pull his attention back to her.

Fury flung out a hand, hitting Breeze in the side of the head. He knocked her toward the door where she sprawled on the carpet. Fury took a step toward Ellie and then another. She nodded at him and inched backward in the direction of the bathroom. She prayed he'd follow her in there. She could lock the door and hopefully he wouldn't be able to throw her around in the smaller space.

"That's it, Fury. Come on, big guy. It's Ellie. Let's go inside the bathroom where we have more privacy." Ellie glanced over to see Breeze on her hands and knees, getting up.

"Breeze," Ellie urged softly. "Leave. Tell them to stay out no matter what."

Ellie backed up more. Fury growled at her and slowly stalked her. She moved closer to the bathroom.

"Come on, baby," Ellie crooned to him. "Come to Ellie. Let's both play nice."

"Fury!" Breeze growled his name.

"Stop it, Breeze. Stay out of this," Ellie demanded. "Don't look at her, Fury. Focus on me. I'm right here."

That scent called to him. Fury sniffed, fighting the daze that gripped his mind, making it nearly impossible to for him to think. He knew rage and pain, so much agony. His vision cleared as he fought the darkness that fogged his mind.

A human woman stood naked feet from him and she looked familiar to him. Her blue eyes were wide, terrified, and he sniffed again, fighting to think. He was back inside his cell, they'd done something to him, and the human had to be responsible but other images suddenly filled his mind.

That human smiling at him, the sound of her laugher, and his hand caressing her cheek flashed through his confused memories. He knew her well, even though he couldn't think clearly. He sniffed again, her scent filling his nose, and more flashbacks replayed inside his mind.

His gaze lowered and pure lust slammed him. He wanted to grab her, throw her down and take her. He hesitated though. He knew he'd hurt her and it mattered to him for some reason that he not do that, shouldn't want that. She was important to him somehow. He fought to push back the haze that dimmed his ability to think. He struggled to remember who she was, why a human would mean a damn thing to him, since they were all his enemies.

More images surfaced in a confused montage. Her smiling while she ate at a table across from him, her sitting on his lap with her arms around him. They were sharing a shower together while she washed his chest with her pale, small hands, and he leaned down to kiss her. Her name was there just on the tip of his tongue and then as he fought with the pure scalding-hot pain, his brain burst with knowledge.

Ellie had become his entire world, the woman who made him happy, and he stumbled a foot closer to her, fighting the rage that threatened to consume him and the painful stabs of agony that threatened to take him to his knees. He needed to hold her, to touch her, and he knew her name. He loved her. Her scent helped him and he needed to get closer to her.

"Ellie," he growled the word.

Something finally flickered inside Fury's eyes, a hint of recognition and real emotion. Ellie smiled. "It's me, Fury. Come to me easy. You don't want to hurt me."

He took big stumbling steps forward and suddenly paused in front of her. She reached for him slowly, wanted to comfort him, and then he had her. His arms wrapped around her waist and her back slammed into the wall hard enough to knock the breath from her lungs. Fury shoved his face into the cradle of her shoulder and neck to breathe against her skin. Ellie sucked in air. Breeze stood in the middle of the room watching them with a worried expression.

"I'm fine," Ellie whispered. "You can leave."

Breeze hesitated.

"Ellie," Fury growled.

Ellie wrapped her arms around his neck tightly, hugging him. "Yeah, baby. It's me."

He growled again but then licked her neck. He panted. His hand around her waist moved to cup her ass, one large hand gripped her soft flesh in a near-bruising hold. Ellie nodded assurances at Breeze over his shoulder. Breeze nodded, backing up. Ellie watched her exit the bedroom and close the door.

"Ellie," Fury growled.

"I'm here."

He shifted his stance. He pressed his chest against hers and one of his hands left her hip. Material tore. Ellie closed her eyes. She tried to calm her breathing.

"Fury? Can you hear me? Talk to me."

He growled. One of his arms wrapped almost painfully around her waist. The other hand gripped her thigh. He forced them open by pressing his hips between hers. She gasped in pain. Fury viciously growled but stopped crushing against her so hard.

"Fury?"

He instantly released her and stumbled away. Ellie trembled as she struggled to gain her balance after he suddenly let her go. Fury dropped to his hands and knees and made a horrible sound filled with pain and misery that make Ellie wince. She lowered to her knees behind him and didn't hesitate to curl her body over his back and wrap her arms around his waist.

"I'm here, Fury. You're going to be fine. Can you hear me? I love you."

He moved suddenly, turned his big, strong body, and it sent Ellie from a bending position to landing on her ass sitting on the carpet. Fury ended up pressed against her in a heartbeat. He curled onto his side facing her, using her thighs for a pillow, and curved his legs around her back. He wrapped his arms tightly around her waist and clung to her. His face pressed into her stomach and a soft whimper came from his throat.

Ellie looked down, seeing him that way that tore her up and tears filled her eyes. She blinked them back. The look of fear and confusion on his face broke her heart. She trembled slightly as she combed her fingers through his hair with one hand while she rubbed his back with the other one.

"It's okay, Fury. I'm here. We're both going to be all right."

"What's wrong with me?" He groaned and held her tighter.

"They think one of the healing drugs you were given is making you a little nuts. It's going to be fine."

He shook his head. "No. They are wrong. I have been on those drugs before but this is different. Sudden." He shivered hard, his big body quivered around her. "It's hard to think and I feel so much rage."

"It's going to be all right," Ellie promised softly. "We're together and I'm going to sit here with you for however long it takes for you to feel better. You aren't going to hurt me. I know you won't because you love me as much as I love you."

His face brushed against her stomach. His tongue came out and he licked the underside her breast. It tickled. Ellie jerked away so he couldn't do it again.

"That tickles."

"You're naked."

"Well, yeah. I needed to get your attention."

"You always have that."

Ellie's gaze ran down Fury's body and noticed that he'd torn open the front of his jeans—the source of that ripping sound when she'd heard material tear when he'd pinned her to the wall. She shivered. If she hadn't calmed him down, hadn't reached him emotionally, he would have taken her against the wall aggressively without care or regard to her pain or his injuries. Ellie continued rubbing him as her fingers brushed through his hair.

"Talk to me. I'm fighting to stay with you but the blackness is so near."

Ellie peered down at Fury's head resting on her lap to discover him staring at her. His dark gaze was filled with confusion when their gazes met.

"I'm right here, Fury." She forced a smile, trying to hide her alarm and worry. "I'm going to hold you until you feel like yourself again."

"Did I hurt anyone? I'm having a difficult time thinking and remembering."

"Everyone is fine." She hoped Breeze wasn't too hurt but she wouldn't bring that up.

He squeezed his eyes closed. "I want you." He growled softly.

Ellie tensed. "Fury? Let me go put some clothes on."

He shook his head. "It distracts me from my rage and it wouldn't matter. I'd still scent you no matter what you wore. You're bleeding. Did I hurt you?"

"No. I got some cuts and scrapes from climbing the back fence to reach you." She turned her foot until she could view it more easily. The cut looked bigger than she thought and she saw a smear of her blood on the carpet. "My foot is bleeding. If you move a little I think I can reach something to put under it. Otherwise I'll get blood on the carpet."

"I don't give a shit."

Ellie laughed. "You say that now when you're not feeling like yourself but wait until tomorrow when we're trying to find a piece of furniture to put over the stain to hide it."

Fury groaned. "I love you, Ellie."

"I love you too. How are you feeling?"

"Rage," he growled. "So much rage and pain. My skin feels on fire."

"Just hold me."

"I don't think I could let you go. Are you sure I didn't hurt you?"

"I'm sure. You didn't hurt me. You just scared the—"

The bedroom door cracked open. Ellie glanced over to the door. Fury tensed, growling.

Trisha's face appeared as she peeked inside. "Are you okay?"

Ellie rubbed Fury's back, trying to calm him. "We're good now," Ellie spoke loudly for all of their benefits, hoping it was true. Her voice softened. "Relax, Fury. It's just Doctor Trisha."

"May I come in?" Trisha whispered. "I need to examine him if I can."

Ellie wasn't sure if he could take other people being close to him as she studied him. "Just hold onto me, Fury. Trisha really needs to examine you so she can help."

"No," he growled. His arms tightened painfully around Ellie as he turned his head to stare up at her. "You're mine. They can't take you from me."

"I'm not going anywhere. I won't move, okay? Please let the Doctor check on you. We'll just stay this way while she does."

Fury took a shaky breath and blinked up at Ellie. He jerked his head in a nod and turned his face into her stomach. Ellie glanced at Trisha.

Trisha stepped into the room slowly and eased out from behind the door. "I need Ted in here too, Ellie. He might be able to identify whatever drug Fury was given by his symptoms."

Ellie winced over her naked state. "Could you hand me something first?"

Trisha stepped over debris to reach the bed. She yanked the sheet from the mattress and hesitantly approached them. She tried to wrap it around Ellie carefully, making sure she didn't touch Fury. Ellie hesitated, realized that to cover herself, the sheet would have to cover Fury too since he molded to her body and wrapped tightly around her.

"That's not going to work. How about giving me one of the shirts in the dresser?" She suddenly remembered that the dresser was facedown. She sighed. "How about the one he took off? Do you see it anywhere?"

Trisha tossed the sheet at the bed and made her way to the corner, carefully stepping on the broken mirror that crunched under her shoes. She picked up Fury's torn shirt and carried it to Ellie. Ellie had to release Fury to put it on. The second her hands left his hair and back, he tensed, hugging her harder, and buried his face deeper into her stomach. Ellie shoved the shirt over the front of her to cover her breasts then caressed Fury again. His hold eased instantly at her soothing touch and he relaxed enough that he wasn't digging his face painfully into her belly anymore.

"I'm right here," Ellie whispered in assurance. "You just hold me. They will figure this out and make you better." Ellie glanced up at Trisha. "I think you can bring him in now. My breasts are covered and you can't see the rest of me with Fury wrapped around me, can you?"

Trish shook her head. "We're doctors anyway. He didn't hurt you?"

"I'm fine. I told you, Fury would never hurt me."

Fury growled in response. Ellie held him tighter, massaging him with her hand on his back and her fingers brushing his hair with the other one. "Shush, Fury. It's fine. Just hang onto me."

Doctor Ted Treadmont entered the room and Justice paused outside the doorway behind him. Justice sniffed, tensed, and his gaze fixed on Ellie with a frown.

"He didn't hurt me. I jumped the back wall and got a little dinged up if you smell blood."

"I know that. We've been listening at the door and heard everything you've said. I am trying to smell him." Justice stayed at the doorway as he carefully studied Fury. "This isn't right, Ted. He smells wrong, not the way he did before with the drugs he's been on for days."

The doctor nodded. "I know. These symptoms aren't from what we've been giving him."

"What's going on?" Ellie glanced between both men.

"The drug we gave him shouldn't have done this." Ted knelt by Fury and Ellie. He opened his bag and glanced over at her. "I need to draw blood. We think that nurse might have given him something else to make him this way. We have to take some blood to test."

Fury tensed and growled but Ellie held him tighter. "Fury? Listen to me. I've got you and you've got me. They are going to help you, okay? Just relax for me."

He nodded against her stomach.

Justice turned and spoke softly to someone out of sight in the hallway. "Go check the nurse's things and the house. Bring whatever drugs you find to us." Justice faced Ellie. "How is he doing?"

"He's doing good. How is Breeze?"

"She's worried about you."

"I'm fine."

Ellie watched Ted and Trisha as they examined Fury. She rubbed him, made soft, soothing sounds often, and talked him in to staying very still as Trisha took blood from his arm. He tensed and growled a few times but he kept holding Ellie, listening to her words. His face stayed pressed against her stomach the entire time.

"Fury?" Ted spoke softly. "How do you feel, son?"

"Rage," Fury whispered. "Horny. Hard to think. My skin burns. Confused. So much pain. I want to fuck Ellie, and if I don't, I think I might die."

Ellie blushed but she wasn't shocked. She knew he was sexually excited. His jeans were torn open with his lap against her hip. He wore boxer briefs and she couldn't miss the feel of the bulge against her.

"Are you experiencing any bloodlust?" Ted reached into his bag and withdrew a vial of clear liquid. He pulled out a syringe next, removing it from the sterile container.

Fury nodded. "I desperately want to tear something apart."

"Son, I won't do it if you don't want me to but can I give you a shot? It will put you to sleep. You will be down for a few hours and hopefully whatever was put into your system will work out by the time you come back around. If something goes wrong both Trisha and I are here to attend you immediately."

Fear gripped Ellie. "No! Tiger said something about how giving him more drugs could kill him."

The doctor met her gaze grimly. "That was concern over another drug but that isn't what we thought he'd been drugged with. I'm fairly certain he can take a sedative. We're right here on hand if we're wrong." He held up a second shot. "That's what this is for if his heart stops. We're prepared but he is suffering. He needs to be sedated."

Fury tensed hard but then he relaxed. "Do it," he growled. "Don't leave me, Ellie." He clutched her tighter.

"I won't let you go," Ellie swore softly.

Ted gave Fury the shot and then nodded at Ellie. "It will only take a few minutes. He'll relax and go to sleep."

"I'm right here, Fury," Ellie whispered to him. "I won't leave your side. When you wake up things will be better, all right? I'll be the first thing you see."

He nodded into her stomach. Minutes passed and she realized Fury's body on hers seemed heavier, nearly crushing her legs. She had to hold him against her chest to keep his head from rolling back at an odd angle. His arms slackened around her waist until they rested against the floor behind her ass. She nodded at Trisha and Ted.

"He's out."

"Let's move him off you." Justice entered the bedroom.

"Let's not," Ellie countered. "I'm kind of naked."

"We'll do it in a way that won't flash you to the guys." Trisha rose to her feet. "Ted, you and Justice take his arms. Close your eyes when you lift him. I'll hand Ellie a towel to wrap around her. After we get her out from under him, she can go inside the bathroom and get dressed while you lift him onto the bed. It's the only place in here not destroyed."

They carefully maneuvered Fury with their eyes closed and Ellie covered her naked body with the towel Trisha fetched. She was pulled to her feet with Trisha's help and then fled into the bathroom. She closed the door and hurried to put on her dirty clothes, still scattered across the floor where she'd left them. By the time she stepped back into the bedroom, the room had filled with a few more people. Fury lay sprawled on his back, unconscious. Ellie moved to his side and sat on the edge of the mattress. She clutched his limp hand.

"He'll be fine," Ted assured her.

"Look at this," Trisha ground out. She held up a dark brown bottle from Belinda's medical bag that had been delivered to the bedroom. "It's Freltridontomez."

Ted cursed. "Damn. Good thing we didn't tranquilize him when he was on his feet. He could have stroked out from the rage at being shot before it took effect."

"What is that?" Ellie glanced at both doctors, wanting an answer.

"It is a chemical that attacks the mind. It sends false signals to the brain that it's in blinding pain without the actual physical discomfort. It usually drives the patient into rage, confusion, and destroys rational thinking. It would explain all Fury's symptoms. He would have progressively grown worse within the hour."

"Why would she do it?" Trisha continued to search through the supposed nurse's bag. "She knew it would be dangerous as hell. From what I've read in the reports they used that drug occasionally on a few Species to force physical fights between their test subjects."

"They did," Tiger growled from the door. "I've been given that shit before. I couldn't even remember my name. I just wanted to kill something and anything that moved would have provoked me. When I'd come out of it I could barely remember what happened and sometimes I couldn't remember anything at all."

Ellie stared at Tiger as he walked into the bedroom and wondered if he was angry that she'd ditched him at Trisha's house.

He shot her a glare. "You are in deep shit with me. Don't ever give me the slip again or steal my car."

"Don't be stupid enough to leave the keys inside the ignition. I told you he wouldn't hurt me," Ellie shot back, angry that he'd get attitude with her.

"I made that decision," Justice sighed. "I feared your life was in danger, Ellie."

"Well, I told you he wouldn't hurt me."

"You got lucky," Trisha intervened. "I've read the reports on a handful of subjects Mercile tested this drug on." Trisha shook her head. "Brutal, insane, killing rage is usually the result. Then again I doubt they ever tried to turn a man on the woman he is in love with."

Breeze took hesitant steps into the bedroom. She'd cleaned her face and had on a new shirt. Ellie studied her with concern. "Are you all right?"

Breeze approached and sat at the end of the bed. She frowned at Ellie. "I'm good. You on the other hand are either very foolish or very in love."

"I'm kind of both," Ellie admitted.

A smile flashed on Breeze's face before she flinched, gently touching her mouth. It looked swollen and a bruise had started to form. Ellie studied the injured area.

"I'm sorry he hit you. I know he normally wouldn't have."

"He wanted you and grew very angry that he had me here instead. I figured that out pretty quick. He could have hurt me a lot worse but he didn't." Breeze darted a glance at Fury. "You chose well, Ellie. He's an amazing male with extremely good control."

"How can you say that after he hit you? You should be pretty upset at him." Ellie didn't understand Breeze's reaction.

"I've seen our males go crazy and they can inflict a lot of pain but he fought it all the way. He only hit me when I touched him or when I tried to stop him from going to you. He didn't try to wound me but instead batted me away with slaps." She hesitated. "He didn't hurt you. You don't know how much he must love you to fight through all that was going on inside him to calm down." Breeze nodded. "He's a good male, a very strong one, and very protective of you. You chose well, Ellie Brower."

Ellie nodded. "Thank you for risking yourself for me."

"This is a love fest." Tiger groaned. "Please stop."

Slade laughed. "I wasn't going to say it but group hug?"

"Stop it," Justice ordered softly. He looked mildly irritated as his gaze darted between his men. "It's sabotage. Slade, go speak to that nurse." Anger tensed his features. "I don't care what it takes but find out why she did this and who helped her."

Tiger's smile faded. "May I go with him?"

Justice studied him with suspicion. "You spent time with that woman. Do you have feelings for her?"

"No. I'm angry. She did this right under my nose. If Slade has a problem terrifying some answers out of her, I don't. I won't kill her but she might wish I would."

"Fine." Justice paused. "Be aware of the security cameras and know the humans will watch. They may not approve of your methods."

"Not a problem." Slade smiled coldly before he turned and strode away.

Ellie watched Tiger follow him until they were out of sight. Her attention shifted to Justice. "Why would someone do this to Fury?"

"You," Ted answered instead. "Well, the relationship you have with Fury has been high on the radar of the media and the hate groups that don't want a fairytale romance."

"I think it's more than that," Trisha declared. "Mercile Industries would love nothing better than if Fury had gone insane and killed Ellie. Let's face it. They look like shit for having kept people locked up inside their research facilities and running illegal experiments on them. They keep stating that New Species are more animal than human, trying to desensitize the media and general public who support them. If a New Species male turned murderous and killed his live-in human girlfriend it would look really bad. Ellie and Fury are the perfect targets since the world is watching them so closely."

"Beatrice Thorton worked for Mercile Industries," Breeze growled.

"Who's Beatrice Thorton?" Ellie frowned.

"She's an ex-employee of Mercile Industries. You knew her by the name she's going by now, Belinda Thomas," Justice said as he walked to the upended dresser and sat on the edge of it.

"That bitch worked for Mercile Industries?" Shocked, Ellie gawked at Breeze for confirmation.

"I recognized her stench when I walked inside the house." Anger deepened Breeze's voice into a near snarl. "I would never forget an enemy. She was the worst. She tortured our people and always pushed needles into us with a big grin. She enjoyed our pain." Breeze turned to Justice. "You sure you never met her?"

"No. She must have only worked on the female side of the testing facility."

"You would think she would have been afraid that one of you might recognize her," Ted speculated.

"Maybe she thought she would be safe since she only worked with women New Species." Ellie glanced around the room. "I mean, the only woman in Fury's life is me. They know I'm not going to recognize her. I worked in the testing facility where Fury was held captive and she didn't work that one. It's public knowledge that all the New Species women live inside a dorm and there aren't supposed to be many of them here. I watch the news and they make it sound as though there's only a handful."

"You worked for Mercile Industries?" Ted glared at Ellie.

"It's not what you're thinking." Justice shot the doctor a frown. "She worked for Victor Helio. You've met him. He approached Ellie when she had a job at Mercile Industries in their corporate offices, not knowing what they really did. He approached her, told her what they suspected, and asked for her help to discover the truth. She smuggled out evidence, risked her life to do it, and gave them enough to get search warrants. Some of the medical and testing reports you've read are ones she stole."

"Oh." Ted relaxed. "You were brave. What made you do it? Did you always want to be a secret spy or work for a police agency?"

Ellie held back a snort. "No. I'm not that adventurous. It just really got to me when Victor Helio came to me and told me what the rumors were. I had to do anything I could to find out if they were really experimenting on people. I was horrified at the concept."

"You're a good person." Ted spoke to Trisha next. "If they are using drugs to attack New Species we need to be aware of it. We need a lockdown on all incoming products that could be affected."

"Starting with the food," Trisha agreed.

"You think it's possible?" Justice looked wary.

"I'm thinking about what I could do if I wanted to sabotage your people, Justice. Contaminating the food would drive everyone crazy," Ted stated grimly.

"Wouldn't it affect humans too?" Justice didn't look convinced.

Ted shrugged. "Sure but I bet they don't care. They are being prosecuted for what they did to you and their only defense is claiming you aren't human. What would hurt New Species more than making at least a good portion of you go nuts enough to turn it into a bloodbath, and the press running with that story?"

"We don't even know if the plot is that big," Justice growled. "I don't want to panic anyone."

"Right," Ted snapped. "I'm going to start looking for something that will counteract Freltridontomez. That way if they use it again we can use darts to deliver an antidote to anyone affected before someone gets hurt. That is the safest thing to do. As I said before, if we sedated them while they are in a full-blown, drug-induced rage it would most likely kill them. They could have a stroke or a heart attack."

Trisha stood. "Do you think we can find something for it? We'll have to work quickly, Ted. We also should order random testing on the water and food shipped in."

"They had some research notes included with the file we got about Freltridontomez. They may have been close to finding a drug to counteract it." Ted collected his bag. "Just because we don't have the end result on paper doesn't mean it's not right there."

"Let's go." Trisha grabbed hers. On her way out she stopped to smile at Ellie. "When Fury wakes up he might have a headache and be sore but he should be fine. If not, give us a call. We'll be at the medical center."

"Wow," Ellie muttered as the couple left. She arched her eyebrows at Justice. "I think my head just spun. Are they like that all the time?"

He nodded. "Ted is what you'd call paranoid but he's the best at what he does. I don't think it is a big-scale plot against us. Eat your meals without fear, Ellie. If they were going to attack our food or water they wouldn't have had to send in a woman to poison Fury with her needles. They would have already attacked us that way."

"Do you think she came from one of the hate groups or Mercile?"

"Mercile makes more sense to me. Two birds with one stone."

"Two birds?"

His eyebrow arched. "You brought them down, Ellie. What better revenge than to make the man you risked your life to save become the man who caused your death? Fury could have killed you. The bad publicity would have crushed us in the press. Ted's right. The only defense they have for their crimes is convincing people we aren't human and therefore it's impossible to abuse us. They're facing criminal charges but we're suing them for money as well."

She let it sink in. "My vote is on Mercile too." She checked on Fury. He slept peacefully.

"I need to make some phone calls, Ellie. I want to check on what this Beatrice Thorton is saying. I'll be in the living room if you need anything."

"You don't have to stay. Thank you for everything today, by the way. Well, except for having Tiger toss me inside a car trunk and kidnap me."

He winced. "I'll be in the other room. We need to stay close to make sure Fury is really fine when he wakes." Justice jerked his head at his men to follow him out.

Breeze stood. "I'm going home."

Ellie gave Breeze a sincere look to convey her gratitude. "You're really a good friend to have come today and I won't forget it. Thank you from the bottom of my heart."

"I'll see you when you come back to work. Take a few days. We're good at the dorm. Don't worry about us."

"Thanks."

Ellie watched everyone leave the bedroom. She was alone with Fury again. She turned on her side and curled against his warm body.

"I love you," she whispered. She just held him, knowing one of them could have died. It scared the hell out of her.

Chapter Twenty

∽

Ellie wanted to go down to the detention center and punch Beatrice Thorton, otherwise known as Nurse Bitch, Belinda Thomas. Tiger and Slade had interrogated the woman until she'd broken and confessed everything. Someone from Mercile Industries had hired her to sabotage the New Species for the bad publicity it would earn. They thought making Fury resemble an unfit animal would turn public opinion in their favor.

Fury had recovered fully but he'd been really upset that he'd lost control the way he had. The blame fell strictly on Nurse Bitch's shoulders for having no morals. The NSO turned the woman over to the authorities to be prosecuted for a long list of crimes but it barely consoled Ellie or Fury.

That bitch had nearly destroyed their lives. She'd picked Fury because he'd been easily accessible after the shooting. She'd just had to be hired to do homecare and bribe a few people on the list to refuse to work for New Species.

Beatrice Thorton had admitted to being curious about what it would be like to have sex with Fury. It was why she'd hit on him and had made Ellie's life miserable. When she finally realized Fury would have nothing to do with her she'd decided to implement her plan while Ellie took a shower so he'd hopefully go insane and kill the woman he loved. It was a vicious scheme and it could have worked in the woman's favor but she hadn't counted on how deeply Fury loved Ellie.

Justice stared at Ellie and Fury grimly. "I swear, she's going to get some serious time. They promised me that she would be made an example of. We have to totally change our security protocols now. We've decided to start schooling some of our people in nursing. That way if we need help in the future we aren't totally dependent on humans for nursing care."

Fury shifted in his seat and glanced around Justice's office. "Did she say if she knew if Mercile would send others?"

Justice's shoulders slumped. "We are sure they will try to infiltrate us again. At least it wasn't as large of an attack as our doctors feared. Our food supply and water were never tampered with. We just have to be very careful of full humans." He gave Ellie an apologetic look. "No offense. I would trust you with my life. It's just strangers we have to be careful with. From now on we do full background checks on any humans who are allowed through the gates."

"We need to rely more on ourselves," Fury concluded. "We have a lot of full humans working here. If Mercile wants to get ugly they could start attempting to bribe them into allowing someone to get past security to cause us harm."

"I'll leave you in charge of that." Justice appeared tired. "It's always going to be a battle for us, my friend. There are always going to be enemies we will have to deal with. Hopefully Mercile will be completely destroyed by the lawsuits and bad publicity. One day I hope they no longer exist. Then all we'll be left to deal with are the humans who think we're an abomination against humanity."

Fury sighed. "Don't forget the arrested Mercile employees are facing a lot of years in prison. I'm sure their families and friends feel rage toward us. There's also the ones who are still out there who avoided arrest. We need to be wary of them. Our people can identify them and this incident has made me realize the danger we pose to them. That woman could have gone after our women who knew what she looked like and could have picked her from a lineup. We were lucky she didn't attack them too."

"That's just another fear we'll struggle with." Justice ran his fingers through his hair.

Ellie glanced at her watch. "Hey, sorry to leave but I have to get to work. The women are expecting me. We're throwing a birthday party and I can't be late."

Fury slowly grinned. "A birthday party?"

Ellie stood and leaned over to cup his face in her hands. "Yes. We have presents, a cake, decorations, and everything. It will be fun."

Fury kissed her. Ellie grinned, backed away, and waved to both men. "Nice seeing you, Justice. See you at home later, Fury."

"Yes, you will," he growled. "You and I have plans now that I have been deemed completely healed."

Heat rushed to Ellie's cheeks when Justice laughed. *Did anyone not know that Fury was cleared for sex this morning? Probably not.* She walked out of the building to settle into her golf cart. She'd missed it. She fished out her key and drove to the women's dorm.

Inside everyone was aflutter with excitement. They were throwing a birthday party for one of the women, getting it ready while she took her class at the New Species school. Ellie took charge. The women had made sure they were home to yell at the birthday girl when she entered the library.

The poor stunned woman jumped a good two feet, looked very confused, but grinned when she realized what they'd done for her. It was the happiest Ellie had ever seen the woman, making it worth every ounce of trouble it had been to plan the surprise party.

By six o'clock Ellie unlocked the front door to her and Fury's house. She'd beat him home and ran for the kitchen. She'd hidden sandwiches at the bottom of the fridge earlier that morning after Fury had left to go to a security meeting. She pulled them out, grabbed a few sodas, a bag of chips from the pantry cupboard, and hurried to the bedroom.

Ten minutes later the front door slammed. Ellie jumped off the bed and darted to the closet. She laughed as she hid inside and waited. Fury always looked for her the second he entered the house. She knew he'd sniff her out pretty quickly and he'd be amused that she'd tried to hide. She heard him coming.

Ellie tried not to laugh as the closet door jerked open. Fury frowned until his gaze slowly raked down her naked body. She grinned.

"It took you long enough to find me."

"Why are you hiding?"

Ellie took a step toward him. "I thought I should at least make you work for it a little."

"Work for what?" His focus stayed on her bare breasts.

"Me." She gripped the front of his uniform. "I thought about waiting on the bed but that was just too easy."

Fury helped her remove his vest and shirt and kicked off his shoes. "I like easy."

She chuckled. "Did you see the picnic I set out? I thought we could get naked, have dinner together, and then maybe watch some TV. That sounds like a great way to spend our evening," she teased.

Fury's lips twitched. "That's fine." He backed out of her range to prevent her from touching him. He unfastened his pants and shoved them down with his briefs. The socks were removed last. Totally naked and aroused, he grinned broadly at her.

"Let's eat." He moved toward the bed.

Ellie followed him. She sat down on the other side of the mattress cross-legged, facing him, flashing her pussy. Fury's dark gaze locked on her lap. He took some long, deep breaths and growled low in the back of his throat.

"What was that, Fury? I didn't quite understand what you said." Ellie allowed her amusement to show in her eyes when he looked up.

Laurann Dohner

"Nothing." He grinned. "This looks really good. I love roast beef."

"I tried to put everything out on the bed that you love." Ellie licked her lips, letting her tongue slowly trace first the lower seam, and then the top.

Fury stared at her mouth. He bit into the sandwich, chewed and swallowed it. "Screw this," he growled and tossed the sandwich aside as he lunged at her.

Ellie hit the bed on her back, laughing as Fury knocked her over and pinned her under him. "The only thing I want to really eat is you."

"What about the game?"

He nuzzled her neck and brushed his lips on her shoulder. "The only thing I am interested in watching is you." He cupped her breast, rubbing his thumb over her nipple. "I am fully healed and plan on doing everything I want to you."

"Did you lock the front door?"

"Locked and bolted. I still keep the handgun inside the nightstand drawer too. I'm going to shoot anyone who comes into this bedroom."

Ellie raked her fingernails down his back. Fury arched against her body and growled. "Easy. Don't excite me too much. It wouldn't take much for me to lose control. I want this to be good for you too."

"Do you trust me?"

Fury didn't hesitate. "With my life."

"Can I be on top?"

Surprise crossed Fury's features but lines slowly appeared at the corner of his eyes as he stared at her. "You want to be on top? Am I crushing you with my weight?" He lifted his chest away from hers to put a few inches of space between them.

She pulled him back down. "You're never too heavy. I love your skin touching mine and I love being under you. I just want to straddle you." Her gaze studied him intently. "Breeze mentioned your males won't allow women on top but I want to be. Will you at least try it for me?"

Fury's jaw clenched. "You want me to submit to you?"

She smiled. "No. I want you to trust me and let me be on top. I think you'll enjoy it."

He rolled them suddenly until she straddled him but he didn't look happy about doing it. "I love you. If it is important to you then I will submit. I can prove that I'd do anything for you, even this."

Ellie's smile fell. He didn't look happy or turned on. He actually looked kind of miserable. *Damn.* She hadn't meant to upset him or have him react badly. She straightened, straddling his stomach. She bit her lip, tempted to have him roll her back under him, but instead she carefully examined his stretched-out body under hers.

Ellie scooted back over his straining erection, happy to see it didn't turn him off in that department, and inched down to sit on his thighs. She leaned forward and licked one of his nipples, tugging the firm nub into her mouth, arching her stomach up enough to put a little space between them when his cock dug into her belly.

Fury tensed under her and growled. Ellie used her teeth to play with his nipple and sucked. Fury's hands gripped her hips firmly but he didn't move. She couldn't miss the way his cock hardened even more against her stomach.

"Ellie," he growled. "It's been too long since I've been inside you. I can't wait anymore. I'm trying to submit for you but I'm not one of your human males. I don't have that patience you keep expecting from me."

She laughed, releasing his nipple, and sat up. Her smile faded. "Relax."

He arched an eyebrow and then lowered his gaze to the protruding flesh in front of Ellie's stomach. His eyes met hers. "Do I look relaxed to you?"

Ellie lifted her hips and gripped Fury's cock. She curled her hand around his stiff shaft and brushed her fingertips down the underside of it, tracing it lightly with her fingernails. He gave a throaty growl and his hands released her hips. He reached up and grabbed the headboard. Wood creaked in protest as his hands clamped down strongly. Her focus shifted to them, noticed his knuckles were white and his muscles grew rigid throughout his body. She stared at him, thinking how beautiful he looked to her.

Ellie lifted up until her pussy was positioned over Fury's cock and sank down slowly, adjusting to him until their bodies were perfectly aligned. She experienced intense pleasure. She ached to have him buried deep inside her and feel what their bodies did together.

She was wet and more than ready to ride him to show him how good being straddled could feel. She moaned as she took him deeper inside her. Every inch of his cock slid snuggly into her pussy as she lowered herself on him until he was fully seated right where he belonged.

Fury threw his head back and growled deeper as wood snapped. His gaze flew up to verify that he'd broken off one of the bars on the headboard. He tossed the wood aside and gripped another one. Their gazes locked. This seemed important to Ellie and he had to admit she looked sexy wrapped over his hips. The feel of her tight, warm sex snug around his cock left him fighting the urge to thrust up into her.

"You're going to kill me."

She started to move on him. "If this is dying, I'm almost ready," Ellie moaned before she slammed down on him, lifted, twisted her hips, and drove down hard again.

Fury released the headboard and reached for her. One of his hands cupped her breast while his other hand slid between their moving bodies. Ellie threw back her head, moaning louder as Fury rubbed his thumb against her clit. Frantic, she moved on him even faster, riding him roughly. Fury growled, his hips thrusting up into her, using his heels on the bed for leverage to slam into her deeper.

He viciously cursed as his cock started to swell, his balls drew up tight, and knew he couldn't hold back anymore. The pleasure experienced every time she drove her body down into him, combined with her muscles clenching around his cock with her pending climax from his thumb massaging her clit was pure paradise. He snarled, trying to fight coming, and managed to hold off until she screamed his name as he sent her over the edge.

Fury shook under her, nearly unseating her as he gave a final thrust up. He groaned loudly as he came. He bucked his hips and groaned deeply from being sent to heaven. Ellie collapsed against his chest, both of them panting.

His arms wrapped around her and pure joy made him grin. Ellie was heaven to him. She'd come into his life when he'd been in hell, an angel of sunshine and hope, even if he hadn't realized at the time why his attraction to her had been so intense. Somewhere deep inside he must have known she was the other half of his soul.

He'd nearly lost her when he'd been drugged and it terrified him how close he'd come to hurting the one thing he loved most. Even insane, he'd known that she was special, that she mattered, and he never would have survived if she'd died. His precious Ellie made life worth living to him. Being with him put her in danger but a life without her wasn't a life at all. He couldn't live without his Ellie.

"So," she panted against his chest. "How was that?"

All the dark thoughts disappeared. Fury chuckled. "I'll submit to you doing this any time."

Ellie caressed him. "I thought you might love that."

"I just love everything about you." He suddenly rolled them to pin her flat under him.

Ellie stared up at him as her legs wrapped around the back of his legs and her arms wound around his neck. "Couldn't take it anymore, huh?"

"I want to make sure you don't try to get up."

"We're locked together. I wouldn't dare try to leave you until that swelling goes down. I told you, I want to make a cuddler out of you."

"You can do that but that's not why I don't want you to get up just yet."

"You just want to hold me? That's so sweet." She kissed his chin. "I love it when you do."

He chuckled. "That's not why either but I enjoy us being connected and holding you is my second favorite thing. I have time to make up." He moved inside her, thrusting gently. "This is my absolute favorite thing to do to you."

Ellie moaned at the instant pleasure, wanted him, but it surprised her. "Again? So soon?"

He nodded, lowering his head until his lips brushed her throat. "Again."

"I so love you," she whispered.

Chapter Twenty-One
ಬ

"Calm down," Ellie laughed.

Fury paced and a soft growl rumbled from his parted lips.

Ellie approached him to grab his arm and pulled him to a stop in front of her. She reached up to caress his cheek. "Nothing bad is going to happen."

"Something dire always happens." He sighed but wrapped his arms around her waist while his intense gaze studied her face. "Are you sure that you don't mind doing it this way? Breeze and some of the females have informed me that I'm making a mistake. They believe you will resent it later. I hope they have been watching too many movies. Breeze reminded me about human families and they think we should have more of your people here."

"They have been watching too many movies. That's true and it's my fault. We watch them almost every day to help them learn about normal life...up to a point. This is what I want. You're my family now, Fury. I love my blood family but they weren't real understanding of our relationship when I spoke to them. I have to face the fact that, no matter what I do or who I'm with, they won't be happy. They will just have to deal with it. If they don't, too bad. This is my life now, here with you. You're everything to me."

Fury chewed on his bottom lip. "What about children? I wish I could give you those but I'm unable." Sadness haunted his eyes. "I'm so sorry."

"Don't be. Do you want to have some?"

Ellie's heart missed a beat at the idea of having a little Fury running around their home. She bet it would be one adorable little baby but she knew it would never happen.

"I would like to." Fury pulled her tighter against his chest. "But mostly I just want you. All that matters is we are together and I am so grateful to have you, Ellie. You are always going to be more than enough to make me happy."

"I would like a few little rug rats myself." She smiled up at him. "We'll work it out somehow. Trisha and Ted are great doctors who might be able to find a way to fix what was done to you and if not, we could always adopt. There are always options. If we never have children, that's okay too."

He nodded. "We can at least talk to the doctors. It would be the first time in my life that I wouldn't mind being tested and prodded. I never believed I'd say those words after all that was done to me inside my cell."

Ellie's heart nearly stilled at the reminder of their past and how they had met. "Will you ever forgive me for what I did to you?"

He met her gaze and held it. "You don't even have to ask that. I already have. You did what you had to do to save us all."

She smiled. "Thank you."

Fury's smile faltered. "Are you sure you aren't going to be sorry for today? Are you certain this is what you want? I need this to be perfect for you."

"Hey," Ellie whispered. "Don't look sad. Being with you makes me happier than I've ever been in my entire life. How many times do I have to keep saying that before you believe me? I love you. If you had any idea how happy this makes me, you wouldn't even think to ask me. I'm positive that this is exactly what I want, just this way, because I'm doing this with you."

The conference room door opened and Ellie twisted her head to glance back. Justice entered and a group of people followed him. Ellie smiled at familiar faces.

"Are you sure, Ellie? We could wait and plan something better, something more traditional."

Ellie met his gaze. "I told you. I don't care where it's held or how it's done, Fury."

"I want nothing to go wrong," Fury growled. "No shooters. No crazy nurses."

Ellie bit her lip hard. She didn't want to laugh. He looked so certain something would go wrong. "This is why we decided to do this today with only a few people clued in to what we're about to do. No one can mess up something they aren't expecting."

"I like your logic."

Ellie moved closer, rising to her tiptoes to brush her lips against his ear. "I love your ass and the fact that you're totally healed up. I can't wait to get you alone."

"Ellie?" Slade spoke.

Ellie turned her head. "I'm talking over here."

"And we're all listening," Slade chuckled while he tapped his ear. "Keen hearing. Glad to know Fury is back to a hundred percent though."

Blushing, Ellie glared at him. "What is it with you guys? Couldn't you at least pretend you didn't hear that?"

Slade winked. "Where would be the fun in that? You blush so cutely."

Fury growled, shooting his friend a warning glare, and Slade moved to take a seat. Ellie shook her head while Fury shrugged.

A white-haired man walked through the door last. He wore a black robe and held a bible in his hand. He took his place in front of Ellie and Fury. His serious gaze traveled around the room.

"I need everyone to please take a seat."

The room became quiet. Ellie saw confusion on a lot of faces as they sat, staring at the couple in front of them with the unfamiliar human male. Most of them had no idea why they had been called to a mandatory meeting but there were a few who smothered knowing grins. Breeze waved at Ellie from a chair in the front. Ellie waved back and then looked up at Fury. Their gazes met and held.

"We're gathered here today," the white-haired man stated loudly, "to join together Fury North and Ellie Brower in marriage." He took a breath.

"Don't say it." Fury gave the minister a scary look. "Don't you dare ask if anyone has any objections. We talked about this."

The man paled and cleared his throat. "Fury, do you take Ellie to be your wife?"

"I do."

The minister opened his mouth but Fury growled again. White eyebrows shot up and his voice lowered. "How much do you want me to cut here?"

Dark eyes narrowed as Fury softly growled again and Ellie bit back a laugh. The minister cleared his throat again.

"Ellie, do you take Fury to be your husband?"

"I do."

"I pronounce you husband and wife." He peered at Fury warily. "Was that fast enough for you? You may kiss your bride. You're legally married."

A wide grin split Fury's features. "No one stopped us."

"Someone would have to be a speed protester to get a have gotten a word in there." Ellie leaned into him and a chuckled. "Now kiss me."

Fury lowered his head and Ellie closed her eyes, her heart racing. Life was never going to be boring with her husband. His mouth took possession of hers and she got lost in the man she loved, in front of a roomful of witnesses.

"Aren't they supposed to exchange rings?" Halfpint whispered the question.

"Oh, they'll be exchanging plenty." Slade chuckled. "I think putting something on her is the last thing Fury wants at this moment."

Breeze laughed. "Um, maybe we should separate them or leave the room because it looks as if he's about to take everything off both of them. They are really excited to be married."

Justice stood. "Let's clear out of here," he whispered, knowing his people could hear him. "Now."

He glanced at the couple kissing at the front of the room, entwined together, and mixed emotions stirred. He was grateful they'd found that much happiness together but at the same time, it made him ache to find it too.

A hand touched his shoulder and he forced his gaze away from Ellie and Fury to meet Tiger's stare.

"They are clearing out," Tiger whispered. "I'll order one of our men to stand outside to prevent anyone from disturbing them. Slade is escorting the minister outside." He paused. "They are so wrapped up in each other that the room could catch fire and they wouldn't be aware of it."

Justice glanced at the front of the room and then grinned. "Let's go." He closed the doors to the conference room when they reached the hallway. "I want that one day," he admitted.

Tiger paused, tilted his head slightly, and watched Justice for a long moment. "I would be too afraid to find and then lose that kind of love."

Justice nodded. "We're free. Anything is possible now if we just reach for it."

Slade walked up. "Are they naked yet and having sex on top of one of the tables?"

"Probably." Tiger grinned. "Justice is getting sentimental and wants a woman of his own. I don't. I enjoy my life just as it is. What about you?"

Slade had a mental image of Doc Trisha and her smile flashed through his thoughts. "I'm undecided but who knows what the future holds."

Print Books:
Cyborg Seduction 1: Burning Up Flint
Cyborg Seduction 2: Kissing Steel
Zorn Warriors 1 & 2: Loving Zorn
Zorn Warriors 3: Tempting Rever
Zorn Warriors 4: Berrr's Vow

About the Author

ᔥ

I'm a full time "in house supervisor" (Sounds *much* better than plain ol' housewife), mother, and writer. I'm addicted to carmel iced coffee, the occasional candy bar (or two), and trying to get at least five hours of sleep at night.

I love to write all kinds of stories. I think the best part about writing is the fact that real life is always uncertain, always tossing things at us that we have no control over, but when you write you can make sure there's always a happy ending. I *love* that about writing. I love it when I sit down at my computer desk and put on my headphones to listen to loud music to block out the world around me, so I can create worlds in front of me.

ᔥ

The author welcomes comments from readers. You can find her website and email address on her author bio page at www.ellorascave.com.

Tell Us What You Think

We appreciate hearing reader opinions about our books. You can email us at Comments@EllorasCave.com.

Why an electronic book?

We live in the Information Age—an exciting time in the history of human civilization, in which technology rules supreme and continues to progress in leaps and bounds every minute of every day. For a multitude of reasons, more and more avid literary fans are opting to purchase e-books instead of paper books. The question from those not yet initiated into the world of electronic reading is simply: *Why?*

1. *Price.* An electronic title at Ellora's Cave Publishing runs anywhere from 40% to 75% less than the cover price of the exact same title in paperback format. Why? Basic mathematics and cost. It is less expensive to publish an e-book (no paper and printing, no warehousing and shipping) than it is to publish a paperback, so the savings are passed along to the consumer.

2. *Space.* Running out of room in your house for your books? That is one worry you will never have with electronic books. For a low one-time cost, you can purchase a handheld device specifically designed for e-reading. Many e-readers have large, convenient screens for viewing. Better yet, hundreds of titles can be stored within your new library—on a single microchip. There are a variety of e-readers from different manufacturers. You can also read e-books on your PC or laptop computer. (Please note that Ellora's Cave does not endorse any specific brands.

You can check our website at www.ellorascave.com for information we make available to new consumers.)

3. *Mobility.* Because your new e-library consists of only a microchip within a small, easily transportable e-reader, your entire cache of books can be taken with you wherever you go.

4. ***Personal Viewing Preferences.*** Are the words you are currently reading too small? Too large? Too... ANNOYING? Paperback books cannot be modified according to personal preferences, but e-books can.

5. ***Instant Gratification.*** Is it the middle of the night and all the bookstores near you are closed? Are you tired of waiting days, sometimes weeks, for bookstores to ship the novels you bought? Ellora's Cave Publishing sells instantaneous downloads twenty-four hours a day, seven days a week, every day of the year. Our webstore is never closed. Our e-book delivery system is 100% automated, meaning your order is filled as soon as you pay for it.

Those are a few of the top reasons why electronic books are replacing paperbacks for many avid readers.

As always, Ellora's Cave welcomes your questions and comments. We invite you to email us at Comments@ellorascave.com or write to us directly at Ellora's Cave Publishing Inc., 1056 Home Avenue, Akron, OH 44310-3502.

MAKE EACH DAY MORE *EXCITING* WITH OUR

ELLORA'S
CAVEMEN
CALENDAR

WWW.ELLORASCAVE.COM

ELLORA'S CAVE
Romanticon

Annual convention
for women who
refuse to behave

17438200R00207

Printed in Great Britain
by Amazon